THE
DEMI-MONDE
SUMMER

ROD REES

Jo Fletcher
BOOKS

First published in Great Britain in 2013 Jo Fletcher Books
This paperback edition published in 2013 by

Jo Fletcher Books
an imprint of Quercus Editions Ltd.
55 Baker Street
7th Floor, South Block
London
W1U 8EW

A CIP catalogue reference for this book is available
from the British Library

ISBN 978 1 84916 507 5 (PB)
ISBN 978 1 84916 663 8 (EBOOK)

10 9 8 7 6 5 4 3 2 1

Typeset by Ellipsis Digital Limited, Glasgow
Printed and bound in Great Britain by Clays Ltd, St Ives plc

EDE

'You can't help getting caught up in the smartly paced story ... well conceived and well executed' *SFX*

'An amazingly quick and enjoyable read' *British Fantasy Society*

'Explosively creative barely defines *The Demi-Monde: Winter*. It blew me away' James Rollins

'It's elegantly constructed, skilfully written, and absolutely impossible to stop reading' *Booklist*

'The writing is state of the art ... exquisitely worked out and told at a cracking pace ... Welcome to holo-hell' Stephen Baxter

'Incredibly entertaining' *The Times*

'Rees makes the book work: the world he's created is a psychopathic nightmare' *Guardian*

'Part *Matrix*, part *Escape from New York*, with a dash of film noir and a whole host of imagination ... Beautifully written [with] a serious kick ass plot' *Falcata Times*

'A fast paced fantasy [that is] very intelligent ... ensures all fans will be on tenterhooks' *SciFiNow*

'If you're looking for a unique and ambitious blend of Cyberpunk, Steampunk, Historical, Dystopian, SF, Fantasy madness, you *have* to check this out' *Zoessteampunkreviews.com*

Also by Rod Rees

The Demi Monde:
Winter
Spring

Contents

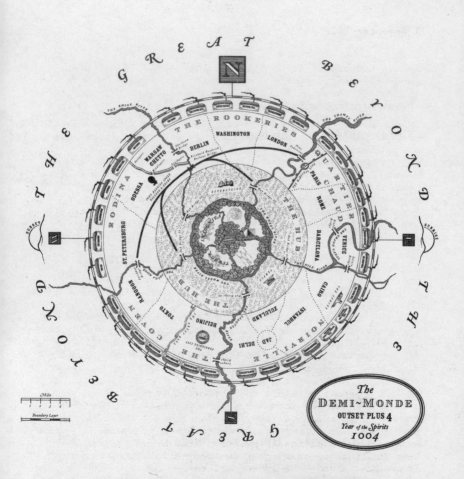

1 November 2018

I have been asked to report regarding the difficulties
currently being experienced with the Demi-Monde Project and
the impact these difficulties might present vis-à-vis the
achieving of the Final Solution.

As the Grand Council knows, using the world's first quantum
computer, ABBA, an engine of immense processing power, we
have developed the Demi-Monde, the most sophisticated
virtual world ever conceived. Recognising that such an
ambitious undertaking would be extraordinarily difficult to
conceal – especially as it involved the clandestine
accessing of DNA data – we chose to disguise the
Demi-Monde's true purpose by persuading the US military to
adopt the simulation as a training ground for their
neoFights.

Using this subterfuge we have populated the Demi-Monde with
thirty million digital duplicates of living people – Dupes –
six million of whom possess the genetic signature
identifying them as proto-Grigorian. In the five years since
the initiation of the Demi-Monde Project these Dupes have
been subject to intense conditioning, notably regarding
their appetite for blood and their living in a high-stress
environment. The final step in producing the desired level
of genetic mutation will however require them to be exposed
to a level of Cavoritic radiation similar in magnitude to
that experienced during the meteor strike of 1795, and, as
it has proved impossible to fabricate Cavorite in quantity
in the Real World, to achieve this intensity it has been
necessary to recreate this singular element virtually in the
Demi-Monde. To this end a Cavorite (or Mantle-ite, as it is
known in the Demi-Monde) reactor – the Great Pyramid – has
been built in the region of the Demi-Monde known as Terror
Incognita. Unfortunately the triggering device – the Column
of Loci – designed to activate this reactor has been waylaid
by the Dupe known as <u>Ella Thomas</u>.

continued over...

Ella Thomas was introduced into the Demi-Monde ostensibly to rescue Norma Williams, the daughter of the US President, herself lured into the Demi-Monde to prevent the US military closing down the Project. To ensure this rescue mission failed, we made strenuous efforts to have a wholly ineffectual individual selected for the task, but as we have belatedly discovered, Thomas is a Lilithi, the most powerful and dangerous enemy of the Grigori. During her sojourn in the Demi-Monde the girl's dormant Lilithian abilities were resuscitated, and thus empowered she has taken control of Venice, her intention now being to ally Venice with NoirVille (the vehemently misogynistic Afro-Arabic Sector of the Demi-Monde), such a move having the potential to fundamentally change the Demi-Monde's politico-military status quo. But worse, Venice is also where the Column of Loci is being held, the upshot being that Ella Thomas (or Doge IMmanual as she is now known) has control of the Column, a wholly unacceptable situation.

(En passant, it should be noted that the one positive aspect of the rise of Ella Thomas is that her relationship with the Dupe known as Vanka Maykov, a glib Russian psychic, seems to be over. Maykov was seen as a disruptive influence in the Demi-Monde but now it appears he has been forced to flee to the JAD, the homeland of the Demi-Monde's faux-Jewish diaspora, the nuJus.)

Compounding these difficulties, Norma Williams has also proven to be more capable than her Real World reputation had led us to expect. Aided and abetted by Burlesque Bandstand, an amoral petty criminal, and Odette Aroca, a truculent French dissident, she has been proselytising the virtues of non-violence and passive resistance, a philosophy known as Normalism. This has had an unsettling effect on the Dupes inhabiting the Demi-Monde, though now Williams has been abducted by Empress Wu and taken to the Coven (the rabidly feminist Sino-Japanese Sector of the Demi-Monde) it is hoped that her baleful influence has been terminated.

Finally, I must report my disappointment with Reinhard Heydrich, the PreLived Singularity (über-psychopath) seeded into the Demi-Monde to take control of the world on our behalf. Despite his early promise (his taking control of two of the Demi-Monde's five Sectors to form the Anglo-Russian empire known as the ForthRight being a prime example), of late he has faltered. This is most marked in his failure to motivate the team of scientists we have provided him with to perfect the Plague weapon which is so vital to the

continued over...

successful implementation of the Final Solution, an incompetence also signalled by his StormTroopers being discomfited by the rebel aristo <u>Trixie Dashwood</u> in the Battle for Warsaw. As Dashwood has now been appointed head of the Covenite army, it is hoped that Heydrich is more effective in his handling of her during the forthcoming invasion of the Coven by the ForthRight.

I acknowledge that a superficial perusal of the above could lead to the conclusion that the setbacks suffered by the Grigori have been many and grievous, but this is not the case. Progress in the Real World has been rapid. <u>Aaliz Heydrich</u>, the daughter of Reinhard Heydrich, has replaced Norma Williams here in the Real World, the Fun/Funs organisation she established goes from strength to strength, and arrangements for the Gathering, the bringing together of all the Fun/Fun members and their parents – the individuals the proto-Grigorian Dupes were based upon – in order that they might be genetically reprogrammed, are well in hand. And with respect to the situation in the Demi-Monde the Grand Council should be aware that I will be personally intervening in the affairs of that virtual world to ensure that remedial action is taken to resolve the minor reverses we have suffered. This being the case, I most strenuously request that the Grand Council does NOT see fit to order a Temporal Modulation to retro-remedy the situation: as we have learned to our cost, the finessing of Temporal Modulations is very difficult and it may be that rather than alleviating the situation it serves only to exacerbate it.

In sum, I do not believe there has been any material impact on the timetable set for the Final Solution which proceeds inexorably towards the planned execution date of 30 April 2019.

I remain Your Humble Servant,

Professor Septimus Bole

Prologue

Rangoon, the Coven

The Demi-Monde: 1st Day of Summer, 1005 ... a few minutes after midnight

Of all the opponents of HerEticalism, perhaps the most dogged and the most troublesome has been the SheTong, a rebel group which seeks to overthrow Her Divine Majesty Empress Wu; subvert the One True Religion, HerEticalism; and prevent Demi-Mondian Femmes entering the glorious state of MostBien. The SheTong is led by Su Xiaoxiao – former concubine of that arch-paternalist and enemy of all Femmes, the pigEmperor Qin Shi Huang, may his soul roast in Hel – a demented and unbalanced Femme unable to throw off the shackles of the specious sociocultural misogynist construct that is heterosexual sex. All members of the ChangGang Security Force are urged to make every effort to locate and destroy Su Xiaoxiao – who has been classified as the Coven's Public Enemy Number One – and her pernicious and destructive organisation.

Circular to all Officers of the ChangGang Security Force signed by Imperial Secretary, NoN Mao ZeDong

Those who would kill must nurture patience.

Su Xiaoxiao waited.

Serene.

Silent.

Still.

Standing formless as smoke, merging into the emptiness of the night.

All her will was concentrated on gauging the correct moment to move. And to do this, she had to have perfect control of her Qi, channelling the energy of the Living until she became one with the Nothingness. As she had been trained, she regulated her breathing, slowing the beat of her body clock, allowing *wu wei* – the effortless inaction of the enlightened soul – to suffuse her mind and her body. She felt herself relax as her body remembered that the harder one tries, the more resistance one creates for oneself.

And as she always did before battle, she found comfort in the words of her great mentor, Sun Tzu.

The Superior Warrior imitates the cobra and lies motionless until the time of striking.

So she stood, swathed from head to toe in her skin-tight black silk *shinobu shōzoku*, invisible in the darkness, indifferent to the monsoon rain that pummelled down on her, oblivious to everything but the study of her prey, waiting until the Amazon turned her back. She was wise to be cautious: the soldierFemme was a dangerous adversary, tall and powerful, her oiled musculature arrogantly displayed by the sleeveless pink jerkin that announced her to be a soldier of the Fifth Legion of Amazons, one of the best fighting units in the whole of the Coven. But this strength, which made Amazons such formidable soldierFemmes, was also their weakness.

Beware hubris: overconfidence makes a warrior contemptuous and contempt of an enemy is the first step towards defeat.

The Amazon turned. Now she had her back to them.

This was the moment. In one fluid motion Su Xiaoxiao adjusted her black scarf – her *tenugui* – so that it covered her face. Now when she moved out of the shadows, only her eyes were uncovered.

Like a black ghost, she drifted through the darkness, avoiding the oases of light spread by the gas lanterns that lined the alleyway, avoiding the puddles of rainwater that patinated the cobbles. She knew to be careful; though they had seen only this one sentry, there might be others. Soon there would be war with the ForthRight and, in anticipation of an invasion, Rangoon's docks had become a military zone, swarming with soldiers day and night as the Coven prepared to resist the onslaught of the ForthRight army.

A sudden movement by the Amazon caused Su Xiaoxiao to flinch back into the night-shrouded safety of a door well, motioning her three *kunoichi* to do likewise. Still as statues, they stood watching as the Amazon moved towards them, rattling the gates of the warehouses as she walked, checking that everything was secure. Satisfied, she began to stroll – blithely negligent of the fate awaiting her – along the alleyway towards the spot where Death was hiding.

Fifteen metres.

Ten metres.

Five metres.

With a touch to the fighter's shoulder, Su Xiaoxiao signalled that the Amazon should be eliminated by Mochizuki Chiyome, her deputy in the SheTong. The girl's black-bladed *tantō* sighed out of its scabbard and for an instant the short steel blade of the knife shimmered in the moonlight. Then Mochizuki oiled forward. A moment later there was a barely audible gasp as she made a *kubi* strike, her *tantō* piercing the Amazon's throat, simultaneously killing her and preventing her from crying out. The soldierFemme crumpled to the cobbles, and Mochizuki dragged her flaccid, lifeless body deeper into the darkness.

The enemy must be dispatched swiftly and without feeling. Terrible surprise is the way of the SheTong.

Wait.

Listen.

Nothing.

The killing had gone unnoticed. There were no shouts of warning, no alarms being sounded, nothing to indicate that a soul had passed to the Nothingness. An uncaring world was oblivious to the death of the Amazon, the only sound accompanying her demise being the distant grumble of the early morning traffic moving through Rangoon's docks. Confident now that no one stood between them and their objective, Su Xiaoxiao ushered her fighters forward and together the four of them crept towards the Anichkov Bridge, their footsteps deadened by the thick crêpe soles of their black canvas boots. And as she stole along, Su Xiaoxiao glanced up towards the Moon, gauging the time. Soon the boat bringing Norma Williams from the WarJunk would be landing in Rangoon and then, for a brief moment, she would hold the fate of the Demi-Monde in her hands. Soon she would decide if it was the destiny of the Demi-Monde to embrace Yin or Yang, darkness or light, salvation or destruction, good or evil. And just for an instant she felt that terrible responsibility resting heavy on her slim shoulders as she remembered the words of the Epigram the iChing had cited in answer to her question as to whether Norma Williams was indeed the true Messiah.

The Flood comes,
Irresistible.
To wash clean the wounds
Sustained by the warrior.
But beware, just as water supports the boat
So in its fury it may swamp it.
Water is the giver of life,
But oft-times
It is the bringer of death.

Yes, the Flood – the Messiah – approached, and her coming

heralded the Time of the Cleansing but there were many who would seek to thwart her, many who would seek to kill her. She was the delicate flower that had to be shielded from the harsh winds of hatred and the savage frosts of ambition. That was the responsibility ABBA had charged Su Xiaoxiao with: to protect the Messiah ... and then to plunge her back into harm's way. A paradox, but such was the Way.

Reaching the end of the alleyway, she paused. She could see the deserted warehouse where she and her fighters would wait for the arrival of the Messiah. Now all they had to do was cross the wide and crowded Maha Bandoola Street unchallenged, a task fraught with danger. Even though it was after midnight, Rangoon's docks bustled; steamer lorries puffed and panted along the road bringing coal to the huge and ominous WarJunks that rocked low and brooding at their moorings; horse-drawn carts dragging artillery pieces rumbled along, the carts' metal-shod wheels snarling and clacking on the cobbles as they made their way to the redoubts that were being built so hurriedly along the banks of the Volga River; and coolieNoNs pushed handcarts laden with boxes of ammunition, their wooden clogs click-clacking as they went. A coffle of slaves covered from head to toe in mud shuffled grumpily along, making their sleepy way back to their barracks after a long day spent digging trenches. And through the whole muddle darted rickshaws bearing officerFemmes and their painted geishas, the rickshaws ducking and weaving through the maelstrom of traffic that had crammed itself into Maha Bandoola Street.

But most dangerous for Su Xiaoxiao and her *kunoichi* was that everywhere there were hundreds upon hundreds of pink-jacketed soldierFemmes marching to take up their positions in the fortified buildings, in the redoubts and in the already flooded trenches, ready to repel the expected assault of the ForthRight Army.

She took a deep breath, reminding herself that at midnight few people were fully awake, most minds were fogged by fatigue or by Solution, then slipped out of the shadows and raced as fast as she could across the street. By the Grace of ABBA, she and her fighters reached the darkness of the opposite side unnoticed and unchallenged. There they settled down in the warehouse to wait. But even as Su Xiaoxiao unslung her M4 and checked its magazine, her eyes were never still, they continually flicked back and forth searching the night for danger.

The Superior Warrior always expects the unexpected.

And then kills it . . .

Part One
Summer Comes

Created by Rosining Nobel, Most Divine Couturier to the House of Worth, as seen in 'In Pure Modes' Un Vogue Vogues Monthly, Summer 1003

Living & More is the dietary and life-style manta of
Un-Fun-DaMentalism designed to detoxify the body and by doing so
purify the Solidified Astral Ether. Fashions are therefore modest and
all-enveloping, designed to conceal, harness and contain the instinctive
libidinous nature of men and (more importantly) of women.

1

New York City
The Real World: 29 October 2018

Whilst I applaud the work of the Fun-Loving Fundamentalists – or, as most people call them, the Fun/Funs – in helping to ameliorate the drug addiction that is rife amongst America's teen population, I remain deeply suspicious of both the organisation and its methods. Sure, the Fun/Funs' Get-Me-Straighter Meter has achieved miraculous results in freeing addicts from their habit, but the question remains: what else is being altered when the GMS Meter is connected to an addict's brain? Sure, Norma Williams talks persuasively about being 'inspired by God', but what is her ultimate ambition? Sure, ParaDigm CyberResearch has been generous in funding the Fun/Funs' work, but is ParaDigm's largesse entirely self-less? Until these questions have been satisfactorily answered, the jury is still out as to whether the Fun/Funs are a force for good or for evil. But let me tell you a secret: my money is on it being the latter.

'No Fun at All: An Enquiry into the Murky World of the Fun/Funs': Odette Aroca, *The New York PollyGazette*

Oddie had no idea how many people were trying to get into the Plaza to hear Norma Williams speak that evening but it was a lot. Tens of thousands of them, in fact, and as the Fun/Funs seemed determined to log the names of everyone wishing to attend the jamboree, there was a bottleneck of mammoth proportions around the auditorium's gates. But finally, after judicious use of her elbows and boots, Oddie managed to squirm her way through the chaos to the front of the queue. There she was faced by a line of Fun/Fun volunteers seated at a long bench table who, as best she could judge in the confusion, were intent on scanning the dog tags – the ID dockets that everyone wore to confirm they were a bona fide citizen of the USA – of all would-be attendees into a Polly.

She nearly baulked. She had an instinctive reluctance to having her dog tag peeped; the government knew enough about her without her *volunteering* information.

But even as she stood debating how to avoid being scanned, there was a surge in the tide of people pressing behind her, and she found herself being rammed up against the table and staring into the face of a guy possessed of too many zits and not enough hair. What he had though was a Valknut badge which signalled that he was a Fun/Fun ... that and an attitude.

'You got an invitation?' the volunteer yelled at her. The noise of the crowd was deafening.

'No, I thought everyone was welcome.'

'Yeah, they are. It's just that so many people have shown up that we can't let them all in. Fire regulations. So, no invite, no entry.'

Oddie wasn't in the mood to be given the go-by: Norma Williams and her Fun/Funs had the makings of a big story and she was determined it would be *her* big story. 'You gotta be pulling my chain. I've just spent an hour being crunched up and touched up while I waited to get to the head of the queue, so don't hit me with all this "you can't come in" shit.'

'Sorry.'

'Fuck that, where's your boss?'

'Look, honey, it won't do any good.'

Oh yes it will. Oddie knew from experience that making a loud and very public demonstration of unhappiness was a great way of coercing any organisation into doing things her way. The squeaky wheel was the one that got the grease.

She raised her voice. She had a *big* voice, but then she was a big girl. 'Don't fucking "honey" me. And dig this: either you get your boss over here or I'm gonna lean across this table and shove that Polly so far up your ass you'll be spending the next week scanning the back of your fucking teeth.'

'Wot seems to be the trouble?'

A big guy in a 'The Fun/Funs are a NonAddictive Substance' T-shirt, speaking with an English accent, and wearing a name tag that read 'Burl Standing', sauntered up alongside the spotty volunteer. His eyes met Oddie's.

Kismet.

They stood and watched Norma Williams perform together, side by side at the edge of the stage. And it was a *performance*. Oh, it might have been billed as 'An Opportunity to Hear about the Fun/Funs' but in reality it was a rally where Norma Williams could be worshipped by her disciples.

She'd seen pictures and PollyCasts of Norma Williams – but then who hadn't? – and had prepared herself to be disappointed. But she wasn't. Sure the girl was smaller than she seemed on the Polly, but then all celebrities were smaller in real life. She was, though, prettier than Oddie had expected and the white lace dress she was wearing was short enough to show off her famously fine legs and tight enough to describe her famously fine curves. And her mass of blonde hair – backcombed to within an inch of its life – flared like a halo around her head when she stood in front of the lights that illuminated the centre of the stage.

But small, beautiful and perfectly formed though Norma Williams was, these attributes were as nothing when compared with the force of personality she radiated. Just standing there acknowledging the cheers and the wild applause of the ten thousand people packed into the hall, Oddie knew Norma Williams was a real, bona fide, twenty-four-carat Star. She had met a load of 'PollyCelebrities' in her time as a stringer for *The New York PollyGazette* and with only a few notable exceptions she had been totally underwhelmed. But just occasionally she had met one possessed of that most elusive quality, charisma. These were the true charismatics ... they had 'It'.

And Norma Williams had 'It' in truckloads. So much so that all the carefully choreographed lighting and stage backgrounds and all the music accompanying her arrival on stage were unnecessary. She was one of those rare individuals who could walk unannounced onto a bare stage and still dominate the theatre and her audience.

The problem Oddie had with people possessed of 'It' was that invariably they were complete and utter bastards who believed it was their God-given right to be treated as 'special'. Oddie had the sneaking feeling that Norma Williams would be a mega-bitch.

'Ain't she wonderful?' yelled Burl into her left ear, giving her a nudge for emphasis.

'Yeah, wonderful.'

And unbelievably fucking dangerous.

Norma spoke for just fifteen minutes, long enough to give what she said substance but not long enough to bore. Like the good performer she was, she left her audience clamouring for more. And it had been an interesting speech as it contained two new announcements of Fun/Fun policy. The first was that the use of the Get-Me-Straighter Meter would be extended outside the USA, with certain selected operatives visiting England, Germany,

Russia and the Ukraine where they would free a million unfortunates from their addictions. The second was that in six months there would be a 'Gathering' in the Nevada desert when all the Fun/Fun converts and their parents would be invited to commune with God and to give thanks for their deliverance from addiction.

The speechifying at an end, Norma took a moment to stand centre stage bowing and waving. Not that Oddie paid much attention; she was distracted by the need to check that her Polly had recorded the girl's performance correctly, and as a result, didn't notice that Norma Williams had come to stand slap-bang in front of her. It was only then that she realised what a big duke Burl was in the Fun/Funs. Even the hyper-nervous security guards were wary of him, and whilst they bustled everyone else backstage away from the girl, they left Burl – and Oddie – where they were.

'So what did you think, Burl?' Norma asked as she towelled the back of her neck.

Oddie almost laughed at how artfully it was done. Using the towel gave the girl an excuse to raise her arms, which in turn caused her short dress to rise even further up her thighs and to press even harder across her tits. She was playing her looks and sex appeal for all they were worth, and from the expression on his face Burl was mesmerised by this little exercise in coquettishness.

'You wos wonderful, Norma, really wonderful. You wos great.'

The girl beamed her thanks and then nodded towards Oddie. 'Aren't you going to introduce me to your friend, Burl?'

'Oh, yus, ov course: this is Oddie. Oddie, this is Norma Williams.'

The two girls shook hands. '"Oddie"?' asked Norma.

'It's short for Odette, my parents are French.'

'And your surname?'

'Aroca,' she answered and it was then that she realised that Norma hadn't released her hand.

'Aroca . . .' Norma murmured, taking a moment to digest this piece of information. 'I've been told about another girl called Aroca. She's an enemy of my father.'

'Not me, Norma, I'm a great admirer of the President. I believe him to be a real beacon of liberty in the world. What he's doing to roll back the PanOptika Surveillance System is vital if we're to have a free and fair society.'

Norma frowned and released Oddie's hand. 'Of course . . . *that* father.'

That father? Weird.

She smiled a bleak, empty smile that sent trickles of fear skipping down Oddie's spine. 'I have a different view of surveillance, Miss Aroca. I am of the firm opinion that surveillance is vital if we are to ensure the security of our great country and to protect its citizens from terrorists, malcontents and other enemies of the state. Only those who have something to hide – something criminal, antisocial or which transgresses the word of God – object to surveillance; good people have nothing to fear. As ParaDigm's advert says: PanOptika watches out for the good guys by watching out for the bad guys.'

'I think you're wrong, Miss Williams—'

Oddie didn't get to finish, being interrupted by a very flustered-looking aide thrusting a piece of paper into Norma Williams's hand. For several long silent seconds she examined what was written there and then looked up to study Oddie very carefully. 'You're a clever girl, Miss Aroca, perhaps even a little *too* clever. My aide has just interrogated ABBA and been advised that you're a reporter for *The New York PollyGazette*. The *Gazette* has been somewhat antagonistic towards the Fun/Funs so I'm not inclined to prolong this conversation.'

'Maybe you should, Miss Williams. Maybe you should try to convert a Doubting Thomas – or even a Doubting Oddie.'

'I find people possessed of your degree of entrenched liberalism, Miss Aroca, incapable of seeing the light.'

'Or perhaps it's your arguments that are suspect. Maybe it's not me who can't see but you who can't convince.'

Norma Williams's lips contracted into a thin, angry line. 'I think you should go now, Miss Aroca.' She turned to Burl. 'Get this girl out of my sight and don't ever, *ever*, bring someone who hasn't been pre-vetted near me again. Do you understand, Burl?' The way the colour drained out of Burl's face indicated that he understood very well indeed.

'Jesus, I ain't never seen her so mad before. You should've told me you wos a reporter. Norma 'ates reporters.'

They were sitting in a Bubble Bar a couple of blocks down from the Plaza. Oddie had chosen it because each of its tables was equipped with a 'bubble' guaranteed to defeat eyeSpies and hence allow those sitting at the table to talk confident that their conversation wouldn't be the subject of cyber-eavesdropping. Her philosophy was that when you were intent on pissing off a company as powerful as ParaDigm CyberResearch, you could never be too careful.

'I told 'er that it wos all a mistake, that you got in because you wosn't scanned properly.' Burl took a swig of his beer. 'Anyways, I guess that's my trip back to London down the tubes.'

'London?' asked Oddie with an encouraging smile.

'Yus, I was gonna be part ov the delegation taking the Get-Me-Straighter Meter to England. There wos to be five hundred ov us going an' we each had to save a thousand addicts. We've got their names on a list.'

Oddie felt her journalistic antennae starting to twitch. 'How could you have their names?'

'Dunno,' said Burl with a shrug, 'but we 'ave. The badges 'ave been made for 'em and everyfing.'

'Badges?'

Burl dug inside his shirt and pulled out a small circular medallion that he had hung around his neck on a silver chain. 'This shows that you've bin saved from addiction.' He leant across the table so that Oddie could get a better look.

The medallion was a simple affair with a Valknut – the emblem of the Fun/Funs – embossed on one side and a symbol of a hand embossed on the other. 'What's with the hand?'

'It shows that Jesus has held out his loving hand to you and you've had the courage to grasp it. We're told that we're never to take it off.'

As she peered at the medallion, Oddie was suddenly conscious that her face was only inches from Burl's. 'I'm sorry I've caused you so much trouble, Burl.'

Burl's big blue eyes blinked. 'Don't matter . . . I like you.'

'I like you too, Burl,' and with that she dipped her head forward and kissed him.

2

Venice
The Demi-Monde: 1st Day of Summer, 1005

```
TO DR JEZEBEL ETHOBAAL HEAD OF THE JAD INSTITUTE OF
METAPHYSICS PO BOX 11/11 + + + GREETINGS + + + PLS B
ADVISED <<ONE WITH NO SHADOW>> IS SAFE FROM CLUTCHES
OF THE BEAST + + + WILL ATTEMPT TO HAVE HIM SMUGGLED
TO NOIRVILLE TOMORROW + + + PLS ENSURE ARRANGEMENTS
MADE THAT HE MIGHT CROSS UNCHALLENGED FROM THERE INTO
THE JAD + + + MAY ABBA GUIDE OUR STEPS AND PROTECT
        OUR SOULS + + + MAMBO JOSEPHINE
```

PAR OISEAU

Copy of PigeonGram message sent by Josephine Baker,
1st day of Summer, 1005

Senior Prelate de Sade, the Supreme Head of the Church of
IMmanualism, gazed out over the crowd packed into the Sala,
a crowd comprising the haute-monde of Venice, all of them
waiting expectantly – reverently, almost – for the newly
crowned Doge IMmanual to speak. With great difficulty de Sade
stifled a smug smile of satisfaction: these, after all, were the
same bastards who just a few months ago had reviled him,
ridiculed him and voted for him to be exiled from Venice.
But now ...

Now he was the second-most important person in the whole
of Venice, outranked only by Her Most Reverend Excellency,

Doge IMmanual I. Now all these arrogant swine had to bend their knee to him.

When the death of Doge Catherine-Sophia had been announced there had never been any doubt as to who would ascend the throne: the people wouldn't have accepted anyone other than the Lady IMmanual, not after the Miracle of the Canal. Recognising inevitability when they saw it, the Council of Ten had hurried through the paperwork and now, less than twelve hours after the death of the previous incumbent, Doge IMmanual was firmly in control of Venice.

De Sade turned and bowed to the new Doge, signalling that it was time for her to address the crowd.

The girl rose to her feet and stepped towards the front of the stage. In acknowledgement of the importance of the occasion she had chosen to wear a diaphanous silver robe that showed off her wonderful body – *all* her wonderful body – in a quite splendid fashion. She was an ineffably beautiful woman and one accomplished in the arts of fiduciary sex, so much so that her audience gazed at her enraptured, ensnared by her beauty.

'All-powerful ABBA,' Doge IMmanual called out in a firm and commanding voice, 'I pray that you will give me the strength and the courage to guide the people of Venice and of the Demi-Monde to Rapture and to victory over the Beast. With this ring,' and here she took a large golden ring from where it lay on a cushion offered to her by a pageboy and placed it on the middle finger of her left hand, 'I wed the CitiZens of Venice to the Word of ABBA and to the Truth of IMmanualism.'

A choir of castrati began to trill away behind the Lady, which, de Sade decided, was, in retrospect, over-egging the ceremonial pudding.

'Members of the Council of Ten, delegates of the Grand Assembly, Patricians of Venice, my lords, ladies and gentlemen, some of you doubted that I have been sent by ABBA to lead the people of the Demi-Monde, but now let there be no doubt. You have asked for a miracle, and I have granted you a miracle. I pledged that Venice would be kept safe from the ravages of the ForthRight, and I have kept Venice safe. The time of doubt and dissension is over: I am the Messiah. Know that any defiance of the Word of ABBA and the teachings of IMmanualism is a device of the Beast by which he spreads mistrust and confusion. Such defiance can no longer be tolerated. Mark this: those who are not with me, body and soul, are my enemies.' She looked around at her audience. 'So I say to you that in this, the most uncertain of worlds, there is one precious certainty: the word of the Doge IMmanual. Follow me and I will bring you safe to Rapture.'

De Sade waited for the applause to die and to ensure that the Lady had finished her speechifying, then made an announcement of his own. 'His Highness, Selim the Grim, Grand Vizier to the court of His HimPerial Majesty Shaka Zulu, comes to honour Doge IMmanual on the day of her coronation.'

And with that the great villain Selim strode into the hall, flanked by a veritable crowd of flunkies. He halted in the middle of the audience chamber. 'Doge IMmanual, I bring greetings from His HimPerial Majesty Shaka Zulu.'

'Welcome to my Court, Grand Vizier Selim, and please convey my felicitations to His HimPerial Majesty. But I would ask, has His Majesty considered the proposition I put to him through your good offices?'

There was a buzz of conversation around the hall, the fools in the Council having obviously not realised that Doge IMmanual had been preparing to take office for weeks. The 'proposition' she was talking about was the result of many hours of long – and very secret – negotiations between her and Selim that had followed their first meeting in the Galerie des Anciens.

'I am commanded to convey to you word that the army of NoirVille is ready to stand shoulder to shoulder with the fighters of Venice in their struggle with the Beast, Reinhard Heydrich.

'And in exchange I will deliver to NoirVille, by the last day of Summer, the secrets of how Aqua Benedicta is manufactured.'

There was another flurry of excited conversation. The formula for Aqua Benedicta was one of the nuJus' most closely guarded secrets. Getting his hands on a supply of the anti-coagulant was the only reason Shaka had agreed to the establishing of the nuJu home in NoirVille, as having exclusive access to the additive had made NoirVille pre-eminent in the Demi-Monde with regards to the trading of blood. If Doge IMmanual was to reveal the nuJus' secret then Shaka would have no further use for them . . . she would be condemning the two million of them living in the JAD – the nuJu Autonomous District set in the middle of NoirVille – to death.

'I take it your holy men have overcome their antipathy to NoirVille being aligned with a Sector ruled by a woman?' Here she looked to the figure of His HimPerial Reverence the Grand Mufti Mohammed al-Mahdi, NoirVille's holiest Man, skulking behind Selim, but he refused to meet her eyes, preferring that Selim spoke for him.

'His HimPerial Majesty Shaka Zulu demanded that our priests go into conclave to consider this spiritual question. This they have done, and they have come to the sage conclusion that as you are the Messiah, you transcend gender and hence an alliance with Venice does not violate the tenets of HimPerialism.'

Very neat, decided de Sade. According to them, the Doge IMmanual *wasn't* a woeMan, but rather ABBA-made Solidified Astral Ether. He stole a glance at the Doge and struggled not to laugh. Standing there clad in her transparent robe, he had to marvel that any man – zadnik or otherwise – could summon up sufficient intellectual or religious flexibility to deny that she was all woman.

Doge IMmanual nodded. 'I am pleased to hear these words. I am a great admirer of His HimPerial Majesty Shaka Zulu, who has welded the disparate people of NoirVille into one tribe. Now, Venice and NoirVille must bring the *métèque* – the Outsiders – to heel. And in acknowledgement of his loyalty I, as the Messiah, will throw my cloak of invulnerability about his HimPis. They are now the chosen of ABBA.'

The Doge waved to a steward standing to one side of the chamber, who strode forward holding before him a golden sceptre surmounted by the entwined runes of *laguz* sinister and *laguz* dexter. 'This sceptre is a symbol that the HimPis of NoirVille are under the protection of the Messiah and of ABBA. And soon they will march to victory in the Demi-Monde. Soon we will begin the Mfecane . . . the Crushing.'

Selim took the sceptre and knelt. 'I accept this on behalf of NoirVille. The HimPis of NoirVille stand ready for your command.'

'And what of the fugitive doge-icide, Vanka Maykov, the murderer of Doge Catherine-Sophia? Have you taken him yet? I understand he is attempting to enter the JAD.'

Maykov again? Why, de Sade wondered, was the Doge so anxious about Maykov? The man's capture and execution seemed to have an urgency his low status hardly warranted.

'Agents of the HimPeril are searching for him even as we speak, Your Excellency.'

A scowl from the Doge. 'I am displeased. Surely, for a ruler as powerful as Lord Shaka, finding one Blank is not difficult.'

By way of a reply the Grand Vizier gestured to one of his lieutenants, who ushered a tall and very broad-shouldered Shade boy forward.

'Maykov will be found, Your Excellency. But, in atonement for the dilatoriness of the HimPeril, His HimPerial Majesty brings you your brother.'

The boy stepped into the halo of light cast by one of the great candelabras that lit the Sala and gave an arrogant wave of his hand. 'Yo, Sis,' he said. 'Long time no see. Septimus Bole sends his regards, and says if yo' don't stop fucking around with miracles and shit then he's gonna get real hot and heavy on yo' ass.'

'Billy?' gasped a stunned Doge IMmanual.

3

NoirVille
The Demi-Monde: 2nd Day of Summer,
1005 ... 01:00

Of all the secret organisations in the Demi-Monde – of which there are many – perhaps the most elusive is the Code Noir. Rumour has it – and there are no facts about the Code Noir, just gossip, innuendo and speculation – that the Code Noir was formed around 975 AC by a group of powerful WhoDoo mambos to oppose the coming to power of the WhoDoo Queen, Marie Laveau (957–984 AC). Reputedly the mightiest mambo ever seen in the Demi-Monde, Marie Laveau was considered by many of her disciples to be the reincarnation of Lilith, a belief supported by her attempts to take control of NoirVille and the vicious manner in which she disposed of her rivals. Marie Laveau was assassinated in 984 AC, a killing ascribed to the Code Noir.

Trying to Pin WhoDoo Down:
Colonel Percy Fawcett, Shangri-La Books

A crack of a rifle, then ...

Zing!

A bullet whizzed six inches or so beyond Vanka's left ear, but he didn't even flinch. He was too depressed to flinch. Flinching was for people who cared if they lived or died.

But some residual, autonomic instinct for self-preservation

persuaded him to crouch lower behind the gunwale of the steamboat that was chugging him across the Nile towards the sanctuary of the JAD. This same instinct provoked him to pull the collar of his mackintosh up to try – in a futile sort of way – to deflect the rain that was lashing down on him. Bang on the stroke of midnight on the first day of Summer the heavens had opened, the monsoon rains had come and they hadn't stopped coming since. Not that Vanka cared. He was past caring.

He'd always scoffed at the plots of some of the soppier penny dreadfuls that related the anguish suffered when a true love was lost, but he wasn't scoffing now. His soul was breaking.

Correction: broken.

He felt empty inside and even the effort to pull his waterproof around his shoulders was too much for his fretted spirits. He actually welcomed the chilled numbness the teeming rain was driving into his body . . . he just wished his mind could be numbed too.

He just wished he was dead.

Crack, crack.

Zing, zing.

Two more bullets whined overhead, seeking to oblige.

'Dis am de last time ah do a gig fo' dem Code Noir cats,' moaned the Shade at the helm of the steamboat. 'Ah don't care how much foldin' dem cats lay on yours truly, nuffing is worth de bad cats cappin' a barrel full o' buckshot up ma ass.'

Vanka stared at the man in an uninterested sort of way. He knew the Signori di Notte – Venice's secret police – were after him, he just didn't give a shit whether they caught him or not. Not after what had happened in Venice. He'd gone to the Doge's Palace to plead with Ella, the woman he loved – what an admission that was for the fancy-free Vanka Maykov to make – to tell her that he wasn't her enemy and that how she was acting was wrong, but instead of the reconciliation he'd hoped for he had found her screwing a guy called Casanova. The sight of her using the man – and he had no doubt as to who was using who in that little tableau – was seared into his memory. It had drained his soul of all happiness.

Crack.

Zing!

'Hey, man,' shouted the Shade, ''ow 'bout yo' gettin' up off yo' sorry Blank ass an' firing back at dem Signori di Notte bastards. Make wiv de dissuasive bang, bang, banging an' such. Don't yo' dig dat it's yos dey're chasing?'

Vanka didn't have the strength. He'd used up what little he had escaping from the Doge's Palace and then, with the help of Josephine Baker, ducking and diving through the backstreets of Venice to the docks. That's where the Code Noir had a boat – and a Shade captain mad enough to run the Nile – waiting to take him to NoirVille. Josephine had bundled him into the boat and had then tried to lure the pursuing bad guys away. Her ruse hadn't worked.

The Shade spun around, hauled out his revolver and loosed off two hopeful shots at their pursuers, but given the way the boat was pitching around on the choppy waters of the Nile, Vanka judged the chance of him hitting something to be somewhere between zero and zip.

'C'mon, man,' the exasperated Shade yelled. 'Pull yo'self together. De badniks am gettin' awful close. Get yo' iron out an' make wiv de lead fusillade.'

Vanka just sat there lost in mournful introspection.

He loved Ella Thomas. She was his everything. Meeting her had given purpose to his whole worthless, directionless, cynical existence. Whilst he didn't have much of a past – not one that he knew about, anyway – she had given him the hope that he might have a future. But now . . .

But now here he was back on the flee, running for his life. He gave a grimace: his life, as far as he could judge, was shit and he'd been served a double helping.

It had to be a double helping because he hadn't just been *betrayed* by the woman he loved, she was now using all her power to have him killed. That's why Josie had got him out of Venice so quickly and why she was so keen for him to make it to the safety of the JAD. Get to the JAD, she'd told him, and he'd have a place to hide. In the JAD he could keep low and wait for the heat to die down.

He was so lost in his despair that it hardly registered that the boat had come to a bobbing halt alongside a pier. They'd made it. Almost without thinking he stood up and stepped ashore.

Immediately the Shade floored the boat's throttle and steered his steamboat off into the night, screaming, 'Yo' one crazy fucking Blank!' as he went.

Crack, crack.

Zing, zing!

Like a sleepwalker, Vanka climbed the slick steps to the jetty, ignoring the shots from the chasing Venetians and the bullets caroming off the stone walls. He should, he supposed, be grateful that they were such lousy shots, but somehow he couldn't raise the energy. But deep down he knew he *had* to find the energy: he was, after all, accused of murdering Doge Catherine-Sophia and, as Josephine Baker had informed him, he did have both the Signori di Notte *and* the HimPeril – their NoirVillian counterparts – hunting him.

Crack, crack.

Zing, zing!

Miraculously he got to the top of the steps without having his head blown off. Ever efficient, Josie had arranged to have a pedicab waiting for him, though the driver seemed less than enthused to be the target of so much hostile attention.

'Get aboard, you Blank bastard!' he shouted as he ducked away from the flying lead. 'Don't yo dig dat dem cats is trying to drill yo?'

Unmoved by the man's entreaties, Vanka waded across the rain-flooded street to the pedicab, climbed aboard and then slumped back into its rickety passenger seat. Even before he'd settled, the driver was standing on his pedals, desperately trying to get the pedicab moving away from their pursuers.

It was as well he did. The chasing Signori di Notte agents emerged at the top of the staircase leading from the river and let loose a flurry of rifle fire. There was a loud bang and a bullet ricocheted off the side of the pedicab.

'An' now ah'm gonna be stiffed fo' a new paint job.' The driver looked into his mirror. 'Ah, fuck, dem cats has only gone and commandeered a steamer.'

The driver pedalled harder, redoubling his efforts to outrun the pursuing agents, but Vanka hardly noticed. He just sat back and listened to the rain rat-tat-tatting on the tin roof over his head.

Fuck, he was fed up.

The carapace of despair that had been insulating Vanka from the danger he was in was finally shattered when the frantic driver swung the pedicab around a corner on only two of the vehicle's three wheels forcing an oncoming steamer to make an emergency stop. As the steamer's head-lanterns washed over the wall of a nearby tenement, Vanka found himself looking at . . . himself.

VANKA MAYKOV
FOUL ASSASSIN OF DOGE CATHERINE-SOPHIA
REWARD OF ONE THOUSAND GUINEAS
MAY BE TAKEN DEAD OR ALIVE.

Fuck, fuck and triple fuck.

To have got the posters printed and pasted so quickly meant that the Lady IMmanual wanted him caught very, very badly. The survival instincts honed by evading numerous enraged husbands finally kicked in: he pulled his top hat further forward over his face and hoicked his collar up higher, hoping as he did so that the black hair dye, imitation cheek scars and the sacrificing of his precious moustache would render him passably NoirVillian. There were, after all, a lot of Blanks living in NoirVille, a lot of Blanks who espoused HimPerialism.

The problem was that, in his experience, a reward of one thousand Guineas had a magical effect on the ability of people to see through disguises.

He tried to shake his negative thinking. He had to keep positive, to keep reminding himself that he had a couple of things going for him: he had Josie and her Code Noir comrades on his side and he had a small fortune sitting in his bank account. If he could get to the JAD safely these in combination should be enough to keep him out of the clutches of the bad guys.

Should be ...

He had to stay alive! Only by doing this would he have a chance of reclaiming his lost love. *That* was the thought that rekindled the fire in Vanka's spirit. Despite everything, he refused to give up the hope that one day the Ella he knew and loved would be returned to him.

For almost an hour they pedalled through the backstreets of Cairo, always keeping the ominous Sphinx – the most sacred religious shrine of the Shades *and* the nuJus – to their left, twisting this way and that until the driver was satisfied that they had lost their pursuers. Finally the driver brought the pedicab to a slithering halt at the edge of a large and very crowded plaza. 'De crossing into de JAD is on de obber side of de square, man. So yo' jump out real quick, before dem cryptos come an' start using ma dick as a target.'

Now came the *really* dangerous part of Vanka's escape, the bit when he had to get through CheckPoint Charlie, through the JAD Wall and into the safety of the JAD.

After disembarking from the pedicab – which took off in a rush – Vanka spent a moment getting his bearings, finally opting to occupy a stairwell looking out over the square leading to the CheckPoint. It was a square packed with a couple of thousand dispirited nuJu refugees who were huddled there waiting for the morning and their chance to enter their HomeLand. These were the flotsam and jetsam of the wars that were ravaging the Demi-Monde, fleeing the death, the turmoil and the persecution that had gripped the world. Forlorn men and women sat around in makeshift camps, guarding their carts and their donkeys piled high with boxes of food, pots and pans, blankets and bedding, and bewildered children. Vanka was surprised: he had read that the NoirVillians were trying to stem this tide, refusing passage across their Sector to nuJus, afraid that they had too many of them settling in the JAD.

Vanka waited for an hour in the pouring rain, waited until he was sure that there were no HimPeril agents lurking in the shadows that surrounded the square, waited until the Border Guard the Code Noir had put the bite on arrived for his shift.

Just as he was on the point of despairing, the bastard finally showed up. But still Vanka chose to remain concealed in the darkness of the doorway, reluctant to leave his hiding place, watching as the sod spent ten minutes smoking a fag and chatting with the guard he was relieving. It was only when he was alone in the booth and had settled down to read his newspaper that Vanka made his move.

Life, decided Border Guard Sorro Anwoo, was mucho de good. He had a great gig scrutinising all the cats who wanted to enter the JAD, a gig that didn't involve too much heavy lifting and allowed him to invest a lot of time running the numbers in the tenement block he called home. Sure, Border Guards weren't paid enough to keep a mouse in molasses, but the possibilities for milking a little action on the side were, like, beaucoup de excellent. Sorro hadn't been in the job more than a month before he realised that whilst most of the nuJu cats trying to haul ass to the JAD didn't have the correct papers, what they usually did have was pocketfuls of long bread. And as the most desperate of these nuJu runners made their move in the late, late black when Sorro was on duty it was a lean night that didn't see him heading back to his crib with at least two hundred Guineas of tax-free income warming his wallet. But that, he decided, was chump change compared with what he would make tonight.

He had been offered a grand – a grand! – to turneth a blind eye when a cat named Jim Tyler showed up at his booth. But that was just chicken feed. That the Code Noir had gone to the trouble to smooth this cat's road in advance told Sorro two things: the first was that the guy taking the promenade powder was important to the max and the second was that if his friends were willing to pay a grand to get this Tyler item into the JAD then they would be willing to pay *two* grand.

So here he was in his booth at three thirty in the morning, idly studying the form guide for the runners in the Istanbul Derby, wrapping himself around a bumper of Solution and just glad to be sitting somewhere cosy and snug outta the rain most grievous, when this real sad sack of a Blank started hammering on his window. He looked real damped out. The only way he could've got wetter was if he'd gone swimming in his clothes.

Sorro eased open the window of his booth a couple of

centimetres to allow him to converse with the merman. 'Sure looks like rain,' he said in a conversational tone.

The man didn't answer, instead he pushed his papers through the slot.

With agonising deliberation Sorro examined said documents. 'Yo' dis "Jim Tyler" item?'

'Yeah,' said the Blank. 'That's what it says on the visa. I was told you'd be expecting me.'

'Ah'm expecting a cat 'bout one eighty-four tall.' He looked up and examined the Blank. 'Check. Black hair. Check, though dey didn't say nuffin' 'bout the hair dye that would be running down de side ob yo' face. Blue eyes. Check. Seventy kilos . . .'

'Look, can we get on with this? I'm drowning out here.'

'Gotta make sure yous de right cat now ain't ah? Cain't have no badniks skedaddling to the JAD wivout de proper authorisation now can we?' Sorro took another long slurping guzzle of his Solution and then slowly – *very* fucking slowly, he didn't dig this Blank cat's attitude – lit a cigarette. After a few languid puffs he gave the Blank a smile. 'Well, ah guess yo' is de cat dem buddies ov yo's bin talkin' to me 'bout, dem cats who want me to turn a blind eye.'

'And?' the Blank prompted.

'Trouble is, mah man, they's paid me to turn *wun* eye and ah's got two of dem. So which wun yo's want me to turn: left or right?'

'How much to turn both?'

'Price is a grand an eye.'

4

London: The Rookeries
The Demi-Monde: 2nd Day of Summer,
1005 ... 02:00

The Heydrich Institute for Natural Sciences in Berlin is famous throughout the Demi-Monde as the foremost centre for enquiry into the functioning of our world and its flora and fauna, indeed the Institute's work regarding diseases and their control is considered as being without peer. Despite the political upheaval in the ForthRight following the Troubles, the Institute still boasts an unrivalled number of prominent Professors including, *inter alia*, Josef Mengele, Robert Boyle, Georges Cuvier, Louis Agassiz and Emil Adolf von Behring, each of them preeminent in their field.

Choosing Your University: ForthRight Press

It was very early, just shy of two o'clock in the morning, and His Holiness the Very Reverend Aleister Crowley's body yearned for sleep. The weeks since the assassination of Beria and the failure of the ForthRight to invade Venice had been very taxing, and the pressure placed by Great Leader Heydrich on his subordinates 'to do something about the Lady IMmanual' had been enormous. But try as Crowley might – and he had been trying mightily hard – there seemed to be no spell, incantation or ritual that had any effect on the witch. Her powers, it seemed, were beyond those possessed by mortal man. And that was why he had sought help from the Spirit World.

He looked up from where he was seated at his desk to check the time by the grandfather clock ticking so ponderously on the other side of his shadow-bedecked study. There were only five minutes remaining before the appointed time of the meeting, and Crowley was confident that his guest would appear precisely as arranged. Septimus Bole was famously exact in his habits.

Crowley took a sip from his glass of Solution, his hand trembling as he did so. It was one of a whole series of glasses of Solution he had been communing with over the past hour as he sought to imbibe a little extra courage, and courage, whatever its provenance, he knew he would be needing in abundance. Bole was, by reputation, a terrifying individual, so much so that Crowley suspected that Heydrich was feigning illness simply to avoid having to meet the bastard. Not that Crowley was terribly surprised: since he had so narrowly missed death by Awful Tower, Heydrich hadn't been the same man, it was as though something had broken inside him. The Heydrich of old wouldn't have been so cowardly as to order a subordinate to take his place at such an important meeting and it was a piece of delegation that Crowley wasn't particularly happy about. Rumour had it that Bole was a man sprung from a nightmare, that he was somehow *inhuman*. Crowley gave a wry chuckle: as Bole was a Daemon, he couldn't be anything other than inhuman.

But . . .

But Daemon though Bole was, there was no denying that he was an ardent and effective supporter of the ForthRight. It was he who had given it the priceless gift of galvanicEnergy and who had made it possible for Heydrich's daughter, Aaliz, to journey to the Spirit World. And with his help the ultimate triumph of UnFunDaMentalism – in both worlds – was assured. Crowley just wished the securing of this assistance didn't necessitate him having to meet with the man. The Faustian bargain Heydrich had struck – that Bole manipulated the Demi-Monde to further the ambitions of the ForthRight and Heydrich, in exchange, had his scientists perfect the V3 plague weapon – was one that Crowley suspected the Great Leader was coming to regret.

The minutes dragged by and then, almost reluctantly, the clock struck two. As the chimes faded into silence, Crowley looked up to find Bole standing staring at him from across the room, having materialised out of nowhere. It had to be Bole; although Crowley had never met him before, that the room had become raw cold was a sure sign of the manifestation of a Daemon. It was as though Bole had sucked all the warmth and goodness out of the room.

Crowley shivered, took a long swallow of Solution and attempted to smile a greeting, but his mouth wouldn't co-operate. Bole wasn't the sort of man who encouraged smiles. He was an uncommonly tall and very, very thin individual, and clad as he was in a tight-fitting black suit he gave the impression of being nothing less than some huge spider. More, with his black top hat perched atop his head and his shaded spectacles resting on his hook of a nose there was a funereal cast to the man, this emphasised by his unnaturally pale complexion and his jet-black hair. Crowley wondered for a moment if Bole was an albino.

Making a determined effort to still his jangling nerves, Crowley stammered a greeting. 'Good morning, Professor Bole. I am grateful you were able to spare the time to visit the Demi-Monde. Please, won't you take a seat?' He gestured to the chair stationed in front of his desk.

Without a word Bole crossed the room, wiped the seat of the chair with a handkerchief he conjured from his sleeve and then, after ensuring the creases in his trousers weren't compromised, settled himself.

As he did so, Crowley had an opportunity to study his sour-faced visitor more closely. The man was younger than he had thought, perhaps only fifty or so, but he looked prematurely aged. His skin had the boiled-owlish pallor possessed by those who spent their life indoors and there were deep shadows under his unblinking eyes suggesting that this peculiar man never slept. In sum, he had a face that might more properly belong to a week-old corpse.

'The Great Leader sends his apologies—'

Bole waved Crowley into silence, finished the arranging of his long legs, flicked a non-existent piece of fluff from his jacket and then let his gaze settle on the mage. 'Let us dispense with platitudes and get to business. I am here, Crowley, at your behest; it was you, was it not, who placed the notice in *The Stormer* requesting that I attend this meeting?' Bole spoke excessively quietly, so much so that Crowley had to lean across his desk to better hear what the man said. His intonation was strange too – clipped and emotionless. As he listened to him, he came to the disturbing conclusion that if engines could be contrived to speak, they would sound like Septimus Bole.

'You are correct, Professor, I was the one who placed the advert. Unfortunately there have been ... problems, problems the Great Leader felt you should be alerted about.'

A deep sigh from Bole. 'It is ever the way, is it not? I ask the incompetents who manage the ForthRight to perform a task, I provide them with the wherewithal to execute said task and I am rewarded with failure. But I trust I will not be *too* disappointed, my mood has already been somewhat darkened by the necessity of visiting this pestilential place at such a ridiculous hour. I find myself quite distracted and in a frame of mind where even the slightest provocation will stimulate quite excessive reprisals. Do you understand me, Crowley?'

Crowley understood the bastard all right: Bole's 'reprisals' were famous within the more rarefied circles of the ForthRight. To gain thinking time, he began to light a cigarette.

Bole leant back in his chair, looking at him quizzically. 'You are permitted to smoke in my presence, Crowley, only if, as a corollary to your noisome addiction, I am permitted to vomit over your boots.'

Cursing himself for forgetting how abstemious Bole was, Crowley stubbed out the cigarette, took a deep breath and began, diving straight to the heart of the matter. There was no way of sugar-coating this particular pill. 'I must report that the Lady IMmanual still lives. More, it seems, her position has been strengthened by her being appointed Doge of Venice, replacing the murdered Doge Catherine-Sophia.'

'I know this,' said Bole with a dismissive wave of his hand. 'The witch has certain . . . abilities and has proven a formidable adversary. That is why I have taken steps to deter her from any further tinkering with the Demi-Monde. There will be no more miracles. But,' and here the man's cold eyes bored into Crowley, 'Venice remains important to us as it is the location of the Column of Loci, an artefact which must – I repeat *must* – be moved with all expediency to its final resting place atop the Great Pyramid in Terror Incognita. You of all people, understand the Column's true significance. You of all people, understand the role the Column will play in the Ceremony of Purification . . . in achieving the Final Solution.'

'The Column is ever in my thoughts, Professor.' Wasn't that the truth. The bloody thing was haunting Crowley: he worried constantly about how to get it out of Venice and on to Terror Incognita and how he would raise it to the top of the Great Pyramid once he got it there. It was the Column which would activate the power of the Great Pyramid and this, in turn, would scour all UnderMentionables from the face of the Demi-Monde.

Bole sniffed. 'I had anticipated that the task of moving the Column would be accomplished with only the minimum of difficulty, but the interference of the Lady IMmanual has thrown these plans into disarray. I had also hoped the ForthRight army would have taken Venice by now, but in this, as in so many other things, I have been disappointed.'

Not as disappointed as those poor sods who had found themselves drowning in the Grand Canal when the Lady performed the Miracle of the Canal, Crowley mused, but he decided to keep this observation to himself.

'Even without the intervention of the Lady IMmanual, an invasion will be difficult, Professor. The Venetian army has been reinforced by the alignment of Venice with NoirVille and with the imminent invasion of the Coven the ForthRight's military resources are stretched very thin. Too thin, our military strategists tell us, to make a renewed assault on Venice.'

'I am alive to the need for the ForthRight to secure its coal supplies from the Coven but it is *vital* that the Column of Loci be brought under the ForthRight's control.' Bole was lost in thought for a moment, then, 'I have intelligence that the Lady is intent on moving the Column to the Temple of Lilith and the only way this might be done is by transporting the Column by river. That will be our chance. You must order your cryptos in Venice to keep the Galerie des Anciens where the Column is housed under constant watch and to send word immediately the Column is moved.'

Crowley gave an eager nod. 'I will ensure that this is done, Professor.'

'But know this, Crowley, with regard to the Column there can be no mistakes. I will hold you personally responsible for any failure. Do you understand?'

Another, though much less eager, nod from Crowley.

'Then let us turn our attention to the invasion of the Coven. It may be that this presents more opportunities than the somewhat prosaic one of securing a supply of coal. Tell me, how goes the development of Vengeance Weapon V3 ... the Plague weapon?'

The change of topic was so unexpected that for a moment Crowley was a little nonplussed. Quickly he scanned his memory of the briefing regarding the ForthRight's secret and war-winning Vengeance Weapons given at yesterday's PolitBuro meeting.

'Not well, Professor Bole. Following the death of the personnel testing the prototype V3 in Warsaw at the end of last Winter there has been a reluctance to authorise its further use until there is an effective antidote. Five hundred personnel died ...'

Bole's cane slashed across Crowley's desk, making him jump back in fear. 'I am careless whether five hundred or five hundred *thousand* died, what I care about is having the plague perfected. The successful refinement of the plague weapon is of the utmost importance.' Shaking his head to demonstrate his disappointment, Bole continued. 'These failures baffle me. Have I not provided you with the very best scientists to produce the plague? Did I not have the likes of Mengele, Newton, Mendel, Boyle, Cuvier, Agassiz and Magnus brought to Berlin to work under your command? And yet still you have the temerity to announce failure. The development of the plague weapon is the most important of all the tasks I have set you, more important even than the defeat of the Lady IMmanual.'

Bole paused for a moment as though collecting his thoughts. 'But where your scientists have failed, Crowley, others have not. The Coven's Dr Merit Ptah is engaged in the development of a plague weapon similar to weapon V3, and this, I am informed, is close to success. I trust you appreciate the danger this poses to the ForthRight.'

Crowley's mouth went dry: he appreciated it all right. He remembered the terrible way the poor sods testing the V3 plague had died. It hadn't been pretty.

'Ptah appears to be a very skilled and accomplished scientist,' Bole continued, 'and the product of that skill and accomplishment resides in her laboratory in Hereji-Jo Castle. You must infiltrate a crypto into the Castle, his mission to steal the Doctor's work and destroy her research facility.'

'But ... but ... Hereji-Jo Castle is, by repute, an impregnable fortress.'

'Indeed it is and once more, Crowley, it seems I must come to your assistance.' He pushed a piece of paper across the desk. 'The Lady IMmanual isn't the only one able to make amendments to the configuration of the Demi-Monde. As you will see from these plans, by the addition of a postern gate I have rendered the Castle a little less impregnable than is commonly believed. A capable and resourceful crypto will now be able to gain access to the fortress.'

'I have such an agent,' Crowley interjected hurriedly. This at least was the truth. The SS had spent years trying to turn one of the LessBiens in Empress Wu's court and finally, by the use of blackmail, they had succeeded. 'I have a highly placed female crypto active in the Coven, a crypto ready, willing and very able to perform such a mission.'

'A woman? I am never comfortable when I am obliged to rely on the more febrile talents of women. It is therefore fortunate that I will have her abetted by three of my own men.' He turned and nodded towards the far corner of the room.

The three individuals – Crowley was loath to use the word 'men' in describing them – standing in the shadows were terrifying. They radiated menace, but being as they were nigh on seven feet tall, this was hardly surprising. But what *was* surprising – bloody unsettling, actually – was their eyes: they seemed to be possessed of cat's eyes, yellow with a black slit for an iris.

Grigori.

'This is Baraquel, Chazaqijal and Sariel,' said Bole casually, as though introducing such strange creatures was a common occurrence. 'They will assist your agent in the stealing of Dr Ptah's formula from her laboratory.' Bole smiled. 'Perhaps if your agent is as well placed as you imply, she might even be able to suborn Dr Ptah ... have her come over to our side.'

As Crowley nodded his understanding, Bole raised a gold pomander to his nose and inhaled deeply. Obviously he found the soot-heavy air of the Rookeries irksome. 'Victory and the conquest of the Demi-Monde are almost within the ForthRight's grasp, but there is still much to be done. You have two principal tasks, Crowley: the Column of Loci must be brought under our control and taken to Terror Incognita, and the secrets of Dr Ptah's work on the plague weapon secured and her laboratory destroyed.'

With that Bole stood up to indicate that the meeting was at an end.

'I can brook no more failure, Crowley,' were his final words as he disappeared back into the darkness.

5

The Doge's Palace, Venice
The Demi-Monde:
2nd Day of Summer, 1005 ... 03:00

That woeMen were created from the most repulsive and despicable creature, the serpent, does much to explain their inferiority. The great Aristotle himself regarded woeMen as simply '*mutilated Men*', a mere receptacle for the Soul of HumanKind which is carried in semen. Father Lotario de Conti in his study of the wiles of Lilith notes that the HIM Book tells us that '*the wickedness of woeMen is greater than all the other wickedness of the Demi-Monde*'. And His HimPerial Reverence Mohammed Ahmed al-Mahdi warns that Man must be ever on his guard against the scheming and pernicious wiles of woeMen as they are an affront to Nature, it being their Lilithian purpose in life to make Men lose their Cool.

An Idiot's Guide to ManHood: Selim the Grim,
HimPerial Instructional Leaflets

Billy didn't like the Demi-Monde: it was too quiet. Where he lived in New York no matter what time it was of the day or night he always knew there were other people about. He could hear the traffic moving in the street three floors below his apartment, he could hear the music coming at him through the tenements' thin walls, he could hear people laughing and shouting and yelling ... he could hear life.

But not in the Demi-Monde. Here everything was hushed. Standing on the balcony of the suite of rooms Ella had given him, all he could hear was the sound of the water lapping in the canals. It was spooky, especially as it was so dark. There were no street lights in Venice and if it hadn't been for the moon he wouldn't have been able to see anything. And to make things worse it hadn't stopped raining since he'd arrived. Billy shivered and pulled his cloak more snugly around his shoulders.

He fucking hated the Demi-Monde. Hated that it was so quiet, hated that it was so dark and especially hated that he couldn't get high. No one seemed to deal in the Demi-Monde.

Worst of all was that he was having trouble getting his head around the fact that the fucking place wasn't *real* . . . it was just a computer game on steroids.

Oh, some of the computer games the nerdniks had played at school were kinda out there with those losers pretending to be orcs and wizards and elves and shit, but this was something else again. This was computer gaming turned up to eleven. Virtual world or not, it was difficult to believe that the Demi-Monde was just digital jerking off and that made it fucking freaky.

But then Bole had warned him that the DM was Weird Central and with a million bucks waiting for him when he got back to the Real World it wasn't too much of a stretch just to stay cool.

Just keep thinking about the dough.

Yeah, the money was the important thing and to earn it all he had to do was keep Sis locked down and stop her making waves . . . or miracles. It was his job to persuade her to stop fucking around playing nigga-in-charge and to haul ass back home.

Not that Ella seemed ready to listen to him; she was really digging this whole goddess trip. That bitch had really put the trembles on him. Bole hadn't said anything about the changes she'd gone through since she'd arrived in the place, but she sure as hell wasn't the same Ella he'd known six months ago. This new Ella was one scary bitch who walked around like she owned the joint, which, from what he could make out, she very nearly did. Nobody messed with Ella. Even de Sade treated her real carefully and from what he'd seen of de Sade he was one cat who really liked to put the hurt on people. He was one mean mother ... but Ella was meaner.

Real mean.

Fuck, she hadn't even twitched when he'd laid the line on her that unless she cut out all the jinky miracle crap then Bole would get hot and heavy on his ass. All she'd done was laugh and tell him that Bole wouldn't dare touch him. And then she'd said that as far as miracles were concerned she was finished for now but she had a doozy up her sleeve scheduled for the end of Summer.

So, as far as Billy saw it, he had no choice: he'd have to cap her. Her performing more miracles would seriously damage his chances of collecting his million bucks.

The problem was *how* to kill her. He'd heard some pretty wild stories about how handy Ella was, how she had sliced and diced some real bad mothers while she'd been in the Demi-Monde. There was even a story going the rounds that some cat had tried to shoot her and she'd *caught* the bullet. Bullshit, of course, but it had decided Billy on a policy of slow and cautious. He'd make sure that he really knew what he was up against before he made his move. But the problem with slow and cautious was that it was fucking boring, especially as there was no prancing powder available to take the edge off life.

He wandered aimlessly back into his room and took his frustration out on a vase of flowers by hurling it against a wall: Billy fucking hated flowers. He was just about to kick the shit out of a marble statue of some dead dude when there was a quiet knock on his door. Billy frowned, wondering who the fuck would be coming to call at three o'clock in the morning. He crossed the room and took a look through the spyhole set in the middle of the door. It was the big guy who called himself Selim the Grim. Selim was OK. Selim was a brother. He might be a backdoor brother but Billy was cool with that: guys being gay just meant there was more pussy for straight cats like him.

He opened the door. Selim wasn't alone, he had two women with him, though as they were swathed from head to toe in black burkas Billy couldn't dig whether they were young or old, fit or fugly.

'Good evening, Duke William, and my apologies for calling on you at such a late hour.'

It took a second for Billy to dig that the 'Duke William' Selim was talking about was him. Ella had laid the title on him on account of him being her brother. He shrugged the guy into his room and shut the door.

'I bring greetings from His HimPerial Majesty Shaka Zulu, who wishes me to ensure that all your desires are being catered for.'

'Why's this Shaka cat worried 'bout me?'

'You are the twin brother of Doge IMmanual, Your Grace, the twin brother of the Messiah. The same blood that flows in her body flows in yours. Our holy men believe that your coming is divinely inspired, after all, according to HimPerialism's most sacred book, the HIM Book, the Messiah cannot be a woeMan but *must* be a Man. They see you as the Man to fulfil that prophecy.'

'No shit?' mused Billy as he poured two healthy glasses of cognac. Cognac was the only thing that had kept him sane since he'd touched down in the Demi-Monde. 'From what I hear, yo' guys in NoirVille are really big on male supremacy and all that shit, right?'

Or more exactly, what PINC told him. It was neat having an encyclopedia stuck in his head.

'That is correct, Your Grace. HimPerialism teaches us that the Fall of Man was brought about by Lilith, the first woeMan, when she tempted Adam to eat the fruit of Yggdrasil, the sacred tree. This ended the Time of Maximum Coolness, the state of Harmony that existed before Lilith's betrayal. As punishment for Lilith's connivance in the Fall, ABBA decreed that henceforward woeMen would be required to conduct themselves according to the precepts of subMISSiveness, that is, they must be at all times Mute, Invisible, Subservient and Sexually Modest.'

'You wanna try telling that to Ella. I don't think she's in the market for submissiveness.'

Selim smiled and took a sip of his cognac. 'And that is why, Your Grace, the powers that be in NoirVille are so pleased that you have come to the Demi-Monde. Although pragmatism has prompted us to put aside our natural aversion to allying ourselves with a people ruled by a woeMan, we live in hope that one day it might be the true Messiah – a *male* Messiah – who sits on the throne of Venice.' He paused. 'You, perhaps?'

'Yeah, well, where I come from, Selim, we kinda see things the same way: with guys on top and bitches underneath, if yo' get my meaning.'

'I am pleased that our opinions have so much commonality. But it would not do for us to get ahead of ourselves. Doge IMmanual is very powerful and has an aversion to having this power challenged. It would be better if, for the moment, we feigned obedience.'

'I'm reading yo', bro.'

'Excellent. Lord Shaka has commanded that I give you this.' Selim clapped his hands and immediately one of the woeMen oiled across the room and placed a small silver bowl on the table to the side of the chair where Billy was sitting. When she removed the lid he saw that it was full to the brim with blue powder.

Billy eyed it suspiciously. 'So what's this shit, man?'

'It is a powder called Dizzi, Your Grace. It's a drug that the NoirVillians are very enamoured of; it is a powerful aphrodisiac much favoured for its ability to stimulate sexual performance.'

PINC had no information regarding Dizzi, which was odd, but this didn't deter Billy. Without thinking, he took up a spoon, dug it deep into the bowl and snorted back the powder long and hard. The effect was both immediate and incredibly stimulating; the fug in his brain caused by the excess of cognac he'd been chugging cleared instantaneously and his senses sharpened. He felt enlivened, energised and his skin tingled. He hadn't felt this charged since he'd come to the Demi-Monde. His prick was already doing the flag salute.

'Wooo-weee . . . the store is open! Fuck, that's bumpin'.'

As was his wont, Billy immediately went back for a second dose, but the spoon didn't make it to his nose, Selim placing a restraining hand on his. 'With regards to Dizzi, it is better to proceed with caution. It takes several weeks to develop a tolerance of its more . . . unusual side effects.'

Billy brushed the hand away and snorted the spoonful up his nose. 'Don't fuss and fret about me, bro. There ain't no chemistry known to man that I cain't handle.'

'I can see you are a man of superhuman strength and tolerance,' said Selim equitably, 'but then, of course, you are the Messiah. And that is why Lord Shaka has seen fit to provide you with a means of slaking these appetites.'

He clapped his hands and immediately the woeMen removed their burkas to reveal that they were young, attractive and very naked. 'These are a gift to you, Your Grace, to do with what you will. Understand they have been well educated with regards to subMISSiveness and will obey your every command.'

Billy got to his feet and wandered across to where the girls were standing. 'My every command?' he asked. 'I gotta tell yo', Selim, ma man, I can get real inventive when it comes to fucking bitches as sleek as these two honeys.'

'Their only duty is to obey, Your Grace.'

Billy felt his spirits rising, along with his dick. Maybe the Demi-Monde wasn't gonna be so bad after all.

6

The JAD
The Demi-Monde:
2nd Day of Summer, 1005 ... 04:00

The most important aspect of a NoirVillian Man's honour code is the maintenance of his Machismo, this being essential if he is to enjoy the respect of his fellow Men. This necessitates a Man acting in a Cool manner, no matter what the provocation or the circumstances. 'Cool' is the most difficult concept in the whole of HimPerialist thought, being readily recognisable in those who possess it but almost impossible to define. The High Priest of Cool, Father Miles Davis, comes closest with this description: *'Cool is possessed by a cat who is in harmony with the Kosmos and has a transcendental inner peace which makes him at one with ABBA and immune to the vicissitudes of the Demi-Monde. Cool is the ability to say "fuck off" without uttering a word.'* As might be supposed, slights to a Man's Machismo are the most common cause of violence within NoirVille.

An Idiot's Guide to ManHood: Selim the Grim, HimPerial
Instructional Leaflets

Vanka pushed the money through the window and waited while the malignant sod of a Border Guard enjoyed himself by counting it. Finally, with a shrug, the guard pulled the lever that opened the large metal gate set into the high wall surrounding the JAD – the infamous 'JAD Wall' – built by Shaka to keep his people away from the corrupting influence of the nuJus. The guard motioned Vanka through.

It was quite a feeling to pass through the gate. For the first time since he'd escaped Venice, Vanka felt just a tad more optimistic about life. Despite the best efforts of the Signori di Notte *and* the HimPeril, he had made it to the safety of the JAD. Not that the JAD seemed to be an overly inviting place.

It was only when the heavy steel gate clanged shut behind him and the guard turned off the gaslights that he noticed how dark it was. There were no street lights – apparently Shaka refused to allow enough gas to be piped into the JAD for it to be squandered on such fripperies – and there were no lights in any of the windows of the heavily grilled storefronts he wandered past. The streets were deserted too.

Luckily, there was still one diehard pedicab driver waiting for those unfortunates entering the JAD. 'You for hire?' Vanka asked hopefully.

'*Feh!* You think I'm sitting here just for zhe good of my health? You think I vanna sit here vaiting for *yolds* like you to come unt ask me zheir stupid questions? Of course I'm for hire, even got a permit to operate so it's all *kosher*. You must be a real *putz* to ask such a question. Vot are you, a NoirVillian, or something?'

'Yeah,' Vanka lied.

The nuJu pedicab driver sniffed and leant back beneath his huge umbrella. Obviously everyone in NoirVille believed that leaving their customers standing in the rain was a great negotiating tactic. He was right.

'It's raining again,' the driver noted, which Vanka decided, as the rain seeped down his neck, was one of the most obsolete observations ever made. '*Azoy*, it's another night most dank unt dismal. Not a night for valking: zhe drains unt zhe sewers can't cut it no more unt every strolling cat's vading ankle-deep in zhe thick brown lotion de motions. *A klug.* Zo, vhere's a *goyisher kop* like you headed?'

'Hotel Copasetic,' answered Vanka. That was the name he had been given by Josie. It was one of the Code Noir's safe houses.

'*ABBA zol ophten!*' said the driver with a mournful shake of his head. 'God forbid! Zhat's in JuGrad, man, zhe most shitful part of zhe whole JAD. Some real nasty *parekhs* strut zheir stuff in JuGrad.' He gave Vanka an unhappy smile. 'If zhe JAD is zhe arsehole of the world, man, zhen JuGrad is half a mile up it. Nah ... I wouldn't wanna go valking up zhere on my lonely; I'd wanna go up zhere in a nice dry pedicab mit a big mean fucker like me riding shotgun.' And to emphasise the point, he patted a huge blunderbuss strapped to the side of his pedicab.

Fucking Hel, thought Vanka, *if the pedicab drivers are using street howitzers, what are the real badniks in the JAD armed with?*

'How much?' asked Vanka, who was fast coming to the conclusion that if he stood out in the rain much longer he'd be in danger of shrinking.

'One hundred Guineas.'

'I think I'll walk,' he said, yanking up the collar of his water-logged coat.

'*Zei nit a nor!* It'll be your funeral, man. But dig zhat in zhe late black zhere is gonna be a load of zadnik-inclined scumboids on zhe prowl around JuGrad looking for action. Lotta zadniks come into the JAD cruising for fresh meat unt zhey gonna really love turd-tumbling zhat soft Blank ass of yours. Jah, a *pisher* like you is gonna be cluster-fucked all vays to Sunday before you've padded a mile. You dig?'

Vanka dug. 'I'll give you fifty Guineas,' he offered, remembering Josie's advice that everything in the JAD required haggling over.

'Fifty Guineas! You vont zhat my children starve? Vot are you, some sort of *gonif*? You trying to svindle me, man?'

'Sixty,' Vanka countered.

'Feh! Vot a *karger*! Okay ... sixty.'

Vanka clambered into the cab and, thankfully, if a little belatedly, out of the rain.

As he was driven through the dark streets, he decided that the JAD fully deserved its reputation for being a shitheap. A busy shitheap: whilst streets near the JAD Wall were empty of traffic and pedestrians, the deeper they drove into JAD the busier it became. Everywhere Vanka looked there were gangs of navvies building pillboxes, erecting huge steel anti-steamer obstacles and garlanding hoops of barbed wire along the sides of the roads. Every intersection was barricaded and every barricade was manned by heavily armed militia. The JAD was a city getting ready for war.

But it hadn't always been like this. Vanka remembered the JAD as it was when the nuJus had first inherited it. Then it had been a part of NoirVille rich with large and ornate buildings, buildings bedecked with domes and cupolas, all arranged so that they faced the direction of the Sphinx, the HimPerialists' holiest monument. Unfortunately three years of being sucked dry by Shaka had left precious little money spare to invest in municipal maintenance. Whereas NoirVille was – thanks to the near-monopoly it had of the blood trade – the richest of all the Sectors in the Demi-Monde, the JAD was poor and this poverty was reflected in its state of decay.

Yeah, a lot had changed since the nuJus had taken over, mainly the image the nuJus had had of being soft touches. They had proved themselves to be tough fuckers, willing to fight to protect their newly acquired homeland.

But what Vanka found even more disturbing than the preparations being made for war was the anti-NoirVillian, anti-Him-Perialist graffiti that decorated the place. As the pedicab bumped and crashed over the smashed-up roads, Vanka was astonished to see the amount of graffiti that crawled over the walls they pedalled past. Shaka might have agreed – in exchange for a regular supply of Aqua Benedicta – to allow the nuJus to settle in the JAD, but there was no disguising what the nuJus thought of him.

The nuJus and the NoirVillians hated one another: the NoirVillians hated the nuJus because they rejected HimPerialism and granted refuge to woeMen fleeing their fathers or husbands, and the nuJus hated the NoirVillians for being obscene, disgusting, misogynistic homosexual bastards.

But like many unhappy marriages, the partners managed to make it work. So when the NoirVillians who liked to walk on the wild side visited the JAD for a little off-HimPerial R & R, they were made to pay. And Vanka in his role as fun-seeking NoirVillian began paying when the pedicab driver pulled up outside his hotel and demanded the fare for the journey. Sixty Guineas was extortion, but having seen some of the no-brows prowling the pavements and having heard the crackle of two firefights, Vanka decided to pay. Anyway, the pedicab driver was a big guy.

'No tip?'

Vanka looked at the guy as though he was demented. 'Yeah ... don't live in the JAD,' he said quietly and then turned towards his hotel.

He had had high hopes for 'the Copasetic': apparently, in reBop – the lingua franca of NoirVille – the word copasetic meant 'excellent'. But whatever the hotel was, it wasn't 'excellent'. The Copasetic was, according to Josie, a 'family-run' hotel, though quite what species the family belonged to she hadn't said. 'Family-run', Vanka decided as he eyed the hotel's crumbling frontage, must be a euphemism for 'shitty'.

Once – a long, long time ago – the building had been truly impressive. Then it had been a wonderful baroque confection of flowing curves and stylised arches, but now it was a flaking, dilapidated remembrance of times past. That somebody had had the bright idea of painting its sandstone exterior a lurid red colour did nothing to raise the tone of the building: it looked like a whorehouse, which presumably was the point.

After enduring the abuse of his pedicab driver – the absence of a tip obviously rankled – Vanka hauled his damp arse across the waterlogged and overgrown front garden, up the hotel's steps, through the scarred wooden door and along the short dark corridor that, he hoped, led to reception. It did, and there, under the uncertain light cast by the oil lamp hanging tenuously from the ceiling by a length of dust-ensnared chain, sat a fat woman reading a very well-thumbed copy of a book. For a long moment the woman didn't look up or in any way acknowledge Vanka's presence, seemingly engrossed in the story she was enjoying.

Vanka coughed.

Reluctantly the woman lifted her head and gave Vanka a smile. He rather wished she hadn't. Dentistry in the JAD had obviously fallen further behind than the town's road repair programme. The few teeth the woman had left – supplemented by two gold incisors – were crooked, stained and signalled her breath was as mouldy as the rest of her.

'*Shalom*,' said the woman, accompanying her greeting with a leering smile.

'I'm sorry,' said Vanka as he mimed incomprehension, 'I don't speak nuJu.' A lie, of course, but while he spoke all of the languages of the Demi-Monde fluently, he guessed that his alter ego, Jim Tyler, a NoirVillian, wouldn't be familiar with nuJu.

The woman winked at Vanka, which he found very disconcerting, until she winked at him again and Vanka decided she was the victim of a rather disturbing nervous tic. He hoped she was, anyway.

'Azoy? Tough shit. Zo ... vot can I do for you?'

'My name's Jim Tyler,' he answered. 'I understand that a booking has been made in my name.'

The woman nodded, stood up, then turned to bend down over her register. Arse in the air, she shuffled through a ragtag pile of paper until she pulled out the sheet she was looking for. 'Jah. I've put you in Room Twenty-Three ... it's our best room ... our *very* best room.' The woman looked at Vanka as though evaluating him. 'It's ten Guineas a night ... payable a veek in advance.'

Stunned by the outrageous price, Vanka dug into his bag and extracted the purse of coins that Josie had supplied him with. The woman eyed the money in a predatory way. 'You vant any extra?' she asked.

'Extra?' answered Vanka cautiously.

'Yah, I'm thinking a *gezinteh* like you might vant something that ain't on the menu.' Another wink. 'Pawn, Dizzi dust ... or, maybe, a sheMan?'

Vanka shook his head. He was about to take offence at the offer of a boy but then remembered that he was playing the role of a NoirVillian.

'No.'

'A girl?' The woman was nothing if not a trier.

'No, nothing.'

The woman shrugged and went back to the study of her book. Vanka looked around the grimy hallway, saw the sign 'Rooms' and moved towards the staircase, his rain-wrecked boots squelching a wet trail that marked his passing.

'*A brokh!*' he heard the woman exclaim behind him. 'I vould lose my head if it vos loose. Tell me, Mr Jim Tyler, how long vill you be staying?'

'All Summer,' answered Vanka, and the depressing realisation was that that might actually be the case.

7

The Coven
The Demi-Monde:
2nd Day of Summer, 1005 ... 05:00

To the HerEticals of the Coven, 'women' is seen as a demeaning, heterosexual, bondage term for the female gender. In order to avoid the linguistic contamination of patriarchal-centric speech, this book uses the HerEtical terms 'Femme' in place of 'Woman' and 'nonFemme' in place of 'Man'. The sublime experience associated with Femme2Femme love, romance and sex is referred to as MoreBienism and those who have come to embrace MoreBienism as MoreBiens. Unfortunately, the tag MoreBien has been lampooned throughout the Demi-Monde, with Femme followers of MoreBienism being ridiculed as *Less*Biens. LessBien is a pejorative, patriarchal word replete with connotations of the suppression and belittlement of Femmes, and will not be used in this book.

The Young Femme's Guide to the HerTory of the Coven: HerTorianNoN Fan Ye, Covenite Textbooks and Periodicals

It was a confirmation of how badly the Coven needed Trixie that not only had they appointed her head of their armed forces, but Imperial Non Mao ZeDong had also agreed – damned reluctantly, it had to be said – that she could meet with Wysochi. The NoN had blustered and prevaricated, complaining that it was not seemly for an officerFemme of her rank to display feelings for an unneutered nonFemme, but Trixie had insisted and, as Mao had come to appreciate, Trixie was a difficult girl to refuse.

And with regard to Wysochi she was *very* determined: she had to know that the man she loved was alive and well. That was why she was sitting, a couple of hours shy of dawn, in a damp and draughty room in the down-at-heel barracks that the remnants of the Warsaw Free Army had been calling home since the beginning of Spring. But none of these discomforts could detract from the happiness she felt seeing Wysochi again. Of all the people in the Demi-Monde he was the only one she trusted . . . the only one she loved.

She knew though that she had to conceal her feelings: Mao – spiteful, vindictive bastard that he was – was sitting at her side watching for behaviour that 'did not accord with HerEtical teachings', having warned her that given the merest excuse, he would terminate the meeting. So every question and every answer had to be couched carefully to avoid provoking his displeasure.

Despite Mao's baleful presence, it was still marvellous to see Wysochi again. Standing there in front of the table she and Mao were seated at, he looked very much as she remembered him from their last meeting a Season ago: big, bold and disrespectful. His face was, perhaps, a little fuller – Coven food, she decided, must agree with him – and he did look remarkably clean. Wysochi had obviously taken a liking to the steam baths the Chinks were so fond of and he looked almost respectable without his habitual frosting of mud and cordite.

Almost.

Clean, she could see every one of the scars he had picked up during the fighting in Warsaw. They made him look like a pirate. 'You're looking well, Major Wysochi,' she began.

'You too, Colonel,' replied Wysochi and he gave her a wink.

For a moment Trixie struggled with the urge to leap up and hug the man, but with Mao in attendance this was impossible. Mao would probably swoon if she did: demonstrations of affection between men and women – between Femmes and nonFemmes – were taboo in the Coven.

'It's GeneralFemme now, Major. Following the death of Jeanne Dark I've been appointed head of the Covenite army.'

Wysochi whistled. 'Congratulations. GeneralFemme, eh? I've gotta say I never thought the powers that be in the Coven would have the intelligence to do something so sensible.'

Mao sucked his teeth to show that he judged Wysochi's observation to be borderline unacceptable.

'I like the shaved head too. Very fetching.'

Trixie ran a hand over her shaven pate and gave a wry smile. 'I was obliged, Major, to have my head shaved in order to conform to HerEtical protocol. Covenite women who have embraced MoreBienism have taken to having this done to show that they have cut all ties with nonFemmes and have no use for sexual objectification. And as the new Commander of the Covenite Army, it was felt necessary that I should dress in accordance with the most rigorous of HerEtical teachings.'

'Hence the overalls?'

Trixie looked down at the plain denim boiler suit she was wearing; only the gold pips on the epaulettes denoted her new status and rank. 'Correct. These are *jiangs*. Every Femme in the Coven wears them.'

'And very nice they must look too,' Wysochi deadpanned.

The conversation faltered for a moment and suddenly Trixie felt very tired and dispirited. She'd had hardly a moment's sleep since she'd been released from prison just thirty-six hours before, her time taken up by a whirl of inspections, parades and briefings.

And all that time festering at the back of her mind was the

suspicion that Empress Wu would eventually betray her and renege on her promise to free the WFA. That was the other reason why she'd insisted on seeing Wysochi, to confirm for herself that he and the rest of the Varsovian fighters were still alive. But the pleasure of meeting Wysochi couldn't rid her of the belief that once her usefulness to Wu was at an end, she and the WFA would be disposed of. She would just have to get her betrayal in first, though for the moment she would bide her time by playing the dutiful and loyal GeneralFemme.

'How have you and the rest of the WFA been treated?' she asked as lightly as she could.

'Oh, we're all fine. We're well fed and allowed to exercise. There's been a little moaning amongst the men about their not being able to see their womenfolk, but other than that all of us are just the same.'

The key phrase of Wysochi's was 'all of us are just the same' which signalled that none of the male Varsovian fighters had been gelded; this, at least, was good news. Trixie turned to Mao: 'Why have my fighters been separated? The WFA makes no distinction between men and women, both fight and die as equals.'

The NoN's face remained totally expressionless. She hated Mao's inscrutability. She liked to see emotion in people; without emotion they were nothing more than automata. This was, she decided, a good metaphor: the NoNs – the eunuchs – of the Coven *were* automata. They spoke like robots, they acted like robots and they even *looked* like robots.

Just as Mao did. There was something disturbingly doll-like about the NoN; he was a little too plump, his skin too smooth and rosy, his pigtail too perfectly coiffed and his black and silver robes too clean and flawlessly pressed for him to be anything other than artificial. But artificial or not, the arrogant bastard had the ear of Empress Wu so he had to be watched.

Without a flicker of an expression Mao raised a hand adorned with excessively long fingernails – these apparently designed to show that he was engaged in intellectual rather than low-caste manual work – and with a disdainful flick of his wrist waved her question aside. 'In the Coven the barbaric and obscene indulgence in heterosexual physical relationships is outlawed, except, that is, for the purposes of officially sanctioned procreation. Whilst in the less enlightened Sectors of the Demi-Monde nonFemmes are encouraged to force their disgusting desires on Femmes, here in the Coven this cannot be condoned. It is unthinkable that we should allow your WFA fighters to rut like animals: it would be an affront to HerEticalism.'

'Apparently, attempts have been made to indoctrinate the WFA's women fighters in the delights of Femme2Femme sex,' interrupted Wysochi.

'Not "indoctrinate",' corrected the NoN sharply, his sing-song voice with its strange Chink accent rising an octave to signal his annoyance. 'They are merely being given the opportunity to understand the philosophy of HerEticalism and to enjoy the sublime pleasures and happiness flowing from the embracing of MoreBienism.'

'LessBienism more like,' grumped Wysochi.

A glare from the NoN. 'That is a pejorative term that is not used in the Coven. If you wish this interview to continue, Preferred Male Wysochi, you will desist from using such foul and offensive language.'

Trixie moved quickly to change the subject. The last thing she wanted was for the meeting to be brought to a premature end by a fit of NoNish pique. 'I asked Imperial Secretary Mao to arrange this meeting so that I could pick your mind, Major Wysochi. Heydrich has issued an ultimatum to the Coven stating that unless trading relations are "normalised" by noon today, a state of war will exist between the ForthRight and the

Coven. I am advised by Imperial Secretary Mao that the Coven will refuse these demands and therefore we must expect the ForthRight to commence its military operations in a little under eight hours. I anticipate that the invasion will be preceded by an artillery bombardment and once the Coven's shore defences have been pummelled to powder the UnFunnies will attempt to force the Volga. So . . . before the Summer is very much older, there will be fighting in the streets of Rangoon. This being the case, I would like your advice regarding how best to make a disposition of my army.'

Wysochi frowned: having been kept in isolation for over three months, he was obviously having a little difficulty getting up to speed with current events. 'Why do the UnFunnies want to invade the Coven? Last time I heard they had their hands full in the Quartier Chaud.'

'They ran into trouble. Our friend Ella Thomas pulled another of her miracle stunts and gave the ForthRight Army the turn-around. There's something of a stand-off going on down there.'

'The Lady IMmanual's up to her old tricks, eh? But that still doesn't explain why the ForthRight has got it in for the Coven.'

'There is a one-word answer to that question, Major: coal. The Coven is refusing to supply coal to the ForthRight until their army has withdrawn from the Quartier Chaud and, as the Coven is the only supplier of coal in the whole of the Demi-Monde, the ForthRight has got a little exercised about it.'

'A provocative thing to have done.'

'Not provocative, Preferred Male Wysochi,' corrected Mao, 'rather it was an act ordained by ABBA Herself. When the iChing was consulted during the Rite of 4Telling, it was ABBA who commanded that the Coven deny the ForthRight coal.'

Wysochi looked at Mao as though the NoN was unbalanced. 'Then it's a shame that ABBA isn't here to do the fighting, because the ForthRight will be coming at you hot and heavy.

Way I understand it, the ForthRight has only got seven, maybe eight weeks of coal reserves, so they'll want to take the Coven coal mines sooner rather than later, otherwise their steamers will go cold boilers. You're in for a hot Summer, GeneralFemme. How many fighters do you have?'

'Trained and combat-ready, about fifty thousand.'

'Fifty thousand! That all? What happened to the Covenite Army?'

Mao answered the question. 'At the order of Her Imperial Majesty Empress Wu, the army was purged of all antiFemme elements when the Coven was proclaimed a HerEtical Sector on the "Glorious Day of Liberation from the evil that is MALEvolence".'

'That was a long time ago.'

'Nine years. And since then most of the nonFemme fighters chose to emigrate to NoirVille rather than volunteer to have their naturally perverse MALEvolent tendencies muted by the process of castration.'

Wysochi didn't say a word but the expression on his face was very eloquent, obviously being of the opinion that given a choice between debollocking and relocating, most men would have been looking to secure the next berth on a barge heading to Cairo.

'We did, however, attract many Femmes from outside the Coven who wished to be part of the Sublime Revolution that is HerEticalism.'

'And now you've got an all-Femme army of just fifty thousand fighters.'

'Correct, Preferred Male Wysochi, though there are a number of NoNs within the Officer Corps. ReverendFemme Dark – may ABBA bring her soul safe to her ancestors – did a fine job of reconstituting the Covenite Army. Her Amazon Regiments are reputed to be some of the finest in the whole of the Demi-Monde.'

Trixie nodded her agreement. 'I inspected them yesterday morning. They're well equipped and look very capable.'

'But there're only fifty thousand of them.'

'Yes.'

'That is why,' continued Mao, 'upon the tragic death of ReverendFemme Dark, Her Imperial Majesty Empress Wu, in her divinely inspired wisdom, appointed GeneralFemme Dashwood as Commander of the Army. Her Imperial Majesty consulted the iChing, which indicated that if the Coven was to defeat the ForthRight then it must put its trust in General-Femme Dashwood. It was, of course, a somewhat unexpected divination but then ABBA works in mysterious ways Her wonders to perform.' Mao took a sip of water. 'Yet, on reflec-tion, ABBA's guidance was not as perverse as it first appeared. As you yourself know, Preferred Male Wysochi, the General-Femme has great experience in leading an army of untrained recruits to victory over the ForthRight. Even as we speak, Femmes are rushing to enlist in the Free Femme Army of Resistance.'

'Terrific,' observed an obviously unimpressed Wysochi. 'And I guess that the ForthRight will be so desperate for coal that it'll throw all its forces at you.'

'Yes,' said Trixie quietly. 'Observation balloons tell us that the ForthRight has ten divisions massed on the St Petersburg side of the Volga.'

'Half a million men . . . nonFemmes.'

'Give or take.'

'Who's commanding them?

'Archie Clement.'

'Shit, not him again. I was hoping someone would have shot him by now.'

This prompted a sardonic laugh from Trixie. 'I tried: that's why I spent all Spring in a Rangoon prison cell.'

'Shame you missed, GeneralFemme: killing that bastard would be worth three months in jail of anybody's time.' Wysochi gave a discouraging shake of his head. 'But here's the problem: military lore has it that to be successful when you attack across a river, you need to outnumber the opposition by five to one. The ForthRight outnumbers you by ten to one, so I guess, to use military terminology, GeneralFemme, you're fucked.'

'Maybe not, Major. There are things which give me some grounds for optimism: the WarJunks of AdmiralNoN Zheng Heii are impressive, as are the rocket batteries managed by CommanderNoN Jiao Yu. And then there's the Geek Fire—'

'That is classified information, GeneralFemme, and should not be discussed with a nonFemme,' warned Mao. 'And might I remind you, Major, that we came here today to hear your advice, not to endure your scatological comments.'

'Then my advice, Imperial Secretary, is to make sure that Archie Clement doesn't take the Anichkov Bridge. If he does, then he'll be able to transport his heavy equipment – especially his armoured steamers – into the Coven, and once he's done that, then you can prepare your NoN arse to receive a non-Femme kicking.'

The NoN leant over the table and gimleted Wysochi with a hard stare. 'Then you should pray to whichever pagan god you subscribe, Preferred Male Wysochi, that that does not happen, because if it does – if GeneralFemme Dashwood were to fail in the ABBA-given task of protecting the Coven – then it will go hard on you and your *gaijin* fighters . . . very hard indeed.' Mao rose to his feet. 'This meeting is over. I am commanded to attend an audience with Her Imperial Majesty in the Forbidding City.'

As a reluctant Trixie followed Mao out of the room, her mind whirred with possibilities. Nodding goodbye to Wysochi, she made the silent pledge that, given a chance, she would shake herself – and her WFA fighters – free of these monsters.

8

The NoirVillian Hub
The Demi-Monde:
2nd Day of Summer, 1005 ... 06:00

Of all the Mantle-ite monuments built by the Pre-Folk none is more enigmatic or mysterious than the Temple of Lilith. And the reason for this is simple: despite one thousand years of effort, the great doors guarding the Temple have resisted all attempts to open them. The secrets within remain inviolate and hence the Temple has become a staple ingredient in the plots of any number of penny dreadfuls, generally being portrayed as the home of vampyres, daemons or women with decidedly accommodating attitudes towards sex.

A Potted History of Penny Dreadfuls: **William Hogarth, Demi-Mondian Komic Books**

The low, ominous drone of the great horn echoed across the emptiness of the Hub alerting the world that a new order had come, signalling – though the Fragiles in their stupidity did not yet realise it – that Lilith had returned.

The girl who had once been Ella Thomas stood motionless, allowing herself to revel for just an instant in the magnificence of the occasion. This must, she decided, be how St Paul felt when he had his revelation on the road to Damascus, when he understood that he had been chosen by God to lead the world to ...

To what?

To Perfection. Yes, to the Perfection that had once been snatched from the world's grasp by a delinquent Nature. But this time there would be no mistake, this time she would make HumanKind perfect.

Now everything was set fair for her to have all of the Demi-Monde kneel before her. She had had Doge Catherine-Sophia eliminated and had assumed control of Venice. She had made alliance with Shaka Zulu – his scruples about aligning himself with a woeMan swept away by his greed to possess the secrets of Aqua Benedicta – and together Venice and NoirVille could outface any enemy. But even more importantly, she had control of the Column of Loci, which would allow her to rekindle the power sleeping in the Temple of Lilith . . . and to conquer the Real World.

Only the question of Vanka Maykov remained unsettled.

The *enigma* of Vanka Maykov, more like. Thinking of Maykov gave her pause. In an earlier incarnation she had loved him and it was an affection that still nagged at her soul. But Lilith wasn't Ella Thomas; Lilith was divine, Lilith was implacable, Lilith had no time for love. So she would use all her power to erase her memory of the man and, hopefully, any feelings for him that might still be lingering in her heart.

So resolved, she took a deep calming breath, stepped from gangplank of the Doge's state barge, the Bucintoro, onto the lush grass of the HubLand and then raised her eyes to gaze along the Divine Way that led to the Temple of Lilith. The Way was invisible to the naked eye – overgrown as it was by a thousand years of neglect – but she knew that only inches beneath her feet lay the sacred Mantle-ite paved road that, in days gone by, worshippers coming to the Temple had used to protect themselves from the ravenous nanoBites. And as the Mantle-ite was invulnerable to decay and to the ravages of time, it would still be there, just as she remembered it, a raised central walkway flanked by two equally wide but lower walkways. As was her right, she chose the central path, the holiest of the three. In times before remembering it had been the Grigori who had walked to her right and the Kohanim to her left, but those days were long gone.

She took the first, tentative step onto the Way. Such was the significance of this simple act that for a second she was overcome by emotion and was forced to stop as the voices of her long-dead sisters whispered in her mind. It took a moment for her to recover her poise. She had come to the Demi-Monde as an ordinary eighteen-year-old girl from New York, but had discovered that she was really something very different.

Very, very different.

The Demi-Monde had awakened her to what she once had been. And with that awakening had come the realisation that she had a destiny, a destiny to lead HumanKind towards a new future. Ella Thomas was no more. The Lady IMmanual was no more. Now there was only Lilith, a Lilith who would soon cause the reincarnation of the Lilithi ... *Homo perfectus.*

And the irony was that it was Bole who had provided her with the means of achieving this resurrection. She stifled a complacent smile. Bole's threat in sending her twin brother Billy to the Demi-Monde had been very eloquent: perform more miracles, tamper with the Demi-Monde again, and Billy would be killed. But delivering Billy to her had been Bole's greatest mistake. He had sent Billy as a warning, but all his presence had done was give her the opportunity to make the Lilithi – the Priestesshood of Lilith – whole again, to enable them to regain all their powers. What Bole hadn't realised was that he had sent her the very thing that would make her ascendancy to power inevitable ... the blood of a Dark Charismatic.

She began to walk along the Divine Way, savouring the

moment, imagining the slick, warm Mantle-ite hidden under the soles of her bare feet, remembering how she had walked along this same path all those thousands of years ago when the world – the Real World – was young. The Way stretched straight and true for nine hundred yards from the Wheel River to the doors of the Temple. She walked slowly, ignoring the rain that beat down on her, ignoring the ululations of her priestesses who followed in her wake, ignoring everything, simply lost to the memories of a time long ago as they were rekindled within her.

Closer now, she could see that the Temple was overgrown by vines and desecrated by a patina of dirt, but despite this neglect, the Mantle-ite walls still glowed green in the moonlight. It was a magnificent, brooding edifice to the power of Lilith.

At the end of the Divine Way the three walkways separated, each leading to one of a trio of enormous doors set in the side of the Temple, each of the doors firmly shut, their bronze locks green and corroded, showing that they had not been open in centuries ... that they would never be opened again except at the command of Lilith. Over the door to the right was the Valknut, the sign of the Grigori; over the one to the left was the five-pointed star of the Kohanim; and over the central one – the Great Entrance – was the sign of *laguz* sinister crossed with *laguz* dexter, the symbol of Lilith.

Ascending the broad stairway leading to the Great Entrance, she was suffused by an almost overwhelming sensation of completeness. It was as though she had gone through her life knowing something was missing but not quite sure what it was, that understanding tantalisingly out of reach.

No longer.

As she walked through the massive propylaeum – the huge archway that decorated the Great Entrance – towards the sealed doors, those long-forgotten memories of the lives of all her forebears came flooding back. Now she was complete, now she was truly Lilith reborn.

She made a silent pledge that soon the Temple would look just as she remembered it from all those thousands of years before . . . that soon its Mantle-ite walls would be scrubbed and clean. Then it would be truly a Temple fit for a goddess, a Temple that symbolised her power and her might. But even dirty and neglected, it was magnificent, each of its walls six hundred and sixty yards long and one hundred and eighty high, with ninety-six fluted columns holding up the massive architraves embossed with scenes from the life of Lilith. It was like the Parthenon writ large . . . but then the Parthenon itself had been just a muddled memory of the grandeur of the Temple that had stood in the lost land Real World scholars had dubbed Urheimat but which she knew better as Atlantis.

Yes, ABBA had created a perfect replica of the Temple she had once presided over in the Real World. It was over eight thousand years since she had last stood before these doors, but then she had stood there as the Goddess Lilith, as Mother Nature . . .

A hugely inappropriate title.

Lilith might have conquered evolution, she might have conquered death, but she had never been able to control Nature. And in a day and a night Nature had unleashed her fury and sent the deluge that had destroyed the civilisation of the Lilithi and thrown those of her people who survived, bemused and leaderless, out into the world.

No, she had never commanded Nature. Only ABBA could do that.

A tear slid slowly down her cheek as the remembrance of the grief caused by that destruction coursed through her. Even now at a distance of eight millennia she was still crippled by the anguish of that terrible day, numbed by the weight of the collective grief of her sisters and daughters and wracked by guilt. She still cursed herself for her hubris, for her inability to see how the world was changing.

She shook her head: this was not the time for recrimination or remorse. This was the time for her to reclaim her place in the world.

She came to stand before the doors that had denied entry to the Temple for a thousand years and reached up towards the six rectangular shapes set into the wall at the door's left-hand side. With a deft flick of her wrist she pushed the first of the shapes upwards and inwards until it clicked out to lie in the palm of her hand. This, the first part of the key, was six inches long and an inch thick with a two-inch notch cut out of its centre. It took her less than a minute to release the five other parts and to assemble them into the shape of Lilith's symbol. The key was complete.

It was this puzzle that had kept the Temple undisturbed since the Confinement.

She took another deep breath, trying to quell her excitement, then placed the key into the slot set to the side of the door and twisted. There was the sound of sliding weights and then gradually the great Mantle-ite door levered itself open.

Lilith stepped across the threshold of the Temple and the Dark made her welcome.

Part Two
The Forbidding Palace

Created by Rosining Nobel, Most Divine Couturier to the House of Worth, as seen in 'ImPura Modes' Un Vogue Vogues Monthly, Summer 1993

This Season in the Quartier Chaud: A-line gowns in primary colours with the nipple taking centre-stage, each varnished a colour that complements the gown.

9

The WarJunk CSS MostBien
The Demi-Monde: 2nd Day of Summer, 1005

Anne Lister, the foremost Sexologist in the Coven, has determined that there is no such thing as love [see: *'Love = Ridiculous'*]. According to Lister, love is merely a nonFemme-inspired construct designed to lure and then entrap self-delusional Femmes into a heterosexual relationship and to have them endure and rationalise all the horrors incumbent on such a relationship without complaint. Of all the weapons in the patriarchal nonFemme's armoury love is not only the most subtle but the most powerful. As Lister writes: *'Anything that can persuade the Femme who is being raped to think the rapist is "Mr Wonderful" has got to be the business.'*

The Young Femme's Guide to the HerTory of the Coven: HerTorianNoN Fan Ye, Covenite Textbooks and Periodicals

I've been kidnapped!

That was Norma's first thought when she finally, reluctantly, struggled awake.

Shipnapped!

She knew she was aboard a ship. Even though she had awoken into pitch darkness, the gentle rocking of her bunk to and fro, the sound of waves washing against the ship's bow and the distant churning of a propeller announced she was in the cabin of a steamship, presumably sailing in the direction of the Coven. Well, that's where Mata Hari had told her she was being taken, anyway.

She sat up and immediately regretted her impulsiveness. Her head swam and her stomach heaved. Gingerly she examined the lump on the back of her head where Mata Hari's pal had whacked her. Thankfully, nothing appeared to be broken, though she'd been left with a thunderous headache as a souvenir of the encounter. She shivered and wrenched the blanket from her bunk, wrapping it around her shoulders. It was a cold, unpleasant night, the rain drumming against the side of the ship.

With her arms outstretched like a blind woman, she felt around in the darkness and after a few moments' scrabbling she found the lamp she was searching for, twisted the knob and, with a spluttering reluctance, the gas mantle flared into life. The faltering light it cast was strong enough for Norma to see that her cabin was small and furnished in a very spartan manner: the bare metal floor looked uncomfortably cold and the furniture bolted to the walls had a very utilitarian air about it. She had the distinct feeling that she was aboard a warship.

She stood up to explore. Another mistake.

She staggered and had to splay her feet to deal with the roll of the ship. Reaching out a hand, she grabbed the back of a chair to support herself, thankful that her captors hadn't thought to chain her hands. She wondered whether this was simply an oversight on their part, but then, she supposed, on board a ship there was nowhere much to escape to.

Curious as to how far her freedom extended, she tottered across the cabin and tried the handle of the door, which, to her amazement, wasn't locked. Hitching the blanket more securely around her shoulders, she stepped out into the narrow gaslit corridor beyond, which ran maybe fifty feet both to her left and to her right. It was deserted: there was no one standing guard so, with no conscious decision, she turned right, the direction opposite to the sound of the propeller. At the end of the corridor was another steel door, which she opened to find herself in a large and quite opulently furnished stateroom. Here a tall, slender woman with long blonde hair and porcelain-white skin sat idly musing a hand on the keys of a piano and, to her right, Norma's abductor, Mata Hari, lay sprawled on a chaise longue busying herself with the cleaning of a large revolver.

The blonde woman looked up and smiled. 'Good evening, Norma, I am so pleased you could join us. I am Lady Lucrezia Borgia, First Deputy to Her Imperial Majesty the Empress Wu. Welcome aboard the Imperial flagship, the WarJunk CSS *MostBien*.'

Lucrezia Borgia ...

Norma scanned back through the history lessons she'd attended in the Real World trying to remember what she had been taught about the woman. Not much: all she could recall was that Borgia had lived in Renaissance Italy where she'd been a noblewoman famed for her beauty and the enthusiasm with which she poisoned her family's political rivals. Not a nice person, which presumably made her another of the Professor's damned Singularities.

Borgia beckoned her further into the room. 'You're up and about a little sooner than we anticipated but, as they say, an unexpected guest is always the most welcome. I suspect, though, that you might wish to repair the damage wrought to your appearance by your recent adventures.' She waved a hand in the vague direction of a door set in the side of the room. 'There is a bathroom to your right and I have taken the liberty of furnishing you with a new outfit. To be blunt, your current costume is a tad revealing for HerEtical sensibilities; it smacks of ImPuritanism and the objectifying of Femme sexuality. Most inappropriate.'

Without a word Norma accepted Borgia's offer and for the next half-hour bathed herself, revelling in the luxury of a seemingly endless supply of piping-hot water and as fine a selection of perfumes and bath salts as she'd ever seen.

Lying in the relaxing suds of the bath gave Norma the chance to think. There was, she decided, absolutely no point in bemoaning the bad luck that had landed her in this predicament. If there was one thing that her time in the Demi-Monde had taught her it was that staying cool was generally a better option than panic. Her days of being the whingeing, helpless victim were now firmly behind her. She had grown up.

So resolved, Norma rose from the bath and towelled herself dry. The 'outfit' Borgia had provided her with looked like a baggy boiler suit made from dark blue denim. Flattering it most certainly wasn't but it was clean and a damned sight more comfortable than her blanket. Resplendent in her new outfit, refreshed and reinvigorated, she strode out of the bathroom to rejoin her hosts.

Borgia clapped her hands when she saw Norma. 'Wonderful! You look reborn, Norma, quite the little HerEtical. And to celebrate your rebirth, might I offer you a glass of wine?'

'That would be great,' admitted Norma, as a steward poured her a glass of Chardonnay, 'though where I come from, Lady Lucrezia, you have something of a reputation for using poison as an ingredient in your cocktails.'

'Very droll, Norma,' chuckled Borgia. 'I do adore Daemonic humour; it is so wonderfully understated. But you needn't be concerned regarding adulterated drinks, the Empress Wu has given specific instructions that you should be delivered to the Forbidding City unharmed.'

'The Forbidding City?'

'The home of Her Imperial Majesty Empress Wu. It was the Empress who ordered you be brought to the Coven.'

'Why?'

Borgia gestured Norma into a chair. 'To answer that I must refer to the iChing. Are you familiar with the iChing, Norma?'

'No.'

'Tush, tush ... I expected more erudition from a Daemon, but no matter.' The woman waved the steward out of the salon and once the three of them were alone launched into her explanation. 'There are many forms of divination practised in the Demi-Monde: the ImPuritans of the Quartier Chaud use their mathematically based preScience, the WhoDooists of the JAD have their stupid seething, whilst the NoirVillians, zadnik animals that they are, prefer the casting of bones. But we Covenites have perhaps the most effective means of all: we have the divinely inspired oracle that is the iChing. By the asking of questions and the simultaneous tossing of coins it is possible to allow the forces of Qi which permeate the Kosmos to be interrogated and understood. It is the most subtle of all the methods used to 4Tell the future and the Empress sets great store by the insights she is offered by the iChing in her quest to establish a MostBien Utopia here in the Demi-Monde.'

'MostBien?' asked Norma.

'The HerEtical concept that the ultimate expression of civilisation will only be achieved when Femmes have gained supremacy in the Demi-Monde and nonFemmes have been relegated to a subordinate role such that their inherent and incurable MALEvolent tendencies no longer infect society.'

'I see,' said Norma cautiously. 'But while this is all very fascinating, it doesn't explain why I was abducted.'

'In the Coven the Rite of 4Telling is performed on the eighty-eighth day of each Quarter. Unfortunately, the Spring reading of the iChing performed just a few days ago indicated that there is a great disturbance in the Qi of the Demi-Monde, Qi being the force which drives the Yin and Yang elements of the Kosmos as they move – as they oscillate – forever seeking balance and harmony.'

Borgia paused to allow Mata Hari to replenish her glass. 'You should understand, Norma, that since the Confinement of the Demi-Monde behind the Boundary Layer, the Yang element – the masculine aspect of the Kosmos – has been in ascendancy, and as a consequence there has been an excess of the masculine essence – MALEvolence – in the world. This has resulted in the wars and the hatreds that have beset the Demi-Monde for the past one thousand years. But we in the Coven have always taken comfort in the knowledge that all things in the Kosmos follow a cyclical path, waxing and waning, and that soon would dawn the age when the masculine Yang will yield, once again, to the feminine Yin. Yes ... until the iChing was consulted during the Spring Rite, it was believed that the rhythm of the Kosmos was moving inexorably towards the Yin, towards the Age of Femmes and the perfection that is MostBien.'

Norma placed her wine glass firmly back onto the table. There was something, just something, in Borgia's tone that told her that what this lunatic would say next was going to be bad news, and bad news was always something to be received with a clear head. No more wine for her.

'The Epigram the Empress Wu was given by the iChing in answer to the question "Has the moment come when Femmes will rule the Demi-Monde?" was ... inauspicious. To the 4Tellers who examined the readings it was apparent that there was a new force at work in the Demi-Monde, which if left unmoderated would destroy the harmony of the Kosmos and prevent the Demi-Monde embracing Yin.'

There was a grim inevitability about what Borgia was saying. 'Me?' suggested Norma.

A nod from Borgia. 'Yes, you. We had at first thought that this baleful influence was created by the one known as the Lady IMmanual, but now we are certain that it is you who endangers the triumph of HerEticalism.'

'I don't see how.'

'The seductive philosophy of Normalism which you have been preaching with such success in the Quartier Chaud promotes a philosophy of peace and non-violence between peoples and between genders. Unfortunately, with respect to HerEticalism, this is an inherently antithetical philosophy in that it denies the complementary antagonism of Yin and Yang and hence rejects the assumption that there is an oscillating rhythm to the Kosmos. Instead of movement and flow you propose stasis and paralysis. But without the dynamic of the eternal – the divine – fluctuation between Femme and nonFemme, between light and dark, between Yin and Yang, the Kosmos will become becalmed.'

Norma couldn't help herself: she laughed. 'Bullshit. The violence associated with the conflict between your Yin and Yang is wrong and to rationalise it on the basis that it's necessary to maintain the natural ebb and flow of Nature is total crap.'

Borgia responded with an indulgent smile, but it was apparent from the way her cheeks went pink that she was struggling to control her temper. 'Not so. This is the intrinsic duality of the Kosmos, a duality that you endanger.'

'You're wrong. The Demi-Monde – any world, for that matter – would be a better place without violence and war. And Normalism is intent on doing just that: encouraging the world to live in harmony.'

'You are a traitor to your gender! All Normalism does is deny HerEticalism the opportunity to triumph.'

'Nuts. You HerEticals don't believe in the duality and the harmony of the Kosmos, if you did, you wouldn't be so down on men.' She remembered Vanka's words to her when, imprisoned in the Bastille, they had debated the politics of revolution: 'No, all you HerEticals are interested in is power, in having your turn at the trough.'

Borgia leapt to her feet, her eyes sparking with anger. 'Enough! I am not here to debate with you, merely to inform you as to why you are being brought before the Empress Wu.'

Suddenly Norma felt terribly bored. Everywhere she went in the Demi-Monde there were maniacs desperate to seize power, to belittle people, and to make life for decent folk more miserable and sordid than it need be. She was becoming increasingly fed up with leaders besotted with power. 'Yeah, yeah, yeah,' she sneered. 'And then what? To be executed? Well, don't think your threats are going to faze me, honey; I've been threatened by experts. And anyway, get rid of me and there are other Normalists ready to take my place. The Normalist movement here in the Demi-Monde is unstoppable.'

'*Nothing* is unstoppable except the ultimate triumph of HerEticalism.' Borgia gave an ugly little laugh. 'We took especial care to have your associates in the Peace Movement abducted with you to ensure that we eliminate Normalism root and branch.' Here she nodded to Mata Hari, who walked over to the cabin's door. When she opened it, Burlesque, Rivets and Odette were pushed inside, guarded by two tall and heavily armed Amazons.

'Look, I don't know wot this is all abart but ...' began Burlesque as he stumbled into the cabin, but he was silenced by the butt of an M4 being slammed into the back of his head by one of the shaven-headed guards.

'You will be silent, Bandstand, or I will have your tongue removed,' said Borgia quietly. 'You should be aware that you and your two colleagues are only alive because your presence will be useful in persuading the Daemon Norma Williams to cooperate with us. But you should understand that if you prove troublesome, then you and the boy will be gelded and your Femme sold into slavery.'

Rivets's pale face drained of the little colour it had. He looked to be on the verge of panicking but fortunately, before he could do anything fatally stupid, proceedings were interrupted by the arrival of an officerFemme. 'AdmiralNoN Zheng Heii's compliments, First Deputy Borgia, but we have come to the disembarkation point. There is a gig standing by to transport AgentFemme Mata Hari and the prisoners to shore.'

10

Rangoon
The Demi-Monde: 2nd Day of Summer, 1005

And the favourite student, Too Zi, enquired of the Master, saying, 'Master, with so much hate and violence in the Demi-Monde how is it possible to retain faith in the ultimate triumph of Goodness in the Kosmos?'

The Master smiled and said, 'All those who seek ABBAsoluteness must mimic the delight of a small child when placed in a room full of dogshit.'

Too Zi frowned. 'I do not understand, Master. How can any remain cheerful in a room full of dogshit?'

'As any child knows, Student Too Zi, when a room contains that much dogshit, there's got to be a puppy in there somewhere.'

The Second Book of the BiAlects, Verse 31

It was a foul night, inky black with rain lancing down, planishing the surface of the river and splashing on the oilskin capes and sou'westers Norma and her three friends had been given to wear. As they were pushed and shoved along the treacherously slippy steel deck of the CSS *MostBien* towards the gig that was bobbing up and down alongside the WarJunk, Mata Hari whispered instructions. 'You will all be quiet: make a sound and you will be silenced by the guards. I say this for your own benefit. At night on the Volga sound travels and the UnFunny artillery lining the shore of St Petersburg needs little excuse to fire.'

As she stepped down into the rocking boat, Norma realised that she was frightened. She might have held her nerve in front of Lucrezia Borgia but, truth be told, she was a very worried girl. As far as she could make out, these HerEticals were as mad as their counterparts in the ForthRight: they were female fascists who instead of directing their lunatic hatred towards nuJus and the other UnderMentionables, directed it towards men.

It was all so absurd.

Yeah, that was the problem with the Demi-Monde, she decided: absurdity. Every idea about how the Demi-Monde should be run had been stretched and twisted until it was a ridiculous parody of what it had been originally and then a demented leadership rammed this twaddle down their people's throats as they screamed 'if you don't think exactly like I do, then you're my enemy'.

It was a depressing situation made more so by the thought that her efforts to change things – which had got off to such a good start – had now been derailed. Norma found herself fretting that while she was being held by these madwomen, she couldn't be out there working to make the Demi-Monde a better and a more tolerant place.

This train of thought was interrupted when Rivets plumped himself down beside her in the gig. In the moonlight she could see that she wasn't the only one who was worried: the mention of being castrated had put the boy into a rare funk. As the boat cast off from the *MostBien* and the sailors began to work the muffled oars, he sat shivering as they buffeted their way towards the riverbank.

As always, Rivets turned to Burlesque Bandstand for comfort. 'Is it right, Burlesque, that these dorks is gonna cut our cocks off?'

'Be quiet!' snarled Mata Hari who was sitting at the bow of the gig peering out into the darkness. 'If you want to keep hold of your penis, little man, I suggest you keep hold of your tongue.'

In response Rivets stuck the aforesaid tongue out at her and leant closer to Burlesque. 'I am not fuckin' 'appy, Burlesque,' he whispered, 'abart 'aving me knob trimmed.'

'That'll only happen if you don't keep shtum,' answered a very tetchy Burlesque. 'Anyway, I fink we wos dead lucky to get orf that ship *tackle intactus*.'

'Oh, yus,' agreed Rivets, his eyes widening in amazement, 'I've bin dead fuckin' lucky I 'as. I gets kidnapped by a bunch of LessBien tarts, spend two nights arse-deep in sewage chained up in the 'old ov a very smelly ship listening to you teaching Odette 'ow to speak Anglo and then get told I'm bin taken to Birdland to 'ave me cock clipped. I don't fink I could stand it, Burlesque, iffn I got any fuckin' luckier.' And as though to punctuate his point, he vomited over the side of the gig.

'Look, Rivets, I know it's a fuck-up, but I wosn't to know that a troupe of fuckin' Amazons were gonna come an' stick their oar in, now wos I? So we've just gotta make the best of it and once we get to dry land, once we're outta these chains, then we'll make a run for it.'

The look he got from Rivets told him that the boy didn't share his confidence. 'I don't fink we're gonna be runnin' anywhere, Burlesque. Way I see it, that Mata Hari cow is going to off us first chance she gets.'

Burlesque shook his head. 'Nah, she won't. Iffn she was going to top us, she'd 'ave done it by now. She wants us alive. Now all we've got to do is look sharp and make sure we get outta this while we can still hit the bass notes.'

Odette edged closer to Rivets. '*Ne t'en fais pas, mon petit* Reevets! 'Ave no doubts that *mon cheri* Burlesque will find the way mostly perfect to – 'ow you say – make the escapes.' She gave Burlesque's arm a squeeze. 'Is 'e not the most wonderful of all the men?'

Norma smiled; Odette's English seemed to be improving by the hour, but unfortunately Rivets was determined not to be consoled. 'Escape, you daft Frog bint?' He rattled his chains. 'We ain't gonna be able to 'ave it away on our toes dragging a couple of hundredweight of best Beijing steel around with us, now are we?'

He was about to say more, but was silenced by the sound of Mata Hari cocking her pistol. Now as they skulled along the river towards the Anichkov Bridge, the Suffer-O-Gette edged even further forward over the bow of the boat trying to make out who was waiting for them on the shore. Suddenly there was a single short flash of a lantern which Mata Hari imitated with the one she was carrying.

'Our friends are here. Prepare to disembark,' she ordered and a minute or so later the gig's keel scraped along the stony bank of the Volga River. They had arrived.

Norma took a quick look around. As best she could judge through the pouring rain, they had landed a couple of hundred yards from the foot of the bridge. It seemed an odd choice of a place to come ashore; she would have thought they would have landed closer to the centre of the Rangoon docks. But she wasn't given much time to puzzle on this before the gig came to a halt and she was shoved out.

There were about ten heavily armed Amazons waiting for them under the command of a tall girl in combat overalls. The girl saluted and then handed Mata Hari a large sheet of parchment which carried a number of impressive-looking seals. 'I am MajorFemme Ito, commander of Amazon Detachment Twenty-Seven. This warrant authorises me to take custody of the Daemon and her confederates, and to transport them to the Forbidding City. Are all the prisoners landed, AgentFemme Zelle?'

It took a moment for Norma to realise that she was addressing Mata Hari using her real name rather than her *nom d'espionage*.

'All ashore, MajorFemme.' Mata Hari turned to her sergeant. 'Release the prisoners' leg-irons; I don't want to have to carry them to the steamer.'

That was when things became decidedly unreal.

As the last of the shackles fell away, Mata Hari raised her revolver and blasted MajorFemme Ito straight between the eyes. The shot was a signal for all hell to break loose as black-clad apparitions materialised out of the darkness. The ninjas looked like characters out of a manga comic, but there was nothing comic about the way they attacked the Amazons. They danced over the rain-slick cobbles with the agility of cats, firing their automatic rifles as they went, decorating the night with blindingly bright muzzle flashes. Amazons began to fall.

'SoldierFemmes to me!' screamed a sergeant as she tried to yank her pistol from its holster. She never managed to do it, being smashed over the head by a length of chain wielded by Odette Aroca.

It was the last Norma saw of the fighting. She felt a strong hand on her shoulder as she was pushed down to the ground with her saviour – one of the ninjas – lying on top of her. The gun battle was brief. It seemed that surprise and Mata Hari's treachery had triumphed over numbers, and after a few minutes she heard an order being yelled for the Amazons to pull back. As the shooting fizzled out, Norma found herself being hauled to her feet.

'Quickly,' snapped the ninja who seemed to be in charge of the rescue mission. 'The Amazons will be back as soon as they recover from their shock and get themselves organised. We must get you to a safe house, Norma.'

Norma?

'Do I know you?'

There was a tinkling laugh and the woman unwrapped the scarf from around her face. 'I am disappointed, Norma, that you have forgotten your friend Su Xiaoxiao so quickly. I was, after all, the first to welcome you into the Demi-Monde.'

A wave of relief washed over Norma. 'Little Su! Oh, it's great to meet you again.' Su Xiaoxiao – Little Su – was one of the few people Norma had met in the Demi-Monde who she liked and trusted. She had been the woman, in those madcap days when Norma had first travelled to the Demi-Monde, who had done everything she could to prevent her being captured by Aleister Crowley, who had warned her about Archie Clement and had told her that she was in danger of becoming one of the Kept. If only Norma had listened to Little Su and not the honeyed words of Percy Shelley, things would have turned out so differently. But then she could never be cross with Percy, he was too dishy for that.

'And I am pleased to welcome you to the Coven, Norma. We have been awaiting your arrival with eager anticipation; we are in dire need of your strength and of your courage. But now is not the time for pleasantries, already our enemies will be regrouping, so I would be grateful if you and your friends would follow me.'

11

Rangoon
The Demi-Monde: 2nd Day of Summer, 1005

The realisation that a relatively small pool of nonFemmes could service the reproductive needs of the entire female population of the Demi-Monde led to the establishment of the Gendercide Committee to examine this issue more carefully. The Committee, which reported in 1003, concluded that a population made up of ninety-nine parts Femmes and one part unCastrated nonFemmes would be viable – and much less violent – than the current equal distribution of the sexes. The Committee also recommended that to enhance the quality of Femme offspring care should be taken in selecting the 'One Per Cent Stock' in order to ensure that these fully functional nonFemmes were well-made, healthy, of superior intelligence, free of congenital illness, and uncompromised by insanity or emotional frailty. The gender balance of the population would be maintained by the adoption of a policy of infanticide aimed at eliminating any excess of male progeny.

HerTory of the YiYi Project: ScientistFemme Dr Merit Ptah,
nuCoven Books

They skirted through the shadows of the docklands, moving quickly, encouraged by the sound of bugles ricocheting through the tight streets and alleyways. Their enemies were now hot on their trail, but, fortunately for the fugitives, the Coven was even more of a maze than the Rookeries, a maze through which Su Xiaoxiao led them with unerring confidence.

As they scuttled through the labyrinthine backstreets, Norma managed to ask Su Xiaoxiao a breathless question. 'How did you know where and when I would be landing?'

'Mata Hari, the SheTong's most valuable crypto,' answered Su Xiaoxiao as she glanced back, checking that all of her charges were safe. 'She sent a PigeonGram informing us where you would be landing. Now, of course, her cover is blown. You should be honoured, Norma, that we were willing to sacrifice the services of such a highly placed crypto just to be able to speak with you.' The Chinese girl gave a grim shake of her head. 'But this is not the place to debate these matters. Soon ...'

'Soon' came some ten minutes later when Norma was ushered up steps leading to the second floor of a nondescript tenement building. Su Xiaoxiao rat-tat-tatted on the door and then whispered into the grille an unseen but very cautious somebody had opened in response to her knocking. Whatever Su Xiaoxiao said worked: the door opened on reluctant hinges and Norma found herself being bustled inside. Immediately two young girls materialised out of the shadows, used picklocks to unfasten the wrist fetters, and once free, Norma and her friends were hurried along a dark corridor to a large room where three men were sitting, arranged along one side of a wooden table. Su Xiaoxiao sat down next to them and waved the four runaways into the seats opposite.

Glasses of scalding hot and very sweet tea were served, and as Norma felt her rain-chilled body begin to warm she took a moment to study her hosts. The three men were dressed in identical robes made of white silk, embroidered with a confection of what looked like the circle and arrow motif Norma recognised as the symbol of masculinity. But their robes were the only thing they had in common: physically they couldn't have been more different. The man in the centre of the trio was tall, slim and quite young, perhaps mid-twenties; the one to his left was older, much stockier and sported a very bushy white beard; and the man to his right was small, almost frail-looking, and his bespectacled eyes darting nervously hither and thither as they desperately sought to avoid meeting Norma's gaze.

They waited while Su Xiaoxiao pulled her cowl from her head and settled herself, the woman looking very petite alongside the men and, with her shaven head, altogether more alien. But just as the months since their first meeting had wrought changes in Norma, so they had in Su Xiaoxiao: now there was a deep sadness in her eyes that Norma couldn't remember seeing during their previous adventures together, and she wore her forty years more heavily.

'So you made it safely, Su Xiaoxiao,' observed the taller of the men.

'It cost the lives of two of my fighters, Pierre-Simon, but if by "safely" you mean that Femme Williams has been brought here unharmed, then the answer is yes.'

'I grieve for your comradeFemmes, but preserving the life of the Messiah is a prize beyond measure.' The man bowed towards Norma. 'Allow me to introduce myself: I am Pierre-Simon Laplace, Femme Williams, formerly *Count* Laplace and erstwhile Director of the Centre for Scientific Enquiry in Paris. Now I am exiled here in the Coven where I function as Adviser Extraordinary to Her Imperial Majesty Empress Wu . . .'

'And as a putative member of her damned stud farm,' grumbled the bearded item to his left.

'Indeed, Karl, but more of that anon. May I introduce my colleagues? To my left is the notorious RaTionalist and curmudgeon Lord Marx, who came hotfoot to the Coven from the ForthRight after the Troubles, Reinhard Heydrich having taken great exception to the pamphlets Karl penned condemning the anti-Royalist Revolution and the cult of UnFunDaMentalism.'

Marx grunted a greeting. 'Pierre-Simon is quite correct, young lady, I am a RaTionalist and would have nothing to do with the occult nonsense being spouted by that charlatan Aleister Crowley. But as Heydrich perceives any criticism as a threat, I was condemned, *in absentia*, to death. Fortunately, thanks to a tip-off from Baron Dashwood, I was able to evade the Checkya and escape to the Coven. And that is why I am here to greet you.'

Laplace continued with his introductions. 'To my right is the distinguished, though somewhat taciturn, expert on all things pertaining to breeding and evolution, Gregor Mendel.'

'I am delighted to meet you,' stammered Mendel in a soft, hesitant voice before busying himself with a forensic study of his glass of tea. The man was so shy that he seemed to have inordinate difficulty interacting with his fellow men and women ... especially the women.

'Mendel is also a fugitive,' explained Laplace, 'in his case, from the Heydrich Institute for Natural Sciences in Berlin. Unfortunately, as he has learnt to his cost, he has leapt from the frying pan into the fire.' Laplace spread his hands. 'So we are all—'

'It is typical of a nonFemme's innate arrogance and presumption of superiority that you should forget to introduce me, Laplace,' scolded Su Xiaoxiao. Her tone might have been light and playful but there was no mistaking that it was a rebuke. 'Therefore, I will introduce myself. I am Su Xiaoxiao and, before his death, I was Most Favoured Courtesan to His Serene Majesty Qin Shi Huang. I have also some small fame as a philosopher and here I admit to being a late and somewhat reluctant convert to the outré doctrine of unBelievability postulated by the Toozian thinker Wen Tiangiang.'

'UnBelievability? Stuff and nonsense!' sneered Marx.

Su Xiaoxiao ignored him. 'Latterly, though, I have devoted myself to the defeat of Empress Wu and the perverse creed that is HerEticalism. To do this I have revived the ancient order of the SheTong.'

'Wot's the SheTong when it's at 'ome?' asked Burlesque.

Su Xiaoxiao laughed. 'Well, according to the ChangGang – the Coven's secret police – we are a ramshackle group of penis-addicted Femmes who are unable to find the courage within ourselves to break free from the bourgeois and unnatural impositions of a socially constructed heterosexuality and usurp the power held by nonFemmes. But in reality it is an ancient order of fighting women. We are Femmes who have pledged ourselves to oppose the more extreme of the solutions being proposed in Court circles to bring about the supposed utopia that is MostBien … the triumph of Femmes.'

Norma nodded her understanding. 'Borgia mentioned that when we spoke aboard ship.'

Su Xiaoxiao's eyes widened in surprise. 'For Borgia to speak so openly means that the HerEticals grow very confident. You have come, Norma, in the very nick of time.'

There was a pause and Norma thought it an opportunity to reciprocate the introductions. 'And these are my friends …' she began.

'We know who accompanies you, their reputation as stalwart supporters of Normalism goes before them,' interrupted Laplace. 'But as time is short – I and my two colleagues must be back in our quarters before our absence is noted – I would prefer if we move directly to business.' He gave Su Xiaoxiao a wry smile. 'With the kind permission of Femme Su I would take it upon myself to iterate the political situation current in the Coven.'

A nod from the woman indicated her agreement.

'Very well. Empress Wu has been the supreme power within the Coven for ten years. A decade ago Wu led the Femme Liberation Movement to victory in the Coven, overthrowing Emperor Qin Shi Huang and replacing Confusionism with HerEticalism as the religion of this ABBA-forgotten Sector.'

'Though she remains a secret disciple of Confusionism,' added Su Xiaoxiao. 'She is addicted to its ability to predict the future.'

'I've never heard of Confusionism before,' Norma admitted.

It was Karl Marx who answered. 'For the simple reason that it is, like RaTionalism, an outlaw religion; it has been banned within the Coven ... except within the Forbidding City.' He sniffed. 'Not that that's any great loss. Confusionism is a remarkably ridiculous philosophy in that it believes – without a shred of evidence – that it is possible to commune with ABBA by the throwing of coins and consulting the Epigrams contained in an ancient book known as the iChing. Twaddle, of course, but for the Empress Wu strangely persuasive twaddle.'

'Lucrezia Borgia mentioned the Empress using the iChing to me earlier this morning.'

Laplace shook his head. 'I am surprised by her candour. The Empress Wu keeps her Confusionist leanings a closely guarded secret.'

'Why?'

'Because Confusionism is linked with an ancient sage called the Master who not only wrote the BiAlects – the teachings which form the foundation of Confusionism – but also the iChing. It would not do for Empress Wu – the doyenne of all that is Femme in the Demi-Monde – to be seen espousing a religion developed by a man ... by a nonFemme.'

'But why is the Empress Wu so anti-men?'

Laplace provided the answer. 'Wu is driven by an aberrational attitude towards sex, having turned penis-envy into a religion which contends that MostBien will only dawn when non-Femmes have been totally and irrevocably eliminated from the face of the Demi-Monde.'

'She wants to get rid ov all us blokes?' interrupted Burlesque.

'Correct.'

'That's bollocks, that is.'

'Very apposite,' murmured Marx.

'Wivout us blokes there wouldn't be any babies.'

'A most pertinent observation, Monsieur Bandstand,' admitted Laplace, 'and, demented though the Empress is, it is a fact which has not gone unnoticed by her and her acolytes. But despite this we believe that Empress Wu is preparing to take the penultimate step to the achieving of MostBien: at her urging HerEtical scientists have developed a Plague that will affect only nonFemmes ... that will destroy all men living in the Demi-Monde.'

'But that's madness,' objected Norma. 'As Burlesque says, it would be suicidal for Wu to deploy such a plague. Destroy men and within seventy years human life will be extinct in the Demi-Monde.'

Laplace glanced towards Mendel. 'It might be best if you took the story up, Gregor: reproduction is, after all, your field of expertise.'

Mendel looked distinctly unhappy to be thrust into the spotlight and for several seconds all he was able to do was ferociously polish his pince-nez, which, Norma assumed, was a displacement activity to mask his shyness. Finally, though, he settled, replaced his spectacles on his nose and in a quavering voice began to speak. 'Although Wu's intentions are never spoken about openly, it has become obvious that several of the more peculiar policies of her regime are not as arbitrary as they first appear. For several years now the Coven has offered sanctuary and a generous pension to nonFemmes ...'

'And immunity from castration,' grumped Karl Marx.

'. . . of proven intellectual ability. As a consequence, the Coven has become something of a haven for those males escaping religious, intellectual and racial persecution in their home Sectors. When I took up Wu's offer of asylum, I thought it nothing more than a piece of whimsy on her part: just as some women collect jewellery and furs, so, I assumed, Empress Wu collected renegade geniuses. But in this surmise I was naive. I have come to the conclusion that the reason I and my intellectually gifted colleagues have been assembled here is to form a stud pool . . . her One Per Cent Stock.' He glanced at the robes he and his colleagues were wearing. 'The emblem shown on this robe indicates that we are . . .'

'Loaded and cocked?' suggested Marx.

'Indeed, Karl, and, as such, are to be shunned by Femmes except when they are licensed to commune with us physically for the purposes of procreation. It is very demeaning.'

Marx winked at Norma, indicating that one man's humiliation was another's good time.

'We believe,' continued Mendel, 'that Wu has now fully stocked her stud farm and hence is in a position to employ a biological weapon she has had developed. She calls this the Plague and it is a weapon designed to kill nonFemmes . . . all nonFemmes except those comprising the One Per Cent Stock. When the Plague is unleashed in the Demi-Monde, those nonFemmes making up the One Per Cent Stock will be held in quarantine safe from its depredations, and when it has passed, having exterminated the rest of the male population, it will be our duty to service Femmes selected for breeding.'

'Sounds like a good gig to me,' observed Burlesque, 'a few hundred blokes having to shag thousands and thousands ov willin' women for a living.' His observation was rewarded by a kick from Odette.

Mendel frowned at the ribald comment. 'That, Mister Bandstand, is the superficial conclusion that a number of my more physically inclined colleagues have come to. Unfortunately I am of the opinion that it may be a very temporary "gig". I have some small expertise regarding the understanding of reproduction and recently I was consulted by a Dr Merit Ptah who is the leader of something called the YiYi Project here in the Coven. Although Dr Ptah was tight-lipped regarding the purpose and the status of this Project, I was left with no doubt that its objective is to prove the viability of parthenogenesis.'

'Wot's that?' asked Burlesque.

'Parthenogenesis, Mister Bandstand, is the impregnation of females *without* male intervention. The ultimate expression of MostBien would be a world without nonFemmes, where every birth is a virgin birth and where every mother is unsullied by contact with a nonFemme or the need for his seed. MostBien would find its apotheosis as a one-sex society. It appears from the scant clues I was given that Project YiYi is well advanced, but quite how close to success it is we do not know. However, we must assume that within a few years nonFemmes will have been rendered extinct.'

'Bugger me wiv a broomstick.'

'An unsavoury metaphor, Mister Bandstand,' observed Laplace, 'but one which does most graphically convey the alarm I and my colleagues feel.'

Norma had the impression that the conversation was running away from her. She understood that HerEticalism's objective was to create a lesbian society, but it was difficult to accept that this involved the extermination of men. 'So what's to be done?'

Su Xiaoxiao took over the discussion. 'We need to discover the status of the Coven's experimentation both with the nonFemme-killing Plague and with parthenogenesis.

Unfortunately the work is so confidential that even using the good offices of Mata Hari' – here she nodded to the woman who was skulking in the room's shadows – 'we have been unable to penetrate the cloak of secrecy which surrounds these projects. It is imperative that we discover where the Plague is being produced and destroy it.' She fixed Norma with a steely stare. 'There is only one place where we are sure this intelligence is held and that is within the Forbidding City. We need someone who is willing to be taken into this, the *sanctum sanctorum* of Empress Wu, and discover the secrets of the Plague weapon.'

For the second time in as many hours a horrible feeling of foreboding descended on Norma. 'Me?'

A nod from Su Xiaoxiao. 'You have been brought to the Coven so that you may be questioned by the Empress's most trusted experts regarding the effect your promotion of Normalism is having on the future of the Demi-Monde. This can only be done within the Forbidding City, which is a sealed world. With the exception of Empress Wu and Imperial Secretary, NoN Mao ZeDong, all those taken into the Forbidding City are never permitted to leave.' She gimleted Norma with a stern look. 'And we must move quickly: Heydrich is preparing to invade the Coven, and it might be that Wu is panicked into doing something precipitous. Time is of the essence.'

Norma gave a sardonic laugh. 'Great: so I get to be taken into the Forbidding City but don't have a snowball's chance in hell of getting out. Look, I don't want to rain on your parade, Little Su, but that lunatic Lucrezia Borgia suggested that Wu wants me out of the picture. I'm guessing that once I'm in the Forbidding City I'm toast.'

'That is, regrettably, the case,' observed Laplace blithely. 'After you have been examined by the Sages of the iChing, you will undoubtedly be put to death. That is the usual way Wu seeks to change the future of the Demi-Monde.'

'Terrific, so for me this is a one-way ticket to the morgue.'

Su Xiaoxiao hurriedly rejoined the conversation. 'Not so, Norma. We too have consulted the iChing and the reading was *most* favourable. The iChing indicates that you are protected by ABBA and that Fate will not allow any harm to come to you.'

'You consult some book—'

'As you will learn, Norma, the iChing is not "some book"; it is a means by which we can allow the Qi of the Kosmos to inform us of ABBA's intentions.'

'Wow, well, that's a real load off my mind. Let me ask a question: has *anyone* who's been taken into the Forbidding City ever escaped from it?'

There was some embarrassed fidgeting. 'Whilst no one has ever escaped from the Forbidding City we are quite confident—'

'Quite?'

'You will have ABBA on your side. And Mata Hari will be there waiting to guide you to safety when you finally escape.'

'Marvellous.'

12

The Forbidding City
The Demi-Monde: 2nd Day of Summer, 1005

Yin and Yang are the binary opposites of the Kosmos, representing, *inter alia*, dark and light, cold and hot, female and
male. But though Yin and Yang are opposites, they are
complementary and mutually dependent: one cannot exist
without the other and they strive unceasingly to create
the balance that will bring harmony to the Kosmos and
ABBAsoluteness to HumanKind. When this is accomplished, Yin will fuse with Yang to create Ying, the ultimate
transcendental Peace. Ying will only be achieved when
Demi-Mondians have succeeded in purifying their
Solidified Astral Ether. Achieving this purity of body,
thought and deed is the ultimate aim of all WunZian
Confusionists, TooZian Confusionists being too pissed to
comment.

An Introduction to Confusionism: Philosopher Xi Kang,
Ping/Pong Publications

Imperial Secretary, NoN Mao ZeDong was of the opinion that
the eating of river cucumbers was a violation of the spirit of
HerEticalism. It was the shape of the things that he found most
objectionable: there was something disturbingly *phallic* about
them and thus it was wrong for any HerEtically inclined Femme
to enjoy putting them in her mouth. They were a distressingly

heterosexual titbit and though he had done his best to rid himself of these reactionary urges it was unsettling to be reminded of what he once was ...

Unfortunately, river cucumbers were a favourite snack of Empress Wu, and as a consequence, Mao's disgust as he stood watching her gulp the foul things down had to remain unvoiced. Empress Wu, having been Blessed by ABBA, was divine and hence beyond criticism, so all he could do was to keep his gaze fixed at a point thirty centimetres or so to the left of the Empress's shoulder and thirty centimetres above it and do his best to ignore the revolting slurping sounds she made as she devoured the damned things. Of course, that the river cucumbers were being fed to the Empress by a naked Fresh Bloom did add a frisson of eroticism to the act, but not enough to make it watchable.

The other small mercy was that this meeting with the Empress was taking place in the Hall of Supreme Harmony, the largest and grandest of all the halls in the Forbidding City and the one that Mao liked the most. It was the hall used only for the most important of meetings and hence it was here that Li – the unbending ritual that suffused and commanded every action of the Empress's servants and that ensured that they always acted as Superior Servants should – was at its most oppressive. This made audiences held in the hall tense affairs, where any violation of Li was summarily – and cruelly – dealt with. And if there was one thing that Mao truly relished, that made his soul soar, it was the meting out of cruel punishments ... especially when the recipient was a Fresh Bloom. Their screams were as music to his ears.

But there were other reasons why he preferred the Hall of Supreme Harmony to all others: it was, in his opinion, the most beautiful of the state rooms in the Forbidding City. He loved the wonderful paintings of dragons – the Empress's emblem – that decorated the room, especially as the dragons were shown in the throes of devouring nonFemmes. He delighted in the beautiful renderings of the torment these grotesquely untrimmed males endured as they were eaten, crushed, clawed and burned by the rampaging dragons. As far as Mao was concerned, in an ideal world – in a *MostBien* world – such would be the fate of all uncastrated nonFemmes. Oh, how he would love to see them suffer for the scorn they had directed towards him and the other NoNs who laboured to make the Coven the haven for HerEticalism it was.

'What news of the Daemon?' The Empress's question snapped Mao out of his reverie.

Fortunately, years of training allowed him to maintain the bland expression with which he permanently dressed his face. It would be better, he decided, that the Empress did not learn of the Daemon's escape, not now the bitch had been success-fully recaptured. Anyway, divulging this would necessitate him criticising Lucrezia Borgia, and that was an activity not conducive to the enjoyment of a long life. Borgia was a *very* vindictive Femme.

As it was the first time he had addressed the Empress that day, he bowed – his body forming the precise forty-five-degree angle to his legs demanded by Li – counted slowly to nine and then stood upright.

'I salute the True Empress, and pray that ABBA grants her Nine Thousand Years of Peace and Contentment. Great Empress Wu, Mistress of the Demi-Monde, of the Great Beyond and of all the Kosmos, Blessed and Much Beloved by ABBA and Defender of the Faith of HerEticalism, it gives me much pleasure to announce that the Daemon is now, even as we speak, en route to the Forbidding City.'

'Good, we would make much enquiry of her.'

Excellent. He so enjoyed the wailing that was the inevitable accompaniment of the Empress's 'enquiries'.

'Yes ... have the Daemon brought here to the Hall of Supreme Harmony. We would examine her and consult with the iChing regarding the disturbances she has wrought to the harmony of the Kosmos.' The Empress paused to slurp down another river cucumber. 'It will be interesting, will it not, to see if the rumours about Daemons being full of blood are true?' she mused. 'Once the divinations are complete, we will have this Daemon whipped and if it bleeds then we will have all the proof we require.'

The prospect of whipping the Daemon caused something miraculous to happen: the Empress smiled, and as she did so there was an almost palpable sigh of relief emanating from those standing in attendance. Perhaps, Mao prayed, she was at last putting the concerns resulting from the less than propitious auguries given by the last reading of the iChing behind her and was once again finding Inner Contentment. She always enjoyed a good whipping.

'And has the *gaijin* Trixie Dashwood concluded her inspection of our defences, Imperial Secretary?'

'She has, Your Majesty,' smarmed Mao, 'and has pronounced herself astonished by the great and profound preparations you have made to repel these upstart heathens and foul heterosexuals the ForthRightists.'

'She made no criticism?'

'It is impossible to conceive that any could criticise your divinely inspired orders, Your Majesty. She has, however, asked that our Reservists be called up.'

'Is this necessary? We are of the opinion that one Femme fighter is the equal of five nonFemmes.'

'Of course, Your Majesty, this is the case, but I felt it wise to allow GeneralFemme Dashwood some independence of action to reinforce the ridiculous notion that it is she who guides and commands our army and navy. She is a great believer in military commanders demonstrating what she calls "initiative".'

Mao stole a quick glance at the Empress to gauge her reaction. The Empress wasn't a great believer in 'initiative', being of the opinion that it was only a short step from 'initiative' to 'sedition'. Luckily for him, she seemed to be in a mood to be indulgent.

'Very well, let her play her nasty little military games. There is something distinctly masculine about that Femme which we find quite revolting. We find it quite astonishing that ABBA, in Her ineffable wisdom, should choose someone so *inappropriate* to be the saviour of the Coven, but we suppose, as ReverendFemme Dark saw fit to have herself killed at such an inconvenient time, ABBA had little alternative. It is, after all, imperative that we have a competent Femme commanding the army, and by all accounts Dashwood is nothing if not competent in matters martial.'

Mao found himself agreeing with his Empress's assessment. That Dashwood was a masculine Femme – the most serious criticism that could be directed at a Femme in the Coven – was undeniable. *Very* masculine, in fact: he had been in attendance when she had attempted to assassinate Archie Clement and had seen at first hand just what a resolute bitch she was.

It was as though the Empress read his thoughts. 'She must, however, be controlled, and left in no doubt that if she disobeys our orders, there will be reprisals.'

'I have ensured that the remnants of the Warsaw Free Army are being closely guarded, Your Majesty, and GeneralFemme Dashwood has been advised that should she act in a manner that may, in any way, be construed as anti-Covenite or anti-HerEtical, then the most severe punishments will be visited upon them.'

'We are inclined to dispose of them now,' muttered the Empress as she held her head back to allow another river cucumber to be placed in her mouth.

Mao shuddered. 'Perhaps it might be wiser to wait until after the ForthRight attack, Your Majesty,' he stammered. 'If word of any culling were to reach the GeneralFemme, it might have a prejudicial effect on her performance.'

The Empress crunched down on the cucumber, then smacked her lips. 'You are correct, Imperial Secretary, we need the *gaijin* to defend us until we are ready to strike back at the ForthRight.' The Empress allowed the Fresh Bloom to dab a cloth on her lips. 'But speaking of culling: how go the efforts of Scientist-Femme Dr Ptah in this regard?'

'I have interviewed the Doctor, Your Majesty, and understand that Project YiYi will soon be completed and the means to eradicate nonFemmes finally within our grasp.'

'In "our" grasp, Imperial Secretary?'

A stupid slip of the tongue and one which had to be remedied whilst he still had a tongue.

'I apologise, Your Majesty: in *your* grasp,' he corrected quickly. 'We are in the final stages of bringing the fermentation vats housed in Hereji-Jo Castle to working temperature. It should be possible to begin quantity production of the Plague within eighty days, with deployment in the rivers on the final day of Summer. Clinical trials indicate that within two weeks of the Plague's deployment the contamination that is the nonFemme population of the Demi-Monde will have been eradicated. If all proceeds to plan, by the fourteenth day of Fall the only nonFemmes existing in the Demi-Monde will be those you have permitted to live, Your Majesty.'

'Effectiveness?'

'One hundred per cent. Any uncastrated nonFemmes drinking water infused with the Plague or coming into contact with a nonFemme who has already contracted the Plague will be dead within ten days.'

'So quickly? It must have a very short incubation period.'

'Four to five days.'

'Contagious?'

'Very. The Plague is transmitted directly, nonFemme to nonFemme, and it is this which makes it so deadly. Every time an infected nonFemme coughs or sneezes, he will infect those around him.'

'You are sure it has no effect on Femmes?'

'Clinical trials were conducted using delinquent Femmes who have refused to indulge in Femme2Femme sex. They were unaffected.'

'NoNs?'

'It is ineffective against NoNs, Your Majesty.' It had been the first question he had posed to that witch Dr Ptah. Mao was no fool.

'How will nonFemmes infected by the Plague die?'

'The Plague is a form of filovirus that is closely akin to the bubonic plague. It attacks the Solidified Astral Ether, causing the lumps – the buboes – which characterise the disease. Death itself comes from necrosis of the body's SAE – it literally melts – and, as might be expected, is hugely painful.'

Mao paused for a moment to relish the thought of the suffering these ungelded bastards would soon be enduring. Then they wouldn't be inclined to laugh at him; then there would be no more snickering behind his back.

Bastards ... he hated them all.

'Excellent,' said the Empress with relish. 'This pain will repay nonFemmes for the suffering they have inflicted on Femmes over the past millennium.' A thought seemed to strike her. 'Is there any way in which nonFemmes can protect themselves from the disease?'

'Only by the strictest of quarantine, as we are doing with the nonFemmes who make up the One Per Cent Stock, but in reality the Plague's onslaught will be so rapid and so devastating that before nonFemmes can take the measures necessary to protect themselves, they will be dead.'

'The One Per Cent Stock will be held safe?'

'They will be moved to special quarters tomorrow and a cordon sanitaire placed around it by Amazons of the First HerEtical Foot. All the water used by the One Per Cent Stock will be drawn from special tanks containing sterilised water. They will remain in quarantine until the Plague has run its course.'

'Excellent. So in ninety days we will be living in what to all intents and purposes is a nonFemme-free world. Then we will be free to devote all our energy to solving the riddle that is parthenogenesis.' Just for an instant the sleepy, almost careless expression on the Empress's face was replaced by one considerably more cruel and calculating. 'So we must hold the ForthRight at bay for ninety days. You will issue orders, Imperial Secretary, that immediately the ForthRight invasion begins, the Gates of the Great Wall are to be sealed and no refugees from Rangoon or Tokyo are to be permitted into Beijing. You will issue a proclamation stating that their Empress demands that all Femmes fight to their last breath to defend the Coven from the onslaught of the heterosexual invaders.'

'And the children?'

'There will be no exceptions.'

Mao was provoked into making an observation. 'The death toll will be enormous, Your Majesty, there are three million people—'

'Let them all die. If by dying they delay the ForthRight's advance until the Plague is ready to be deployed, then that is a sacrifice we are willing to make. If by dying they enable the Demi-Monde to enter the blissful state of MostBien, then that is a sacrifice we are willing to make.'

The prospect of so much suffering delighted the Empress to

the extent that she was persuaded to indulge in another river cucumber. As Mao averted his eyes, he caught sight of one of his assistants signalling to him from across the room.

'I am pleased to announce, Your Majesty, that the Daemon known as Norma Williams has been delivered to the Forbidding City.'

13

The Forbidding City
The Demi-Monde: 2nd Day of Summer, 1005

HerEticalism abhors the sexual objectifying of Femmes. Decree 998/undressing: In Praise of DeMureness demands that all Femmes refrain from dressing and acting in an immodest or provocative manner which may be construed as having the intent to inflame the heterosexual libido. In response to this Decree, Covenite clothing designer Jiang Qing introduced the all-in-one boiler suit made from blue denim which has now become the near-ubiquitous uniform of Femmes within the Coven. Colloquially these are called '*jiangs*', or, as the word has been corrupted in the rest of the Demi-Monde, 'jeans'.

The Young Femme's Guide to the HerTory of the Coven:
HerTorianNoN Fan Ye, Covenite Textbooks
and Periodicals

Norma's rearrest by the Amazons was easy to stage. When she emerged from the safe house, day had most definitely dawned, the rain had eased a little and the streets were crawling with pink-jacketed soldiers searching for her, so it was a simple matter for her and her two escorts to 'accidentally' bump into a pair of Amazons. After a suitably convincing sword fight, Norma found herself once more wearing a set of manacles and riding in the back of a closed steamer guarded by a very resolute-looking CaptainFemme.

Her journey to the Forbidding City took just over an hour, and when the steamer finally wheezed to a halt and the doors were thrown open she found herself attended by a tall, portly man in flowing silk robes embroidered with golden dragons who was standing, protected from the rain by a large pink umbrella held by an enormously muscular guard. He bowed to Norma. 'I am Imperial Secretary Mao ZeDong, First Administrator and Most Senior NoN in the Court of Great Empress Wu, Mistress of the Demi-Monde, of the Great Beyond and of all the Kosmos, Blessed and Much Beloved by ABBA and Defender of the Faith of HerEticalism.' The man's voice was peculiarly high-pitched and he spoke in a strange lilting manner but this, Norma supposed, was what happened when a guy had his nuts chopped off. His English, though accented, was, however, impeccable.

It would, Norma decided, be impolite not to return the bow, but even as she did so she found it impossible to take her eyes off the man … off the *former* man, she corrected herself. Covenite NoNs were famous throughout the Demi-Monde but this was the first time she had ever seen one of these exotic creatures up close.

Of course she recognised the Dupe, having studied his image on the Polly back in the Real World when she had been preparing an essay on the history of Communist China, though she had never imagined Mao ZeDong looking quite so … divine. The pictures she'd seen had always shown him dressed in an artless military uniform with a forage cap plonked atop his melon of a head, so the long moustache, pigtail and over-elaborate robe came as something of a surprise, as did the mist of heavy perfume that shrouded him. Unfortunately, the perfume wasn't heavy enough to disguise the unmistakable odour of urine that clung to his clothes.

Odd.

'You are not permitted beyond this point, CaptainFemme,' Mao advised as he handed the officer a sealed warrant. The Covenites seemed obsessed with paperwork. 'This is the authorisation indicating that I have taken ownership of the prisoner. I and my GuardNoNs' – he indicated the two oversized men standing behind him – 'will now take responsibility for the Daemon.'

As the steamer puffed away, Mao bowed Norma towards a bright yellow palanquin, itself adorned with the same dragon motifs he wore on his kimono. 'You are to be brought to the Forbidding City, Femme Williams, and to do this we must cross the Bridge of the Heavenly Divide.' He pointed a finger towards the preposterously narrow bridge that spanned the huge moat that circled the City. 'We must ride in the Imperial Palanquin as the bridge is built to break under the weight of a steamer.'

Norma and Mao clambered inside the litter, which was lifted onto the shoulders of four brutally strong BearerNoNs who immediately set off at a trot, carrying them across the hundred-metre span of the bridge. As they went on their swaying way, Mao kept up his commentary. 'The Bridge of the Heavenly Divide is the only way in and out of the Forbidding City. Beneath us is the Moat of UnMerciful Vengeances, its deep water covering a myriad of sharpened spikes designed to deter even the most determined of attackers.'

It was then that a series of distant explosions rocked the quietude of Beijing. Curious about what was happening, Norma glanced out of the window and saw, on the other side of the Coven, beyond the Great Wall, trails of artillery shells looping over from the ForthRight and smashing into Rangoon. The war with the ForthRight that Su Xiaoxiao had been so anxious about had obviously begun.

'That's ForthRight artillery, Imperial Secretary, so I've got a feeling that soon you're going to need all the deterring you can get. By the look of it, the ForthRight is preparing to invade.'

Mao dismissed her comment with a negligent wave of his hand. 'The ForthRight is of no concern; the Covenite army will brush these disgusting UnFunDaMentalist pig-dogs aside with no more effort than I might use to swat a fly.'

Yeah, right.

With a shrug Norma turned her attention back to the study of the wonders of the Forbidding City. One of the more peculiar aspects she noted was that they appeared to be going *uphill* and, as she had always understood the Demi-Monde's Urban Band to be flat, this came as something of a surprise.

Mao explained. 'The Forbidding City is built on a motte formed from a circular outcrop of Mantle-ite precisely one kilometre in diameter which rises fifty metres above the surface of the Demi-Monde. It is unique in all of the Demi-Monde. Scholars speculate that it was formed by our Ancestors, the preChinks, at the same time they constructed the Great Wall.'

The palanquin came to a rolling halt and Norma was helped to disembark by a BearerNoN. She was grateful to be back on her own two feet; her trip across the bridge had left her feeling as queasy as she'd been aboard the WarJunk.

Coming to stand beside her, Mao pointed to the massive gates that towered over them. 'These are the Meridian Gates which bar the way into the utopia that is the Forbidding City. Only a select and privileged few ever see the wonders that are hidden behind them.'

The gates *were* impressive: at least a hundred feet high, coloured a deep, foreboding red, and set into the huge wall that circled the City. They looked incredibly formidable. Studying them, Norma decided that maybe Mao's dismissive attitude towards the ForthRight was well grounded; it was difficult to imagine any artillery being powerful enough to smash them down.

Their approach had been observed; from high up on the walls a gong sounded and immediately the gates began to open. Giving Norma yet another bow, Mao motioned her ahead of him and into the City. 'This is the private domain of the Empress Wu. Only the most honoured and beautiful of Femmes and the most faithful and loyal of NoNs are allowed to live in the Forbidding City, and of course, once they are within the City walls, none are ever permitted to leave.'

Terrific.

'None of them?'

'Only the Empress and, of course, myself may leave the City.'

Abandon hope all ye who enter here ... especially if your name's Norma Williams.

Entering the Forbidding City was like stepping into a fantasy world of pagodas, swooping yellow-tiled roofs, red-brick walls, immaculately paved courtyards and a plethora of statues of dragons. But the thing that impressed Norma the most was how *clean* the City was: so clean that it looked for all the world like a Disneyfied version of a Chinese palace.

And the Femmes and NoNs who were scuttling about the place were as curious as their setting. All the girls were dressed in beautifully embroidered kimonos – no boiler suits for them – their shaven heads decorated with elaborate silver tiaras rendered in the shapes of leaves and birds. But the NoNs populating the City seemed determined not to be outdone: their robes were equally fine and their penchant for make-up gave their faces a peculiarly dramatic and other-worldly cast.

'So there are no men – nonFemmes – within the Forbidding City.'

'No. Such a thought is disgusting to HerEticalism; only NoNs are permitted to grace the Forbidding City.'

'That seems a rather draconian policy.'

'Not at all,' said Mao as he guided Norma through a side door and along an elaborately decorated corridor, 'it is eminently sensible. Undiluted and unrestrained masculinity is anathema to HerEticalism ... indeed, MALEvolence is anathema to the very concept of civilised behaviour. The Forbidding City is MostBien in microcosm; it shows what the Demi-Monde might be if it was freed of the contamination of unneutered nonFemmes.'

'But isn't becoming a NoN a sacrifice? Don't you miss being a man?'

'Are all Daemons this blunt, Femme Williams?'

'Only the Yank ones.'

'I see. Then I must tell you that it is not a sacrifice, rather it is a relief. I am honoured to be a NoN and thus to have been freed of the burden of MALEvolence. By becoming a NoN, ABBA has seen fit to lift the burden of children from my shoulders in order that I might dedicate myself more fully to the service of ABBA's anointed representative in the Demi-Monde, Her Divine Majesty Empress Wu. Castration is not a loss; rather, it is a cleansing.'

'But doesn't being isolated here in this feminist utopia of hers mean that Empress Wu is a little cut off from her people ... from reality?'

'It is necessary because Her Celestial Majesty Empress Wu must be shielded from ordinary mortals who might be blinded by her divinity. That is the reason why she inhabits the Forbidding City, only leaving it to attend to matters of the utmost importance.'

Norma was about to ask more questions but it seemed they had reached their destination. The NoN led her into a room that reminded her of an indoor swimming pool populated by half a dozen chubby men each clad in nothing more than a loincloth.

'These BodyNoNs will prepare you for your audience with Her Divine Majesty.'

'Prepare me?'

'In the Forbidding City only those Femmes attired as a MoreBien – as a Femme who has embraced the tenets of HerEticalism – may gaze upon the Empress. And to disport yourself in the manner of a MoreBien, Femme Williams, you must embrace DeMureness.'

They shaved her head. And after being washed, scrubbed, oiled, perfumed and then dressed in yet another hugely unflattering boiler suit – this time made from green silk – she was led by Mao along the corridor to a second set of doors. These were very grand affairs, embossed with silver dragons, guarding what Norma could only assume was 'a Very Important Place'.

She was right.

'This is the Hall of Supreme Harmony,' explained Mao in a hushed and reverential voice, 'the very centre of the Demi-Monde. Here resides the Dragon Throne and it is here you will be given audience with Empress Wu. Your soul should sing, Femme Williams, at the honour the Empress bestows upon you. Few are granted the privilege of entering the Hall of Supreme Harmony and of gazing upon the divine form of the Empress Wu.'

He waited for a few seconds, obviously expecting a reaction from Norma, and seemed decidedly miffed when he didn't get one. 'You must steel yourself, Femme Williams, such that you are not overwhelmed by the magnificence you will experience. Many faint when they see the Hall for the first time, overcome by their feeling of awe.'

'Don't fret yourself: I've been to Vegas and nothing can top that.'

Mao scowled and then decided to ignore the comment. 'Such was the ABBA-inspired genius of the architect of the Forbidding City, the NoN Nguyen An, that at noon – as it now is – the sunlight streams into the Hall of Supreme Harmony making the room appear to float in the air, to become one with the Nothingness. But do not be afraid. If you find yourself beset by fear, focus your attention on the bronze statuettes guarding the marble platform at the centre of the Hall where sits the Dragon Throne, or breathe in the fragrance of the *Phoebe nanmu* hardwoods brought by the preChinks from Terror Incognita to build the Hall. If all else fails, meditate on the shining sphere of silver that hangs from the ceiling: the Sacred Pearl of Wisdom.'

'Don't worry, I'm cool.'

'An unnecessarily vulgar NoirVillian expression, but no matter. When you enter the Hall of Supreme Harmony, you will see a black line marked on the floor: you will walk up to it, kneel and then kowtow, knocking your forehead to the ground nine times. Failure to do this will be a mark of deep disrespect for which the reward will be summary execution at the hands of the Amazons guarding Her Divine Majesty. You will not speak until spoken to, you will not gaze directly towards Her Divine Majesty and you will address her as "Your Majesty" at all times. When you first address her, you will also say, "I salute the True Empress, and pray that ABBA grants her Nine Thousand Years of Peace and Contentment."'

Even as she repeated the salutation to herself, the doors of the Hall of Supreme Harmony swung open and Norma found herself being ushered into a room of such scale and such daunting luxury that it took her breath away. Vegas, she decided, had nothing on this. Indeed, she was so awestruck that before she quite realised what she was doing she had crossed the room, knelt at the black line and performed the requisite genuflections.

'You are a very *small* Daemon, Norma Williams,' came a lilting, musical voice from the stage in front of her. 'We are *most* disappointed.'

14

The Forbidding City
The Demi-Monde: 2nd Day of Summer, 1005

Fresh Blooms – the nuFemme concubines who inhabit the Forbidding City and who are famed for their transcendental beauty – are a staple of Covenite Romantic Fiction. Although CRF is widely derided in literary circles as being 'simplistic', 'derivative' and 'borderline pawnographic', these novels have proved enormously popular with lower-class Femmes. Of course, it must be admitted that the plots of these Romances are typically anodyne, generally following a variation of what has come to be called 'the CRF story arc': a young, lovely though somewhat wayward Fresh Bloom is seduced from the ways of MoreBienism by a dashing but wicked nonFemme; she discovers that he is plotting to assassinate our beloved Empress; with the help of her true love – typically a lusty and erotically inclined servingFemme – she comes to understand the sublime nature of MoreBienism and of Femme2Femme sex and to finally defeat the dastardly schemes of the evil nonFemme. Tripe admittedly, but tripe which has done much to promote the cause of HerEticalism throughout the Demi-Monde.

An Examination of Covenite Literary Traditions: Elizabeth Carter, BlueStocking Press

Fresh Bloom Dong E scuttled through the vast and ornate corridors of the Forbidding City, or rather she scuttled whilst doing her very best not to *appear* to be scuttling. Haste and anxiety were frowned upon in the Forbidding City: here in the private realm of Her Celestial Majesty Empress Wu, all had to be peace and tranquillity, nothing was allowed to disturb the *wu wei* that pervaded this, the Centre of the World. But though outwardly Dong E displayed the bland, emotionless expression demanded of all Fresh Blooms, inwardly her mind was a whirl of possibilities and fears.

Fears.

Fears that this might be the moment when she was to be told that she was no longer a particularly *fresh* Fresh Bloom, that at the age of nineteen she would have to yield to another nuFemme – a *younger* nuFemme – that this was the time when she would join her ancestors, the brief moment when she had brought beauty to the Forbidding City and pleasure to Empress Wu over. Fears that it might be the time that she would be Plucked.

But not only was this a chilling possibility, it was also a depressingly likely one. She was, after all, the oldest of all the Fresh Blooms.

She pushed this fear brusquely to one side. She was still the most accomplished dancer of them all and just two days ago the Empress had complimented her on her rendition of 'The Solitary Orchid' which she had played so wonderfully on the *guquin*. And it didn't do to forget that only the previous night she had been chosen to come to the Empress's bedchamber to perform the Ritual of the Entwining Ivy. Concubines who had so recently received *chong* – sexual favour – from the Empress and who had performed so skilfully – and enthusiastically – to assist her in keeping her Yin and Yang essences in balance were not candidates for Plucking. And despite her advancing years she was still the most beautiful of all the Fresh Blooms . . . and the cleverest.

Anyway, Fresh Blooms were not Plucked by the Empress; that was the role of the Guardian of the Imperial Bedchamber, the much hated NoN Mao, and as the audience she had been summoned to was to be graced by the Empress, the NoN would not be performing a duty as prosaic as a Plucking in her presence. The Empress would never soil her hands or her soul with something so *masculine* as a Plucking.

So there must be another reason why she had been summoned to attend the Empress. And it had been a very urgent summons; she had not even been given sufficient time to have her face enlivened by a wash of lavender water or to enquire of the iChing which colour of kimono would be most auspicious for the trials ahead. It was most perplexing. What, she enquired of herself, could be so urgent as to warrant such a violation of Li?

She almost laughed. The reality was that the inhabitants of the City – especially the younger ones – took delight in flouting the soul-sapping rules and regulations propounded by Li. Of course, the penalties levied on those found to be perpetrating such violations were severe, but this only added a flavouring of excitement to proceedings. As a result, the City was – under its stiff and unbending surface – a hotbed of illicit assignations, illegal love affairs, clandestine intimacies and forbidden intrigues.

As she neared the Great Gates that guarded the entrance to the Hall of Supreme Harmony, Dong E gradually eased her pace, taking deep breaths, slowing her body clock and allowing *wu wei* to infuse her Solidified Astral Ether. The securing of *wu wei* was the goal of all good Confusionists . . .

Silently Dong E rebuked herself. There were no Confusionists any more; they had all been swept aside by the tide of the

Femme Liberation Movement, by the Yin Revolution. Now all Femmes were HerEticals, and though the thought processes of Confusionism still pervaded the Forbidding City, it was not wise to mention them. Fresh Blooms were not even supposed to be aware of the teachings of Confusionism – especially not of TooZian-inclined Confusionism. But when you were as clever as Dong E, it was remarkable what could be gleaned simply by standing silent during audiences and listening. And then, of course, there were the banned books she had read in the Gallery of Literary Profundity and the lessons she learnt during her illicit meetings with PhilosopherNoN Xi Kang.

She came to the Great Gates, protected as always by two implacable GuardNoNs. She bowed. 'Fresh Bloom Dong E comes to attend the Most Precious and Revered Great Empress Wu, FemmeDated by ABBA to be the Ruler of all the Demi-Monde.'

Although they recognised her, as Li demanded, the NoNs pretended that she was a stranger, eyeing her very suspiciously before returning the bow. Finally though – after the passage of the requisite amount of time required by Li – the CaptainNoN made a careful scrutiny of the List of Honoured Attendees and then made to open the Gate, but before he could turn the handle, Dong E stepped forward and placed a tiny hand on the eunuch's arm. 'A moment, Most Honourable CaptainNoN,' and with that she turned towards one of the enormous mirrors that decorated the corridor. The urgency of the summons she had received, Dong E knew, would be no excuse for a slovenly appearance. That she would appear before the Empress without make-up – subtle, almost invisible make-up to be sure, but vital when a Fresh Bloom had reached the venerable age of nineteen – was one thing, but it would be a gross violation of Li if she should be in any other way careless in her dress or her demeanour. It might even hasten the day when she would be Plucked.

The girl who peered back at her from the mirror was perfect. She was tiny, delicate and ineffably beautiful – as all Fresh Blooms were required to be – her skin flawless and unblemished, her eyes bright and sparkling – she would keep them downcast during the audience in order that the Empress did not become disturbed by the intelligence they signalled – and her mouth small, with well-formed lips. It was a mouth she would keep as tightly closed as she was able during the audience; Imperial NoN Mao had commented just the previous week that her mouth – pretty though it was – housed a too-sharp tongue. The weals from the beating he had inflicted on her arse when she had made the quip about NoNs being able to go about their duties unseen but not unsmelt still smarted.

She lifted a perfectly manicured hand, the pearlescent varnish on her long fingernails twinkling in the light of the gas lamps that lined the corridor, and made a minute – and totally unnecessary – adjustment to the neck of her kimono. This done, she turned to the three OracleNoNs who had accompanied her and examined them in an equally diligent fashion. Each of them carried a wooden box – heavily inlaid with renderings of Epigrams taken from the iChing – and inside each box was one of the three Celestial Coins used by the Imperial TongJi, the shaFemme responsible for the casting of the iChing. That Dong E had been ordered to bring the Celestial Coins to the audience was also an oddity and a violation of Li. Usually the Celestial Coins were only used when the iChing was being consulted during a Rite of 4Telling.

Her critical eye confirmed that each of the OracleNoNs' appearance was all that it should be, so she nodded to the CaptainNoN, who pushed open the gates to give her entrance to the Hall of Supreme Harmony beyond.

*

Even with her eyes downcast as she tripped lightly towards the line embossed across the floor of the magnificent room, Dong E could see enough to realise that this would be no ordinary audience. The Empress Wu, seated on the Dragon Throne at the very end of the Hall, was attended by the Imperial Secretary, Mao ZeDong . . .

Stinking pig-dog that he was and the way he was eyeing her showed that his pernicious heterosexual tendencies hadn't been *totally* extinguished by his gelding. Mao, she was sure, desired her.

. . . who was both Guardian of the Imperial Bedchamber and the most powerful of all the NoNs charged with administering the Coven. Mao's attendance signalled that something very important and very serious was to take place, and that she had not been summoned just to entertain and arouse the Empress.

She took a surreptitious glance around the Hall. She saw, standing in front of the dais upon which the Dragon Throne sat, that hideous creature the Imperial TongJi, swathed as always in her black leather robes with her face obscured by a mask concocted from intertwined leather strips and filigree silver. From the brief experiences Dong E had of observing the 4Teller at work she knew the creature was as horrible on the inside as she looked on the outside. She was a Femme who revelled in inflicting pain, as Dong E had learnt to her cost when she had once been gifted to the TongJi for a night by the Empress.

But strange though the TongJi was, this afternoon there was someone even stranger kneeling in the centre of the room, but fear of tripping up – what a violation of Li *that* would be – meant that Dong E was unable to study this person in any detail. All she could see was that this someone was a small, slim *gaijin* Femme clad in green *jiangs*. The peculiar thing was that she had never heard of a *gaijin* being allowed entry to the Forbidding City.

How odd.

She reached the line embossed across the centre of the Hall, kowtowed, knocking her head nine times on the ebony floor as the Ritual of Supplication demanded, and then intoned, 'Fresh Bloom Dong E salutes the True Empress Wu and humbly beseeches ABBA to grant her Nine Thousand Years of Peace and Contentment.'

'You may rise and approach the Great Empress Wu,' Mao commanded in his piping voice. 'Have the OracleNoNs place the Celestial Coins in the drums.'

There was going to be a reading!

Hiding her excitement behind a mask of inscrutability, Dong E swayed back up to her feet and signalled to the OracleNoNs that they should place the Coins in the three drums set in front of the throne. Spinning the Coins in the drums was a vital part of any reading of the iChing, this allowing them time to interact with the Qi that suffused the Kosmos and for ABBA to work Her will on the outcome of the 4Telling.

Once the coins had been placed in the drums, Mao squeaked a brusque 'You may depart the Imperial Presence, Fresh Bloom Dong E.'

But just as she was retreating backwards towards the Kowtow Line, the Empress spoke. 'No, Imperial NoN Mao, we wish the Fresh Bloom to remain.' The Empress gimleted Dong E with a fearsome look. 'Fresh Bloom Dong E, we understand that your Anglo is that of a native speaker. Is this the truth?'

Dong E bowed. 'Yes, Your Majesty. I have been blessed by ABBA with a great facility in that tongue.'

'Blessed?' sneered Mao. 'To be able to converse in the pig language of the *gaijin* is not a blessing, Dong E, it is a curse. Anglo and all the other pagan tongues should not be uttered in the Forbidding City and most certainly not when we are gathered to contemplate the auguries of the iChing.'

'The Daemon does not speak or comprehend Chinese,' observed the Empress.

Daemon? Was the Empress suggesting that this small and unremarkable nuFemme kneeling before the throne was a Daemon? Dong E decided to pay closer attention to the creature: relating its idiosyncrasies would make her the centre of attention when she returned to the Pavilion of Delicious Delights. The other Fresh Blooms would be *so* jealous.

'If we are to interrogate her, we must either use Anglo or we must have an interpreter. As Dong E is the most accomplished of all the Fresh Blooms in this regard, her assistance in this matter will be invaluable.'

Dong E sensed Mao's unhappiness. Whilst the Empress and Mao were fluent in all the languages of the Demi-Monde, the other courtiers and advisers gathered in the Hall were not. It was a dilemma for the NoN: if he insisted – *tried* to insist – on her quitting the Hall of Supreme Harmony then the majority of the Court wouldn't understand a word that was spoken to or by the Empress's 'guest'.

'This is a most profound transgression of Li, Your Majesty,' bridled Mao. 'Ritual has it that only those who have attained the Ninth Level of Celestial Competence may be permitted to attend a Rite of 4Telling and, if my memory serves me correctly, Fresh Bloom Dong E is only of the third level.'

The Empress waved the NoN's objections away. 'This Rite is itself a transgression of Li, as is the presence of a Daemon in the Forbidding City. Come, Fresh Bloom Dong E, and stand beside us.'

Amazing, thought Dong E as she trotted forward and up the nine steps that led to the Dragon Throne. Only when she had been summoned to her bedchamber to provide physical comforts had she been as close as this to the Empress. It was an unbelievable sign of preference and, as she could see from the expression on Mao's face, it was not one of which the NoN was particularly enamoured.

This matter concluded, the Empress addressed the Daemon with Dong E providing the interpretation. 'You are a very *small* Daemon, Norma Williams,' she said with a perfectly pitched element of disdain in her voice. 'We are *most* disappointed.'

The Forbidding City
The Demi-Monde: 2nd Day of Summer, 1005

The iChing gives its advice to the Soul consulting it by making reference to one of 512 Epigrams. Three coins are thrown nine times to produce a NonaGram made up of nine lines (or, more accurately, of three TriGrams), the lines being either broken or solid – Yin or Yang – and the answer to the question posed as the coins are thrown discovered by reference to the 512 Epigrams – one for each possible NonaGram – described in the iChing. The lines used to construct the TriGrams are:

Yin Line
The Female. A Broken Line, represented by 0 (zero) and referred to as the Nothingness.

Yang Line
The Male. An UnBroken Line, represented by 1 (one) and referred to as the Unity or ABBA.

The binary nature of the lines produced and the spiritual realities which underlie them have been the focus of much debate. Although '1' refers to the Spiritual Unity and Perfection expressed by ABBA and '0' to the Nothingness of the Kosmos, it is 0 which comes before 1 in order to achieve mathematical synchronicity. The great Confusionist philosopher Wun Zi argued that on this basis Femmes come before nonFemmes in the hierarchy of the Kosmos. The response of Too Zi is recorded as being 'bollocks'.

Religions of the Demi-Monde: Otto Weininger, University of Berlin Publications

Disappointed? Fuck you too, Norma riposted silently.

It wasn't as though Empress Wu – and she assumed the tiny woman seated on the throne *was* Empress Wu – was much to look at either. Quite striking in a weird sort of way but anyone having that much care and attention lavished on them would have looked just as good. The problem Wu had, decided Norma, was that she looked like a doll: she was a small, fragile woman in her mid-thirties who had a complexion that had the appearance and the warmth of porcelain. This, coupled with her over-elaborate robes and the golden crown resting on her head, gave her a rather fey look. But the most unsettling thing was the woman's eyes: there was real steel in her gaze, which, from Norma's experience, betokened that she was one of the psychopaths – the Singularities – ABBA had used to stock the Demi-Monde.

Careful, Norma.

Mao spoke, his Chinese rendered into excellent English by the beautiful girl standing next to Empress Wu. 'Yes, Your Majesty, this is the Daemon known as Norma Williams. She is the Daemon who has promoted the specious and subversive philosophy of Normalism, which teaches that violence is wrong and that the peoples of the Demi-Monde should live in peace and harmony. As such she is a proponent of the reviled concept of Ying.'

Obviously overcome by the horror that was peace and harmony, Mao took a moment to compose himself. 'Know this,

Daemon, Her Majesty Empress Wu is much disappointed in you. The shaFemmes who profess knowledge of the Land of the Spirits contend that Daemons are fearsome creatures possessed of horns and a tail and whose breath stinks of fire and brimstone but you are quite ordinary.'

'I'm a New York Daemon,' Norma explained. 'The ones you're referring to come from LA. They're really freaky; they've got tails and horns . . . the whole nine yards. Shit, they're so wacked out on the West Coast they even elected Schwarzenegger as governor.'

The Empress frowned as she tried to understand what Norma was saying, studying her suspiciously before continuing. 'But tell me, Daemon: is it true that you and your kind have blood flowing freely in your bodies?'

'It is true, Your Majesty. I'm full to the brim of Château Neuf de Gore.'

'Disgusting. Such a thing is a perversion of Nature.' There was another brooding silence. 'And are you the creature who has by conjurations and a glib tongue so traduced the CitiZens of the Medi that they have denied the commands of those set to rule over them? Are you the creature who has by cunning artifice persuaded them to espouse the pernicious and unholy creed known as Normalism?'

It wasn't quite the way Norma would have chosen to describe what she had been doing in the Medi, but what the hell. 'Yes, I was the leader of the Normalist movement, but I'm light on the cunning artifice. I left that to the ImPuritans. Their artifices were as cunning as hell.'

That was a statement that gave her beautiful interpreter some difficulty.

'And by your order was that foul monument to the false creed of UnFunDaMentalism and Biological Essentialism known as the Awful Tower caused to fall?'

Now, she decided, wasn't the time to quibble or to mention Burlesque Bandstand's role in that little faux pas. 'It was.'

'And by this means you did assassinate the barbarian Lavrentii Beria?'

'Yes, all ten thousand tons of the tower landed on the bastard's head so I guess he's very, very dead ... and very, very flat.'

'Remarkable,' continued Wu. 'You will not be aware, being a base Daemon, that your activities in the Medi have caused a most profound disruption to the Qi of the Kosmos and to the harmony of the Demi-Monde. Is that not so, Imperial TongJi Fu Shi?'

For the first time the tall and incredibly skinny woman who looked as though she was dressed as an extra in a horror movie spoke, using a voice that reminded Norma of the sound made when nails were dragged over a blackboard. 'That is so, Your Majesty. We have made most careful and precise calculations and it would seem that the presence and activities of this Daemon have wrenched the balance of the Kosmos asunder. The 4Tellings of the iChing made on the eighty-eighth day of Spring showed that there had been a fundamental and inauspicious shift from previous divinations. This Daemon, by its foul and pernicious meddling in the affairs of the Demi-Monde, threatens to disrupt the harmony of the Kosmos and to prevent the dawning of the Second Age of Femmes. It must die.'

Oh shit. Here we go again.

From her vantage point at the side of the throne, Dong E had an excellent view of the Daemon, and she had to admit that the Empress was quite correct: the Daemon was a disappointment. The form the Daemon had taken was that of a young girl – it was probably about Dong E's age – quite small, though with the more voluptuous figure of a *gaijin*. It could, Dong E decided, be classified as *quite* pretty by those Femmes with a taste for the more unrefined and rumbustious of MoreBien activities, but, to her mind, the Daemon's weather-beaten complexion and oddly shaped eyes meant that it could never be truly classed as beautiful.

She was so lost in her examination of the Daemon – and having to concentrate hard to interpret the creature's peculiar syntax – that she almost missed the TongJi's statement that the Daemon threatened to prevent the dawning of the Second Age of Femmes.

Even Dong E's usually impeccable composure struggled to cope with this revelation. It was a fundamental belief enshrined in HerEtical dogma that the Demi-Monde was now on the cusp of entering the Second Age of Femmes, when Yin – the female essence – would rise and Yang – the male essence – would decline. This would be the Age when nonFemmes would be replaced by Femmes as the dominant gender in the world. And for this belief – this *certainty* – to be challenged was unthinkable; it undermined the very foundations of HerEticalism.

'But before this Daemon is sent to meet its Ancestors,' intoned the Imperial TongJi, 'we must, with it in attendance, once again consult the iChing. In the presence of the Daemon the resulting 4Tellings will be of the highest order, nothing will be withheld and nothing will be denied.' The TongJi turned towards the Empress and bowed: 'With your permission, Your Majesty, I would begin the Rite of 4Telling.'

A nod of agreement from the Empress and immediately the TongJi began her preparations. Never having seen a Rite of 4Telling performed before, Dong E was fascinated by what unfolded before her. Incense burners were lit allowing strong and very pungent smoke to fill the Hall, and hard, discordant music suffused it. As she swayed to the music, the TongJi drank from a golden chalice then she danced and wailed for ten interminable minutes. It was incredibly boring.

Finally though the TongJi's performance ended and, arms outstretched, she screamed out her first question to the Kosmos. 'Oh ABBA, Omniscient, Omnipotent and Omnipresent Power in the Kosmos, Creator of All Things and Director of the Living, we ask you to heed our question and have the iChing guide our steps along the Way. Merciful ABBA, is the New Age of Yin upon us, are we to enter the Second Age of Femmes?'

Immediately the OracleNoNs rotated the three drums and then allowed the Celestial Coins to fall to the ground to form the first line of the Nonagram. They repeated this nine times until all nine lines were complete and had been inscribed in blood on the floor before the Dragon Throne.

The TongJi stared at the NonaGram for long silent seconds, seemingly frozen in fear.

'What does the NonaGram say?' prompted an impatient Empress.

'It is the NonaGram known as the Cruel Disappointment,' announced the TongJi. 'This relates to the four hundred and fifty-seventh Epigram of the iChing, which says:

It is the Time of the Changing.
That which has gone Before cannot be Preserved,
That which was to Come cannot be Sustained.
Fate weighs heavy on the Foundations of the Kosmos,
Shoulders bow and backs break,
And all that was Certain is made Doubt.
So the Dark wails in Torment.
So the Rivers, stirred by the Wind, seep away,
To be replenished by the Cleansing Flood.'

There was not a sound in the room as those present absorbed the 4Telling. Dong E knew this particular Epigram was always associated with an inauspicious outcome: it wasn't called Cruel

Disappointment for nothing. It was obvious to her that the iChing was advising the Empress Wu that the presence of the Daemon – the Cleansing Flood no less – in the Demi-Monde was resulting in an elemental change in the way the Demi-Monde was ordered. And the reference to the Rivers was *very* disturbing: the Empress often wore kimonos embroidered with the figure Kăn which represented Water and symbolised that she was the one destined to come after the Supreme Yin, Lilith. She wouldn't like being advised that she was destined to 'seep away'.

Dong E stole a quick look at the Empress who had gone very pale. This was an augury she had neither expected nor wanted.

'Ask the iChing how this Change can be prevented and the transition of the Demi-Monde to the Second Age of Femmes preserved,' the Empress snarled.

A very uncomfortable TongJi shuffled her feet. 'With the greatest of respect, Your Majesty, it is impossible to ask the iChing *how* a change might be effected; it is only possible to ask if a certain course of action is wise or imprudent.'

The Empress slapped a hand down angrily on the arm of the Dragon Throne, snapping a jewel-encrusted fingernail as she did so. Not a good omen, decided Dong E. 'Then ask it this: will the death of this Daemon return the Demi-Monde to the True Path? Will the death of the Daemon permit the dawning of the Second Age of Femmes?'

Dong E translated the question for the benefit of the Daemon and was surprised to see that it merely shrugged the threat aside. This girl might be a *gaijin* Daemon but its calm demeanour indicated that its soul – if Daemons *had* souls, that is – was possessed of *wu wei*. It was an interesting consideration: despite what people like Mao might say regarding the spiritual immaturity of *gaijins*, perhaps they were as capable of attaining the sublime state of ABBAsoluteness as Covenites.

Again the TongJi performed her ritual, but this time, when her arms were thrown wide, the question she announced to the Kosmos was more brutal. 'Merciful ABBA, might we turn aside from the path that Fate has given us? By the destruction of the Daemon known as Norma Williams, will we be able to usher in the Second Age of Femmes?'

Once more the drums were turned and once more the Coins fell, allowing a second NonaGram to be painted on the floor.

'It is the NonaGram known as the Warning,' said the TongJi in a tremulous voice, the shaFemme looking as though she was in danger of passing out, 'and the Epigram to which it relates is the very last in the iChing. It is Epigram number five hundred and twelve.'

This wasn't the TongJi's lucky day, decided Dong E, the auguries don't get much worse than this. Number five hundred and twelve was ABBA's Epigram, which warned HumanKind that though ABBA was all-good and all-benevolent, She was not indulgent of Her creations. It was the most portentous of all the Epigrams and the most feared. There was a moment's pause as the TongJi calmed herself. 'This Epigram says:

It is the Fate of all creatures to believe
That they are Greater than ABBA.
But they are just HumanKind,
Created from Nothing to be returned to Nothing.
Only ABBA remains,
Tolerant of Good and Intolerant of Evil.
Beware. ABBA will punish
Those who would be gods and who
Persuade Fools to kneel before Lies dressed as Truth.'

'Solution,' snapped the Empress and Dong E had never seen a ServantNoN move more quickly to deliver a drink. The Empress was radiating anger. 'Are we to understand that ABBA will punish us if we harm this Daemon?' The question was spoken in such a quiet voice that the words were barely audible.

Astonishingly, both the TongJi *and* Imperial NoN Mao seemed to be stricken mute, neither of them daring to tell Empress Wu – ABBA-blessed as she was – that she was in danger of offending ABBA.

Even before she quite realised what she was doing, Dong E had spoken. 'With all respect and humility, Your Majesty, it is impossible to conceive that this is the message conveyed by the Epigram.'

'Be silent,' snapped Mao.

'No ... let the girl speak. Her words please us.'

Ignoring the look of undiluted hatred Mao aimed in her direction, Dong E continued. 'You are Divine, Your Majesty, ordained by ABBA, therefore it is unthinkable that ABBA, in all Her wisdom, would seek to punish one such as you. Certainly it appears that we are advised that to destroy the Daemon would be to transgress the Way ordained by ABBA, but perhaps the iChing wishes you to be more subtle in your treatment of the creature. There are other ways, are there not, of negating the Daemon's baleful influence, ways that stop short of killing it. Could we not, say, *protect* the Daemon by keeping it here in the Forbidding City, held in solitary confinement?'

Dong E was impressed with herself: she had found a way of giving the Empress what she wanted – the neutralising of the Daemon – without violating the advice yielded by the iChing. And she had saved the Daemon's life ...

This last thought gave her pause: why was she so concerned about a *Daemon*?

'I must beg that you forgive this impudent and ridiculous interruption, Your Majesty,' spluttered Mao. 'And know that

Fresh Bloom Dong E will be punished most severely for this violation of Li.'

'No,' came the quiet reply. 'She will not be punished.' The Empress leant forward. 'Ask the iChing this, TongJi: if the Daemon was to be kept safe and well here in the Forbidding City, would ABBA deem this to be a transgression of Her will?'

Once more the TongJi asked her question, once more the drums turned and once more the coins were read. The third NonaGram painted on the floor was that of the ninety-ninth Epigram, the one known as the UnDecided. A frown creased the forehead of the TongJi: this was not the response she had been expecting from the Oracle.

'What does this Epigram say?' prompted the Empress.

'It is one of the iChing's most perplexing statements,' stuttered the TongJi. 'It reads:

Can Good be born of Evil?
Can Poison beget Life?
Can Fire quench the Thirst?
Only you can answer,
And, as in all things, the answer is the question.
So question yourself.
Peer into your soul.
There you will find yourself
Peering back.'

'But what does it mean?' demanded the Empress.

'As I say, Your Majesty, the UnDecided is the most devious of all the Epigrams and its meaning is elusive. My own interpretation is that the Daemon is the Poison, the Evil and the Fire which will rack our world and therefore it must be eliminated.'

'Hmmm. And what of you, Dong E? What is your interpretation?'

In truth, Dong E didn't have a clue, but as she had learnt during her years in the Forbidding City, when in doubt, always give the answer the Empress most wanted to hear. 'That the keeping of the Daemon safe here in the Forbidding City will remove her mischievous influence from the Kosmos, such that the Demi-Monde can proceed into the Second Age of Femmes without let or hindrance.'

Empress Wu gave a distracted nod. 'I believe you have correctly interpreted the will of ABBA, Fresh Bloom Dong E. There will be no more 4Tellings. You may leave us, Imperial TongJi, this ritual is now completed.'

Very sensible, thought Dong E. The Forbidding City was a hotbed of gossip and rumour at the best of times and if the Empress posed any further questions and the iChing's answers were similarly inauspicious, the bad news – that the Second Age of Femmes was off the agenda – would be quickly known to everyone in the City.

But ever the one to ensure that the rumours percolating through the Forbidding City were the rumours she personally approved of, the Empress Wu announced in a loud voice, 'Let it be known that the iChing has confirmed that by holding the Daemon safe in the Forbidding City we have removed the final obstacle standing between Femmes and their attaining of the long-dreamt-for state of MostBien. By making the Daemon as an empty vessel we usher in the Second Age of Femmes.'

16

The Forbidding City
The Demi-Monde: 2nd Day of Summer, 1005

And the Master's favourite pupil, Too Zi, approached him, saying, 'Master, I have listened diligently to your sermon when you advised that "Movement is necessary for those who find themselves weighed down by old troubles and the pain of ferocious bindings. Unburden yourself fully, but ensure to open lots of windows afterwards."' The pupil shook his head and said, 'But though I have heard, Master, I do not understand.'

To which the Master replied, 'Life's just shit, kid.'

Third Book of the BiAlects, Verse 45

Calling the Daemon an empty vessel was an unfortunate insult, decided Dong E as she left the Hall of Supreme Harmony. Empty vessels are full of the Nothingness and hence replete with *wu wei*.

Interesting.

As she had been taught by PhilosopherNoN Xi Kang, there was great power and strength in the Nothingness that is *wu wei*. The spaces between the spokes of a wheel, the void that is the Kosmos, the invisible flight of an arrow ... all were examples of the Nothingness, but none was as powerful as non-violence, the power to fight without fighting.

And as this Daemon was the proselytiser of this strange

philosophy of non-violence, Normalism, it was little wonder it – correction, *she*; only humans could embrace *wu wei* – was blessed by ABBA. ABBA, after all, was the ultimate embodiment of *wu wei* and the Nothingness.

Dong E shook her head, trying to clear it. A Daemon being possessed of *wu wei* was an intriguing thought, so intriguing that she wasn't inclined to return to her quarters as Mao had commanded her. Instead of turning left towards the Pavilion of Delicious Delights, she turned right towards the Gallery of Literary Profundity. Luckily for her, it was the Time of the Replenishing of Bodily Strength and the corridors of the Forbidding City were deserted as everybody took luncheon.

Still Dong E knew she had to be careful. The Gallery of Literary Profundity was out of bounds to Fresh Blooms as knowledge and learning were believed to make them lose that oh-so-cherished glow associated with the first awakening of FemmeHood. But for her these unofficial visits to the library and her chats there with Xi Kang were what made her tedious life in the Forbidding City worth living. Breaking the rules and violating Li was exciting. Better, she had decided, to die seeking knowledge than to die of boredom.

She came to the servants' door of the long-neglected library and, after taking a quick look around to check that she was not being watched, eased it open. Taking a deep breath she shimmied her way inside, steeling herself against the putrid onslaught of the millions of gently mouldering sheets of paper the library was home to. This was the second and inferior library of the Forbidding City and it was where all the discredited texts, the scrolls containing outdated opinions and the tomes relating to obsolete theories were housed, only protected from destruction by the belief that words once written became the property of ABBA. Without this injunction the whole lot would have been turned to ash years ago.

The size of the library showed just how much heterodoxical philosophy had been concocted over the years. The Gallery of Literary Profundity was, by Dong E's estimation, almost five hundred metres square, at least fifty metres high and was criss-crossed by a perplexing maze of floor-to-ceiling bookcases each crammed full of books, rolls of parchment and document boxes. It was also home to the Coven's most irascible HerTorian, the PhilosopherNoN Xi Kang.

Silent on her slippers, Dong E tripped through the vast room, feeling intimidated as she always did by the cliffs of books that loomed over her. It was pitch dark, there were no windows and no gaslights in the room, so all she had to guide her was her memory of previous visits and the smell wafting towards her from the cubicle set in the furthest corner of the library where Xi Kang had built his home.

She rounded a final bookshelf and by the light of a near-gutted candle standing on a rickety table could just make out the huddled form of the old NoN as he lay on his cot swathed in a threadbare blanket. Braving the smell – a concoction of mustiness, neglect and urine – Dong E bent down and gently shook the NoN by the shoulder.

'Revered PhilosopherNoN Xi Kang, it is me, Fresh Bloom Dong E. I have come to visit you. Look, I have brought you a present.' With that she placed a small bottle of Sake Solution on the side table.

The NoN grumped off the blanket, stretched and then made a grab for the bottle. He took a long, long guzzle. 'Excellent. Fuck, that was good. Just what a man – a former man – needs to wake him up in the morning.' He gave his arse a deep and very profound scratch. 'It is morning, is it not?'

'No, afternoon.'

'Date?'

'It is the second day of Summer, one thousand and five.'

'No kidding. Summer already, eh? Fuck, doesn't time fly when you're enjoying yourself. I thought it was still Spring.'

He took another swig from the bottle, then swung his skinny legs off the cot and let out a loud fart. Dong E was forced to turn her head to protect herself from the smell and to avoid watching the NoN peeing into a rusted bucket. The NoN was a truly repellent individual: excessively tall, excessively thin, excessively dirty and excessively disrespectful to Li. He reached up a grubby hand, gave his bald head a rub and then pushed his feet into his sandals. 'Afternoon you say? Too fucking early to be drinking, so I'll pretend it's midnight; time is, after all, an infinitely malleable concept. What did the Master say about Time? Ah, yes, *The sands of time flow so don't let it get in your sandwiches, otherwise you'll be eating desert.* Absolutely no fucking relevance to what we're talking about but that's the Master for you.' He drained the bottle and smacked his lips. 'Fucking good Solution, though it comes to a sorry pass when brainless whores like you are provided with better rations than intellectuals such as me, but the Demi-Monde is, as the Sage Too Zi often remarked, a world that has been fucked over more times than an ImPure hooker, so perhaps I shouldn't be so surprised.'

Dong E's indulgent smile was hidden in the darkness. It was hardly surprising that Xi Kang had been exiled to this, a forgotten part of the Forbidding City; the rather scatological philosophy of the TooZian branch of Confusionism he espoused had never been popular in the more refined circles of the Coven. And since the triumph of HerEticalism the study of Confusionism was only permitted within the Forbidding City and here the only interpretation of Confusionism considered legitimate was that of the Great Sage – and Femme – Wun Zi. Only her rendering of Confusionism's greatest work – the BiAlects – was now considered valid. As a result, TooZian

Confusionists, such as Xi Kang, had been shunned and banished from the presence of the Empress. The poor sod had been lucky to avoid execution for blasphemy and sedition.

The old NoN cocked his head to one side. 'What's that noise?'

The distant rumble of gunfire had been going on for so long that Dong E hardly noticed it. 'Oh, that. We haven't been told *officially* but the rumour is that the ForthRight Army is attacking Rangoon. What you can hear is the sound of our artillery.'

'*Our* artillery? Fucking nonsense: more like the UnFunnies' artillery. Maybe if I get lucky, one of their gunners will land a shell on Wu's head.' He looked over to Dong E and gave her a twisted grin. 'Anyway, enough of this chitter-chatter: to what do I owe the pleasure of your company?'

'I have been present at a ritual of 4Telling conducted by TongJi Fu Shi ...'

'Incompetent WunZian cunt,' muttered Xi Kang.

'... where she consulted the iChing regarding a number of questions posed by the Empress Wu.'

The old NoN froze. 'You were present at a 4Telling held in the presence of Wu? You heard the questions? You saw the NonaGrams which were cast?'

'Yes, yes and yes,' Dong E answered, hardly able to keep the triumph out of her voice.

Xi Kang gave a sniff. 'A whore like you would never have been permitted to attend a 4Telling in my day. No surprise there though: standards have been going to shit ever since the Yin Revolution.' The NoN spat on the floor. 'Fucking Femme Liberation Movement ... or rather unFucking Femme Liberation Movement: I hope all those bitches die of rampant vaginitis.' He pushed a scrap of paper and a stub of a pencil towards Dong E. 'Write the NonaGrams down for me.' Even in the flickering candlelight she could see that the NoN was aquiver to know what had happened during the 4Telling: he might have been able to disguise the excitement in his voice but there was no concealing the trembling of his fingers.

'And if I do that, will you promise to interpret the Changes for me?'

This was the great insight that PhilosopherNoN Xi Kang had shared with her during their many candlelit discussions, that the BiAlects and the iChing had been written to reflect the two disparate aspects of the Kosmos: Yin and Yang. The Master had chosen to articulate this dualism through the antagonistic Voices of the mythical Sages of the Ancient World, Wun Zi and Too Zi, the pair locked in continual and unresolved debate over the purpose and ultimate fate of HumanKind. Unfortunately for a TooZian like Xi Kang, since the advent of HerEticalism the Yang insight of Too Zi had been expunged and it was blasphemy to even mention that almost every NonaGram cast had a Yang shadow that added shading to the initial WunZian – Yin – reading. And it was this 'Change' reading that Dong E wished Xi Kang – the last of the TooZian scholars – to explain to her.

'I might,' said Xi Kang slyly. 'But the question is, what are you offering in exchange for my unique knowledge of the Changes?'

'Another bottle of Sake Solution?'

'Tush ... a mere bagatelle. You demand deep and profound insights into the Kosmos, insights that only I can give you, and you offer me a bottle of Solution in return. You'll have to do better than that.'

'What do you want?'

'The Sage Too Zi taught that all those intent on under-standing the concept of Confusionism had to espouse the Philosophy of Get.'

'The Philosophy of what?'

'Fuck, what's happened to the standard of education while I've been trapped in this shit-hole? You young people know precisely fuck-all. No, it's not the Philosophy of What, it's the Philosophy of Get. As – according to TooZian philosophy – there is no ABBA, no Paradise and hence no Purpose to Life, then there is absolutely no fucking point in trying to be good, therefore the whole aim of life is to Get Laid, Get Drunk, Get High and Get Even. Hence the Philosophy of Get.'

'And that's your philosophy of life?'

'You bet . . . or rather Get. It's the philosophy of all TooZians.'

'And you want me to help you pursue this philosophy?'

'To be more exact, just one part of it: I want you to help me to Get Even.'

'I don't understand.'

'Then let me explain. When that malignant, man-hating bitch Wu took over the Coven ten years ago, she deprived me of all the things I loved: my cock and my access to narcotics and a copious supply of Solution. As a consequence, I am now denied the ability to Get Laid, Get Drunk and Get High. All I am left with is the ability to Get Even and this, my beautiful Fresh Bloom, is what you must assist me in achieving, if, that is, you wish me to help you with your quest for TooZian knowledge. If I translate the NonaGrams you give me, you must promise to perform me one service in exchange.'

'What service?'

'Fuck knows. I'll tell you after I've studied your NonaGrams.'

Dong E wrote out the three NonaGrams and handed the paper to Xi Kang, who examined them carefully for several long minutes. 'Do you remember precisely how the Coins fell when each of the lines of the NonaGrams was formed?' The bantering tone had gone: this was a serious question posed in a serious way.

She had known from her previous discussions with the NoN

how important this was and had memorised which lines had been formed from two heads and one tail – to create a Changing Yang line – and which had been formed from two tails and one head – to create a Changing Yin line. She indicated on the paper which were the Changing lines and Xi Kang quickly drew the new NonaGrams.

'Fucking fascinating,' he admitted. 'Fascinating and somewhat troubling. Tell me, was there anything peculiar about the individual who was the subject of these questions?'

'She's a nuFemme . . . and she's a Daemon.'

'A Daemon! Are you totally fucking stupid? Why didn't you tell me before? This changes' – he laughed at the unintended play on words – 'everything.' With that he grabbed a candle and ambled off into the darkness that shrouded the room, leaving Dong E to scrabble along in his wake. Finally after five minutes of meandering through the shelves the NoN came to the bookcase he was searching for.

'Unfortunately, my pretty little whore, the tome I am seeking is on the very top shelf.' With some difficulty he slid a very rickety ladder along the bookcase. 'My age and sense of self-preservation preclude me from mounting the ladder.' He laughed. 'Indeed, since that witch Wu had my manhood removed I am unable to properly mount anything, so I would be grateful if you would scuttle up to the top shelf and retrieve a volume entitled *Daemons, Messiahs and Other ABBArational Beliefs*.'

'You want me to go up there?'

'Why yes, you won't be able to reach the fucking thing otherwise.'

Dong E drew a finger over a volume parked on the shelf next to her: the dust covering it was *very* thick. She looked down at her white and cream kimono, the silver embroidery glinting in the candlelight. 'I go up there and I'll get filthy. My kimono will be ruined and then everyone will know I've been up to mischief.'

'Then it is fortunate that I have a solution to your dilemma.'

It took a real effort for Xi Kang to hold back the tears as a naked Dong E slowly ascended the ladder, leaving him on the ground holding her kimono, the ladder and his breath. She was a wonderful girl and, despite his teasing of her, he had always been impressed by her sharp intelligence. And, of course, she also had an arse which reminded him of freshly plucked plums.

Or something like that.

He sighed: in another life he might have . . .

He stopped himself. No, he wouldn't: she was the daughter of a man he had both liked and revered and hence he would have treated her with the utmost respect . . . even when she was naked. Fuck it, he was the girl's godfather.

But it was a very *nice* arse.

Again he berated himself. Such musings were nothing more than self-inflicted torture: he was an old man, bereft of his cock, so musing about young and beautiful girls was an exercise in futility. It was nine years now since he had – reluctantly – acceded to become a NoN and until today he had almost managed to forget what it was like to be a real man. Not that he'd been given any choice in the matter: the alternative to gelding being execution, the public humiliation of his family and the murder of Dong E. At a stroke – a very painful stroke and one which he did his best not to think about – he'd been converted from an active and contented man into . . .

Well, he wasn't actually sure what he'd been converted into. Other than the loss of his penis there had been other changes: his beard had become sparse, his muscles had softened and he had found himself packing on weight.

He had tried to compensate for this bodily deterioration by

undertaking a strict regime of exercise. By his estimation, one circuit through the meandering alleys formed by the library's bookshelves measured two kilometres, and every day he trotted around them ten times, carrying the six overstuffed volumes that comprised the complete works of the sage Kwan E're. It pleased him that he was the only man in the history of the Demi-Monde who had ever found a use for the crap Kwan had written.

Frightening though these physical changes were, it was those wrought on his personality that had been most disturbing. He seemed suddenly bereft of energy, his will becoming almost as weak as his body, and he had become more docile and tractable, unwilling to engage in the heated arguments he had so delighted in before he was chopped. It had taken huge effort on his part to retain the irascibility that all TooZians were so proud of; he'd had to work fucking damned hard at being unpleasant and obnoxious. That he'd succeeded, he saw as his greatest victory. Indeed, he had been so unpleasant and so critical that that unPrick Mao had exiled him to the corner of the Gallery of Literary Profundity.

Bastard.

Incompetent bastard.

But he wasn't defeated yet and, with the help of Dong E, he might yet turn the tables on Wu. He might still be able to Get Even.

With a shake of his head he brought himself out of his reverie. 'You are possessed of a beautifully pert arse, my naked little whore. It is a shame you are condemned to have it admired only by that witch Wu and by a broken-down NoN.'

'You are very kind, NoN Xi Kang,' he heard the girl call down to him. He was pleased to note that despite standing stark naked at the top of the ladder, the girl still managed to retain her *wu wei*. There was a grunt and a cough. 'It is almost impossible to see up here; the books are filthy.'

'We are fortunate that they are still here. The first inclination of that philistine Wu was to burn them; she said that the works of Too Zi were an insult to all Femmes and a stain on the memory of Confusionism. Claptrap, of course, but what more can you expect from a LessBien extremist like her?'

'The word "LessBien" I find insulting and offensive, NoN Xi Kang.'

'Tough fucking luck. Maybe you should give heterosexuality a try. Get yourself a fully functioning nonFemme and indulge in a little *chong* time with him. You might like it.'

'HerEticalism teaches us that heterosexual sex is merely a means by which nonFemmes seek to dominate Femmes. Heterosexuality is a form of social indoctrination designed to promote and sustain a state of Patriarchalism within the Demi-Monde.'

'Bollocks, of course, but very well quoted bollocks. If you are ever reincarnated, my delicious little strumpet, you will make a fine parrot.'

'I am much more than a parrot. For Femmes to be truly free of the servitude imposed upon them by nonFemmes, the brutal and unhygienic quasi-political regime that is heterosexual sex must be dismantled and destroyed. And to do this Femmes of the Coven must cease collaborating with their oppressors and realise that when a Femme is violated by a nonFemme, all she is doing is demonstrating her own oppression and showing her contempt for her body and individuality.'

'That, if I'm not mistaken, is a quote from that pile of pseudo-intellectual effluent entitled *Dealing with the Infestation of nonFemmes: The Decontamination of the Demi-Monde* and written by that bulldyke LessBien bitch Dr Barbara Agemedes. It's horse-shit: I was so disgusted with the book that I used its pages to wipe my arse. It was the only thing they were good for.'

'I refuse to stand naked at the top of a ladder debating

HerEticalist dogma with you, NoN Xi.' There was another grunt and the candle the girl was holding quivered in the darkness. 'You are fortunate that I have found the book you are searching for.'

'Originally,' began NoN Xi, as he lolled back on his cot and watched Dong E dress herself, 'Confusionism was developed as a confrontational religion. The Master who wrote the philosophical work that underpins Confusionism – the BiAlects – believed that only through open and fervent debate and argument would the ultimate truth of the Kosmos be revealed. It is the aim of all Confusionists to reconcile the two diametrically opposed voices of Wun Zi and Too Zi, and by doing so to discover the harmony of all knowledge and thought, and to merge Yin and Yang. This merging will create the Sublime Harmony called Ying, and the achieving of Ying will bring peace and tranquillity to the Kosmos.'

Dong E frowned: Mao had mentioned Ying in connection with the Daemon. 'I'd never heard of this Ying of yours before today.'

'Of course not. The last thing Wu wants is for people to appreciate that there was an alternative to MostBien . . . Ying.' He smiled. 'Tell me, what is the full title of the iChing?'

'The iChing: The Book of Small Change.'

'And the "Small Change" refers to what?'

'The three coins used in consulting the iChing, which when tossed reveal the NonaGram leading to the Epigram which answers the question posed.'

'Total bollocks. The "Small Change" actually refers to the ability of most NonaGrams to exist in two forms . . . to *change* between the WunZian and the TooZian form of the NonaGram and hence reveal both the Yin *and* the Yang aspect of the relevant Epigram. And that's just what we are going to do now:

look at the alternative TooZian answers to the questions posed by that incompetent cow TongJi Fu Shi.' He flicked through the crisp pages of the book Dong E had brought down from the bookcase. 'The most important Change is the one pertaining to Epigram five hundred and twelve. This converts, in its Yang form, to Epigram one, the Harmony, which reads as follows:

> To end, we must begin
> Guided, but unguided.
> Free, but bound by the Harmony of wu wei,
> The Peaceful Anger of the Truth.
> There will always be Darkness,
> But the Flower that Delights shows the Other Way.
> She turns our eyes from the Water and towards the Sun
> And saves the Messiah sent by ABBA,
> Who would lead us to the glory that is Ying.'

'I don't understand.'

'No one fucking understands. Most TooZians think the Master wrote it when he was pissed. But now, its meaning is obvious.'

'Not to me.'

'I doubt that. You might be a whore with a body that would inflame the dead, but you are a clever little thing ... for a Femme, that is.'

'I still don't understand.'

'Very well, let me explain. It seems that your Daemon is the Messiah – and you've got no idea how distasteful it is for an atheistic TooZian like me to say those words – who has been sent by ABBA to lead HumanKind to a state of Perfect Harmony that fuses Yin and Yang in Ying. The Messiah is in peril and it is incumbent on you to save her.'

'Me?'

'The Epigram couldn't be more precise: "*But the Flower*

that Delights shows the Other Way." That is obviously a reference to you – a Fresh Bloom is a flower, isn't it? – and having seen you naked, if ever there was a "Flower that Delights", it's you. As for the "Other Way", well, that must be the spurning of the perverted misandry of HerEticalism, the rejection of MoreBienism and the embracing of Ying.'

'I can't do that.'

'You must: it goes on to say that you will be the one who *"turns our eyes from the Water and towards the Sun"*, you will be the one who turns her eyes from the Yin of HerEticalism to the Ying of understanding.'

'But I can't betray the Empress on the say-so of one Epigram.'

'I thought you might be reluctant. That's why I had you bring down this volume, *Daemons, Messiahs and Other ABBArational Beliefs*. I think you should read it and then decide. It's a load of bollocks but it's quite persuasive bollocks.'

'I've never heard of it. Who wrote it?'

'I did,' said Xi Kang.

'Oh,' said a surprised Dong E as she eyed the thick book warily. 'But much as I would like to read it, I can't: books are banned in the Pavilion of Delicious Delights.'

'Then let's make it simpler,' and with that NoN Xi Kang ripped a dozen pages out of the book. 'Try the abridged version.'

The Forbidding City
The Demi-Monde: 2nd Day of Summer, 1005

The favourite pupil, Too Zi, asked the Master, 'Why does Man have such an affinity to violence?'

And the Master replied, 'Man's big problem is having a surfeit of Qi, and his stupid behaviour is the result of his desperate attempts to rid himself of this superfluity. When he is young, he does this by trying to fuck anything with a ticking body clock, and when he is in his prime, he does it by fighting other Men. Of course, by the time he reaches old age and his Qi is depleted, he is so desperate to reclaim his youth that he *still* goes around fucking and fighting.'

'And what is the answer to this dilemma?' asked Too Zi.

'Wanking,' replied the Master as he disappeared into the bathroom.

The Fifth Book of BiAlects, Verse 37

Life with the rest of the Empress's concubines in the Pavilion of Delicious Delights was not one that Dong E found conducive to private study and reflection. Every moment of every day was confined and encoded by Li. Li informed them what it was appropriate to wear, which songs it was most propitious to sing, and which board games it was permitted to play. Li told them when to wash, when to eat, when to rest ... everything. And to ensure that Li was meticulously adhered to, there was always the hateful presence of NoN Mao ZeDong noting and punishing every indiscretion and every violation of protocol committed by the Fresh Blooms.

In this monitoring Mao was enthusiastically aided and abetted by Noble Consort Yu Lang, the most senior of all the Empress's concubines and hence her favourite, and being the favourite, she was permanently worried that her position would one day be usurped by a younger and fresher rival. She was suspicious of any Fresh Bloom who seemed to be finding favour with the Empress and hence Dong E's invitation to attend the Rite of 4Telling had been very badly received.

The interrogation commenced immediately Dong E returned from her adventure in the Gallery of Literary Profundity. 'You were summoned to an audience in the Hall of Supreme Harmony, Fresh Bloom Dong E. This is a rare honour for one so low. Come, tell me what occurred.'

Dong E bowed. 'You must forgive me, Noble Consort Yu Lang, but I have been pressed most earnestly by Her Majesty to remain silent regarding what I saw and heard in her presence.'

Yu Lang bridled and slapped her fan angrily onto the palm of her hand. She beckoned to her GuardianNoN, the repulsive Wang Jingwei. 'NoN Wang Jingwei, this nothing of a Fresh Bloom refuses to divulge what happened this morning when she was called to the Hall of Supreme Harmony. Have you ever heard such insolence?'

The fat NoN shook his head so hard that his jowls wobbled. 'Never! It is the duty of all Fresh Blooms to be obedient to those placed above them and, if I may say so, there are none more elevated in the Imperial Seraglio than yourself, Noble Consort Yu.'

Servile bastard.

'Come, no more of this nonsense, Fresh Bloom Dong E, tell Noble Consort Yu Lang what transpired this morning.'

Again Dong E bowed. 'With the deepest and most profound regret, Revered GuardianNoN Wang Jingwei, I must decline to tell you. I am bound by oath to remain silent on these matters. It grieves me most earnestly to refuse your commands, but my pledge to Her Imperial Majesty cannot be denied.'

They beat her. Using a cane, they beat her. But no matter how hard they slashed it across her bottom, she refused to speak and eventually Wang Jingwei called a halt – obviously concerned about the trouble there would be if the Empress called for Dong E that night and she was unable to walk – and he and Yu Lang left her sobbing and alone locked in an ante room with only a candle for company.

Which was what Dong E had planned all along.

As soon as she heard the key turn in the lock, Dong E stopped crying, dried her eyes and took a few moments to regain her composure. She had deliberately antagonised Yu Lang knowing that as punishment she would be condemned to a couple of hours of solitary confinement, and this, she had learnt, was the only way she could achieve privacy. She retrieved the sheets of paper Xi Kang had given her from where they were hidden down the back of her kimono – where their presence had saved her from the worst of the caning – and settled back to read.

Then, just as quickly, stopped reading.

No wonder *Daemons, Messiahs and Other ABBArational Beliefs* was a banned book. In the first few lines Xi Kang denied the existence of ABBA, and as this, in turn, denied the divinity of Empress Wu it was an opinion that was punishable by death. To be caught reading such seditious material would lead to a very swift and very painful Plucking. Dong E took a quick – and totally unnecessary – look around the room before allowing curiosity to drag her eyes back to the page.

She read for ten minutes and the more she read the more she came to understand why Xi Kang – TooZian radical that he was – had been banished to the Gallery of Literary Profundity, especially when he opined that *once the amount of Qi within the Demi-Monde rises to a Critical Level (nineteen years from now in the year 1005 AC) . . .*

This year!

. . . then the world will self-destruct in an orgy of violence, an event which I named the Big Bang . . . or, as those of a religious bent prefer to call it, Ragnarok. A study of the religious tracts indicates that Ragnarok will signal a shift from Yin/Yang dualism to a merging of Yin and Yang, creating a harmonised Demi-Monde suffused with Ying. It will be at this moment when the Messiah – whose manifestation is foretold in all Demi-Mondian religions – will arrive to lead the faithful to ABBAsoluteness.

This was sacrilege of the most pernicious kind. It was the bedrock of HerEticalism that the Demi-Monde was about to enter the Second Age of the Femmes, the Millennium when Femmes would achieve mastery – MISStery – of the world and nonFemmes, with their passion for violence and mayhem, would be removed from power. But what Xi Kang was suggesting was that there was another interpretation of the movement of the Kosmos, that the Age to come was not one dominated by Yin – the female essence – but one that would usher in the Time of Perfect Harmony, of Ying, the elegant and perfect merging of the female and the male essences, the combining of Yin *and* of Yang. And again Dong E was struck by the similarity this concept had with Normalism, the non-violent creed of the Daemon Norma Williams.

Worse was to come with Xi Kang arguing that there would be a Messiah sent by ABBA to lead the people of the Demi-Monde to ABBAsoluteness . . . to oneness with ABBA. Again this was a disturbingly heretical suggestion. Whilst the coming of a Messiah was fundamental to many of the religions of the Demi-Monde, it was strenuously denied by HerEticalism. How could it be, HerEticalism asked, that ABBA would need to send a Messiah to the Demi-Monde when She already had a representative in this world in the guise of the ABBA-blessed Empress Wu? It was Empress Wu, all Covenites were taught, who was the Messiah. It was she who would bring Femmes to the precious state of MostBien and who would drive MALEvolence from the world.

But if Dong E was to believe Xi Kang, the message was clear: the Messiah would be a Daemon ... just like this Norma Williams.

Astonishing though this was, it was a paragraph towards the end of the extract that turned her astonishment into incredulity.

It is the struggle between the Messiah and the Beast that forms the basis for the Final Conflict. But the Messiah will not fight alone, having the help of PaPa Legba (sometimes called the Trickster, or the Wily Fox), the Warrior (sometimes called the Battle-Maiden or grim Surt) and, finally, the Fresh Bloom, destined by Fate and her Ancestors to come to the Messiah's aid when all have deserted her.

A Fresh Bloom was destined by Fate to come to the Messiah's aid!

For a moment Dong E sat stunned. Then she checked the imprint date shown on the fly of the mutilated book. The book had been printed long before she had come to the Forbidding City, long before she had been named a Fresh Bloom. It was a strange and a very upsetting coincidence.

Dong E sat for long minutes in silent consideration of what she had read trying to attain *wu wei*. Once she had accomplished this she delved into her pocket and drew out the three coins she used when consulting the iChing, settled her body and mind, voiced her question – *What is to be my role with regard to the Daemon?* – and then with a dexterity honed by much practice threw the three coins nine times.

The NonaGram created gave her considerable pause. Like all

Fresh Blooms, she had committed the five hundred and twelve Epigrams of the iChing to memory so she knew what the sixty-sixth one said, and as she sat in that dark and dank room, she felt the heavy hand of Fate on her shoulder. Now she understood that she was the girl destined to save the Messiah.

> *So like an island*
> *Alone in a raging sea,*
> *Like a lamp*
> *Shining in the darkest night,*
> *So Good must resist Evil.*
> *Know you this:*
> *To deny is to surrender,*
> *To kowtow is to submit,*
> *You, the Superior Soul, must Stand.*

'Why me?'

'Why not?' countered Xi Kang.

'But I'm a nothing. I'm just a Fresh Bloom and a not very important Fresh Bloom at that.'

'ABBA moves in mysterious ways.' Xi Kang stopped himself. 'Bollocks, I must be going senile. We TooZians don't believe in ABBA so it's impossible for Her – or perhaps Him – to move at all. So let's just say that you have been ordained by Fate to do this great task.'

'That's a cop-out: Fate is just another name for ABBA.'

Xi Kang took another long gulp from the bottle of Solution Dong E had brought as a gift. 'You got me there. I always thought the Master, when he was writing the BiAlects, never really had his heart in it when he was composing the parts relating to the non-existence of ABBA. What did you think of my book?'

'Disturbing ... infuriating.'

'Excellent! I have always been of the opinion that a book that doesn't infuriate at least half of its readers isn't a book at all, it's a brochure. So which bits did you find especially troublesome?'

'Well ... the part that says a Fresh Bloom will come to the Messiah's aid when all have deserted her. Is my Celestial name really used in ancient mythology?'

'Frequently.'

'It might be just a coincidence.'

'Could be, but somehow I don't think so. Rather I'm inclined to think a prophecy made at a distance of two thousand years that turns out to be true smacks of divine guidance ... fuck ... smacks of Fate. It seems, my deliciously beautiful wanton, that you have a great role to play in deciding the destiny of the Messiah and hence of the Demi-Monde.'

'And it *is* the Daemon who is the Messiah?'

'That's what the iChing says.'

'Well, it's one thing to be tasked with saving the Messiah, it's quite another to actually do it. She's being kept incommunicado in an apartment in the Pavilion of Silent Repose, an apartment guarded twenty-four hours a day by GuardNoNs.'

Xi Kang shrugged. 'And now we come to the payment I can demand for providing you with the insight into the Changes. This Daemon, after all, has got to eat and to have her laundry done, and you are a very pretty *little* trollop ...'

Part Three
The Column of Loci

18

Venice
The Demi-Monde: 8th Day of Summer, 1005

Little has come down to us from the days before the Confinement. In the chaos that accompanied the final defeat of Lilith, efforts – misguided, but eminently understandable – were made by the new rulers of the Demi-Monde to eradicate all records of those terrible days. It is said that the smoke from the pyres made of the books of Lilithian lore blotted out the Sun. Miraculously, one book survived the conflagration: the infamous *Flagellum Hominum: The Scourge of HumanKind*. This epic work, supposedly written by Lilith herself, is believed to contain all the knowledge and the enchantments of the Lilithi – the followers of Lilith – but even here there is uncertainty. Most of the book is written in the – as yet – undeciphered Pre-Folk A script and hence the vast majority of what it contains is unintelligible.

Religions of the Demi-Monde: **Otto Weininger, University of Berlin Publications**

'I wish to see the Column.'

Nikolai Kondratieff bowed, using it as a means of hiding the apprehension he felt sure was reflected on his face. The sudden appearance of the Marquis de Sade – or, as he was now, *Senior Prelate* de Sade – was a disturbing event. But what made his appearance all the more disconcerting was that he was accompanied by Grand Vizier Selim the Grim and Doge IMmanual's twin brother, Duke William, both of whom, if the scuttlebutt was to be believed, were mad, bad and dangerous to know.

Having met Selim before at the unveiling of the Column, Kondratieff was prepared for how intimidating the man was but nothing could have prepared him for how threatened he felt to be in the presence of Duke William. The boy brought the darkness with him.

Duke William looked just as Kondratieff imagined he would: big and brutal. He was tall, like his sister, and very powerfully built, his jacket struggling to contain his broad shoulders. But it wasn't his size that so alarmed Kondratieff; it was the fact that the boy seemed to be a mass of twitches and tics. His feet were incessantly tap, tap, tapping on the floor, his hands were continually touching and teasing his elaborate coiffure and his left eye was beset by a nervous tremor. He gave the impression that he was having the greatest of difficulty containing his passions ... that he was borderline out of control. Kondratieff knew instinctively that he was a Dark Charismatic ... an InDeterminate and very evil force of Nature.

This was the swine who had caused Kondratieff to order the running of the Future History Institute's Data Analysis and Evaluation machinery – the DAEmon – day and night for the last week as he tried desperately to assess the impact the boy's sudden appearance in the Demi-Monde would have on the future. And the results had all been bad. Whilst Kondratieff was confident – well, relatively confident – that the Temporal Modulations he and de Nostredame had been making would prevent Doge IMmanual from achieving mastery of the Demi-Monde, her brother's unexpected manifestation had thrown these plans into disarray. Now it was time for desperate measures.

'That will be my pleasure, Your Holiness ... Your Highness

... Your Grace,' Kondratieff smarmed, masking his feelings of disgust with a smile. 'It is not often that the Galerie des Anciens is graced by the presence of three such noble visitors.' He did his best to keep even the merest hint of sarcasm from inflecting his voice, but it was difficult. Only a few weeks ago de Sade had been one of the most detested men in the whole of Venice and now here he was, strutting around as one of its most important personages. Only a few weeks ago Selim had been one of the most feared enemies of Venice and now here he was, promenading around as though he was thinking of buying the city. And, if the rumours circulating Venice were correct, such were Duke William's perverse appetites that his natural habitat was deep in the sewers of civilisation.

All three were men to be very, very wary of.

Kondratieff turned up the gas mantles dotted around the walls of the hall housing the Column, revealing it in all its glory, glowing green in the flickering light and standing an imposing six metres tall. He could see from de Sade's expression that even though he had seen the Column before, he was still awed by its size and power: he circled it carefully examining the inscriptions rendered in Pre-Folk A etched into each of the six faces. These were the inscriptions that Kondratieff's friend Professeur Michel de Nostredame had translated, revealing them to voice chilling predictions regarding Ragnarok and the End of Days.

'Magnificent, isn't it?' Kondratieff suggested.

Duke William yawned. 'It's just some big piece of stone,' was his assessment as he lounged down into a chair and lit another cigarette. 'Boring to the max. Blasé-blah-blah-blah!'

De Sade ignored his charge's imbecilic observation. 'More than magnificent, Kondratieff, it is also of great metaphysical significance, so much so that the Doge IMmanual, in her divinely inspired wisdom, wishes the Column moved to a home more befitting its importance.'

Kondratieff mimicked bewilderment. 'A home?'

'After discussions with His Highness, Grand Vizier Selim, it has been agreed that the Column be given a permanent home in the Temple of Lilith that stands in the HubLand bordering NoirVille.'

The last thing Kondratieff needed telling was where the Temple of Lilith was. All preHistorians knew where the Temple was, which, unfortunately, was about all they did know about it. The Temple was a vast Mantle-ite structure set slap-bang in the centre of the NoirVille Hub and that had – so legend had it – been the place where Lilith had worked her magic. It was from the Temple that she had drawn her occult power.

Of course, this was all conjecture. The Temple had been sealed by Lilith before the Confinement and no one – and a great many mages had tried and failed – had managed to prise its doors open since. Not that there had been any *recent* attempts: following the triumph of HimPerialism in NoirVille the Temple had been declared taboo, the guardians of HimPerialism apparently believing it to be inappropriate for Men who practised Man²naM sex and who followed the precepts of Machismo to venerate a temple celebrating the cult of the Dark Witch, Lilith. The last time Kondratieff had seen the Temple it had been barely visible beneath an overgrowth of ivy.

'I am surprised,' lied Kondratieff. 'I understood that His HimPerial Reverence Mohammed al-Mahdi is strongly opposed to efforts being made to open the Temple.'

'The political situation has changed somewhat, Kondratieff,' said Selim airily. 'With the rapprochement of NoirVille and Venice it is thought vital that there should be some symbol of this burgeoning friendship and what better symbol could there be than the reclaiming of the Temple of Lilith?'

Kondratieff frowned. 'To reclaim it, Your Highness, the Temple has first to be opened and that has defeated the Demi-Monde's best minds for over a thousand years. The devices and

conjurations Lilith used to close the Temple have proved themselves to be impervious to attack and beyond the wit of
HumanKind to avoid.'

A condescending chuckle from de Sade. 'You will have
noticed, Kondratieff, that Doge IMmanual is quite apt at doing
that which mere mortals such as you and I find impossible. She
is, after all, the Messiah sent by ABBA to lead us through
Ragnarok and on to Rapture.'

Kondratieff hoped the bland smile he gave as a reply was
sufficiently convincing. The Lady IMmanual wasn't so much
the Messiah as the *Beast* who would lead HumanKind over a
cliff and plummeting into the Abyss.

'You will be pleased to hear, Kondratieff, that Doge IMmanual
has opened the Temple and intends to rededicate it on the final
day of Summer, on Lammas Eve. We will need the Column transported to the Temple by then.'

Despite himself Kondratieff gawped, astonished by the blithe
manner in which de Sade described the enormously difficult
task of moving the Column to the Hub. 'At the risk of sounding
a little defeatist, Your Holiness, I would remind you that the
Column is very big and very heavy. It weighs almost two
hundred tons.' Images of steamer-crawlers dragging the Column
across the Hub came to mind. They weren't particularly reassuring images. 'And with it being Summer, the nanoBites are
very active in the Hub. I am therefore at a loss as to how such
a feat might be accomplished.'

If the way he waved Kondratieff's concerns away was any
indication, de Sade seemed utterly careless of the obstacle
presented by the nanoBites. 'That is why I have come to visit
you today, Kondratieff. You are one of Venice's foremost scientists, so the Doge IMmanual wishes you to assume the
responsibility of organising the transportation and erection of
the Column. My thoughts are that it should be encased in a

metal cylinder and floated down the Nile to the Wheel River where it can be brought ashore at a landing point opposite the Temple.'

Kondratieff felt the furrows on his brow deepen. De Sade wasn't listening to him. 'An ingenious plan, Senior Prelate, but one which still leaves us with the conundrum of how to move the Column from the landing point, across the Hub, and thence to the Temple. As I say, the nanoBites are very active at this time of year.'

'Being built of Mantle-ite, the Column is impervious to attack.'

'Unfortunately, the steamer-crawlers and the navvies needed to haul the Column are not.'

'Tut, tut, Kondratieff, you must learn to trust the ABBA-guided wisdom of Doge IMmanual. She has advised me that there is an ancient Mantle-ite road leading from the Wheel River to the Temple which has become overgrown and forgotten. Even as we speak, workmen are clearing it. The majesty of the Divine Way will soon be revealed.'

A Mantle-ite road? There were no records in the ancient literature of there ever being such a road. Despite himself Kondratieff felt a quiver of excitement. Opportunities beckoned and this was not the time for further demurral. 'Then I would be honoured to undertake the management of transporting the Column to the Temple.'

Honoured was an understatement: this was an opportunity made in heaven.

'Very good, Kondratieff. You should be in no doubt as to the importance of this commission. The opening of the Temple and the unveiling of the Column on Lammas Eve will be a historic event and one attended by the leaders of both Venice and NoirVille. You would do well not to fail. Liaise with Admiral Bragadin regarding any vessel you might require to tow the Column to the Hub.'

'Be assured, Your Holiness, that this project will receive my fullest attention.'

'Excellent. And I look forward to your presence at the Sala del Maggior Consiglio this afternoon to hear the Doge IMmanual address the Grand Council. All loyal Venetians will wish to attend.'

Absent-mindedly Kondratieff bowed the three men out of the room, his mind already racing with possibilities ... murderous possibilities.

Master of preScience and of 4Telling though Kondratieff was, it was beyond even his expertise to know *precisely* when the sky would open and the monsoon rains would come washing down. Folklore had it that 'on Summer afternoons the rain starts at two and finishes at three and by then, my friend, you'll be as wet as me', but actually the start and finish of the afternoon rains wasn't quite as precise as that. Currently he had one of his graduate students delving through the weather records of Venice to try to establish the pattern – and like every other natural event in the Demi-Monde, there *would* be a pattern – but he'd only gone back sixteen years and as yet there was no apparent cyclicality in the timing of the monsoons.

Today the rains had tarried – until twelve minutes past three, to be exact, and Kondratieff was a *very* exact man – and as a consequence, when he had left the Sala after hearing the Doge speak he had been caught outside without an umbrella.

But he hardly noticed the rain which beat down on his top hat; he was too distracted by what he had heard in the Doge's Palace. Standing in the midst of the crowd, Kondratieff had come to understand the future the Doge IMmanual saw stretching out before the peoples of the Demi-Monde and, as far as he was concerned, it was a very bleak future indeed. Doge IMmanual was intent on leading HumanKind to Perfection. She

had even used the Confusionist expression 'ABBAsoluteness' –
oneness with ABBA – to describe her ambition in this regard,
an ambition that would necessitate the 'remodelling' of
HumanKind. Doge IMmanual wasn't so much intent on
changing the future as changing HumanKind.

But what Kondratieff had found most troubling was the final
statement of the Doge: 'To build anew, we must first destroy.'
And what it seemed that she and her new ally Shaka Zulu were
intent on destroying was anybody who wasn't prepared to bend
a knee to IMmanualism. It was a vision of the future that frightened Kondratieff; as a scientist he celebrated freedom of
thought and this, he suspected, would be one of the first free-
doms that Doge IMmanual planned to remove. Perfection, as
far as he was concerned, betokened sterile uniformity.

A steamer panted past, washing cold and very scummy water
over his boots, and rather than brave the torrential rain any
longer, he elected to duck into a café and wait until the storm
clouds passed. Enjoying a cup of café au gore would be quite a
pleasant way to while away an hour and enable him to do a
little uninterrupted thinking . . . thinking about how to get rid
of Doge IMmanual *and* her venomous brother.

To defeat the Beast he would have to take matters, reluctantly, into his own hands. His cogitations were interrupted by
the arrival of an unexpected visitor.

'Hey, Nikolai, baby, mind if I grab a stump to rest my rump?'

Kondratieff looked up, and found himself looking into the
large brown eyes of a heavily veiled woman. Or more accurately,
a *woeMan*: she had to be a NoirVillian, only NoirVillian females
dressed in burkas like the one that shrouded the woman's body
from the top of her head to the soles of her shoes. She was also
a very determined woeMan: before he had an opportunity to
protest the intrusion, the woman had shimmied into the seat
opposite his.

'Ain't you going to make with the meet and greet, Nikolai? I'm Josephine Baker and it's a pleasure to finally beat gums with the great Nikolai Kondratieff.' And with that the woeMan pulled back her veil and shrugged down the hood of her burka. She held out her hand and Kondratieff gave it a tentative shake.

He had to do a double take. He *did* recognise Josephine Baker; he had seen her perform in La Fenice nightclub three or four Seasons ago and the girl was unforgettable.

As casually as he was able, Kondratieff took a look around the café checking to see if there were any of Venice's hated secret police lurking nearby; Josephine Baker was, after all, one of the most wanted people in Venice. 'I don't believe there is a man in the whole of the Demi-Monde who would fail to recognise you, Miss Baker ... and nor would the Signori di Notte. I understand from the newspapers that you are being urgently sought by the authorities in connection with the escape of Vanka Maykov.'

His caution obviously tickled his guest. 'Don't worry, Nikolai, I made sure I wasn't being tailed. Anyway, no one is gonna dig who I am when I'm hidden under a burka.' She ran a hand over her shaven pate. 'And even without the burka any cat seeing me will think I'm a good little IMmanualist. Course, I'm gonna have to wear a wig when I'm back in the JAD: I don't wanna give the hepcats in the Code Noir the impression that I've gone rogue.'

Despite himself, Kondratieff laughed. In a way the girl was right: with IMmanualism now the *religion du jour* in Venice, an increasing number of women were aping the new Doge by shaving their heads. 'The problem, my dear Miss Baker, is that even such a drastic ruse is unable to disguise either your beauty or your ethnicity.'

Josephine giggled. 'Wow, Nikolai, I didn't dig that you were such a smooth-talking cat. I'll have to watch you. But don't worry about my ethnicity: since the alliance between Venice and NoirVille, this burg is awash with Shades.' She shook her lovely head. 'Nah, no one is gonna spot me, not the way I shuck and jive.'

Kondratieff nodded his understanding, though he wished he could share the girl's confidence. A woman as lovely as Josephine Baker drew attention as readily as a magnet drew iron filings, and it took just an instant for attention to mutate into recognition. The girl was correct though, there were a *lot* of Shades in Venice – especially soldiers sent to reinforce the Venetian army against an attack by the ForthRight – but none of them, he suspected, had her sexual charisma.

'Delighted as I am to meet you, Miss Baker, you presumably appreciate that your being in Venice constitutes a considerable risk.' He left unsaid that his consorting with an Enemy of the People was also a considerable risk for *him*.

'Yeah, I dig that to the mostest and if it wasn't for the heavy spiel Jezebel Ethobaal asked me to lay on you I'd already have hightailed it to the JAD.' She lit a cigarette and took a long calming drag. 'You'll be glad to hear that Vanka made it to the JAD okay. Way I dig it, Vanka was a friend of yours.'

Time to be cautious, decided Kondratieff. In Venice even the walls had ears ... and very often spyholes. 'An acquaintance, nothing more. But I am pleased to hear that he is safe: there was something strangely likeable about the man.'

'Yeah, Jezebel got really hot and heavy on the subject of Vanka Maykov and bringing him safe and sound to the JAD.'

Kondratieff nodded again. Dr Jezebel Ethobaal had tormented him all through Spring with demands that he keep Vanka Maykov – the One with No Shadow – safe and with Ethobaal being leader of the Code Noir and the world's foremost practitioner of WhoDoo she was a difficult woman to deny. And her having sent one of her foremost agents – Josephine Baker – to talk to him directly rather than sending him a PigeonGram indicated that she was intent on becoming even more demanding.

Kondratieff ordered fresh coffee for them both and waited until it had been served before continuing. 'I have to say I was surprised by the importance Jezebel Ethobaal placed on rescuing Maykov.'

'Nikolai, you gotta dig that Vanka's the big barracuda. He's the guy who could help us defeat the Beast. The trouble is the Lady IMmanual knows it too: our cryptos in the Doge's Palace tell us that she got really bent outta shape when she heard he'd vamoosed.'

Kondratieff played the naif. 'Why? My understanding is that Vanka Maykov is little more than a confidence man ... a trickster.'

'Trickster ...' Josephine mused on the word for a moment. 'Yeah, that's who Vanka Maykov is: the Trickster. So tricky that he doesn't have an aura.'

Kondratieff gave an absent-minded nod. He already knew about that peculiarity of Maykov's, but there were other things that made the man remarkable. Ever since he'd tried to have HyperOpia make predictions about Maykov and the program had come back saying that as far as it was concerned he didn't exist, Kondratieff had known he was ... different. So different that it was as though he'd appeared out of thin air five years ago. Of course, Kondratieff had his own theories as to who – or more accurately, *what* – Vanka Maykov was, but as these were somewhat unorthodox, he kept them to himself.

'I appreciate that a lack of an aura is unique, Miss Baker, but that in itself is hardly enough to substantiate the Doge's enthusiasm for having the man executed. Maybe the Doge's lust for vengeance is simply jealous pique; she and Maykov were, after all, lovers.'

'It ain't jealousy, Nikolai. Truth is Vanka really creeps that dame out. She's scared of him.'

'Why?'

It was Josephine's turn to look nervously around to check there were no eavesdroppers. 'Some of the senior WhoDoo mambos, Jezebel amongst them, think that Vanka might be an emissary of the Great Bondye – of ABBA – that he might be PaPa Legba, the keeper of the gate that divides the Demi-Monde from the Spirit World. That's why, now he's safely in the JAD, we're gonna have him attend one of our séances. If he is who we think he is then he'll be able to have us defeat Doge IMmanual ... Lilith.'

'You don't sound terribly confident.'

'We're not. Lilith is a very powerful mage ... maybe too powerful for us to take down. That's why we need Vanka's help.'

'When are you planning to hold this séance of yours?'

'Soon ... as soon as I get back to the JAD.'

The conversation faltered as Kondratieff sipped his coffee and Josephine lit another cigarette. It was Kondratieff who broke the silence.

'Then if you think you have the beating of Doge IMmanual, why have you taken such a risk to come to speak with me?'

'Jezebel Ethobaal asked me to deliver this. It's a gift to thank you for the help you've given to the Code Noir.' From her large canvas shoulder bag Josephine extracted a leather-bound book, which from the look of it was many hundreds of years old. 'This, Nikolai, baby, is one of only five surviving copies of the *Flagellum Hominum*, more commonly monikered as—'

'*The Scourge of HumanKind*. Yes, it's one of the most famous of all relics from pre-Confinement history.'

Famous certainly, and very, very rare. What Josephine Baker was holding in her hand was worth a small – correction, a *large* – fortune. By reputation it was a compendium of all Lilith's wisdom regarding matters relating to the Spirit World, though of course, being written in the language of the Pre-Folk, until the discovery of the Column, no one had ever been able to translate it.

'Jezebel said you'd dig its importance. She asked that you read the verse in the book relating to Loci's Column. It's a real nastygram. I've marked it with the slip of paper.' With that she passed the book to Kondratieff, who took it reverently into his hands.

The tome was as fragile as it looked and the pages brittle with age. Gently he opened it to the place marked. 'It's written in Pre-Folk A,' he noted.

'But you're a real longhair when it comes to digging the Pre-Folk A inkings.'

'A *recent* expert, Miss Baker: the language has only just been deciphered. Anyway, understanding is one thing, but fluency is quite another. To translate this will require time.'

'Then I'll give you the ten-centime tour. Thanks to Professeur de Nostredame's unBabelising of Pre-Folk A, Jezebel has managed to decipher the contents of the book and the heavy-duty revelation is that the Column you have housed in the Galerie des Anciens has beaucoup de much occult significance.'

'That we already know, Miss Baker. And the question which comes to my mind is "so what?"'

'There's a new face in town—'

'Billy Thomas.'

'Got it in one, daddyo. That cat's a real piece of strange.'

'How so?'

'He's a loose cannon and the feeling is that he ain't the type of cat who'll wanna play second banana to his sister. Our worry is if someone like Selim the Grim takes him under his wing he could become as big a threat as she is.'

'You're too late, Miss Baker, that's already happened. Selim brought Duke William to the Galerie des Anciens this morning to view the Column.'

'Shit. I should've known that Selim would be sniffing around . . . he's one fly guy. The important thing is to keep Selim from getting control of the Column. According to the *Flagellum*, in the final struggle between the Messiah and the Beast whoever has control of the Column is gonna end up as top cat.' Josephine allowed the waiter to refresh her coffee, to give him time, Kondratieff suspected, to absorb the import of what she was saying. 'Jezebel has asked me to urge you to do everything in your power to prevent the Column falling into the hands of the badniks. You gotta know that if they succeed in tapping into the Column's power, then it's curtains for the good guys. It'll be Lucifer who emerges triumphant from Ragnarok . . . Duke William.'

Kondratieff gave a doleful shake of his head. 'Dr Ethobaal flatters me if she thinks I am able to influence matters with regard to the Column. The Column is *already* in the hands of Doge IMmanual and she has already issued orders that it is to be moved to the Temple of Lilith.'

Now *that* piece of information stopped Josephine Baker in mid-puff. 'That's beaucoup de bad news. Is there anything you can do to prevent that going down? If the Column gets to the Temple then we'll all be hurtin' for certain.'

Kondratieff shook his head. Since his meeting with de Sade that morning he had thought long and hard about the Column and had come to the conclusion that the order he had been given to transport it to the Temple presented him with a unique opportunity to destroy Doge IMmanual's poisonous brother . . . and, *en passant*, to give him the chance of destroying Heydrich and UnFunDaMentalism.

For a moment he resisted the temptation to share his plan with Josephine Baker. Having made a quick calculation of the risks and benefits of confiding in her, he had come to the hard-headed decision that as the probability of her being captured by the Signori di Notte was well over fifty per cent – she was much too noticeable for it to be otherwise – it would be imprudent for him to reveal his intentions to her. But as the girl had risked her life to meet with him, for once in his life Kondratieff decided to cast caution to the wind. He leaned closer.

'Very well, Miss Baker. Let us assume that you and your fellow WhoDooists are successful in stripping Lilith of her powers, then it will only remain for us to dispose of Duke William and to position the Column atop of the Great Pyramid.'

'Sounds easy if you say it quick.'

'Indeed . . . but I have a plan,' and for the next five minutes Kondratieff explained what he was intending to do.

When he had finished, Josephine Baker sat back in her chair and whistled. 'That's a real ballsy play, Nikolai, and you dig that for you it's a one-way ticket to endsville?'

'I know . . .' Kondratieff trailed off. Josephine Baker had verbalised that which he had so desperately tried not to think about . . . that to destroy Duke William he would have to sacrifice his own life.

For several moments the pair of them sat in an uncomfortable silence. Then Josephine Baker took Kondratieff's hand in hers and gave it a squeeze. 'Let me thank you on behalf of the Code Noir and the people of the Demi-Monde for what you are intending to do, Nikolai. It takes a steamer-load of moxy to go up against the Beast.' She checked her watch. 'I better be going. Knowing what I know now I can't take any chances of been picked up by the badniks. Shit, I still can't believe that you're serious.'

'Oh, I'm *very* serious, Miss Baker, but before you go I need you to do me a service. I want you to stand up from this table, slap me and then storm out of the café.'

'You're kidding me!'

'No, I'm not!'

'Why?'

'It'll be my insurance policy if we have been spotted together.'

With a nod of understanding Josephine Baker stood up, moving so quickly that she knocked her chair over. Then she glowered down at Kondratieff. 'Man, you're one big disappointment, Nikolai,' she announced in a loud voice. 'I thought you were a stand-up guy, but now I see that when the heat is on, I've gotta number you amongst the missing. Pardon me while I commune with the cobbles.' With that she slapped him hard around the cheek then flounced out of the café, not even pausing to secure her veil around her face.

Even Kondratieff wasn't sure if she had been play-acting.

19

The NoirVille Hub
The Demi-Monde: 10th Day of Summer, 1005

Twins have a special place in preConfinement mythology, being seen as the embodiment of the duality of the Kosmos, or, as Confusionists would have it, of Yin and Yang. Folk mythology contends that twins are conceived only by a woman who has had coitus with a Daemon and hence twins are supposedly blessed/cursed with supernatural powers and abilities. That Lilith had a twin brother, Lucifer, has only added weight to the widely held superstition that the birth of boy/girl twins is especially portentous: such twins are generally thought to embody the good and the evil of the Kosmos.

Myths and Legends of the Demi-Monde: James Sallusius,
ForthRight Books and Periodicals

'Behold, Your Grace ... the Temple of Lilith!'

Billy Thomas braced himself against the sway of the Bucintoro as the Captain brought the ship alongside the stone jetty and then looked to where de Sade was pointing. Thankfully, the rain had eased a little so he could see, maybe a mile or so inland from the river, at the end of an arrow-straight road, a huge – make that a *fucking* huge – temple standing alone and majestic slap-bang in the centre of the grass-land the Dupes called 'the Hub'. It looked like one of those temples they had in movies like *The Lord of the Rings*, all columns and statues and shit, though he couldn't ever remember any of them glowing green in the sunlight. Well, not so much glowing as *shining*: the Temple looked perfect and perfectly clean, which, he guessed, wasn't surprising given the army of people de Sade had had scrubbing and polishing it.

Still, it was a weird building to see rising out of the grass prairie, but then everything in the Demi-Monde was weird to the max. Especially his sister. Yeah, in his opinion, Ella was taking all this Doge IMmanual shit too fucking seriously by half.

'This, my Prince,' de Sade prattled on, 'is the centre of all power in the Demi-Monde. This is where Lilith – the greatest mage ever to walk the Nine Worlds – conducted her rites.'

As he stood listening to this crap, Billy found it difficult to keep a straight face. But that was the deal he had cut with Bole: to enter the Demi-Monde and make like he believed all this Lilith baloney his sister and her main man, de Sade, were laying down. Humour them. And for a million bucks he was willing to do most anything, even stand on the deck of a ship dressed like Gandalf's gay brother in a golden robe (now *that* was a picture he sure didn't want posted on Facebook; the KY cru would be sniffing around him in no time flat) surrounded by sixty almost naked bitches and being told by de Sade that he was gonna be taking part in the Ceremony of the Leaping or some such heavy-duty bullshit. What made things worse, he hated the fucking crown he had planted on his head. Bling was one thing but this made him feel like a total prick. But Ella had insisted, and whatever Ella wanted, Ella got. She was the big enchilada in the Demi-Monde.

Yeah, all this religious crap was getting right up his ass.

There *were* compensations. He was living large and now that Selim had hooked him up to a regular supply of Dizzi he could go through life with everything sunny. Then there were these really toned priestesses de Sade had brought along for the ride to the Temple and as he had discovered, fucking a Dupe was just as much fun as fucking a Real Worlder. And with him being a Duke and the brother of Doge IMmanual, every one of these priestess honeys was more than willing to frolic and fuck.

Yeah, role-playing a Duke was kinda cool in a screwed-up, off-beat sorta way and with all this ImPuritan shit the girls in Venice believed in, since he'd arrived in the Demi-Monde he'd been laid all ways and sideways.

'It is truly magnificent, is it not, Your Grace?' murmured de Sade.

For a moment Billy wasn't sure if he was talking about the Temple or the really stacked Shade priestess with the tight ass he'd be putting the moves on later. It was difficult to tell with de Sade. When it came to women, de Sade was as down and dirty as Billy, but at the same time he came on like he really believed all this IMmanualism shit.

'The Temple? Yeah, man, it's banging. Real awesome.'

'Are you ready to attend the Ceremony of the Leaping?'

Billy tore his gaze away from the girl. He had no doubt whose bones he'd like to be leaping right now, but the problem with being, like, a main man in Ella's little fantasy world was that he couldn't just stand there checking out the talent and trying to decide which one he'd like to fuck next. No, he had to look real serious and religious and shit which was difficult with sixty naked girls parading around him. He felt like a kid let loose in a candy store.

'Yeah,' he murmured as the priestesses began to disembark. 'I'm cool.'

Despite his professed insouciance, it was a very reluctant Billy who followed de Sade into the Temple. The Demi-Monde might be a very trippy place, but as trippy places went, the Temple of Lilith was up there in a class of uno.

Fuck, it was scary. Big – nah, cancel big and substitute fucking *enormous* – and empty. In fact, it was so big and so empty that every sound ricocheted off the walls and ceiling in a really spooky way, the slap of his sandals on the stone floor reverberating around the immense hall that opened before him. It even stank scary, having that musty, dusty smell you could taste, the sort of smell that lodged at the back of your throat as though it was intent on choking you.

'The roof of the Temple is remarkable, is it not, Your Grace?'

Looking up, Billy had to admit de Sade had a point. The roof seemed to have been made from glass, though this PINC gizmo Bole had shoved into his head was telling him it was actually one unbroken and unbreakable sheet of transparent Mantle-ite – MantlePlex – which stretched the full length and width of the Temple and which allowed sunlight to stream in, making it as bright inside as it had been in the open air.

The problem Billy had was that as the light struck the MantlePlex roof, it caused images to be cast around the Temple – images of snakes – so wherever he looked, he saw the fucking things wriggling and squirming around the floor and the walls. Snakes like the ones he had embroidered on his robes. All this IMmanualism crap Sis kept mouthing off about seemed to be really big on snakes.

The Temple gave him the jumps.

De Sade seemed to sense his concern. 'Don't be afraid, Your Grace, there is nothing to be frightened of.'

Billy bridled. 'Yo' dissing me, bro? Yo' saying that I'm a coward? This is Billy Thomas yo' talking to, and Billy Thomas ain't scared of nuffing.'

Obviously shocked by the boy's reaction, de Sade gabbled an

apology. 'I am sorry, Your Grace, I did not mean to imply—'

'Okay, I'm good. But just remember that Billy Thomas ain't no bitch.'

'Of course, Your Grace,' and a nervous de Sade bustled Billy up to a huge slab of red stone.

'This, Your Grace, is the Altar of Lilith, once the most sacred place in the whole of the Demi-Monde.'

'Yeah, great.'

'It is indeed "great", Your Grace,' agreed de Sade, obviously not hip to Billy's indifference. 'Unfortunately, the Altar is incomplete: the Column that once stood to its side on that hexagonal base,' and here he pointed to the six-sided platform a couple of yards behind the stone slab, 'is missing. But now the Column has been discovered. It was the one we visited in the Galerie des Anciens . . .'

Yeah, and what a drag of a day that had been. Billy fucking hated museums.

'. . . and once it is returned to its rightful resting place, the Temple will be reborn.'

De Sade's explanation was interrupted when a trumpet note echoed through the Temple. 'The Ceremony of the Leaping is about to commence, Your Grace. If you would come this way?'

The courtyard that de Sade led Billy into was vast, but what really caught his attention was that there seemed to be some form of athletics contest taking place there.

'This is the Ceremony of the Leaping,' explained de Sade. 'It is an ancient tradition performed on the tenth day of Summer, a tradition last performed when the Demi-Monde was young. It is a ceremony in which the priestesses demonstrate their prowess by pitting their strength and agility against one of the most fearsome of all creatures, the aurochs.'

Billy felt PINC telling him that the aurochs was a huge species of wild bull – extinct in the Real World – that had been one of the most dangerous creatures ever to roam the earth. In fact, looking across to the far side of the Temple, he decided he didn't need PINC to tell him that, he could see for himself.

At one end of the courtyard a group of men were attempting to control what looked like an oversized bull. The animal was fucking immense. It had a shoulder height of way over eight feet with a huge head that sported a pair of long and savagely sharp horns. Jet black in colour – except for a white stripe running down its spine – the beast looked big and powerful and really, really pissed, tossing its head around and bellowing like billy-o as steam rose from its flanks. Instinctively Billy edged back: if that mother went on the rampage, it would crush and gore a lot of people before it was grounded and he wasn't of a mind to be one of them.

The aurochs was such a handful that it was giving the guys trying to keep hold of the ropes they had tied around its neck one hell of a time; it needed ten of them to stop the thing stampeding free. As best Billy could make out, the bull handlers were trying to manoeuvre it towards a long, narrow corridor, the sides of which had been built from six-foot-high tree trunks. *Thick* tree trunks: they did, after all, have to contain two tons of angry bovine. The corridor – runway more like – ran straight as a rule for the one hundred yards that stretched from one side of the courtyard to the other, but what its purpose was, Billy had no idea. It wasn't long before he found out.

After a lot of prodding with spears the handlers managed to edge the aurochs into the runway, where the evil-tempered bastard stood pawing the ground and giving off some seriously bad vibes.

Immediately this had been done, there was another blast of the trumpet and a very tall girl – a black like Billy – who was naked apart from a half-mask walked towards the end of the runway opposite to the one where the aurochs was making waves. She was an imperious-looking piece who moved like a dancer.

Nice.

A priestess bowed to the girl and then opened a gate giving access to the runway, girl and aurochs now facing each other along the length of the wooden corridor. Immediately it saw the girl, the bull's attitude changed: whereas before it had been kicking up one hell of a ho-ha, now it quietened, eyeing the girl ominously, its breath coming in short sharp pants. It might have been quieter, but the beast seemed all the more dangerous because of it. All the aurochs's anger was now focused on the girl.

Again the trumpet sounded, there were shouts from the handlers, the tethers were released and with a great roar the huge bull hurled itself towards the girl. The power of the aurochs was incredible; it charged down the runway like an express train, shaking the ground as it ran. Even standing fifty yards away, Billy could feel the vibrations shuddering up through the soles of his feet and could smell the hatred the bull gave off.

And then something fucking strange happened. Instead of standing there pissing herself, as Billy reckoned any sane person would do when a couple of tons of irate aurochs was heading at high speed in their direction, the girl began to run *towards* the aurochs.

Crazy fucking bitch.

Fascinated by the prospect that in about five seconds a beautiful piece of black ass would be reduced to guacamole, Billy watched goggled-eyed as aurochs and girl tore at one another, amazed by how fast the girl could run. Seriously fast. But if her speed was amazing, what happened next was right outta DC comics. Girl and aurochs met midway along the runway but, rather than the truck wreck of a collision that Billy had been expecting, the girl suddenly leapt at the aurochs and using its horns as a fulcrum, executed a full somersault, flying way over the bull's back to land – fucking gracefully – at least ten yards beyond it.

Now Billy had seen Polly footage of Olympic gymnasts, but he was willing to lay good money that none of them – *none* of them – would have been able to do what that girl had just done. It wasn't just the timing of the leap, which had been fucking amazing; it wasn't just the height of the leap, which had been fucking amazing; and it hadn't been the distance she'd covered, which had been fucking amazing. No, what had been *really* fucking amazing was how effortlessly she had done it. Shit, the girl had actually incorporated a double twist into her leap and that, as far as Billy was concerned, was just taking the rise.

And it wasn't only him stunned by what the girl had done: the aurochs was pretty perplexed too. The thing slid to a halt – which, when you weighed close to two tons, were travelling at the thick end of twenty miles an hour and didn't have the benefit of brakes, was no mean feat – and attempted to turn around. The thick wooden walls of the runway prevented it doing this which went down like the proverbial weighable inflatable. The aurochs went apeshit, leaping up and down and using its horns to rip the shit out of anything there was to rip the shit out of, which mainly consisted of the wooden walls of the runway.

But the aurochs's humiliation wasn't finished. Barely had the girl landed but she'd performed a pirouette and with a hop, a skip and a jump had landed gracefully square on the aurochs's back, then tumbled forward and, once more using the horns as her barre, had sprung a dismount outside the runway.

Un-fucking-believable.

All the priestesses and the handlers began to applaud, the

protests of the aurochs being ignored. And then, much to Billy's surprise, the bull leaper turned to walk towards him.

Woh, this must be my lucky day.

He tried to stand up straighter and to look more Dukely; the prospect of screwing this honey was really jingling his jangles. And as she came nearer, he had a chance to study this remarkable girl up close.

Looking at her, Billy could see there were subtle differences in her proportions that marked her out as someone – as *something* – different. The mouth that peeked out from under her mask was just a little larger than Billy would have expected and her neck was just a little thicker. Her chest – he noted *en passant* that she had really great tits – was much more barrel-shaped than was normal in a woman, and from what Billy could make out from a cursory examination of her arms, the configuration of the muscles was . . . wrong; a number of the muscles seemed to have been rearranged and emphasised at the expense of their colleagues. It was as though she had been remodelled . . . re-engineered . . . redesigned.

Yeah, she looked odd. Different.

The girl came to a halt just a pace in front of him and then with a flourish pulled the mask from her face. It was Ella.

Shit, my sister's built!

He had to do a double take and for a moment wondered why he hadn't recognised these physical oddities of hers before. It was only then that he remembered that Ella – back in the Real World – had had a peculiar reluctance to show off her body. He'd never seen her in a swimming costume and she had always worn dresses with sleeves. Sure she'd worn short skirts, but her legs, as best he could judge, were the only normal thing about her.

'Well, what did you think?' she asked.

For a moment Billy didn't know what to say, stunned into

silence by the thought that it was his sister – his *sister* – who had done the bull leaping, that it was his sister who had just done what he judged to be impossible and that it was his sister who seemed to be physically so different. Shit, she didn't even seem to be breathing hard.

'Billy?' she prompted.

'Shit, Sis, yo' the bomb, fo' sure. That was awesome. Way I see it you'd have to be a fucking mutant or something to do what yo' just done.'

Wasn't that the fucking truth.

Ella laughed and then, taking him by the arm, led him out of earshot of the others gathered in the Temple. 'That's a very insightful observation, Billy. Yeah, you really do have to be a mutant to perform in the bull run: no normal man or woman could ever move as quickly as I did or have the strength to perform the gymnastics you've just seen me perform.'

'Oh yeah? Then how come you can do it? Way I see it you ain't no mutant.'

'You're right, Billy, I'm not a mutant, but neither am I human. I am Lilithi. I am *Homo perfectus*.'

Fuck, where were the cats in white coats when you needed them?

20

The NoirVillian Hub
The Demi-Monde: 10th Day of Summer, 1005

And the Master said, 'There will be ultimate harmony in the Nine Worlds. Though the Yin/Yang of the Kosmos will ebb and flow, wax and wane, finally all will be in balance, all will be in harmony. When the pans of the Scales of Life are set equal, *wu wei* will suffuse the Kosmos.'

Puzzled, the favourite student, Wun Zi, asked, 'Tell me, Master, what should I do to further this harmony and to help the scales of the Kosmos move into balance?'

To this the Master replied, 'Get that interfering fuck ABBA to take His – or possibly Her – thumb off the right-hand pan.'

The Eighth Book of the BiAlects, Verse 27

A couple of Ella's priestesses led Billy from the courtyard to an ante-room while Ella changed. And, boy, when she re-appeared, he knew he was gonna have real trouble getting used to her wandering around in an ankle-length robe that stuck to her body like glue and gave everybody and his father a great idea about the goodies hidden beneath. And with the horned crown she had perched on top of her shaven head she looked like she was dressed to attend a really loco Halloween party. The problem was that with such a serious, far-out look on her face he guessed she wasn't in the market for doing a lot of trick-or-treating.

But then Ella had never been one for the lighter side of life. Back in the Real World she had been a real nerdnik, a straight-A student who didn't do drugs, didn't mess with boys and was about as much fun as a kick in the nuts ... pretty much the same as she was here in the Demi-Monde.

She ordered the servants out of the room and, when they were alone, turned her black, empty eyes towards him. When she spoke, her voice was misty, faraway. 'Lammas Eve approaches, Billy, the time of the Awakening. And the reality is that I am not as I once was: Ella Thomas is gone and in her place stands Lilith, the first Goddess.'

'Wha'? Ah, c'mon, Sis, keep it real. What yo' laying on me? This is Billy yo' talking to. Yo' don't have to play-act with me.'

Ella laughed. 'I can understand your surprise, Billy. It must come as a shock to hear your sister announce that she is the reincarnation of an eleven-thousand-year-old goddess ...'

Right on the fucking money!

'... but that is the reality.'

'How?'

'How did this happen?' She gave a rather disconcerting little laugh. 'By serendipity. My enemies were trying to destroy me here in the Demi-Monde but instead they woke Lilith from her slumbers, woke the power that was dormant within me. Serendipity, Billy, just as it is serendipity that Septimus Bole – the son of my greatest enemy – sent you to the Demi-Monde to try to control me, and by doing so has made my triumph inevitable.'

What the fuck was she talking about?

'Yes, Lilith is risen again. I am returned to cleanse both the Demi-Monde and the Real World of the contaminants that are the Grigori.'

'Grigori? Nigga, please; this is some ultra-weird science yo' droppin' on me.'

'I'll explain in a moment,' Ella crooned. 'But for you to truly understand the miracle that has occurred it is necessary that I first tell you about the *real* history of our world . . . of the Real World.' Then as Billy stood there, his sister began to circle him, finally coming to stand out of sight behind him. It was really fucking disconcerting.

'Try to imagine our world as it was eleven thousand years ago, a world held fast by an everlasting winter, tight in the frozen grip of the last Ice Age. Then it was a vast frozen wasteland, a land where the few beleaguered examples of *Homo sapiens* huddled in a haven beside what is now the Black Sea.'

Billy stood silent: Ella, by his reckoning, had flipped.

'Then the Black Sea was a large freshwater lake, an oasis of fertility in a brutal world. And it was into this world that a woman was born, her coming marked by the impact of a meteor that bathed the land in a strange green radiation . . . a radiation that changed her . . . improved her. That woman's name was Lilith and thanks to the meteor she came to possess an intellect exceeding any who had ever lived. Such was her genius that she alone realised that for HumanKind to survive there must be cooperation, that the selfishness and individuality of the hunter were traits that would lead to the destruction of the tribe and to the extinction of the race of *Homo sapiens*. But there was more to Lilith than simple genius: she was blessed with the miracle of Atavistic Thought Inheritance.'

'What?' As Billy stood there open-mouthed, he wondered if they sold weapons-grade psychotropics in the Demi-Monde. He had a sneaking feeling he was gonna need them. This bitch had issues.

'Atavistic Thought Inheritance is an example of those occasional and arbitrary evolutionary leaps made by Nature. The first Lilith was a mutation ... a freak of Nature ... the first person to be able to convey ancestral memory – instinctive *and* acquired knowledge – to her daughters. The whole of the knowledge and the experiences of that first Lilith was transmitted to her daughters *at birth*, and her daughters, in their turn, passed this knowledge – supplemented by the knowledge they themselves acquired in their lifetime – to their daughters.' Ella sighed. 'I am the last of the Lilithi, but because I possess Atavistic Thought Inheritance I am simultaneously the first Lilith incarnate. I am the Lilith who carries the accumulated wisdom of five hundred generations of the Lilithi, the descendants of Lilith.'

'Ah, c'mon, Sis, yo' blowing me smoke.'

Ella ignored him. 'For the Lilithi the body is not the decaying prison of the soul that it is for Fragiles, those unfortunates who make up the majority of humankind. Our souls are not condemned to die with our bodies; they live on in our daughters. Atavistic Thought Inheritance makes the Lilithi immortal, so that a thousand years is as nothing to us. And the Lilithi used the knowledge they acquired to bring peace and prosperity to their tribe, and as the years went by, Lilith was elevated to the status of the Supreme Goddess, and as a Goddess her word became law and all bowed before her.'

Reluctantly Billy asked a question, almost afraid of what the answer might be. 'Okay, whyn't yo' school me some more? What was the name of this tribe?'

'The Adin, though you would better know them as Atlanteans. Lilith's people were the ones who inhabited the lost world of Atlantis.'

Billy couldn't stop himself: he started to laugh uproariously. 'Kill that shit, Sis, you've got to be yanking my chain. First you lay the line on me that you're eleven thousand years old, that you're the reincarnation of a long-dead Goddess with a really far-out ability to transmit knowledge through the generations, and now you start gassing that you're a refugee from Atlantis.' He shook his head. 'Shit, Sis, when we get back to the Real World you don't wanna waste your time becoming a geneticist ... you wanna be a scriptwriter. James Cameron will just love you.'

Ella's voice hardened. 'You may mock, Billy, but what I have told you is the truth. And as they watched and studied the world around them, the Lilithi determined to manipulate the bloodlines of mankind. They determined to better Nature, to breed three new species of humankind. The first of these were the Lilithi, *Homo perfectus*: the priestesses who alone bore the gift of Atavistic Thought Inheritance.'

'Hey, girl, yo' gotta stop all this madness. Yo' can't be sayin' that yo' a different *species* to the rest of us cats?'

Ella came to stand in front of Billy and gestured to her body. 'Of course. You have the evidence of your own eyes, Billy, you have seen me perform the Leaping. No one human could have done what I did and the explanation for this is simple: the Lilithi are *not* human. Just as Neanderthal man was inferior to *Homo sapiens*, so *Homo sapiens* are inferior to the Lilithi. We Lilithi were bred and refined over thousands of years to produce a species of woman that is physically and mentally superior to *Homo sapiens*. It was we who understood that the potential of *Homo sapiens* is circumscribed by their bodies, so by selective breeding we overcame these physical obstacles. The apotheosis of three thousand years of eugenical effort is seen in me.'

With a flourish she threw wide her arms, opening herself to examination, and despite his instinctive reluctance – she was his *sister*, after all – Billy found himself studying her. As he did so, he came to the worrying conclusion that perhaps – just perhaps – what she was saying wasn't all froth and fiction ... and that there should be a law against sisters looking that good.

'The second of these new species created by the Lilithi were the Grigori, *Homo callous*, the race of warriors charged with protecting the people of Atlantis.' Ella let out a long, dispirited sigh as though recalling the Grigori brought back sombre memories. 'Young men, like you, Billy, are dangerous: males in every species known in Nature are at their most ferocious when they are in their physical prime and are searching for a mate. So, we bred the Grigori to achieve a paedomorphic aspect, to be a species that preserved these juvenile urges and angers ... we bred them to prevent the onset of a more equitable and peaceable maturity. The Grigori were the troublesome and destructive juveniles who never grew up.'

For a moment she seemed lost in her reminiscences. 'The Grigori were never many in number, but even though they were so few, their reputation for ferocity and skill in battle made them figures of myth and superstition. Even today their names resonate ... Satan, Azazel, Semiazaz.'

'So what happened to the Grigori?'

'We Lilithi might have conquered evolution, Billy, but we could not control Nature. And in a day and a night Nature unleashed her fury and destroyed the civilisation of the Lilithi and smashed the cities of Atlantis. Nature sent the Deluge that drowned Atlantis and threw those of her people who survived, bemused and leaderless, out into the world.'

'Whoa, slow the flow, Sis. Is this the same Flood they used to talk about in Bible class?'

'It is. As the earth warmed after the last Ice Age, the enormous glaciers that covered the planet began to melt and the meltwater created vast lakes in the middle of North America and Russia, great lakes trapped behind shrinking glaciers and melting mountains of ice. One day, eight thousand years ago, these walls crumbled and the huge melt lakes released enormous quantities of water into the oceans, creating gigantic tsunami. The land bridge between Atlantis and the Mediterranean – the Pillars of Hercules – was destroyed, and the freshwater lake that was the Black Sea, and the city of Atlantis that bordered it, were inundated.'

Ella was silent for a few moments as though overcome by the emotions rekindled by these memories. 'The work of three thousand years destroyed in moments, drowned under a thousand feet of sea water. Only two thousand Atlanteans survived, less than one in a hundred. The few surviving Lilithi wandered the earth as a broken people; our gift of Atavistic Thought Inheritance meant that we not only shared all our knowledge, but also our experiences. We felt the pain of a sister's death as vividly as if it were our own and the destruction of so many of our Lilithian sisters emotionally crippled us. Numbed by collective grief, we retreated from the world. We slept, until I was roused here in the Demi-Monde.'

A miserable tear coursed slowly down Ella's cheek. 'But the worst was that the Grigori also survived, becoming a pernicious diaspora, spread like seeds on the wind, deracinated and disgruntled. They fled north into Russia and Europe, and east to the Indus, infecting the race of Man as they went. For the first time they bred outside their species and so their penchant for violence and evil began to infect the rest of HumanKind. Like the Lilithi and the Kohanim – the third race created by Lilith – the Grigori were never meant to breed with those who were not of their kind ... but the Grigori were wild animals who could not be tamed or domesticated.'

'Wild animals?' Billy prompted.

'You must understand, Billy, that the Grigori are a different people – a different species – from Man. They are stronger, taller, quicker, free of the restraint imposed by conscience.' She laughed. 'The Grigori have *no* conscience. Oh, they have other weaknesses, but they are not fettered by moral scruples.'

She took a moment to calm herself. 'And as the Grigori bred with Man so a hybrid species emerged . . . the Dark Charismatics . . . psychopaths . . . mongrel Fragiles infected with the Grigori's evil. The Dark Charismatics are the bastard progeny of the Grigori . . . or as the rest of the world knows them, vampires.'

'Shit, Sis, yo' sayin' these Grigori of yours are vampires?' He could hardly keep the mocking tone out of his voice.

'Yes. They had been bred to rule the night, when their enemies were at their weakest, and as the years passed so they began to fear daylight. More . . . we fed them blood to promote their growth and they became addicted to its taste. But though they shunned daylight, though they craved blood, still they were the greatest warriors the world has ever seen.'

'Ah c'mon Sis, if these Grigori cats of yours were so amped, how come they didn't conquer the whole known?'

Another laugh from Ella. 'The Grigori were never the most fecund of species and, remember, it is difficult for two different species – no matter how close they are on the Tree of Life – to interbreed, so only very rarely was the union of Grigori and Fragile fruitful. That is why there are so few fully functional, fully aware Dark Charismatics loose in the world.'

'Then how did the Grigori survive?'

'They were – are – nurtured and sustained by their bastard children, the Dark Charismatics, and in return for this succour they infused the Dark Charismatics with their hatred of the Jews.'

Oh fuck.

Billy tried to keep the disbelief out of his voice. 'What the fuck have the Jews gotta do with all this?'

'The Kohanim – the proto-Jews – were the third race created by the Lilithi. Before we discovered the secret of writing, we needed a class of administrators able to remember the genealogical history of every man and woman in Atlantis. Only in this way could we, the Lilithi, ensure that the characteristics we bred for were evident in the mating pair and in their offspring, but to remember so much data required a mind of the most prodigious capacity. So we bred a special race, the Kohanim, with a talent for memorising copious amounts of information. The Kohanim were the ultimate eugenicists, controlling, as they did, the breeding of the people of Atlantis. It was the Kohanim who decided who should mate with whom, and which child should be allowed to live and which to die. Is it any wonder that the people of Atlantis came to hate them? None more so than the Grigori, whom the Kohanim were charged with controlling ... and, when necessary, with culling. The Grigori loathed them with a passion.'

'Okay, Sis, lay it on me: what happened to the Kohanim?'

'Like all of the people of Atlantis, when the Deluge came, most were destroyed, but a handful survived and fled east into Mesopotamia splintering into sects and rival factions as they went, and interbreeding with the peoples they met on their travels. This miscegenation eventually spawned the Jews. The Jews are the by-blows of the Kohanim.'

This was all becoming too much for Billy. He looked around, spotted a bottle of cognac, poured himself a glassful and took a long, long swig. If he was to handle all this Lilithi, Grigori, Kohanim and Atlantis bullshit, he'd have to do it blasted. What he wouldn't give for a couple of lines of Dizzi.

'Look, Ella ... Sis, I don't wanna rain on your parade, but ain't it a little far out that no one in the Real World has ever heard about Lilith and Atlantis? Yo' telling me there ain't no records ... myths ... that sort of shit telling us about what went down?'

'Oh, there are memories of Lilith but they are distorted by time. I have been transformed from a goddess into a daemon. My symbols became the symbols of evil: the wise snake became the devil incarnate; the Tree of Knowledge that gave us the fruit that made the mind soar and resonate in harmony with the Kosmos became the bearer of the bitter fruit of temptation; and the crescent horns that I wear as my crown, the symbol of the Lilithi's hegemony over the night and of my role as the Queen of Heaven, became the horns of the devil.'

His sister was quiet for a moment as though gathering herself to proceed. 'But now Lilith has returned to finish what was interrupted all those thousands of years ago ... making humankind perfect.' She smiled at Billy. 'And that is why Septimus Bole has sent you here, Billy, to prevent the second coming of the Lilithi.'

'Why would he do that?'

'Because Septimus Bole is a Dark Charismatic – a by-blow of a Grigori – and the Grigori are frightened of me ... of the Lilithi. They know that the Lilithi will one day return and find a way of destroying them and correcting the mistake we made of allowing them to mate with Fragiles. They know that one day we will find a way of purifying humankind and of eradicating the contamination of Dark Charismatics. Now, after all these years I am come to fulfil this destiny.'

Utterly mad.

'Even as we speak, arrangements are being made to bring the Column of Loci back to its rightful resting place in the Temple, and once it is here, the power of the Temple is restored ... the power of Lilith is restored. On Lammas night I will conduct a ritual that will begin the Awakening of the Lilithi and to do that I need your help, Billy.'

Billy sure as hell didn't like the way Ella looked at him when she said this: he had the freaky feeling that she was laughing at him, but having seen the way she'd handled that aurochs he decided to play it cool.

'Me? Like as always, I'm here fo' yo', Sis. After all, we's family?'

Ella gave an unsettling little laugh. 'Yes, we are family. And being my twin, Billy, your ... assistance will make me all-powerful. It is Fate that you have been sent here just as the final battle between the Lilithi and the Grigori is to be fought. And you, Billy, are my most powerful weapon in this struggle.'

Suddenly Ella spread her arms wide and, in a voice so loud that it filled the Temple, cried out, 'ABBA, I am come again. I have come to reclaim the Nine Worlds. I have come to bring Perfection to the Kosmos. I am Lilith reborn.'

Man, this bitch is swinging off her hinges.

21

Venice
The Demi-Monde: 10th Day of Summer, 1005

Last comes the Time of Trysting | When those who would rule must vie
Joined in their final ferocity | The prize so precious, so profound
Who will wield the staff of ABBA? | Who will place it atop the Pyramid?
For the victor the spoils of life | For the vanquished the lament of death
Such is the Way.

Book 3, verse 27 of the *Flagellum Hominum*:
Translated by Jezebel Ethabaal, JAD Academic Press

Kondratieff heard the arrival of the Signori di Notte even before they were announced. He heard them banging on the door of his house, he heard them shouting at his housekeeper demanding to know where he was, and he heard them pounding up the stairs to his study.

It took them less than thirty seconds to do all that but it was enough time for him to place the precious copy of the *Flagellum Hominum* and his plans for the bomb back into their hiding place under the floorboards and to assume the look of aggrieved innocence so necessary when dealing with members of Venice's secret police.

As the door of his study was barged open, he turned in his chair to greet his visitors, who consisted of a young and very florid-faced captain and two impressively large constables. 'Are you Docteur Nikolai Kondratieff, Head of the Future History Foundation?' the captain demanded.

'I am.'

'Good,' and the captain stood to one side to allow a fourth man to enter the room.

Kondratieff recognised him immediately: few Venetian men were as tall as the Abbé Niccolò di Bernado dei Machiavelli or as addicted to the use of perfume. But no perfume known to man was powerful enough to mask the aroma of duplicity that bedecked Machiavelli. Kondratieff loathed both him and his extraordinarily supple loyalties. Put simply, the man was a turncoat. Doge Catherine-Sophia had barely stopped twitching before he had converted to IMmanualism, had pledged his allegiance to the new Doge and had begun ridding Venice of anti-IMmanualists. And as head of the Signori di Notte he was ideally placed to do just that. He was, without doubt, the most unprincipled man in the whole of Venice.

Kondratieff corrected himself: he was the *second*-most unprincipled man in the whole of Venice. The premier exponent of these deplorable talents was the Senior Prelate of the Church of IMmanualism, the Marquis de Sade, but it was a bloody close contest.

Machiavelli came to a halt a pace in front of Kondratieff's desk and glared down at him. Closer now, the feeling of unease he engendered was stronger, his faux-holiness making the hairs on the back of Kondratieff's neck tingle and sweat start under his armpits. Silently he counselled himself to remain calm; his life depended upon it.

'CitiZen Kondratieff, we have reason to believe that you are a fellow-traveller of the crypto and WhoDoo agitator Josephine Baker.'

Kondratieff shrugged. 'And good morning to you too, Abbé Niccolò, I am pleased to see you looking so well—'

'Answer the question!'

To buy thinking time, Kondratieff tried to prevaricate. 'I do not believe you have asked a question. You have made a statement. Questions, or so I was taught at school, are generally constructed in the interrogative form.'

Machiavelli snorted his frustration. 'Are you a fellow-traveller of Josephine Baker?'

'Why don't you ask the woman herself?' An important question: if the Signori di Notte had taken her then he was a dead man. Under torture she would be forced to admit that he'd been in contact with Jezebel Ethobaal and to tell all about his plans to disrupt the Lammas Eve ceremony.

'The agent provocateur Josephine Baker has evaded capture, spirited to the JAD by her fellow Code Noirists. So I ask you again: are you a fellow-traveller of the woman?'

A feeling of intense relief washed over Kondratieff. 'Would you be so kind as to define for me the term "fellow-traveller"?'

Another snort. 'One who aids and abets an Enemy of Venice and gives succour to those who would deny the divinity of Doge IMmanual.'

'Then the answer to your question is no.'

The curtness of the answer obviously threw Machiavelli a little. He was probably used to those he interrogated stammering out a longer-winded denial but as Kondratieff had learnt during his time in the service of Doge Catherine-Sophia – *may ABBA rest her soul* – when mouthing moonshine it was always best to keep answers concise.

'You lie. We have reliable witnesses who report that you conversed at length with the woman on the afternoon of the eighth day of Summer in the Café Florian. Do you deny having met her?'

'No.'

A frown dressed Machiavelli's brow; this was obviously another unexpected response. 'And what was discussed at this rendezvous?'

Kondratieff shrugged. 'It wasn't a "rendezvous" as that presupposes advanced knowledge of the meeting, of which I had none. I had never met Miss Baker before and she came up to me unexpectedly whilst I was sheltering from the rain in the café. She seemed quite beside herself, telling me some poppy-cock about how the Column of Loci was important in determining the outcome of Ragnarok. She asked that I help her to steal the Column, a request I declined. Hearing this, Miss Baker became very agitated and stormed out of the café. The café was quite crowded so there must have been several witnesses to the encounter.'

'You didn't report this incident to the authorities?'

'Why should I have? I had no idea that Miss Baker was a – how did you so wonderfully describe her? – ah, yes, a crypto and WhoDoo agitator. If I reported every crackpot who crosses my path I would have precious little time for my work.'

Machiavelli eyed Kondratieff suspiciously, his foot tapping nervously on the wooden floor of the study as he did so. Not quite certain if he'd put the floorboard back correctly, Kondratieff found himself wishing the man would desist.

'I must also ask why you had one of your servants purchase five thousand boxes of matches.'

Kondratieff stifled his surprise: he hadn't realised he was being watched so closely. 'Such an exciting life you secret service types lead, eh, Abbé Niccolò? Whatever will you be up to next: delving into my dustbins, perhaps?'

'Answer the question!'

'I have an idea regarding how the manufacture of matches may be made safer for the poor girls who labour to produce them. It is a simple idea but one I am confident will eliminate the scourge known as Phossy Jaw. To do this I must test the effectiveness of my matches against those already available on the market. Hence the purchase of so many boxes of matches.'

For several long seconds Machiavelli searched his face for connivance. Then, 'I must ask you to accompany me to the station for further interrogation.'

This was not good news. Kondratieff had no illusions regarding his ability to withstand an 'interrogation'. Time, he decided, to call Machiavelli's bluff. 'Am I right in supposing that you have the authorisation of Senior Prelate de Sade to interrupt my work?'

'In matters of Sector Security I am answerable only to the Doge herself.'

'As you wish: it is just that I had been led to believe by the Senior Prelate that the removal of the Column of Loci to the Temple of Lilith takes precedence over everything. I can only hope that this interview isn't just sabre-rattling on your part, Abbé Niccolò, because I am on a very tight schedule and any delay could mean that the deadline' – he had to suppress a smile; 'deadline' was *such* an apposite word – 'for the delivery of the Column is missed.' Kondratieff smiled. 'May I see the *lettre de cachet* verifying your right to arrest me?'

The two men locked stares but it was Machiavelli who looked away first, bluff called. 'No *lettre de cachet* has been issued.'

'Ah,' murmured Kondratieff, 'so this is an *unofficial* visit.'

'You should be grateful that you have such powerful protectors, Kondratieff. Very well, you will remain free but remember that you are being watched night and day.'

'That is a task your agents will find very easy to perform. I will have little time to leave this house until my plans for the transportation of the Column to the Temple are complete.'

When – with much bad grace – Machiavelli had gone Kondratieff spent two long hours sitting by the window watching the rain shimmy down the panes of glass as he tried to shake off the feeling of panic that had settled on him.

He just thanked ABBA that he'd had the 4Sight to have Josephine Baker pantomime a brusque – and painful – departure from the café. That she had left in such obvious dudgeon had muddied the waters and made Machiavelli unsure as to his culpability, but it had been a damned close-run thing and Kondratieff felt himself seriously shaken by how near he had come to being arrested. He wasn't built for adventure or intrigue; he was just an academic and by no means a hero. But that was what Fate was demanding of him, to play the hero, a role he had spent his life trying to avoid.

Thanks to the power of his HyperOpia program, he was able to 4Cast the Future of the Demi-Monde with some exactitude and this had, inevitably, necessitated his becoming involved with the nefarious manipulation of that Future, but he had always tried to make the nips and tweaks he made to the historical continuum as subtle and as slight as possible. His had been the gentle hand on the tiller of Fate. But with regard to the threat posed by the Lady IMmanual and her odious brother, a gentle hand would not be enough. Together these baleful twins were the embodiment of his oft-cited temporal avalanche, a historical juggernaut, barging a path to the Future with all the subtlety of an armoured steamer. And avalanches were difficult things to steer: the WhoDoo mambos might be able to neutralise the power of Lilith, but to defeat Duke William Kondratieff's calculations showed that brutal and decisive action would be needed.

But . . .

But whilst mathematics was unwavering in its precision and cold-blooded in its certainty, the same could not be said about *him* and, unfortunately, he was the one ordained by Fate to execute the sentence handed down by preScientific arithmetic. Fate, by giving him the responsibility of purging the canker that was Duke William from the body of the Demi-Monde, was obliging him to become a mass murderer ... and to destroy himself in the process.

How, he wondered, would history remember him: as monster or martyr? Would his name be respected or reviled?

Another long, doleful sigh. It mattered not: he would be dead when the history books were written.

The thought of his impending death persuaded him to check his design for the bomb's fuse mechanism again, and he pulled the blueprints from their hiding place under the floorboards. This done, he spent several minutes auditing his calculations and, as he had concluded the dozen times he had done this before, he judged them to be correct. Of course, the data relating to the effects of a concentrated dose of Mantle-ite radiation were scant but he was confident that it would be more than powerful enough to trip the detonator. The design he judged to be foolproof, the only flaw he could see was that he would be given no time to escape: the moment the fuse was triggered, the bomb would detonate.

It was a suicide mission, a thought so troubling that Kondratieff found his hand had begun to tremble. He had to take a moment to settle himself.

Even as he sat there pondering on his imminent death the clock in the corner of the room chimed. He checked the time by his pocket watch: de Nostredame's guest would be arriving soon, so with a fatalistic shrug of his shoulders Kondratieff collected up the blueprints and made his way up the stairs to the top of the house.

The knowledge, supplied courtesy of Machiavelli, that his every move was being watched by the Signori di Notte, necessitated his moving between his house and that of his collaborator, Michel de Nostredame, via the attic that ran the length of the ten houses making up the terrace on the northern side of Calle del Fabbri. Only in this way would he avoid the agents standing watch outside his house.

Thankfully de Nostredame had a fortifying glass of Solution waiting for him when he emerged coughing and covered in cobwebs and dust from his journey through the attic. His friend was not alone; sitting next to him on his couch was a well-made man, sporting a tremendously bushy beard and a large and very prominent nose. The beret he wore attested to his having artistic pretensions, a surmise that was confirmed when introductions were effected.

'Nikolai, I have the honour of introducing you to Auguste Rodin,' de Nostredame announced. 'Auguste, may I, in turn, present the Demi-Monde's most eminent Future Historian, Docteur Nikolai Kondratieff.' The two men shook hands, Kondratieff somewhat in awe of the man many regarded as the Quartier Chaud's greatest living sculptor. 'Auguste has agreed to help us in our little adventure, Nikolai. He is a great patriot and is as aghast as we are by the evil that has taken control of Venice and which now threatens the Demi-Monde. Like us, he believes the Doge IMmanual to be the Beast ... the harbinger of the Dark.'

Rodin nodded vigorously. 'That is true, Docteur. I have only recently fled the Medi for Venice and now I find that the evil I was trying to evade is once more snapping at my heels. The purging of non-IMmanualists in Venice has begun and the Signori di Notte are arresting those whose only crime is to not believe. Many of my friends have already been thrown into prison and I fear that it will not be long before I join them. I will do everything I can to bring justice and fair government back to the Quartier Chaud.'

'Then let us be about it,' said de Nostredame.

Without further ado Kondratieff laid his blueprints out across Nostredame's cluttered table, one end of the sheets secured by a bottle of Solution and the other by the Professeur's pipe. Kondratieff coughed to clear his throat and then began. 'We had thought that defeating the evil that threatens the Demi-Monde would simply necessitate the neutering of the power of Doge IMmanual – the Beast – but now her brother walks amongst us and by our calculations he is as great a threat to the peace of our world as his sister. It has fallen to Michel and myself to prevent him securing power in the Demi-Monde.'

'How? He is guarded *very* closely.'

'Have you heard of the Column of Loci, Auguste?' asked Kondratieff.

Rodin chuckled. 'Of course. As a sculptor, I am naturally fascinated by the work of the Pre-Folk. I have visited the Galerie des Anciens to view the Column on several occasions.'

'Excellent. But what you will not know is that the Column has a key role to play in the outcome of Ragnarok, in deciding who will emerge triumphant in the final struggle between good and evil. That is the message conveyed to us in the *Flagellum Hominum*.' With that Kondratieff drew the copy of the book from his satchel and placed it on the table. 'The translated *Flagellum Hominum* tells us that the Column of Loci possesses great power: that it is a huge conductor of occult energy … energy stored in the Temple of Lilith *and* in the Great Pyramid. I have been advised that the Doge IMmanual intends to take the Column to the Temple of Lilith where it will serve as a means of regenerating all of Lilith's power. It is my intention to create an imitation Column and to substitute the fake for the original. It is this ersatz Column that I will deliver to the Temple of Lilith.'

'To what end?' asked an obviously perplexed Rodin. 'Surely all this will do is interrupt the Ceremony of Awakening … it will do nothing to destroy the power of Doge IMmanual or of Duke William.'

'The introduction of the fake into the Temple when Duke William and his supporters are gathered together gives us an unprecedented opportunity to eliminate the whole pack of them in one fell swoop.' Kondratieff tapped a long finger on his plan. 'The imitation Column will be one gigantic bomb designed to detonate during the ceremony to be performed on Lammas Eve.'

It took a moment for the sculptor to appreciate the full implications of what Kondratieff was saying. 'The papers say there will be four hundred people attending that ceremony. You wish me to abet you in their slaughter?'

A nod from Kondratieff. 'It is the only way. Four hundred lives sacrificed to preserve millions.'

An ashen-faced Rodin rose unsteadily to his feet, rattling the glasses standing on the table as he did so. 'I must have a moment ... this is barbaric ... I must ...' He took a gulp of Solution and then crossed the room to stand by a window. There he remained, alone and silent, for several minutes, obviously locked in confused consideration of what he was being asked to do. Finally he turned to de Nostredame. 'Michel ... we have been friends for many years ... are you sure this terrible scheme proposed by Docteur Kondratieff is necessary?'

'It is,' replied de Nostredame firmly. 'We have run our 4Telling program, HyperOpia, several times and the answer is consistent. We must destroy Duke William. Believe me, Auguste, both Nikolai and I take this step with the greatest reluctance. We are not murderers by inclination – far from it – but Fate would have us become so.'

'But I am an artist, not an assassin.'

'And I am a mathematician,' said Kondratieff quietly, 'and Nostredame here a preHistorian, but if we wish to preserve the Demi-Monde from evil we can no longer simply walk by on the other side. As Edmund Burke said: all that is necessary for the triumph of evil is for good men to do nothing.'

'But what of Heydrich? Surely by destroying Duke William *and* the leaders of Venice and NoirVille we will simply make it easier for that bastard to take control of the Demi-Monde?'

De Nostredame laughed. 'One tyrant at a time, Auguste. We have other plans for Heydrich.'

Rodin took a deep breath and then drained his glass. 'Very well, I will help you.'

A relieved Kondratieff turned back to his blueprints. 'For our plan to be successful, the counterfeit Column must be a perfect duplicate of the real one. This is the task we would set you, Auguste, to carve the simulacrum.'

Rodin walked over to the table and made a long and very close study of Kondratieff's plans. Cogitations over, he ran a hand through his mane of hair and addressed the two scientists. 'Technically, it is very straightforward, the major challenges are your requirements that the imitation must be a perfect match for the original and, of course, that it be hollow.'

Kondratieff said nothing, waiting for the sculptor to continue.

'What is the timetable? When must this imitation Column be finished?'

'By the eightieth day of Summer.'

Rodin whistled softly. 'Difficult. If I were permitted to use my assistants—'

'It is imperative that no one other than you knows about this work. If the Signori di Notte were to discover what we are about, then the punishment will be severe.'

Rodin nodded solemnly, acknowledging what Kondratieff said made sense. 'Very well, I will work alone in the smaller of my two studios, the one situated on the island of Murano. I will tell everyone I am engaged in a secret work commissioned in honour of the Doge IMmanual, a commission to be unveiled on Lammas Eve.' He gave a wry chuckle. 'That, at least, is the truth.'

'There's a harbour in Murano, is there not?'

'Yes, but why . . . ?'

'We will effect the switch of the two Columns – the real for the fake – there when we are loading them into the pontoons designed to float them down the Nile.'

'A pontoon?'

'It's a fancy name for a watertight steel cylinder with a keel and a rudder. The imitation Column will be sealed inside one of them so that it can be floated down the Nile to the pier on the Wheel River opposite the Temple of Lilith.'

'It will be difficult to effect such a substitution without it being seen,' mused Rodin.

'Difficult, but not impossible. We will bring the *real* Column to Murano ostensibly to be fitted into the pontoon, and once it is there we will make the switch.'

Again Rodin lapsed into silence, then, 'Whilst I applaud the audacity of your scheme, Nikolai, I would be remiss if I did not point out a failing. The Column of Loci is made from Mantle-ite and, as you know, Mantle ite emits a green glow.'

De Nostredame laughed. 'Have no fear, Auguste, Nikolai here has thought of everything. Inspired by the illusions perpetrated by a man called Vanka Maykov, he has found the solution to this little dilemma in the use of matches.'

De Nostredame's second guest arrived an hour after the departure of Rodin. In contrast to the refined and thoughtful sculptor, Peter Nearchus was uncouth and unpleasant. Big and overweight, the sets of cheek scars he wore – which announced to the world that he was a HimPerialist . . . a *Blank* HimPerialist – making him look uglier than he was. Kondratieff disliked him on sight ... disliked him, but needed him. He was the man who had to be persuaded to build the second pontoon. Nearchus was the greatest shipbuilder in the whole of the Demi-Monde.

Once the introductions were complete, Nearchus was all business. 'So, de Nostredame, what's all this cloak-and-dagger stuff about? I hate coming over to Venice now that black bitch of yours is in charge. I don't care what our priests say: it's a violation of the sacred teachings of HimPerialism that NoirVille should be cooperating with a woeMan. By rights woeMen shouldn't be allowed to run anything bigger than a knocking shop.' He gave a chuckle. 'Yeah, the only time woeMen should be in a position over Men is when they're straddling them.'

The man, Kondratieff decided, was a pig. Listening to Nearchus, he found himself amazed that someone as disgusting as this misogynistic oaf should have been blessed by ABBA with so much talent, but ABBA was often inclined to imbue the most unworthy of Demi-Mondians with genius.

'Yeah, I hate that Shade cunt with a vengeance. And by signing a pact with the witch, Shaka Zulu has insulted ABBA and slighted the Machismo of every one of us who calls himself a Man. It's bad enough us allowing that nuJu scum to set up the JAD slap-bang in the middle of NoirVille without us co-operating with a woeMan. I don't know what NoirVille's coming to. Shaka's going soft, losing his Cool. It's time he handed over to someone like Pobedonostsev.'

Kondratieff said nothing: he had never fully appreciated the enmity and the hatred that existed between the Blanks and the Shades in NoirVille. But even so, the thought of that madman Pobedonostsev running NoirVille made his SAE turn cold. Maybe, though, this was a division in the HimPerial ranks that they could exploit.

De Nostredame saw the opportunity too. 'What would you say, Peter,' he smarmed, 'if I was to give you a chance to rid the world of Doge IMmanual *and* Shaka Zulu?'

The piggy eyes of Nearchus settled on de Nostredame. 'Okay, I'm listening.'

For the second time that afternoon Kondratieff pulled a set of diagrams out of his satchel. 'We wish this built ... built in secret.'

The blueprints showed the design for the steel pontoon.

'What the fuck? I'm already building one of these. The head of the Venice Armoury – a fucking idiot called John Dixon – placed an order for a pontoon identical to this one just last week.'

'I know,' said Kondratieff quietly. 'John Dixon is the man I commissioned to design the pontoon. Now we want you to build a *second* one, but to do it in such a way that no one, least of all John Dixon, learns about it.'

'But why?'

And Kondratieff explained his plan to Nearchus and, as he did so, the man became more and more excited.

'You're gonna detonate this bomb of yours on Lammas Eve?'

'Correct.'

'And Doge IMmanual and Shaka Zulu will be attending.'

'I know.'

Nearchus's eyes sparkled: the prospect of the ruler of NoirVille – the *Shade* ruler of NoirVille – being eliminated was obviously a tantalising prospect.

'What's going to happen to the real Column?'

'We have plans for it,' said Kondratieff carefully, 'plans that are no concern of yours.'

Nearchus studied the blueprints of the pontoon for a few moments. 'Okay, I'm your man. It's time Shaka was sent to meet his ancestors. I'll build the pontoon in our Number Two yard, that way nobody will twig what we're up to.' He looked up from the plans and studied Kondratieff intently. 'When d'you want it for?'

'By the eightieth day of Summer.'

Nearchus rolled up the plans. 'Then I better not hang around here gassing.'

Kondratieff watched Nearchus go. The man had performed just as the HyperOpia program had predicted he would. Now he only had one problem to solve: finding a steamship to tow the second Column to Terror Incognita. And for the solution to that puzzle he would have to turn to Su Xiaoxiao.

It was nearly midnight when Kondratieff placed his magnifying glass to one side and spent a moment massaging the bridge of his nose in a vain attempt to ease the pain that was racking his mind. He always got a headache when obliged to write in the tiny script needed for the messages to be carried by pigeons, and with a message as complex as this one, legibility was of the essence. There could be no mistakes regarding what he was asking and no misunderstanding of the importance he attached to the request he was making.

These were without doubt the most important thirty words he had ever written.

He laboured for over three hours to ensure that every minute letter of the message was crafted for clarity, but even so he wondered if Su Xiaoxiao and the SheTong would be able to do what he asked. The Demi-Monde was a world beset by war and hence the procuring of a steamship of sufficient power to tow a pontoon was an immensely difficult task. He had tried and failed to find one in Venice, and now that he was watched night and day by Machiavelli's agents, it was impossible for him to sneak across to NoirVille to organise one there. Su Xiaoxiao was his last hope.

Satisfied, Kondratieff put down his pen, opened the cage, took out the bird and deftly sealed the message ring around its leg. Then with a silent prayer he tossed the pigeon into the night and watched it wing its way towards Rangoon.

22

NoirVille
Thr Demi-Monde: 14th Day of Summer, 1005

Glorious though the reign of Shaka Zulu was, it was not without its controversies. Permitting the establishment of a nuJu homeland – the JAD – in the centre of NoirVille in exchange for the supply of Aqua Benedicta might have made the Sector one of the wealthiest in the Demi-Monde, *but* it created deep divisions within the ruling elite. The rapprochement with Venice might have been an astute move politically and militarily, *but* it outraged more conservative religious leaders for whom cooperating with the Doge – a woeMan – was a violation of the sacred tenets of HimPerialism. And finally, the decision to accept *non*Shade male refugees – Blanks – into NoirVille might have been necessary to replenish a population depleted by the exodus of woeMen to the Coven following the triumph there of the Femme Liberation Movement, *but* the racial tensions between Shades and Blanks cast a long shadow over NoirVille.

The HisTory of NoirVille: Ibn Duraid,
First NoirVillian Press

'I must admit to being surprised – *pleasantly* surprised – to have received your message, Nearchus,' murmured Konstantin Petrovich Pobedonostsev, HimPerial Secretary to the Court of His Majesty Shaka Zulu and tutor to Crown Prince Xolandi, as he toyed with the quail Nearchus's chef had taken almost two days to prepare. As the man picked at his food, Nearchus was reminded of a scrawny chicken pecking away at its corn, just as Pobedonostsev's whining, wheedling voice pecked away at his patience. But these antipathies he would keep well hidden: Pobedonostsev was a powerful and petulant man and, in Nearchus's experience, powerful and petulant men were best placated rather than antagonised. Pobedonostsev was, after all, leader of the ultra-secret Brotherhood of a Purer SAE, the Blank supremacy party in NoirVille.

The man placed his fork down. 'Yes, you have always been a loyal member of the Brotherhood, Nearchus, but the intelligence you have communicated regarding the Column of Loci presents us with great – with *HisToric* – opportunities.'

Time to double my price, decided Nearchus. Loyalty to the Brotherhood was one thing, but business was business.

Pobedonostsev pushed his plate away, the quail only half consumed, then smiled at Nearchus which, contrarily, made him more repulsive than ever. He was thin to the point of gauntness, all sunken cheeks and narrow lips and eyes, his skeletal appearance emphasised by his baldness, by his tiny tortoiseshell glasses and by the excessively tight black uniform he was wearing. Nearchus couldn't identify the uniform – probably it was that worn by members of the Elevated Order of Tight-Arses and Sycophants – but whichever it was, the uniform made Pobedonostsev look like a desiccated crow.

The crow spoke. 'Indeed, the import of your revelations is such that I have taken the liberty of inviting His Holiness to this meeting.' Here Pobedonostsev nodded towards Aleister Crowley, seated to his right.

At the sound of his name Crowley sat up a little straighter in his chair and squared his shoulders. It didn't help: in the flesh he was a disappointment. The Supreme Head of the

Church of UnFunDaMentalism might be tall and imposing and – with his bright robes and outlandish jewellery – have a suitably exotic appearance, but there was an air of desperation about him. He looked to be a man under pressure, which was presumably why he had risked his neck to come to Cairo to speak with Nearchus in person. And this, in turn, indicated the importance the powers that be in the ForthRight attached to their understanding of Kondratieff's plans.

Maybe triple the price?

'Again, I am honoured,' Nearchus charmed as he raised his glass in salute of both Crowley *and* his financial good fortune.

The three men quaffed their Solution and Nearchus took the opportunity to ponder on the amazing turn of events his meeting with Kondratieff had precipitated. As a senior member of the BrotherHood of a Purer SAE, he had known that the BrotherHood and the ForthRight had been edging – somewhat warily, it had to be admitted – towards an alliance, but he had never realised that matters had come so far. Of course, on fundamental matters of religious doctrine UnFunDaMentalists like Crowley and Blank supremacists like Pobedonostsev were in agreement – that woeMen were an inferior species; that UnderMentionables, notably nuJus and Shades, were fit only for extermination; and that the people chosen by ABBA to rule the Demi-Monde were the Blank races – but . . .

But still each side's instinctive suspicion of the other had made a formal alliance difficult. Both sides were led by very ambitious men who believed that they, and they alone, had been called by ABBA to purify the Demi-Monde and to rule in His name. It had been the emergence of the Lady IMmanual that had made them more amenable to collaboration. Now it appeared that his uncovering of Kondratieff's plot had finally persuaded the two sides to ignore their suspicions and unite against Doge IMmanual and Shaka Zulu.

Pobedonostsev placed his glass carefully back on the table and nodded encouragingly to Nearchus. 'I would be grateful if you would summarise for His Holiness's benefit the details of Kondratieff's plans.'

'As you wish, HimPerial Secretary. Kondratieff is intent on creating a replica of the Column of Loci and it is this replica that will soon be en route to the Temple of Lilith. The replica is, in fact, a bomb, which Kondratieff intends to detonate on Lammas Eve, destroying the Doge IMmanual—'

'And all the other guests gathered there,' interjected Pobedonostsev, 'guests who will include Shaka Zulu and his court, and that upstart Duke William.' The man could hardly keep the excitement out of his voice: he loathed Shades almost as much as he loathed woeMen.

'Excellent,' murmured Crowley. 'That will be a fearsome blow struck in the cause of Aryan supremacy.' A sip of his Solution. 'And what, Nearchus, will be the fate of the *real* Column?'

'Here Kondratieff was evasive, but, as his housekeeper was amenable to bribery, I was able to have sight of his confidential notebooks. I can tell you that the genuine Column will be taken to Terror Incognita where forces opposed to the ForthRight will seek to erect it on top of the Great Pyramid. For what reason I have no idea, but I do know he intends to approach Su Xiaoxiao and the SheTong to help him do this.'

'Su Xiaoxiao!' Crowley sneered. 'That troublemaker, though I doubt that after the invasion of the Coven by the ForthRight army either she or her ninja hooligans will be in any condition to assist Kondratieff in this endeavour. But we must be wary. Be aware, Nearchus, that the placing of the Column on the summit of the Great Pyramid is an occult act of enormous metaphysical significance, so much so that it is vital – *vital* – that it is performed only by those loyal to the True Religion, UnFunDaMentalism. Tell me, Nearchus, how will the real Column be taken to Terror Incognita?'

'In a second pontoon currently being constructed in my ship-yard. The plan is that Su Xiaoxiao will seize a steamship capable of towing the pontoon, sail it to the harbour on the Isle of Murano on the final day of Summer ...'

'Lammas Eve,' observed Pobedonostsev somewhat unnecessarily.

'... take the pontoon containing the real Column under tow and bring it to Terror Incognita.'

'Where does Su Xiaoxiao believe she can find such a steamship?'

'The plan is that she will steal it from the ForthRight.'

Crowley scratched his chin as he pondered what Nearchus had said. 'This presents us with an opportunity to take the Column. When, in your opinion, would it be best to intercept the pontoon?'

'It would be imprudent for the ForthRight Navy to attempt to take the Column whilst it is in Venice. If they were spotted by NoirVillian or Venetian shore batteries ...' Nearchus left the sentence unfinished; the power of the guns sited along the banks of the Nile was famous throughout the Demi-Monde. 'My advice would be to allow Su Xiaoxiao to steal the steamship, take the real Column under tow and for the ForthRight Navy to intercept the pontoon when it is en route to Terror Incognita, ideally at the junction of the Nile and the Wheel, at a point beyond the range of the shore batteries.'

'And that is just what we will do,' announced Crowley, rewarding his decisiveness with a swig of Solution. 'You have done well, Nearchus. This is an ABBA-sent opportunity to rid the Demi-Monde of two of the most formidable enemies of UnFunDaMentalism, Shaka Zulu and Doge IMmanual, and to ensure that the Column of Loci is in the possession of those who follow the True Religion.'

An enthusiastic nod from Pobedonostsev. 'That is so, Your

Holiness. It will only remain to destroy the Crown Prince Xolandi, and the Shades in NoirVille will be leaderless and hence ripe for elimination. And once their fate has been settled, it will be the turn of the JAD and the nuJu scum squatting there to be scoured from the face of the Demi-Monde.'

'The Final Solution will be in our grasp,' Crowley smarmed.

'The Final Solution,' Pobedonostsev breathed as he raised his glass, and the other two men joined him in his toast. 'To a wholly Blank world, where UnderMentionables have been exterminated and where woeMen are content in their ABBA-ordained role as subordinate helpmates to Men.'

Part Four
The Battle for the Coven

Created by Rossing Nóbel, Most Divine Couturier to the House of Worth, as seen in 'In Pure Modes' Un Vague Vogues Monthly, Summer 1003

In the Coven, Her Eticalism preaches an abhorrance of the sexual objectifying of Femmes. In response clothing designer Jiang Qing introduced the all-in-one boiler suit which has become the near-ubiquitous uniform for Femmes. Colloquially this suit is called the 'jiang'. This imprecation for restraint does not apply in the Forbidding City and hence the NoNs (eunuchs) there parade in opulent splendour.

23

Rangoon
The Demi-Monde: 35th Day of Summer, 1005

The greatest designer of armoured steamers is undoubtedly Isambard Kingdom Brunel, the genius behind the IKB class of Metropolitan Pacification Steamers that have become the armoured steamer of choice for all governments within the Demi-Monde. So it is little surprise that the SS-Ordo Templi Aryanis's Materiel and Munitions Commissariat approached Brunel's company – Pantechnicons of Distinction (London) Limited – to design and manufacture a new breed of river steamer. And the results of this collaboration were revolutionary. The Monitor-class armoured fighting vessel is without peer in the quest for river supremacy.

Excerpt from article entitled 'The Final Frontier:
Riverine Warfare in the Second Millennium':
The ForthRight Engineer, Fall 1004

By Trixie's estimation, the ForthRight's bombardment of Rangoon was far heavier and more intense than any she'd endured during the Siege of Warsaw. And it wasn't just the quantity of the shells that fell in a never-ending stream on the poor sods skulking in the ruins of the city, the calibre of the guns was bigger too; if she wasn't mistaken, the UnFunnies were using siege mortars. The shells were so heavy that every time one fell near the concrete redoubt she was using as her command headquarters, the whole place shook and a trail of dust drifted down from the ceiling, thickening the dank atmosphere and coating everyone cowering there with a frosting of beige powder.

But Trixie's biggest concern wasn't with the shaking of the redoubt: to her stunned surprise, her hands had started shaking too.

After the weeks of bombardment she'd endured in Warsaw she'd thought she was immune to the terror of an artillery barrage, but it seemed not. She jumped every time she felt the vibrating impact of an explosion, and worse, thirty-odd days on since the first shell had landed, her nerves were shredded. Now all she felt like doing was curling up in a ball, closing her eyes, stuffing her fingers in her ears and pretending this wasn't happening ... wasn't happening to her *again*.

Not that she could allow herself to show fear. She was a general and generals couldn't display the same weaknesses as ordinary soldiers. But it *was* difficult: the shelling never relented, pummelling the city twenty-four hours a day. Clement had learnt from the debacle of the Warsaw Uprising and was obviously intent on holding his invasion back until both Rangoon and its defenders had been flattened.

And now that moment had come. Just a few minutes shy of dawn on the thirty-fifth day of the war, the bombardment had paused, indicating that the ForthRight attack was imminent and the UnFunnies were preparing to launch their invasion barges against Rangoon. In a few short hours the fate of the Coven would be settled. This was Trixie's moment of truth.

She took a deep breath, trying to get control of herself. This was one of those times when she missed Wysochi the most; missed his strength, his courage and his certainty.

'Status of the WarJunks?' she snapped towards her Chief of Staff, pleased that her voice didn't betray her fear.

Efficient as ever, CommanderNon Jiao Yu gave her an immediate update. 'We have had semaphore messages from AdmiralNoN Zheng Heii advising that the WarJunks *MostBien*, *Wu*, *Dark*, *Borgia* and *Ptah* are in position a few hundred metres from Hub Bridge Number Four. They are just fifteen minutes' steaming time from Rangoon.'

Trixie sighed: five WarJunks wasn't enough. Intelligence reported that Clement had twenty of the ForthRight's new Monitors patrolling the Volga, and, though the considered opinion amongst naval experts was that the Coven's WarJunks were more powerful and tougher than the Monitors, odds of four to one were simply too great to be overcome.

'Send a signal that Heii is to hold his position. Inform him the invasion is anticipated to begin within the hour, and when the order is given to attack, he is to concentrate his assault on the enemy's drifter barges. His first priority is the destruction of the troop transports.'

Jiao Yu relayed the order and a communicationsFemme began pulling the levers that operated the semaphore.

'Are the rocket batteries in position?'

Jiao Yu bowed. 'Seven batteries are in position and their rockets are ready to be launched at your command, General-Femme. I must respectfully report that the eighth has been destroyed by enemy artillery fire.'

Trixie nodded. She didn't need anybody to tell her that: she'd seen the fireworks display from the observation port of her bunker. The prematurely ignited rockets had created mayhem as they whizzed around like demented comets before smashing into the ground and turning the downtown district of Rangoon with its tightly packed wooden houses into an inferno. It was the one time Trixie had been pleased to see the rains: she simply didn't have enough fighters to bring the blaze under control. If the rain didn't douse the flames, then Rangoon would just have to burn.

'How many salvoes of rockets do we have?'

'Five per battery. Each salvo will constitute twenty rockets.'

Trixie made a quick calculation: seven batteries, five salvoes, twenty rockets per salvo, giving a total of seven hundred rockets, each with a warhead of one hundred kilos of high explosive. Seventy tons of death and destruction plummeting down on the UnFunnies. Impressive, but again, not enough. If each battery had *fifty* salvoes, then, maybe, she could smash the UnFunnies' invasion barges where they were berthed and end the invasion before it began, but all five salvoes would do was discomfort the invasion fleet.

Trixie gave a rueful smile: she didn't want to discomfort the UnFunnies, she wanted to kill the bastards. This was her time to take revenge for all the suffering and pain Heydrich and his cronies had inflicted on her and her family.

'You will hold your fire until I give the word and then concentrate your fire along the St Petersburg docks. I want to burn the barges when they are packed with StormTroopers.'

Another bow from the NoN. Jiao Yu was a good soldier; he would do his duty and, more importantly, would do what she fucking told him to do. She was just thankful that all the NoN officers had accepted her appointment with similar grace, but unfortunately it had been different with the female officers. There had been more than a little bitching in the Femme ranks when she had been elevated to command the Covenite army, and there were no bigger bitches than the Trung sisters currently standing sullen and silent in the corner of the bunker.

Let 'em stew.

Now for the key question. 'Status of the Geek Fire?'

This was the Coven's ace in the hole. Jiao Yu seemed to

brighten a little: he had obviously been as impressed by the weapon as Trixie had. 'Everything is in order, GeneralFemme Dashwood. All five of the reservoirs are full and all the siphons are ready to discharge immediately you give the order.'

'I understand that one of the siphon valves – the one controlling the reservoir nearest to the Anichkov Bridge – is giving problems.'

'I have had Leading EngineerNoN Li Chang check the valve and he has pronounced it fully operational.'

'Good.'

BANG! Another mortar shell landed nearby and Trixie had to pause to let the reverberation of the huge explosion dissipate. Absent-mindedly she brushed concrete dust from her *jiangs* and was pleased to see her hand had stopped shaking. 'You must understand, CommanderNoN, that I intend to deploy the Geek Fire *after* the first wave of invasion barges has landed.'

Even Jiao Yu's formidable inscrutability was tested by this pronouncement. 'With the greatest of respect, GeneralFemme Dashwood, it is against all the precepts of war to allow an invading army to gain a foothold—'

'We are heavily outnumbered, CommanderNoN Jiao Yu, and the only way we will defeat the enemy is by securing local superiority. By allowing the enemy to land and *then* deploying the Geek Fire we will be able to destroy the barges intended to reinforce the first assault and leave the troops who have already made shore vulnerable to counter-attack.'

'The evacuation of civilians from the western side of Rangoon has still not been completed, GeneralFemme; I am concerned that these tactics will lead to a great many casualties. The fighting around the landing points will be fierce.'

Trixie took a deep breath. This was one of those moments when a military commander had to be hard-hearted, when the few had to be sacrificed for the greater good. 'I know, but we have no alternative. The Empress has decreed that the gates in the Great Wall are to remain closed, so there is nowhere for refugees to go to escape the fighting.'

One of Jiao Yu's eyebrows twitched as he registered the veiled criticism of the Empress. 'It is the belief of Her Majesty that should the gates be opened, those in Rangoon and Tokyo will fight with less enthusiasm. She has ordered that there can be no retreat: the army and the people must understand that if the enemy is victorious, they will die.'

Trixie said nothing. It was unbelievably callous of the Empress to leave her people to suffer like this. And not only callous, it was, in her opinion, bad strategy. The panicked civilian population of Rangoon and Tokyo were already making her army's work difficult, and anyway, she knew from her time in Warsaw that soldiers who were worried about the fate of their loved ones didn't have their mind on killing the enemy.

'I understand. And that's why we must not let the enemy advance beyond their initial landing grounds. We must destroy them on the shores of the Volga. I am relying on you, CommanderNoN Jiao Yu.'

Again Jiao Yu bowed his acceptance of the order, even as a signalFemme handed him a message.

'It appears, GeneralFemme Dashwood, that the first of the barbarians' invasion barges has been observed preparing to leave its moorings.'

'Then fire the rockets.'

At precisely seven in the morning the order came down to Comrade Captain John Worden that he had the honour of leading the assault on Rangoon. It was a proud moment for Worden and he had to fight hard to stop himself whooping with excitement as he shouted his instructions to the officers of the ForthRight Fighting Ship, the FFS *Heydrich*, ordering the vessel to go to action stations. But it wasn't just a proud moment: it was also a historic one. The *Heydrich* was the first Monitor-class ironclad ever deployed by the ForthRight Navy and Worden was determined that, come Hel or high water, he would prove worthy of the honour he had been given in commanding her.

Caught by the tide, the *Heydrich* rolled against her moorings and Worden had to steady himself against a guard rail. Designed to sit menacingly low in the water – most of her bulk sat below the waterline safe from enemy fire – the *Heydrich* was a bitch of a ship to handle, especially in an ebb tide. Beautiful she wasn't, graceful she wasn't: the *Heydrich* was an uncompromising and brutal weapon of war, line and aesthetics having been sacrificed for strength, power and stealth. Yeah . . . stealth. With only the huge double-gunned turret, the smokestack and the pilothouse Worden was currently occupying standing proud of the deck, the *Heydrich* was almost invisible to attacking warships.

Worden took a look along the length of his ship, checking that all was as it should be. Satisfied, he picked up a megaphone and shouted to the group of tars standing ready by the hawsers tethering the *Heydrich* to the two troop-transport barges he was responsible for towing safe across the Volga.

'Are the barges secure, Midshipman?'

'All secure, Comrade Captain.'

'Then cast off.' Worden didn't pause to watch them carry out his order – they were good men who knew their business – instead he called down the speaker tube to his second-in-command sweating away in the fetid bowels of the *Heydrich*. 'Full steam ahead, Mr May.' He listened while his order echoed along the *Heydrich*'s one-hundred-and-seventy-foot length to the engine room. The first indication Worden had that his order had been received was when the ship began to tremble as the engine's two huge pistons began to reciprocate. Then the propeller bit and the *Heydrich* slid its massive thousand tons slowly – almost reluctantly – away from the dock. But barely had the warship got under way, barely had she picked up any momentum, when there was a huge tug from behind as the hawsers ran out of slack and the *Heydrich* took the first of the barges she was hauling under tow.

'Battle stations. Close all watertight hatches and doors. Load guns.'

Hardly had the order been issued than all Hel was let loose. The noise of the pounding pistons of the *Heydrich*'s steam engines and the clanging of the hatches as they were slammed shut were as nothing to the shrieking, screaming, nerve-shredding howl that suddenly enveloped the *Heydrich*. Worden's world seemed to explode in a twisting turmoil of fire and noise. All around the Monitor were ear-killing explosions and, as the *Heydrich* pitched and yawed, a deafened and bemused Worden flinched back as the armoured skin of the ship was peppered with shrapnel. There was a huge *BANG* and though the ship's hull comprised two feet of oak and four inches of steel plate, the force of the explosion was such that he had the distinct impression that the walls of the ship bowed inwards. Worden was hurled against the side of the pilothouse and it was only by making a mad grab for the guard rail that he prevented himself tumbling down the stairwell into the innards of the ship. For several stunned seconds he lay on the deck before an instinctive sense of duty forced him to his feet and persuaded him to shove his head out of the observation porthole. The scene that greeted him was one of flaming carnage.

Rocket attack.

There had been whispered rumours within the SS that the Chinks were developing surface-to-surface rockets based on the design that had made life so dangerous for the ForthRight's Zeppelins, but he had never imagined that they would be so powerful. The whole of St Petersburg docks seemed to have been reduced to a burning chaos, but worse, one of the rockets had struck the second of the two barges the *Heydrich* was towing, turning it into a floating bonfire. As he watched, he saw screaming soldiers, burning from head to foot, leaping into the river.

'Damage report,' he yelled into the speaker tube.

It took a moment for Lieutenant May to respond, and when he did, he sounded shell-shocked. 'We took a hit amidships, Comrade Captain. Nothing too serious. Couple of timbers cracked and one man killed by flying splinters.'

With a grim nod of understanding, Worden turned his attention back to the two barges the *Heydrich* had in tow. He made a mental scan of the second barge's inventory, reminding himself that it was transporting all the reserve ammunition and grenades for use by the two hundred SS StormTroopers carried by the first barge. He was shouting orders before he was even conscious he'd made a decision: 'Cut barge number two free.'

Almost as soon as the words were out of his mouth three burly sailors carrying axes raced down the *Heydrich*'s deck, scrambled across the hawser to the first barge and then disappeared in the direction of the second. When the *Heydrich* leapt forward, Worden knew his order had been carried out and the burning barge had been cut adrift. It wasn't a moment too soon: even as he watched, there was a huge explosion that sent the *Heydrich* pitching and waves crashing over its low sides. The second barge had exploded.

There was no time to bemoan its loss or to grieve for the fifty StormTroopers destroyed in the explosion. Satisfied that the *Heydrich* was still river-worthy, Worden turned his telescope towards Rangoon and watched open-mouthed as wave after wave of rockets speared skywards. It was a terrifying sight to see them arch through the air – their progress marked by the trail of fire they left in their wake – hover for a moment at the apogee of their trajectory and then plummet, wailing like daemons, back Demi-Monde-wards. Fortunately for the *Heydrich*, the target of the whiz-bangs seemed to be the docks, which were now receding rapidly in the ship's wake, the fury of these devastating salvoes being borne by those Monitors and barges still waiting to sail. Breathing a sigh of relief, Worden pulled his hip flask out of his back pocket and took a calming swill of Solution, wondering as he did so what else these bastard Chinks had up their sleeves.

He didn't have long to find out.

'Five enemy WarJunks to port!' screamed the lookout.

Five . . .

As Worden scanned the smoke-shrouded river searching for sight of the enemy, he knew it was going to be a long and very dangerous day. He just hoped ABBA was inclined to smile on him.

Satisfied that her orders regarding the deployment of the rockets were being carried out, Trixie turned – reluctantly – to the Trung sisters who were waiting impatiently in the far corner of the bunker. They were tiny women – almost childlike – but had an air about them carried by those who had seen more than their fair share of fighting: they had, after all, commanded the forces of the Femme Liberation Movement that had stormed the Forbidding City during the fighting in 995 AC. They were tough cookies, but they were also disaffected.

After interviewing the officers she'd inherited from Jeanne Dark it quickly became apparent that the most accomplished and the most aggressive of them all were the two Trung sisters,

Trac and Nhi. The problem, Trixie suspected, was that they might be just a touch *too* aggressive, and when fighting a defensive war, aggression had to be leavened with discipline. They were also the officers who had objected most strenuously to her appointment, the elder of the pair – Trung Trac – seeing herself as Jeanne Dark's natural heir. And in Trixie's experience, resentful subordinates were unreliable subordinates.

But resentful or no, Mao had insisted that they be appointed as Trixie's joint second-in-command – he had flatly refused to allow her to employ Wysochi in that capacity – so she and they just had to make the best of it.

'ColonelFemme Trung Trac, you have been given command of the Covenite army defending the shores of the Volga. It is your responsibility to destroy the first wave of enemy invaders and to prevent them breaking out of their beachheads.'

The woman bowed, but not quite as deeply as Li demanded. *Bitch.*

She was an ugly woman, the left side of her face deeply scarred where it had been burnt when a Zeppelin had crashed near her. She had escaped death by inches.

Shame.

'The Covenite Army will not fail Empress Wu or the Divine Faith that is HerEticalism,' she answered in her piping voice. 'Have no doubt, GeneralFemme Dashwood, that we will repel all attempts by the heterosexual defilers to pollute the haven of MoreBienism that is the Coven.'

Not just a bitch, Trixie decided, but a pompous bitch.

'And you, ColonelFemme Trung Nhi, have command of the forces dedicated to defending the Anichkov Bridge. It is imperative that the bridge is held. If the ForthRight takes the bridge, then they will be able to reinforce their beachheads and we will be outflanked. The fate of the Coven lies in your hands and those of your fighters.'

'The Fifth Legion of Amazons will hold the bridge,

GeneralFemme, on that you have my word as an Officer and a gentleFemme.'

Trixie stood silent for a moment. Then she addressed all those gathered in the bunker. 'The ForthRight invasion of the Coven has begun. We are outgunned and outnumbered, but I have been outgunned and outnumbered before and I have been victorious. Remember that if you fail, then the evil that is UnFunDaMentalism will cast its long shadow over the Coven and everything you hold dear will be lost. May ABBA be with you.'

And with me.

24

Rangoon
The Demi-Monde: 35th Day of Summer, 1005

Several studies have been undertaken to examine the
emotional and psychological impact of gelding, but the
most extensive is the one conducted by prison reformer
Elizabeth Fry (*A Study of the Most Beneficial Effects of Castration
on the Mood and Manners of Recalcitrant Prisoners Held in Coven
Prisons*). Whilst Fry majors on the overwhelmingly positive
effect of gelding – the vast majority of those studied
became noticeably more placid and tractable after treatment – there was, however, a significant coterie of
nonFemmes who did not respond in a satisfactory manner.
Indeed, the anger and resentment towards HerEticalism
and the Coven evinced by these recidivists makes it essential that any NoN not responding positively to gelding be
summarily executed.

Castration's Too Good for Them: Jeanne Dark, Covenite
Instruction Manuals

AdmiralNoN Zheng Heii used the TooZian breathing techniques
he'd been taught as a boy to regulate his Qi, this ensuring that
the meridians criss-crossing his body were clear and that the
energy he drew from the Kosmos could flow more easily.
Tonight he would journey to join his ancestors and he was

determined that he would make that journey as a Superior Man, with his soul suffused with *wu wei*.

Yes ... tonight Zheng Heii would act in a Superior and an Honourable manner. Tonight he would act as a *Man* and not as a NoN.

Instinctively his fingers touched the medallion at his throat, the one that had belonged to his father and that had been passed to him by his beloved mother. It bore the Epigram *Tui*, denoting the Eldest Son, and it was the Eldest Son to whom the ancestors gave the responsibility of defending a family's honour. The medallion was Zheng Heii's most treasured possession, his mother having given it to him when she had informed him that his father had been killed defending the Forbidding City and the Emperor against the HerEtical forces of the Femme Liberation Movement. And then his mother had committed *jigai* – ritual suicide. It had been Zheng Heii who had found her body, her face beatific in death, the image of his father clasped in her hands and her legs tied together to ensure that even in death she remained a Superior Woman. As he had gazed down at her, so beautiful and so perfect, he had sworn that, one day, he would avenge both of his Most Honoured and Beloved Parents.

Wu in her arrogance had never suspected the hate that Zheng Heii had nurtured these ten years, the bitch confident that by gelding him she had made him biddable. But tonight she would understand that the fires of hate still burned bright in his soul, a hate that could only be doused by revenge. And tonight, ten years to the day after his mother passed across the Final Void to be with her ancestors, he would have that revenge.

The WarJunk *Wu*, the flagship of his little flotilla, rolled as she was buffeted by the ebb tide of a river swollen by the monsoon rains, but Zheng paid little heed, his mind concentrated on the orders he would be giving in the next few minutes, orders that would determine whether all his planning and connivance – and the falsification of the war game scores at the Beijing Naval College – had been in vain. By skilful manoeuvring he had managed to appoint NoNs loyal to him and to the creed of Confusionism to the command of three of the five WarJunks. They might have been reduced to the status of NoNs but this did not detract from their being good and resolute Men. He just hoped three would be enough.

Zheng Heii turned to his captain. 'CaptainNoN Weng, signal the other WarJunks that they are to assume Battle Formation Alpha, the Wolf Pack.'

CaptainFemme Andrews commanding the WarJunk CSS *Dark* gave the signal to acknowledge that the message from Heii had been received, but though she was willing to admit to receiving it, whether she understood it was quite another matter. Whilst she would concede that AdmiralNoN Zheng Heii was a genius – his lectures at the Beijing Naval College were the ones she never missed – and that the tactics to be adopted tonight had been simulated many times in war games, she had never been convinced of their *appropriateness*.

To her way of thinking, when a force such as theirs was to be deployed against an enemy that outnumbered them but that was encumbered by the need to tow and protect sluggish troop barges, then the Wolf Pack was not the best battle formation. To use the five WarJunks the Coven possessed en masse – as the Wolf Pack demanded – was, in her opinion, a mistake. It made the WarJunks vulnerable to fire from shore batteries and susceptible to being surrounded by enemy warships. It also negated the effective use of what Andrews believed was their most potent weapon: the huge ram that the WarJunks had on their prows. It was Andrews's belief that there wasn't a ship on the river that would be able to resist being rammed by a WarJunk.

Better, she had proposed, that the WarJunks operate Lone Wolf-style, each of them being given an area of the Volga to patrol. Such tactics, she believed, would create the maximum confusion in the enemy fleet and lead to the maximum number of sinkings. But though this seemed eminently logical to her, whenever her Lone Wolf tactics had been played out in the war games conducted at the Naval College, the tonnage sunk was always less than that achieved by Zheng Heii's Wolf Packs. It was as though the dice had been weighted against her. And so, reluctantly, she had had to concede, and tonight the five WarJunks would operate as a single unit.

'Steer towards the centre of the Volga,' she ordered. 'Bring the *Dark* between the *Borgia* and the *Ptah*.'

Battle Formation Alpha demanded that the WarJunks proceed up the Volga in line abreast, sweeping all enemy vessels before them, then, just two hundred metres from the Anichkov Bridge, the WarJunks in positions two and four – the *Dark* and the *MostBien*, commanded by Andrews's friend CaptainFemme Hôjô Masako – would drop back to create the W pattern demanded by the formation. This would allow the WarJunks to bring the maximum number of their guns to bear on the enemy without fear of hitting a friendly ship.

'HelmsFemme reports we are now alongside *Borgia* and *Ptah*.'

With a nod of acknowledgement Andrews used her telescope to study the dark, brooding shape sailing to port, the low, triangular superstructure of the WarJunk cunningly designed to deflect enemy shells.

'Lookout reports that the *Ptah* has veered off course, CaptainFemme. It is now only a cable-length from us.'

'Send a signal to the *Ptah* asking it to be more diligent in keeping station.'

Andrews shook her head in mock-despair. Typically fucking useless NoN riverFemmeship: the dickless bastard, CaptainNoN

Matsei Iwane, commanding the *Ptah*, couldn't even keep his ship pointed in the right direction. ABBA only knew how he had graduated ahead of her in the class of '01.

But there was more to her dislike of the *Ptah*'s commander than his poor riverFemmeship: there was something about the way Matsei Iwane looked at Femmes that told her he had never truly accepted the teachings of HerEticalism. There was something disturbingly heterosexual about the NoN.

She raised her glass to verify that the idiot was altering course. He wasn't, and what was more he'd forgotten to batten down the hatches covering the *Ptah*'s gun ports. It was a surprise that – very briefly – turned to astonishment when the *Ptah* fired a point-blank broadside into the *Dark*.

'Er, Comrade Captain, you ain't gonna believe this but the lookouts report that the Coven's WarJunks have started firing at each other.'

Worden snatched up his glass and trained it downstream. Sure enough, it appeared that three of the WarJunks sailing towards them were now pouring fire into the other two. Such was the ferocity of the bombardment that the ships under attack had already begun to list; they'd be gone in a matter of minutes.

'What the devil?'

'Lookout says that one of the WarJunks has run up a white flag. Seems like the Covenite Navy is intent on surrendering.'

Trixie thought CommanderNoN Jiao Yu was going to cry. His cheeks had gone scarlet and his bottom lip was trembling.

'What's the matter, CommanderNoN?'

Jiao Yu bowed. 'GeneralFemme Dashwood ... it is with the greatest grief that I must report to you an act of gross treachery performed by AdmiralNoN Zheng Heii. I have received a message from Naval Observation Station Three stating that they have seen the WarJunk CSS *Wu* and two others loyal to Zheng Heii firing on WarJunks commanded by Femmes. The *Dark* and *MostBien* have been sunk.' More lip-trembling: the NoN looked as though he was going to pass out. 'The traitor Zheng Heii was then seen to surrender three WarJunks to the pig UnFunDaMentalists.'

Trixie took a deep, deep breath, trying to remain calm. It was at moments like these when real leaders showed their steel: it was easy to lead when things were going right, it was quite another thing to lead when everything around you was turning to shit. She nodded and then gave Jiao Yu a grim smile. 'Okay, these things happen. Just be thankful that this treachery won't materially affect the outcome of the war. The WarJunks are – were – an important part of our armoury, but not vital.' She gave the NoN an encouraging smile. 'Don't worry, we'll defeat the ForthRight without them.'

Jiao Yu was not in a mood to be reassured. 'Again, with the deepest of respect, GeneralFemme, I fear that when this news is communicated to the Forbidding City, the retribution inflicted on NoNs will be terrible. The Empress Wu will undoubtedly take the actions of Zheng Heii as an indication that the loyalty of all NoNs is suspect.' He paused. 'The Empress Wu can be very ... decisive when it comes to removing those she sees as threats to the HerEtical cause.'

'I see.' And what Trixie saw was that if Wu initiated a purge of NoNs, then any hope she had of defeating the UnFunnies was gone. NoN officers held a great many key positions in her army and without them the Coven's military would be reduced to chaos.

'Is Heii typical of all NoNs? Do I have to watch out for all of you?'

'No, GeneralFemme; although Heii was revered as a great

military strategist there was always a suspicion amongst NoNs that his castration had not subdued the MALEvolence in his soul. And of course, though he was much respected, his influence was greatest in the navy, rather than the army.'

'Okay. Then there is only one solution: we must not allow the message regarding Heii's treachery to be transmitted to the Forbidding City. That way we'll prevent the Empress doing anything precipitous.'

'But to withhold intelligence from the Empress is treason.'

'No, it's war.'

'But how?'

'The Signalling Station is three rooms down from us. I suggest you take some GuardNoNs loyal to you and commandeer it.'

'The signalFemmes will object.'

Trixie gave Jiao Yu an empty smile. 'Stop that signal and you give your fellow NoNs a chance of living. Don't and by evening you'll all have been put up against a wall and shot. The choice is yours.'

For a long moment Jiao Yu was silent as he struggled, Trixie supposed, with the idea of doing something so unorthodox. Finally he unclipped the holster that held his sidearm and bowed to Trixie. 'If you will excuse me for a moment, GeneralFemme.'

Although she had tried to shrug off Heii's treachery, Trixie knew the war was going badly; just four hours in and she could sense the feeling of defeat in the air. The WarJunks had been betrayed and the rocket attack, though spectacular, hadn't done more than delay things. Now the only shot she had left in her locker was Geek Fire.

The belief within the War Council of the Covenite Army was that Geek Fire should be used as a deterrent, that it should be ignited in advance of an amphibious landing to repel the attackers, but Trixie had decided that this was hokum. It was better, in her opinion, to wait until the ForthRight army had landed, the fight had been engaged and *then* to ignite it. In this way the force already on Covenite soil would be cut off from reinforcements and the maximum number of landing barges would be caught in midstream by the conflagration. It was a strategy that required an iron nerve and exact timing.

Immediately the first of the ForthRight troop barges was ashore and the Covenite defenders had come to grips with the advancing StormTroopers, messages had flooded into the Command Post, begging, demanding, pleading that the fury of the Geek Fire be released. But still she refused to give the command.

Trixie glanced towards Jiao Yu: the NoN seemed tremendously bucked up after shooting the two recalcitrant signalFemmes. Killing people obviously agreed with him. 'How many enemy barges have reached Rangoon?'

'The best estimate we have is around fifty.'

Fifty barges meant that just ten thousand StormTroopers had made it to Rangoon; not enough to persuade her to spring her trap. 'Hold the siphons closed until two hundred barges have made shore.'

A quizzical look from Jiao Yu. 'With the deepest of respect, GeneralFemme Dashwood, we understand that the fighting around the Anichkov Bridge is severe. ColonelFemme Trung Nhi is already demanding reinforcements.'

'She has five thousand fighters, more than enough to hold the bridge *and* to repel an attack from the SS who've landed. Tell her there will be no reinforcements and that she must stand firm.'

The NoN bowed and then disappeared in the direction of the signal room – now manned exclusively by NoNs – leaving Trixie alone to ponder whether she'd made the correct decision. A somewhat breathless Jiao Yu returned barely a minute later. 'We are advised, GeneralFemme Dashwood, that over two hundred enemy barges have now landed.'

'Then open the siphons and flood the river.'

It was a simple enough order, but the consequences, she knew, would be horrific. Geek Fire was a treacherous mixture of bitumen, palm oil, resin, rubber and other secret ingredients that floated on water and when ignited erupted in a fury of fire and poisonous vapour. It was a devilish weapon. 'Siphons open!' came a shout from one of the SignalNoNs.

Now the five siphons positioned at equal distances along the bank of the Volga would be spewing the liquid held in the reservoirs – these, thankfully, housed in concrete bunkers near the Great Wall safe from the artillery shells raining down on Rangoon – into the river, where the tide would spread it along its course. Then an igniting rocket would be fired and the whole lot would go up in a ferment of fire, flames and fumes. Anything remotely flammable – like a ForthRight troop-transport barge and the SS bastards inside it – wouldn't stand a chance.

Ten minutes passed and then Jiao Yu bustled back into the command room. 'Everything is in order, GeneralFemme,' he advised Trixie. 'We are ready to fire the ignition rocket.'

'Then do it, CommanderNon. Let's fry up these bastard UnFunnies. Let's give 'em a foretaste of Hel.'

Wysochi had ignored his guards and with a couple of the other WFA officers had climbed up onto the roof of their barracks to get a better look at the Battle for Rangoon, but, much as he admired Trixie's battle acumen, he had to admit that what he saw had him worried. That the ForthRight had already secured a couple of footholds along the Rangoon side of the river was bad enough, but what really concerned Wysochi was the lack of Covenite artillery deployed to keep them from being rein-forced. In fact there seemed to be nothing much being done to prevent the waves of ForthRight troop-transport barges reaching Rangoon and consolidating the gains the UnFunnies had already made.

Where were all the WarJunks he had heard the guards talking about?

The only thing he could think of was that Trixie had some-thing really evil up her sleeve, but even he hadn't imagined it would be as evil as it turned out to be. The combination of surprise and heat he experienced when the whole river exploded in a cauldron of twenty-foot-high flames was such that he was forced to take two shocked steps back and it was only by grabbing on to a chimney pot that he stopped himself tumbling off the roof.

'What the fuck?' he spluttered as he was blanketed by a cloud of sulphurous, choking black smoke.

'Geek Fire!' shouted one of his young lieutenants over the noise of the boiling river, the screams of dying men and the incessant artillery fire that was falling on Rangoon. 'There've been a lot of rumours about it. Guess it had to be these sneaky Chinks who ended up perfecting it, seeing that they've always been devils when it came to alchemy. I feel sorry for the poor sods in those barges.'

Wysochi wasn't sorry for them. 'Fuck 'em ... fuck all UnFunnies, I hope they burn slow,' he growled, though as far as he could see, there wasn't much chance of that. The fire was so intense that any UnFunny barge caught in it would be barbecued in an instant. And there would be a lot of StormTroopers being barbecued tonight, the fire enveloping the river had engulfed a veritable fleet of barges and even through the black smoke Wysochi could see that several were already ablaze. He gave a grim smile, realising that Trixie had really foxed them, and if the fire burned long enough those StormTroopers already ashore would be cut off and made easy meat for the Covenite army.

And then disaster struck.

25

Rangoon
The Demi-Monde: 35th Day of Summer, 1005

Investigations made regarding the incendiary weapon deployed with such effect by the Covenite Army during the initial phase of Case White – the invasion of the Coven – have as yet failed to reveal the constituents and method of manufacture of the so-called 'Geek Fire'. This weapon was awarded the highest security classification by the Coven's Administration, and unfortunately the inventor of the weapon, ScientistNoN Chang Po-tuan, appears to have been amongst those NoNs purged for 'crimes against the Coven' following the defection to the ForthRight of AdmiralNoN Zheng Heii.

Checkya Report Number 71288-CoV
dated 68th day of Summer, 1005 AC

The suspect valve at Pumping Station Number Three which serviced the largest Geek Fire reservoir malfunctioned. It was an important valve, the one intended to prevent blowback, to prevent the flames from the already burning Geek Fire retreating along the fuel lines and into the reservoir. The consensus later was that Leading EngineerNoN Li Chang was a confederate of Heii's and deliberately sabotaged the valve, though as Li Chang died in the ensuing explosion, the truth of the matter would never be known. But whatever the cause of the valve's malfunction, the consequences were apparent to everybody in Rangoon: the huge fuel reservoir positioned opposite the Anichkov Bridge exploded with a blast that was heard and felt for a radius of five miles. Trixie had never seen anything like it. The Demi-Monde erupted in three-hundred-foot-high gouts of flame.

Even sheltered within her bunker, even with her arm thrown across her face, Trixie was still hurled backwards by the blast and the SAE of her right cheek scorched by the flames that engulfed the redoubt. Immediately the semaphore vanes – bent and twisted by the heat, but still operating – began to clatter and a moment later a somewhat charred Jiao Yu came scurrying into the Command Centre. 'I must advise you, GeneralFemme, that the reservoir servicing Pumping Station Number Three has exploded.'

No kidding, thought Trixie as she brushed cinders from her *jiangs*.

'It seems that half of the buildings in Rangoon are now on fire. ColonelFemme Trung Nhi has also advised that her fighters were badly affected by the blast, the Amazon regiment defending the Anichkov Bridge being almost totally annihilated. The few who survived are unable to present any credible opposition to the SS. The ColonelFemme urgently requests reinforcements.'

It took Trixie only a moment to assess the situation. She knew that a commander as able as Archie Clement wouldn't let an opportunity like this slip by him, and as soon as his men had recovered from the shock of the explosion, they would attack the Anichkov Bridge with a vengeance. And once the bridge was in enemy hands, the game would be well and truly up.

'Bring up the reserves,' she snapped to a rather glassy-eyed Jiao Yu.

'We have no reserves, GeneralFemme Dashwood,' he stammered. 'ColonelFemme Trung Trac ordered them to the western part of the city to defend against the ForthRight forces landing there.'

'I gave no such command . . .'

The silent answer she received from Jiao Yu was eloquent: the officerFemmes, aggrieved that command of the army had been given to an outsider, had obviously decided to bypass her and by their disloyalty and disobedience had endangered the whole of the Coven. But this was no time for recrimination. Trixie needed reinforcements to hold the bridge and she needed them fast. 'Send a message to the barracks where the WFA fighters are being held. I want them released and I want them armed.' She began to furiously scribble a message on a page she'd torn from her notebook. 'Have this given to Major Wysochi . . .'

Something made her look up. CommanderNoN Jiao Yu was staring at her as though she was mad. 'That is unthinkable, GeneralFemme Dashwood . . . utterly unthinkable. It is a violation of all HerEtical dogma to have uncastrated nonFemmes fighting alongside Femmes. It would be an endorsement of their MALEvolence. I cannot obey such an order.' He shook his head vehemently to emphasise the point.

A strange calmness descended on Trixie. Like the good commander she was, she didn't see the confusion and the chaos of war, instead she saw with great clarity what needed to be done to salvage the situation. She unclasped her holster.

'CommanderNoN Jiao Yu, I command this army. My orders have been betrayed twice today but, believe me, I will not allow them to be betrayed a third time. If you want the Coven to survive, that bridge must be held, and to do this I need fighters. Thanks to Trung's treachery, the only fighters I have to reinforce the bridge are those belonging to the WFA. So I'm giving you a direct order to free and arm these men and women so that we might save the Coven from the ForthRight.' She stared directly into the NoN's eyes. 'Are you still telling me that you refuse to obey my order?'

The NoN swallowed and looked around the room for support. There was none, every other soldier suddenly very busy doing something that avoided them having to look in Jiao Yu's direction. He glanced nervously at Trixie and then at the pistol she had drawn from her holster. Finally he bowed. 'I will obey.'

From his perch atop the roof Wysochi saw the express rider galloping towards the barracks and knew instinctively what would be the contents of the message the man was carrying.

'Captain, get the fighters together and lined up in ranks on the parade ground ready to march.'

The young captain gawped at Wysochi. 'March where, Major?'

'To war, Captain. The WFA is back in the business of killing UnFunnies.'

It took them half an hour to deploy and another thirty minutes to get to the arsenal where their weapons had been stored, so it was an hour after he had received the message that Wysochi and three thousand of his WFA fighters approached the Anichkov Bridge. Just a single look told him that the situation was desperate. As best he could judge in the confusion, whilst the bridge was still clear of the enemy, the defenders were in danger of being flanked on both sides by StormTroopers who had landed after the Geek Fire had faltered.

'Captain,' he bellowed, 'take one thousand men and secure our right flank and you, Lieutenant, take the same number and secure our left flank.' Wysochi did his best to sound confident but his assessment was that the position was untenable. He could see the ForthRight's armoured steamers already massing on the St Petersburg side of the river ready to force the bridge and it was only a matter of time before the sheer weight of the

SS would overwhelm his small army. But it was equally obvious that if the bridge was lost, there would be little hope of saving Rangoon.

He turned to the knot of Covenite officers standing, looking dazed and confused, a little way from him. 'Who's in command here?'

A small woman dressed in a filthy and tattered boiler suit peeled away and walked unsteadily over to Wysochi. As she got closer, he could see that the arm that hung limply at her left side was badly burnt and her eyes had the glazed expression of someone in shock. This, he knew, would be difficult.

'I am ColonelFemme Trung Nhi, Commander of the Second Covenite Army. And may I ask who has given you – a nonFemme – authority regarding the defence of this bridge?'

'I am Major Feliks Wysochi of the WFA and I and my fighters are here by order of GeneralFemme Dashwood.' Wysochi handed the woman the piece of paper delivered by the express rider.

Trung Nhi read the order. 'This is wholly improper. It is an insult to HerEticalism that an uncastrated nonFemme be given command of Femmes.'

Wysochi felt his temper flare. 'Look, ColonelFemme Trung, in ten minutes about a hundred armoured steamers are going to come trundling over that bridge and unless we get ourselves organised, they ain't gonna stop trundling until they've flattened the whole fucking Coven. So what I want is for you to deploy your fighters—'

'I will not take orders from a nonFemme!' Trung snarled. 'You and your kind are not needed here, Major Wysochi. We in the Coven have struggled long and hard to rid our Sector of the vile, patriarchal contamination you represent, so we do not need your offer of help now.'

'But the UnFunnies are coming.'

'And we will fight them, but we will fight them as free

Femmes, not as docile women eager to sublimate themselves and their identities to beasts such as you.'

A baffled Wysochi led the WFA fighters east from the Anichkov Bridge along the bank of the Volga. He had no alternative, Trung Nhi – the maniac – had threatened to have her fighters fire on the WFA fighters unless they withdrew and that would have just made a difficult situation impossible. Having been told that Trixie had her Command Post on the Hubside of the bridge, he'd decided to march his ragtag army there to get orders, which he hoped would involve skedaddling out of the Coven while they still had a chance to skedaddle. He'd had enough of these lunatic dorks to last a lifetime.

When he finally got to Trixie's command bunker, his welcome wasn't quite what he'd been anticipating. 'Wysochi? What the fuck are you doing here? I gave you an order to defend the bridge.'

As he and his fighters had just spent the last thirty minutes fighting their way through the alleys and backstreets of a burning Rangoon to get to the bunker, Wysochi wasn't in the mood to be given a dressing-down.

'And fuck you too . . . GeneralFemme, ma'am. For your information, that LessBien nutcase Trung Nhi told me and my fighters that we weren't wanted.'

'I put you in command, not her!'

'That order might have been given, but it certainly wasn't obeyed. If I had insisted then the chances are that those mind-dead Amazons would have started firing on my fighters and, much as I'd have loved to have shot the mad bitch, it didn't seem a particularly productive way to go about saving the Coven.'

Scarlet with fury, Trixie turned on CommanderNoN Jiao Yu. 'You knew this would happen, didn't you?'

The fearful NoN took a step back. Wysochi didn't blame him; Trixie in a rage was an intimidating sight. As he saw it, the NoN would be bloody lucky if he got out of the bunker without being shot. Fuck it, *he'd* be lucky to get out of the bunker without being shot.

'I did not *know*, GeneralFemme. I suspected, but I did not know. You must realise that Trung Nhi is a Suffer-O-Gette, one of the most radical of all HerEticals. She hates nonFemmes: it is impossible for her ever to accept orders from one of them.'

For several long moments Trixie stood stock-still, only the tapping of her right foot on the concrete floor signalling her agitation. Finally she spoke and, thankfully, it seemed she understood what the NoN had said. 'Has there been any word from ColonelFemme Trung Nhi?'

'The last message from her was received thirty minutes ago.'

'You have observers . . .'

'They report that armoured steamers have successfully crossed the Anichkov Bridge and that the Second Army is retreating back into Rangoon.'

'And the First Army?'

'ColonelFemme Trung Trac reported that she believed herself to be in danger of being encircled by ForthRight forces to the east and to the west and would be retreating to a defensive line on the border of the Industrial Sector.'

Trixie leant over the large map of the Coven that was spread across the table in the centre of the redoubt. 'If the UnFunnies have taken the bridge, then they have driven a wedge between what's left of the First and the Second Armies. All we can do now is fall back and provide a rearguard to allow as many fighters as possible to escape. We'll form a defensive line around Rangoon's Blood Bank.'

Jiao Yu was provoked into protesting. 'Surely we must counter-attack? We must try to retake the bridge.'

'One of the Confusionist generals I remember reading about,

a chap called Sun Tzu, always taught that in war you should reinforce success and starve failure. And that, CommanderNoN Jiao Yu, is just what we're going to do. There's no way we can recapture the bridge and, now the ForthRight has brought their heavy vehicles across, Rangoon is toast.' She gave the NoN a wry smile. 'I deem my responsibility to Empress Wu fulfilled. I have done my best to command her army in defence of the Coven but I have been betrayed by my officers. Therefore I feel free to pursue the war against the ForthRight in any way I see fit.'

Part Five
The Séance and the Rise of Duke William

Created by Rising Nobel, Most Divine Couturier to the House of Worth, as seen in In Pure Modes Un Vogue Vogues Monthly, Summer 1003

The fashions of Noir Villian Men are designed to display the perfection and symmetry of their bodies (as described by Father Eugene Sandow) whilst Noir Villian woeMen are clad in a manner reflective of their obedience and subordination to Men and their espousal of the creed of subMISSiveness.

26

The JAD
The Demi-Monde: 41st Day of Summer, 1005

When Shaka Zulu demanded, as a condition for his agreeing to the establishment of a nuJu homeland on the territory of NoirVille, that a wall be built sealing the JAD from the rest of the Demi-Monde, this met with no objection from the nuJu negotiators. And the reason for this was simple: the nuJus did not regard the wall as something designed to seal them *in* but rather as a device to keep the rest of the Demi-Monde *out*. Whilst Demi-Mondians have oft complained of nuJu arrogance and aloofness, they have never appreciated *why* the nuJus adopted such an attitude. The simple truth is that the nuJus wished to hold themselves apart from the rest of the peoples of the Demi-Monde to prevent their race being infected by interbreeding with what they call the Dark Charismatics, the mongrel breed of Humans and Grigori. To preserve this racial purity, nuJus scorned any who married outside their tribe, because outside the tribe they knew Demi-Mondians had become contaminated. This is the reason why nuJus employ matchmakers to bring nuJu boys and girls together, this to ensure that neither of the partners shows signs of possession, of being in thrall to Dark Charistmatics.

History of the JAD: Rabbi Schmuel Gelbfisz,
JAD Journals and Books

As hotels went, the Hotel Copasetic was right down there with the worst of them. Vanka, in his time wandering around the Demi-Monde, had stayed in some real fleapits but never, ever, anything to compare with the Copasetic. The room he was occupying was despicably shabby, the food the restaurant served poisonous and the staff incorrigibly rude and inefficient. The only decent conversation he'd had since he'd come to the JAD had been with the tailor Josephine Baker had sent to equip him with a suitably JADdy wardrobe.

Boredom had provoked him to read everything there was to read in the hotel, to the extent that he was now fully conversant with every one of the ingredients of Abercrombie's Amazing Macassar Oil and could recite – word-perfectly – Mrs Beeton's flatulence-inducing recipe for *brioche pain perdu*. Indeed, his desperation for mental stimulation had been such that he had even tried to engage the receptionist in conversation, an exercise he abandoned when he had realised his efforts were being misconstrued and the woman had begun winking at him with real purpose.

Having been holed up in the place for forty days and forty nights, Vanka knew he was on the brink of going stir crazy but the note he had received from Josephine Baker delivered courtesy of the tailor had been very firm on the matter: under no circumstances was he to leave the hotel until he received word from the Code Noir that the coast was clear. So he'd sat in his room and waited ... and waited ... and waited. He'd had nothing to do except eat and sleep ... although he had tried to do as little of the latter as was humanly possible. Vanka hated sleeping. When he slept he was visited by the Dream, and though when he woke he couldn't for the life of him remember what it was about, he was left so wrung out and upset that he knew it hadn't been a pleasant experience. Every night he was visited by the Dream and every morning he woke tired, confused and very troubled.

The upshot was that Vanka came down to breakfast that morning exhausted. Not that the prospect of breakfast did anything to raise his spirits: as the broken-down old waiter ladled a great mound of very obnoxious-looking *matzo brei* onto his plate, Vanka found himself fantasising about bacon and sausages. He pushed the plate to one side and contented himself with munching absent-mindedly on a stale bagel, wondering as he chewed when – *if* – he'd ever get out of the JAD. He wished Fate would come to his rescue.

It did.

'Excuse me, younk man.'

Vanka looked up to see an old man – seventy years old, if he was a day – standing at the side of his table, with a hand outstretched in his direction. He was a tall man, dressed in a well-worn black suit with a kippah atop his bald head, and this, together with his thick accent, proclaimed him to be a nuJu. '*Gut morgen.* I am Rabbi Schmuel Gelbfisz,' the man announced, 'unt I am delighted to meet mit you, Mr ...'

'Jim Tyler.' Vanka took the proffered hand and shook it carefully. It was like grasping a sheath of brittle twigs. 'How can I help you, Rabbi Gelbfisz?'

The man waved the bony hand. 'You zee, Mr Jim Tyler, zhat ve are zhe only two guests occupying zhe whole of zhis enormous unt somewhat dilapidated dining room.'

Vanka nodded, and then raised a 'so what?' eyebrow.

'Vell ... it zeems to me zhat it is zhe height of absurdity zhat I should zit over zhere' – again the hand was waved, though this time in the direction of the empty tables lining the far wall of the dining room – 'unt zhat you should zit over here. *Feh!* Is it not ridiculous zhat ve should continue to ignore one anozzer? Fate has placed us in each ozzher's company unt I am loath to spurn zhe overtures of such a vilful deity. Perhaps, zherefore, you vould permit me to join you?'

'Well, actually—' Vanka began, but before he could formulate a polite demurral, the man was making himself comfortable in the chair across the table from his.

'Gut. I am alvays delighted to make new acquaintances, especially zhose, like you, who are newcomers to zhe JAD.' The man gave a beaming smile: old he might be, but he was an arresting individual who must, Vanka decided, have been a dog for the ladies when he was young.

Vanka bowed to the inevitable and prompted the conversation forward. 'You say I'm a newcomer to the JAD, Rabbi Gelbfisz: am I that easy to spot?'

'Jah, of course. You sport zhe typical expression of a first-time visitor to zhe JAD, zhat cocktail of bemusement unt incredulity I call zhe "JAD look" which is similar to zhat vorn by a man who has just taken a cucumber up zhe *keister*.'

Despite himself – the last thing he wanted to do was to encourage this strange man – Vanka laughed, finding himself intrigued by the old rabbi with the pixie eyes. 'Do all newcomers have this "JAD look"?'

The rabbi helped himself to a spoonful of Vanka's abandoned breakfast. 'Jah, every von of zhem ... especially zhose zadniks from NoirVille mit a penchant for communing mit vegetables.'

Vanka smiled. 'I'm not surprised. The JAD isn't anything like I imagined. It's *very* different where I come from.'

'*A brokh.* I often zay how remarkable it is zhat zhe JAD unt zhe rest ov zhe Demi-Monde could have deviated zo far, zo quickly.' The rabbi sat silent for a moment as he munched suspiciously on the *matzo brei*. 'Zhe JAD is an anthropologist's vet dream, is it not? How vonderful to be able to study zhe manner in vhich a population, shunned unt isolated as ve nuJus have been, can develop in such strange unt different vays. It is proof zhat evolution is alive unt vell.' He took a sip of his coffee, eyeing Vanka as he did so. 'Perhaps zhat is vot you are, Mr Tyler, an anthropologist?'

With a panache honed by practice, Vanka trotted out his cover story. 'No, I'm a writer. I've been commissioned to do a book about the music that has grown up in the JAD since its inception. I'm especially interested in the JAD's own brand of dance music, the stuff called reBop.'

Rabbi Gelbfisz chuckled as he poured a life-threatening amount of sugar into his coffee. 'Azoy? Your investigations must be at a very early stage, Mr Tyler. ReBop is a style of music zhat has not been popular mit nuJus for several years now. Zhe younk JADniks have come to embrace vot zhey call klezmerJad.'

'You seem to know an awful lot about it.'

A snort of derision. 'I have not alvays been old, Mr Tyler. Vonce, long before I vos ejected from my homeland by zhose anti-nuJu bastards who masquerade as UnFunnies, I vos' – he gave Vanka a wink – 'in zhe idiom of zhe day, slack, slim unt sent. I played trumpet . . . jah, trumpet, in a vigged-out combo called, unt here, Mr Tyler, you must remember I vos *very* younk, zhe Zink Zonk Zombies.' Rabbi Gelbfisz smirked at the recollection. 'Jah, it is true, vonce zhis old *alter cocker* vos pretty good at blowing on a horn . . . unt at having his horn blown.' He gave a mischievous little giggle before continuing. 'Zhey vere interesting times, zhough vhen I think about vot I used to vear – zoot suits in pastel colours, mit drape jackets unt peg-leg trousers, vide-brimmed fedoras – I am acutely embarrassed. I must have looked a real *schloomp*.'

Rabbi Gelbfisz's gaze seemed to harden for a moment. 'Zo, who do you write for, Mr Tyler? Your accent is strange. Your Anglo is too gut for you to be a native speaker.'

Careful, thought Vanka, *this guy's a lot sharper than he would like you to believe.*

'Oh, I'm an Anglo, through and through,' Vanka lied. 'I was born in the Rookeries. And as for who I write for: I'm freelance,

I just hunt down stories and then sell them to the highest bidder.'

'I myself come from Rodina. I escaped from Varsaw during zhe Troubles.'

'You were very sensible.'

'Jah. I have vatched zhe genocidal efforts of zhe UnFunnies regarding my home district mit much interest. Vhen zhat *momzer* Heydrich decided to racially unt religiously homogenise zhe ForthRight, I knew it vos time to take a runavay powder.'

'It must have been terrible.'

'*Azoy*. It vos, Mr Tyler, it vos. Unt zhe biggest regret I have is zhat zhough I anticipated zhe betrayal of zhe nuJus by Heydrich, I failed to convince zhe rest of my family to accompany me into exile. Even my cousin Louie – unt believe me, Louie ain't no *schlemiel* – told me that I could include him out. But zhe good thing vos zhat zhey got lucky unt headed for zhe Great Beyond vhen zhe Lady IMmanual parted zhe Boundary Layer. Jah, vot zhat girl did in Varsaw vos marvellous . . . a real miracle. She saved three million of my people unt zhat ain't *bobkes*; it's three million people who are alive today because of vot zhat girl did. Us nuJus owe her big time.'

It took Vanka a moment to disentangle what the rabbi was saying, and when he did, he wasn't happy being reminded about what Ella had been . . . and what she had become.

'Which is vhy, Vanka Maykov, ve nuJus had to think long unt hard before ve let you come here to zhe JAD.'

At the admission that this old nuJu knew his real name a frisson of fear trickled down Vanka's spine. He took a quick look around to check his escape route and, as he suspected it would be, the restaurant's exit was now guarded by two big, burly men.

Fuck.

*

'You know who I am?'

'Of course. You should dig, Vanka Maykov, zhat ve nuJus know everything zhat goes down in zhe JAD . . . everything.'

'Then why—?'

'*Zorg zich nit.* Don't worry about it, I ain't gonna shop you to zhe HimPeril. I have come to meet mit zhe famous Vanka Maykov unt to see for myself if he is a *mensch* – a stand-up guy – or a *klutz*. Unt I am pleased to tell you, Vanka Maykov, zhat you are okay, zhat you're vot ve nuJus call a *gooteh neshumen* – a good soul.'

'Why is that so important?'

'Because zhese are dangerous times, Vanka Maykov, unt zhe dark clouds gather. Zhe Beast is abroad unt vhile ve nuJus don't vant to become involved mit sorting out zhe mess you gentiles have made of things, ve know ve must help zhe forces of light. Okay, it's a begrudging help but vhen a people have spent a thousand years being beaten like dogs, you can understand zhat zhose dogs are reluctant to come to zhe defence ov zhe vons doing zhe beating. But needs must vhen Loki drives unt by our reckoning zoon, because of zhe interference of Doge IMmanual, zhe whole of zhe Demi-Monde vill be engulfed in war . . . zhe JAD included.'

'I saw the preparations you were making to resist an invasion when I came to the hotel.'

'Ov course, war vill come, on zhis you may be sure. How can it be ozzervise mit so many hotheads unt racists amongst both zhe Shades unt zhe nuJus?'

'Why should it come to fighting? I thought the Shades and the nuJus had reached a modus vivendi: you got your HomeLand and the Shades got the blood trade. Wasn't that what the MANdate said, the one signed with Shaka Zulu?'

'Jah. But zhere are zhose in NoirVille, like zhat *draykop* Pobedonostsev, who loathe us mit a passion unt who vill not rest until ve have been eradicated. Unt, of course, zhere are nuJus who make zhe claim zhat *all* of NoirVille should be ours unt zhat all zhe Shades should be kicked out of zhe Sector. Zo you zee, Vanka Maykov, zhat compromise is difficult, especially now it zeems zhat Doge IMmanual is intent on breaking our monopoly of Aqua Benedicta. Jah, war comes. How can it be ozzervise vehn zhe Beast valks zhe Demi-Monde?'

'And who do you regard as the Beast?'

'Doge IMmanual, of course. Zhe vay ve nuJus see it, zhe girl who saved our people in Varsaw ain't zhe same girl who's just crowned herself Doge in Venice unt has hooked up mit zhat *shtik drek* Shaka. Like I say, our cryptos tell us zhat Doge IMmanual has zhe secrets ov Aqua Benedicta unt zhat she is going to disclose zhese to Shaka Zulu in exchange for his support in conquering zhe Demi-Monde. Vot zhis tells us zhat she ain't zhe Messiah ... she's zhe Beast. Unt I guess even a greener like you can dig zhat ve in the JAD ain't really enchanted about zhe prospect of Shaka's Himpis making a surprise visit. *Feh!* Zhe cleaning ... zhe dusting. Unt zhat is vhy ve had to think zo carefully about letting you come to zhe JAD, Vanka Maykov. Harbouring you vill piss off Doge IMmanual unt zhat ain't a healthy thing to do.'

Vanka gave a mournful shake of his head. 'And the worst thing about this is I don't know why she hates me so much.'

'*Oy vay!* Such bad luck to believe you are hated mitout reason. But zhere *is* a reason: she hates you because you are zhe man mit zhe power to defeat her.'

'Me?'

'Jah, you. You are more zhan you appear, Vanka Maykov ... much more.' Gelbfisz pushed a piece of paper across the breakfast table. 'If you go to zhis club tonight, zomebody will be waiting for you. Listen to zhat somebody slowly unt zhey vill tell you how Doge IMmanual might be defeated. But understand zhis: ve nuJus don't want Doge IMmanual harmed; ve want her *dis*armed. Vhen she vos vot she vos before she is vot she is, she did us nuJus a big favour. Unt now it is payback time. You dig?'

'Yeah . . . disarmed, and that's exactly what I want.'

'Gut. But be careful, Vanka Maykov. Zhe HimPeril are looking for you, zo keep your eyes peeled.'

Rabbi Gelbfisz drained his cup of coffee, then checked his watch.

'*Gants goot.* Unfortunately, Vanka Maykov, now I have to go attend zhe Sin-All-Gone; today I am reading from Epistle Sixty-Six of zhe Book of Profits, zhe vun dealing mit zhe coming of zhe Messiah. It has been most interesting talking mit you, unt perhaps we vill meet again. Fate vill decide.' He held out his hand and the pair of them shook. 'And as you are feigning an interest in jad music, Vanka Maykov, I should leave you in zhe style of my youth.' He smiled again, the twinkle back in his eyes. 'Zo, Vanka Maykov, I plant you now unt dig you later.'

27

Venice
The Demi-Monde: 41st Day of Summer, 1005

The teachings of HimPerialism are enshrined in the HIM Book, the most sacred book in the NoirVillian religious corpus, which contains, according to HimPerial theologians, the inerrant and infallible Word of ABBA. The text of the HIM Book was translated by the great mage and scholar Cab Calloway in 505 AC from original Pre-Folk manuscripts which were unfortunately destroyed during the Great War of 512.

An Idiot's Guide to ManHood: Selim the Grim, HimPerial
Instructional Leaflets

Billy fucking loathed being cooped up in the Palace. He liked it when he and his buddies went out on the town, raising hell. Okay, so Ella had told him he had to stay confined within the Palace 'for his own safety', but he hadn't and that was why he had been summoned to an audience with his sister.

He hated these sessions. Not only was Ella totally fucking crackers – her believing that she was the reincarnation of this Lilith item and had been born in Atlantis proved that – but she had also begun to look at him in an odd way, like she was sizing him up for a coffin or something.

Really fucking freaky.

And today, when he had been called to her chambers, she

seemed intent on not just looking at him sideways but talking to him sideways.

'I have received word from the captain of the Signori di Notte detachment assigned to protect you that your carousing has become excessive. Last night, it seems, you were involved in a brawl over a woman.'

Billy fidgeted just like he had done when he'd been four years old and Dad – the drunk bastard – had caught him torturing that cat. He hated being told off. Fuck it, he wasn't a kid any more. And the truth was, he liked kicking up a little dust with his new cru, knowing that it didn't matter what they did or who they hurt. Everything in the Demi-Monde was just make-believe and everyone living in it – 'cept him and Sis – was only a fucking Dupe.

Fuck 'em.

'I cannot allow you to endanger yourself, Billy.'

'Ah, c'mon Sis, what are yo', my mother? Yo' treatin' me like some house nigga or such. I gotta get busy otherwise I'm gonna blow a fuse.'

'I'm not your mother, Billy, just someone who cares about you. You must understand that you have an important role to play in my achieving mastery of the Demi-Monde – and the worlds beyond – more important than you could possibly realise.'

Yeah, yeah, yeah.

'So it's important that no harm comes to you; that you are kept safe. I want you to promise that there will be no more of these stupid escapades.'

Yadda, yadda, yadda.

'Sis . . .' Billy began and then stopped, not quite sure how to proceed. He didn't like how cold her eyes had become and anyway it was fucking difficult to know what to say to your sister when she was lying on a couch looking too slinky by half. He had to look away.

He took a deep breath before replying. Selim had told him to stay frosty, that he wouldn't have to put up with this shit for much longer.

'Okay, Sis, I'll stay home from now on.'

Like fuck.

During the couple of weeks Billy had been in Venice he'd fallen in with a group of other young nobles who had a passion for wine, women and debauchery that was almost as fierce as his, and it was to these he turned that night. And such was the skill of this gang of upper-class hooligans that despite the guards Ella had set to watch him, they still managed to smuggle him out of the Palace. Fuck what he'd promised her: without a little occasional R & R in no time flat he'd be as nuts as she was.

They had a great night, so much so that it wasn't until the early hours – after five hours of heavy drinking – that the four of them – Billy, Bajamonte, Marco and Badoero – quit the brothel and staggered back in the direction of the Palace singing and shouting and on the lookout for more devilment as they went. They found it as they were crossing the Piazza San Marco.

'Hey, will yo' stalk this guy,' screamed Billy as he pointed to a well-dressed, middle-aged man who was walking towards them with a young woman on his arm. Billy manoeuvred himself in front of the man, blocking his progress. 'Yo, man, where d'ya think you're going?'

'I am going home, sir, and I would be obliged if you would step aside.'

The Dupe's haughty attitude got right up Billy's ass. 'Back da fuck up, bro. Yo' coming at me or something? All I'm askin' is if yo's going home to fuck this sweet piece of pie?' He waved a hand towards the girl, then used it to flick the man's top hat from his head. As it landed on the cobbles, Bajamonte trod on it.

The old guy eyed the four boys nervously. 'Please ... sir ... your language ... this is my daughter.'

Billy smirked and stretched out a hand to run his fingers down the girl's cheek. She flinched back in disgust but not before PINC had told Billy that the girl was Isabella, daughter of Duke Pietro Gradenigo, and a real high-class piece of action. 'Yo' daughter? Nah, this ain't yo' daughter, I think this is yo' whore,' and with that he made another lunge for the girl.

Now Duke Gradenigo might have been a lot older than Billy and he might have been a little out of shape, but the big advantage he had was that he wasn't drunk. He defended his daughter by giving Billy a shove on his shoulder that sent him tumbling into the gutter. That was when things started to get a whole lot uglier.

Drunk or not, Billy didn't like being dumped on his ass by some old guy and he sure as hell didn't like it when his buddies started to laugh at him. Sour-faced, he levered himself – with some considerable difficulty – back up to his feet and slowly drew his knuckleduster from his pocket.

Knuckledusters were Billy's weapons of choice in the Real World. He liked the sound they made when he drove them into a face, liked hearing bones crunch, liked seeing skin split and blood flow, liked it when the poor fuck he was hitting had to spit out teeth and blood and snot. He felt connected when he used a knuckleduster and that was why one of the first things he'd done when he'd arrived in the Demi-Monde was to have one made. It was a beaut too: two pounds of brass studded with half-inch steel spikes.

'Right, you fucking Dupe, you're gonna pay for that. You know who I am? I'm Duke William, brother of the Doge, and nobody messes with me. I'm gonna smash your fucking eyes out.'

'You would not dare! I am Duke Pietro Gradenigo, a member of the Council of Ten—'

A savage blow to his right cheek shut the Duke up. Billy followed it up with a punch to his midriff. With a *woof* the Duke doubled over just in time to take a second shot to the side of the head which laid him out cold across the cobbles. Billy didn't hesitate: he gave the man four good kicks.

'No!' screamed the girl and like a man roused from a dream, Billy stopped stomping on her father and turned his attention to her.

'Strip her,' he growled and there was something in his look that persuaded his three friends to disregard her father's rank and do just what Billy told them to do.

The girl put up one hell of a fight, clawing and kicking at the men as they tore at her clothes, and it was this that saved her. Her screaming and shouting roused the tenants of the rooms bordering the piazza, the most truculent of whom was an old woman who had the room directly above the spot where the struggle was taking place.

Her window crashed open. 'What's going on?' she yelled. 'Leave that poor girl alone.'

'Go to bed,' Billy hollered back. 'Ain't nothing to do with yo'. This is the Doge's work.'

'Loki's work more like!' and with a strength that belied her advanced years the woman pushed at one of the heavy stone gargoyles that decorated her balcony, sending it crashing to the ground fifty feet below. En route it struck Bajamonte Tiepolo on the head, killing him instantly. The sight of Bajamonte lying dead on the cobbles and the sound of police whistles was enough to persuade Marco and Badoero to take to their heels. Billy had no option but to stagger along in their wake.

'Explain!' the Doge shouted as she swept into the library where de Sade was working.

De Sade stood up from his desk and bowed, unnerved by the

fury that inflected the Doge's voice. 'It seems your brother and three of his friends went carousing last night and during the course of the evening they beat Duke Pietro Gradenigo to within an inch of his life and attempted to rape his daughter. They were only persuaded to desist when a neighbour' – here de Sade checked his notes – 'a Lady Lucia Rossi, tipped a large stone carving onto the head of Count Bajamonte Tiepolo, killing him outright.'

'Damn.'

The Doge began to pace rapidly backwards and forwards across the room, wringing her hands as she went. De Sade had never seen her as vexed as this. He'd known she would be angry about what her fool of a brother had done and that was why he'd decided to delay bringing her the bad news until the morning. Somehow, though, she had found out earlier.

'Is Duke William all right?'

Now *that* was a surprising question. The political implications of her stupid, vicious knucklehead of a brother nearly killing a member of the Council of Ten were enormous, but here she was fretting about the bastard's health. He would never have thought that someone as cold and hard-nosed as Doge IMmanual would have cared a damn for anyone who had embarrassed her as her brother had done.

'Yes, he is unharmed. I understand he is now asleep in his room. He was very drunk, my Doge. If I might be so bold, we must think of how to manage this unfortunate affair. It might be better to send your brother into exile: the family of Duke Gradenigo are baying for his head ... they want revenge.'

'No. He will remain here in the Palace, there will be no exile and there will be no punishment.' She stopped her pacing and turned to de Sade. 'I thought, First Prelate, that I had given you express instructions that Duke William was to be guarded at all times, that these escapades of his were to cease.'

'That is so, my Doge, but unfortunately your brother is disinclined to be guarded. He likes to go on what he calls "Dupe hunts", and to do this he uses all manner of contrivances and disguises to evade those I have set to watch him. Your brother is a very cunning individual.'

The Doge's eyes sparkled in anger and for a moment de Sade was very afraid. He had seen her when she had fought the Grigori called Semiazaz and when she had performed in the Ceremony of the Leaping. There was no denying that the Doge IMmanual was different from other Demi-Mondians just as there was no denying that if she wished, she could snap his neck like a twig.

Thankfully, she seemed to get a grip on her emotions. 'Very well, I suppose it is unfair to blame you for Duke William's truancy. He's spent his life avoiding school, avoiding work, avoiding the police and avoiding responsibility. All he likes doing is fighting, fucking and getting high. But it is essential that he is kept safe . . . *essential*.'

With a loud, despairing sigh the girl seated herself on a couch. 'Come, de Sade, sit next to me. I am in need of your advice.'

De Sade swallowed. In the weeks since he had hitched his wagon to the star that was Doge IMmanual he had spent many hours regretting that decision. There was something wrong about the girl, something decidedly . . . frigid. Oh, she took pleasure in matters of the flesh – he had the scratches on his back to prove it – but it was as though her soul was dead. But now the die was cast, so with a smile he sat down beside the girl.

'It is important in the days to come that I have standing by my side a man I can trust implicitly, who will not baulk when I do the things I must do to ensure the Lilithi rise again.' She laughed. 'You see, First Prelate, how far I trust you: other than

Prince William, you are the only one who knows that I am Lilith come again and that soon the Lilithi will be reborn. And in this matter the safe keeping of Duke William is vital.'

De Sade shuffled nervously as the girl unbuttoned his jacket, delved a hand inside and began to caress his chest. 'May I enquire why, my Doge?' he asked in a strangled voice.

'You understand that Duke William is a Dark Charismatic, do you not?'

Only with the greatest difficulty did de Sade prevent himself from jumping.

'I had suspected as much, my Doge, he has an almost insatiable appetite for inflicting pain.'

'Yes, a lack of empathy and an addiction to cruelty are the defining characteristics of all Dark Charismatics but then you would know that, wouldn't you, de Sade, being one yourself?' She laughed. 'Oh, Billy isn't a particularly *powerful* Dark Charismatic – he's too stupid to be that – but he most certainly is one of that foul breed.'

This candour caused de Sade's eyebrows to arch in surprise: the girl's tone was contemptuous. It was as though she hated her brother.

'In my world he'd be classified as a γ Class Singularity . . . a low-level psychopath. All γ-Class Singularities are the same, they revel in close-up violence and torture. They like getting their hands bloodied and hearing the screams of their victims as they torment them.'

'I understand that you regard Dark Charismatics as your enemy, my Doge, and this being the case I am at a loss—'

'As to why I am so eager Prince William be protected?'

'Indeed, my Doge.'

'On Lammas Eve we will conduct the Ceremony of Awakening, when the latent powers of my priestesses will be revived. There is one thing vital if these powers are to be brought into bloom.'

'And that is, my Doge?'

'Blood,' she said simply as her hand wandered from his chest and snaked lower.

'Why blood?' he asked as calmly as he was able, distinctly distracted by the way she had begun to unpick the buttons tethering his trousers.

'In the Real World all the most powerful rituals of the Lilithi necessitated the priestesses drinking blood ... the making of human sacrifices.'

'Human sacrifices?' De Sade didn't like the squeak that seemed to have inflected his voice.

'Yes. The Lilithi are irrevocably associated with blood. Originally we believed that blood was the divine fluid, the means by which our race memories could be passed from one generation to the next, that blood was the vehicle for the inheritance of that knowledge. Of course, as our understanding of the mechanics of heredity grew, so we came to appreciate that blood's role in the inheritance of familial traits is trivial, but by then its symbolism was deeply ingrained in our rites.'

The Doge pushed her hand inside de Sade's now open trousers, making it difficult for him to concentrate. Manfully – hah! – he tried to keep the burgeoning excitement out of his voice. 'But what has this to do with Prince William?'

'The most powerful blood that can be used in these ceremonies is that of a Dark Charismatic. And Billy being my twin makes his blood doubly potent. Therefore, Billy must be sacrificed so that the Lilithi may rise again. And that is why you must find a way of keeping him safe and docile until Lammas Eve. I am relying on you, de Sade, and if you succeed . . .' She leant back on the couch, offering herself to the man.

Grand Vizier Selim the Grim had to turn away from the spyhole, disgusted as he was by the sight of a Man coupling with a woeMan. It was a despicable, unnatural act which turned his stomach. But then, this was Lilith herself who he was spying on, and she was the woeMan responsible for all the evil in the world.

Standing there in the gloom of the secret passage, Selim took a moment to settle himself, to still the abhorrence he felt that his beloved NoirVille had seen fit to align itself with a city-state ruled by a woeMan such as this ... a woeMan so addicted to the pleasures of the flesh as to be careless of the sacred vows of subMISSiveness.

But ...

But the Grand Mufti had determined that Duke William was the Messiah, and Selim had been ordered by His HimPerial Majesty Shaka Zulu to protect and keep the boy safe until the time was right for him to usurp his sister. Once the secret of Aqua Benedicta was theirs then Doge IMmanual would be of no further use to them ... then the True Messiah, Duke William, would be ordained as ABBA made SAE ... then Doge IMmanual could be disposed of.

Selim felt his racing body-clock slow and the queasiness he had felt at being obliged to witness such an obscene act subside. He was pleased by his restraint: he had made it a rule never to allow the more choleric emotions to control his actions and tonight Doge IMmanual had demonstrated the value of such forbearance.

Of course, the Doge being a woeMan made her all the more prone to emotional outbursts and it had taken only a whisper in her ear from one of the servants who had accepted Selim's coin to alert her to the events concerning her brother. It had been her anger at the news that had driven her from her room to search for de Sade, and it had been her anger that had persuaded her to confront him in the library where he had been working on his papers. And whilst the more private chambers of the Palace had been carefully checked for spyholes, the library had not.

Selim had listened intently to what the Doge said, his attention particularly piqued when she had spoken of the importance to the Ceremony of Awakening of using Duke William's blood. That the same blood ran in the Doge – Duke William's twin – opened up many intriguing possibilities.

28

The JAD
The Demi-Monde: 41st Day of Summer, 1005

In Confusionist philosophy the goal of all those who follow the Divine Way is the attaining of ABBAsoluteness, the state of being united – Body, Mind and Soul – with ABBA. This concept is, however, found in other religions of the Demi-Monde, where it is referred to as the Nothingness, that ineffable state which exists between the material and the spiritual worlds and which all those wishing to commune with ABBA must visit. Those who seek to travel to the Nothingness in order to attain ABBAsoluteness must first ensure the purity of their Solidified Astral Ether, this allowing the Holy Ghost to bring them to uncorrupted communion with ABBA.

Religions of the Demi-Monde: Otto Weininger,
University of Berlin Publications

It was approaching midnight when the pedicab Vanka had hired to take him to 'Club Tzatske' – the name of the rendezvous on the slip of paper Rabbi Gelbfisz had handed him – deposited him at the end of a tight cobblestone alley. Though the rain had eased, the gutters were still awash and the cobbles slick and shiny, the alley stretching out like a ribbon of black liquorice, at the end of which, perhaps fifty yards from where he was standing, Vanka saw a flickering blue light illuminating a sign that read 'Club Tzatske'.

The Tzatske looked to be a real slaughterhouse, so much so that Vanka hesitated before surrendering the relative safety of the main road for the uncertainty of the gloomy alleyway. But as the alternative was to go back to his shitty little hotel room and stay there for the rest of his natural, he pulled up the collar of his coat, settled his top hat hard down on his head and, making himself look as big as he could, walked to the club.

Miraculously, he wasn't ambushed by rippers en route.

The entrance to the club was bracketed by a couple of over-muscled toughs in tight suits, their bowler hats pulled over their eyes and cigarettes smoking between their lips.

'Yous a *petit blanc* ... a NoirVillian whitey?' asked the taller of the two doormen without taking the cigarette out of his mouth.

Vanka nodded.

'Yous looking for a gut time?'

'Yeah, I'm looking to hear some jad.'

'Good place zhis, man. Best jad in zhe whole ov zhe JAD. Beaucoup de hot.' He winked at Vanka, who was fast becoming fed up with this particular nuJu mannerism. 'You come to see JoJo?'

'JoJo?'

The boy tapped a nicotine-stained finger against a poster that showed a semi-naked girl doing peculiar things with a trumpet. That she was wearing a mask, Vanka put down to an attempt to spare her family some deep embarrassment and to avoid legal action from the manufacturers of the trumpet. 'JoJo ... zhe best jad singer unt zhe best pair of tits in zhe ...'

'... whole of the JAD?' suggested Vanka. 'Okay, I'd like to hear JoJo.'

'Five guineas.' The boy held out his hand and with great reluc-

tance Vanka filled it with money; the JAD was getting to be a
very expensive place. The boy examined the coins carefully
then nodded his approval. 'Okay. You vont drugs? Cocaine,
laudanum, Dizzi?'

'No.'

'Yous *sure*?' The boy seemed genuinely surprised.

'Yeah.'

The boy tossed Vanka a dismissive glare, then nodded him
through the club's doors, signalling him to use the dimly lit
stairway beyond. This Vanka did, edging slowly up the stairs,
moving carefully so as not to trip on the cracked linoleum
covering the steps. It was difficult in the rancid gloom to see
where he was going, so he simply followed the sound of the
music drifting towards him.

He reached the top of the stairs then – arms outstretched
like a blind man – edged along a dark and narrow corridor
until he reached a door. This he pushed open only to find the
Tzatske pushing back, hitting him with a cacophony of noise
and smoke that made him flinch away in disgust. Taking a deep
breath, he shoved his way inside, hardly able to see where he
was going, blinded and confused by the gloom, the tightly
packed people and the dense cigarette smoke. How Gelbfisz's
agent was meant to find him in this bedlam he had no idea.

Like the rest of the JAD, the club had seen better days: the
peeling paintwork and cracked lampshades attested to that, but
what Vanka found most unsettling were the murals dotted
around the place, murals that lampooned Shaka as a rampant
zadnik in congress with various luminaries of the HimPerialist
movement.

One mural was particularly upsetting. It showed Ella – in her
guise of Doge IMmanual – getting it on with Shaka. It was quite
a good representation of her too, and for a moment Vanka felt
all the anguish of his lost love come flooding back.

Pushing these doleful thoughts to the back of his mind, he pulled at the collar of his shirt and loosened his cravat. It was no wonder the doorman had said the Tzatske played hot jad, the heat in the club was intense and although he had only been there for a few moments, sweat was already sliding down his cheeks and he could feel his shirt sticking to his back. Now all he wanted was to get to the bar and treat himself to a long, cold beer.

He rounded a corner and found himself standing at the lip of a balcony that swept around the building in a huge semi-circle. Looking down through the thick swirls of smoke, he saw, twenty feet or so below him, a girl fronting a jad trio, crooning a type of music Vanka had never heard before. This, he assumed, was Gelbfisz's klezmerJad. Then, just for a moment, the smoke clouds parted to reveal JoJo, or, as Vanka knew her better, Josephine Baker.

Vanka had to do a double take, but it was Josie all right: even disguised beneath a scarlet-coloured wig and her face hidden behind a mask, there was no mistaking her. He'd know that body anywhere and there was a lot of that body on display: the diaphanous material of her loose top served only to colour her breasts rather than to hide them, and her black skirt, made from woven strips of rubber, was short, tight and presented her superb legs wonderfully well.

Pummelled and pounded by the music, entranced by how Josie sang and danced, dizzy from heat and smoke, Vanka descended the winding staircase that led to the dance floor. There, through the haze, he saw a waiter gesturing to him and he automatically steered towards the man.

'Got a spare booth over by zhe wall. Best booth in zhe whole of zhe JAD. It'll cost you five guineas.'

What alternative do I have?

Vanka pressed the coins into the waiter's hand and followed him as he shimmied his way between the sardined tables to the booth.

'Zafer here,' said the waiter, gesturing to the shadowed alcove. 'All zhe pimps sit on zhe side ov zhe room vhere you vere standing. It's raised up a bit; zhey can keep an eye on zheir *putani* from zhere.'

Vanka sat down just in time to hear Josie make an announcement that the band was taking a fifteen-minute break, and to warm applause, she and her musicians trooped off stage. Vanka ordered a beer, and as the waiter served it the boy whispered into his ear. 'You wanna meet JoJo?'

'Nah, I'm waiting for somebody.'

The waiter leant closer so there was no chance of his being heard by any of the customers sitting nearby. 'Yeah, I know, unt zhat somebody's JoJo. You want zhat I bring her over?'

Vanka smiled. So Josie was Gelbfisz's agent. 'Yeah, that would be good.'

The waiter oozed over to Josie, who pantomimed giving Vanka the once-over, patted a hand against her bobbed wig and then, with a careless aside to one of her friends, sashayed across to his table. When she arrived at Vanka's booth, the pair of them spent a few seconds silently assessing one another, Josie examining Vanka as though she'd never met him before and Vanka desperately trying to avoid his gaze drifting towards the girl's breasts which were so obviously displayed under her transparent top.

With a casual elegance Josie held out a long slim hand and said in a loud voice, 'Greetings, gate, I hear you're looking to palpitate. Jakob sayeth you're interested in pumping pelvises with yours truly.' She gave Vanka a wink to encourage him to join in the play-acting.

Vanka took the hand and shook it . . . and then found the disturbing Josie holding on to it for a beat or two longer than was strictly necessary. The girl was an incorrigible flirt. 'That's right. My name's Jim Tyler. Would you care to join me for a drink?' Josie gave an indifferent shrug and then oiled down into the proffered seat.

Once settled, she edged closer to Vanka, pushing her mouth – and other parts of her body – closer to him. It was very distracting. 'Good to see you, Vanka,' she whispered. 'How you doing?'

'Not bad,' Vanka lied. 'What's with the JoJo alias?'

'It's my reBop name. I use it when I'm beached between gigs: it helps keep creditors off my tail.' She waved to the waiter, who seemed to know from experience what Josie's preference was; the glass of gin and gore materialised almost immediately. She lifted her glass in salute. 'Cheers, Vanka. I'm glad to see you're still in one piece. I was beginning to worry. Gotta tell you, you're one warm number these days, those cats from the HimPeril been really shaking the foliage trying to find out where you're hanging. You better keep a low profile or for you it's endsville. You dig?'

'I dig,' and he took a nervous look around at the Tzatske's clientele. For someone who was advising him to stay under-cover Josie had a peculiar idea about places to rendezvous.

She must have understood his concern. 'Don't worry, Vanka, the Tzatske's a cool place. It's under the protection of Schmuel Gelbfisz who's got the biggest kahunas in the JAD.'

'Yeah, I've met him. He seemed like a good guy.'

'He is. Schmuel's a hepcat who's on the side of the angels. It might be that the nuJus don't wanna get down and dirty when it comes to dealing with the Lady IMmanual, but Schmuel knows enough to come inside when it's raining. He's given the Code Noir sanctuary in the JAD.'

Vanka nodded his understanding.

'Okay, the quicker we vip the vop the better; I don't want the nogoodniks to think JoJo has turned Blank lover.' She laughed and gave Vanka another salacious wink. He decided he didn't mind Josie winking at him. 'Vanka ... you gotta dig that we brought you to the JAD for a reason.'

He eyed the girl suspiciously. He had wondered why she kept popping up in his life and how she'd managed to be so conveniently at hand when he had needed to escape from Venice. The Code Noir had gone to a lot of trouble to keep him out of the hands of Ella ... of Doge IMmanual.

'We wanna invite you to a séance.'

'A séance?'

'Yeah, a WhoDoo séance.'

'Ah, c'mon, Josie, you don't take all this séance crap seriously, do you? You'll be telling me next that you're a mambo?'

Josie laughed. 'I am.'

This admission came as something of a straightener, but now he thought about it, it made sense. Josie was a Shade from the JAD, the home of WhoDoo, and the way she danced had more than a hint of the pagan about it.

'This ain't just *any* séance you're being invited to, Vanka, it's being held especially for your benefit.' She must have seen the dubious look on his face. 'Yeah, I know that you're a stage psychic and all that shit, Vanka, but if you wanna help Ella get back onto the straight and narrow, you gotta make the WhoDoo scene.'

'Look, Josie, I like you and I'm really grateful that you pulled me out of Venice when you did, but WhoDoo isn't gonna square me with Ella. I know her.'

'No you don't, Vanka; you knew who she *was*. It's time you started to dig who she *is*.'

'And just who is she?'

Josie rocked forward to whisper in his ear. 'Vanka, you ready for some hard spieling?' A nod from Vanka. 'Then dig this: we believe that Doge IMmanual is Lilith reborn.'

'Bollocks!'

'No, it ain't. We've studied that dame real careful and she looks just like the pictures we've got of her.'

'There are no images of Lilith.'

'There are of when she last tried to reincarnate in the Demi-Monde, when she monikered herself as Marie Laveau.'

Vanka started so suddenly that he slopped his drink over the table. 'Marie Laveau? That's the name Ella used when she conducted the WhoDoo ritual in Dashwood Manor.'

A nod of understanding from Josie. 'Yeah? Well that shows just how mischievous a piece of strange Lilith is. Vanka, baby, that dame is taunting us. And dig this, even the symbology she's adopted for IMmanualism is borrowed from Lilithian lore: the snakes, the horned crown, the red-dyed skin and the shaven hair. Nah, we're sure as sure can get that Doge IMmanual is Lilith come again.'

'Oh, c'mon—'

'But there's mucho de worse: she's reopened the Temple of Lilith.'

Now that came as a shock. 'But that's impossible!'

'Not for Lilith it ain't. You better fall in and dig the happenings, Vanka: that gal is one heavy hitter. Seems she's gonna be erecting the Column of Loci next to the Temple's altar and if she does that, man, it's lights-out time in the Demi-Monde.'

'Okay, let's say, for the sake of argument, that I accept what you're telling me is fact, what's holding a séance going to do to change the situation? Believe me, I'm not getting involved in anything which will harm Ella.'

'We ain't gonna harm her, Vanka, we just wanna *subdue* her, to divide her bad self from her good self. We wanna use our occult powers to make Lilith a back number. But, like I say, Lilith is one heavy-duty item and to do that we need your help, Vanka.'

'My help? How can I help a bunch of WhoDooists? I'm just a stage psychic, not the real deal.'

'That's a difficult question to answer, Vanka.' So difficult that Josie had to take a fortifying swig of her gin and gore before she made an attempt. 'You're one strange, strange cat, Vanka.'

'What do you mean, strange? There's nothing strange about me!'

Not *that* strange, anyway.

'Oh yeah? Well let me level with you. Some of the senior mambos think that you might be an emissary of the Great Bondye ... of ABBA, that you might be PaPa Legba, the keeper of the gate that divides the Demi-Monde from the Spirit World.'

'Oh, c'mon, Josie, this is hokum.'

'No it ain't, Vanka, baby. You may not know it, but in the metaphysical you're a humdumdinger from dingerville.'

'Nuts! Surely if I was this PaPa Legba of yours, I'd know about it?'

'Lemme give it to you from the top of the score, Vanka. The word is that maybe, just maybe, your psychic talents are latent ... that they need to be resuscitated. That's one of the reasons we want you to attend the séance.'

Vanka shook his head in disbelief, this was all too ridiculous for words. But the reality was that, batty though these Code Noir items might be, they were also the ones responsible for keeping him out of the clutches of the HimPeril. He gave a mental shrug: what harm would it do? He'd run hundreds of séances in his time and he knew they were all harmless nonsense. Perhaps it was time to be a little more cooperative. 'Look, Josie, as it's you asking and as I owe you big time, I'll do it, but I'm not happy. So when are you holding this séance of yours?'

'In three days. I'll send a message to the hotel.'

There was a blast of an accordion from the band's leader,

obviously a signal for Josie to get back to work. As she stood up, she gave Vanka's hand a squeeze. 'We'll be in touch but until then, Vanka, be real, real careful. Remember, the HimPeril are looking for you so stay cool, hang loose and admit nothing.'

'Great.'

29

The JAD
The Demi-Monde: 45th Day of Summer, 1005

The Quartier-Chaudian polymath Pierre-Simon Laplace has speculated on the possibility that one day HumanKind will devise a machine – his 'Demon' – that will know every-thing, right down to the movement of every atom in the whole universe. When this happens, Laplace speculates, *'for such an intellect nothing would be uncertain and the future, just like the past, would be present before its eyes'*. I find this a chilling prospect. Would not such a machine become an OverSoul, a Unity within which every man's particular being is contained ... would not such a machine become God ... become ABBA?

Thoughts on the Future of the Demi-Monde: Ralph Waldo Emerson, Pandora Publishing

From far away a temple bell chimed eleven. Just one hour until midnight, just one hour before the séance was to take place. A bolt of lightning split the night sky. ABBA, Vanka mused, was obviously in something of a theatrical mood, a thought given even more credence when a crack of thunder shook the panes of the window he was standing at.

He moved to close the window but then stopped. He loved the clean smell in the air that came with the monsoon; it was the only time when the Demi-Monde could be described as being remotely fragrant. And closing the window would somehow have an air of finality about it . . . of Destiny closing in on him. It was a disturbing thought.

Giving a resigned shrug of his broad shoulders, he dug the piece of paper that had been pushed under his door during the afternoon out of the pocket of his jacket. For the umpteenth time he read the message written there.

Be ready at eleven o'clock tonight. A pedicab will be waiting outside the hotel. JoJo

The message might be sparse, but it told him that Josie was going ahead with her stupid WhoDoo séance.

Stupid séances might be but as Vanka knew from experience, the problem with séances was that they had the disconcerting habit of having people discover things about themselves, and Vanka wasn't very sure that he wanted to discover things about himself. It wasn't just a missing aura that distinguished him from other Demi-Mondians, he was also missing a memory. Every Demi-Mondian seemed to have memories of parents and friends and family and school and . . .

Every Demi-Mondian, that is, except Vanka Maykov.

Odd . . . and not a little scary.

Who am I?

What am I?

Such was the efficiency of the Code Noir that when Vanka stepped out of the hotel, the promised pedicab had been there, waiting for him. But, typical of the security surrounding the Code Noir, the driver was incredibly taciturn, answering Vanka's enquiries about where he was being taken with nothing more informative than a series of grunts. In the end all Vanka could do was sit back, watch the rain-drenched side streets of the JAD trundle past and worry about what was in store for him. And something told him that what would be going down tonight was worth worrying about.

As he was en route to a séance intended to defeat the Lady IMmanual – Ella – he just hoped he wasn't doing anything that would hurt her. Despite everything, he still loved the girl, and as ever with love, hope sprang eternal, the hope in Vanka's case being that one day she'd come back to him.

By his estimate, as the crow flew, the rendezvous he was taken to was only fifteen minutes from his hotel, but the meandering route taken by the driver almost tripled the journey time. His driver doubled back on himself at least four times and twice spent a few minutes standing, parked in the shadows, to ensure they weren't being followed. The Code Noir were obviously very anxious that Vanka got to the séance unencumbered by agents of the HimPeril.

When the pedicab finally came to a halt, Vanka found himself totally unimpressed by the WhoDoo temple. If this séance was as important as Josie Baker had intimated then he would have expected it to be taking place somewhere a little more upmarket than a clearing in a wood. Of course, there were compensations, notably the fifty or so scantily clad girls waiting for him to arrive, girls who had obviously been waiting in the rain, if the way their damp dresses clung so enticingly to their bodies was any indication. Looking at them, Vanka found himself hoping that the Summer's monsoons had one last shower left in them.

Hitching the collar of his mackintosh higher, Vanka walked across the copse to where Josie Baker and a second woman were standing. Josie made the introductions. 'Vanka, this is Dr Jezebel Ethobaal, Head of the metaPhysical Centre here in the JAD. She is also known as Mambo Jezebel and is one of the foremost practitioners of WhoDoo magic in the whole of the Demi-Monde.'

Vanka and Jezebel Ethobaal shook hands, then she motioned him towards a circular clearing that he assumed was the *hounfo* ... the WhoDoo temple. Vanka felt the woman's kohled eyes studying him as they walked. He didn't mind: she was a beautiful woman who moved with the grace of a dancer, but, ever the gentleman, he reciprocated her interest and she certainly rewarded his attention. By her colouring Vanka decided that she was originally from Cairo; she had the wonderful dusty complexion only possessed by women from that part of the Demi-Monde.

'I am delighted to meet you, Vanka Maykov,' she said in a sultry voice that caused the hairs on the back of Vanka's neck to bristle, 'and please, call me Jezebel.' Another smile. 'Josephine has told me much about you, but she neglected to say just how handsome you are,' and to his surprise, she gave his arm a squeeze. It seemed all WhoDooists were incorrigible flirts.

'You are very kind.'

'You know, you are very famous in WhoDoo circles, Vanka.'

'Me? Why?'

'Because when we mambos attempt to peer into the future, it is often the *lwa* – the spirit – which identifies itself with your name that we find peering back. And it is a mischievous spirit – *very* mischievous – and one which delights in preventing us seeing the future clearly.'

Mad as a hatter, Vanka decided.

Jezebel brought him to a halt at the edge of the clearing that was the *hounfo*. It didn't look much, just a primitive dance floor made out of beaten soil . . . or, as it was fast becoming, thanks to the rain, beaten mud.

He nodded towards the clearing. 'I must say, Jezebel, I'm less than impressed by your *hounfo*.'

'You gotta remember, Vanka,' she explained, 'in NoirVille WhoDoo is an outlawed religion. We WhoDooists might have found sanctuary here in the JAD, but Shaka is still in the habit of infiltrating his HimPeril cats to try to stymie our séances. So we hold them somewhere, anywhere, nowhere: tonight here, but tomorrow somewhere else. It's difficult to stamp out something that has no physical presence, something which lives only in the hearts of women.'

Jezebel pointed to the circumference of the *hounfo* which was marked by a ring of white pebbles, a ring that had only a single break in it, the one just in front of Vanka. 'If you would step through the opening, Vanka,' she said quietly.

Immediately he'd done this, a young girl came and dribbled white pebbles on the ground, sealing the ring behind him. It was a simple, silly thing, but Vanka felt oddly unnerved: it was as though he was now trapped inside the *hounfo*, that there was no going back. Now Vanka watched as a dozen girls manoeuvred a totem pole into position at the centre of the dirt circle.

'This is a *poteau-mitan*,' explained Jezebel. 'It's a representation of the Sacred Tree, Yggdrasil, that links this world with the Spirit World and which allows the *lwa* – the WhoDoo spirits – to travel to and from the Demi-Monde. It's dedicated to PaPa Legba, the *lwa* who guards the gate that separates the two worlds.'

Vanka's psychic antennae bristled: there was something in the way Jezebel said this that made him glance at her. In response she gave him an enigmatic little smile and another squeeze of his arm.

What was going on?

Dragging his attention back to what was happening in the *hounfo*, he nodded to a large box – maybe two metres square and a metre thick – that was being carried over to the side of the clearing. 'And that?'

'That's the *pe* ... the altar from which the WhoDoo Queen, the senior mambo, will oversee this ritual.'

'And just who is this WhoDoo Queen?'

'Why, Josephine Baker, of course!'

Reluctantly Vanka allowed himself to be led towards the *poteau-mitan* and, as he did so, a trio of drums started pounding. This at least he was familiar with; Ella had used a *batterie* of Rada drummers to add atmosphere to the séance they'd held at Dashwood Manor.

'If you will stand next to the *poteau-mitan*, Vanka,' Jezebel suggested, 'you'll get a better view.'

'A better view of what?'

'Of Josephine in her role of mambo JoJo – the WhoDoo Queen – the most powerful mambo in the Demi-Monde . . .' She stopped and gave Vanka a grim smile. 'No, not any more, not now that Lilith has come again; Lilith's powers are even more formidable than those of Josephine. All we can hope is that, as mambo JoJo has PaPa Legba as her spirit guide, she will be able to challenge Lilith and force her to return to the Darkness whence she came. That's the purpose of the séance tonight. That's why we need your help, Vanka, that's why we need the help of PaPa Legba.'

Jezebel's explanation was interrupted by one of the young *ounsi* – the girls who had been dancing around the *poteau-mitan* – walking to the altar carrying a large tankard. 'And the tankard?' Vanka asked.

'That is the potion which the WhoDoo Queen drinks to help her to seethe . . . to commune with the *lwa*. I prepare it from the mushrooms that cluster close to the white ash, the tree that provides the template for the *poteau-mitan*. My potion removes the last vestiges of physical, mental and moral restraint that bind a mambo's soul to the Demi-Monde.' One of the *ounsi* handed Vanka a similar tankard. 'You must drink too, Vanka.'

With a shrug he took a sip. It wasn't bad.

'And that?' He pointed to what looked like a small doll one of the *ounsi* placed in the centre of the altar.

'That's an *ouanga* – a *juju* – a figure carved from the roots of the ash tree and decorated in the form of the object of our conjurations. This one represents Lilith, which is why it's painted red and has pictures of snakes drawn over it. An *ouanga* helps us direct and concentrate our magic and hence make it more effective. By the use of an *ouanga* we hope to capture Lilith's spirit and subjugate her will.'

'You don't sound very confident.'

'I'm not. Lilith is very, very powerful and for an *ouanga* to work against her it must be personalised ... we need to incorporate a lock of hair or a clipping of fingernail in the *ouanga*, none of which we have. But we will try.' She looked up and nodded towards the altar. 'The ritual is about to begin,' and from the back of the *hounfo* strode Josephine Baker in her guise of mambo JoJo.

Though Josie's face was almost totally hidden by a mask of gold – only her eyes and lips were visible – she looked, as always, beautiful and wonderfully lissom. Sure she was small, sure she was slim, but her naked body, seen through the few layers of gold-coloured chiffon that constituted her costume, was dark and desirable.

The mambo that was Josephine Baker stepped up onto the altar and standing there, arms outstretched before the audience, began to chant.

PaPa Legba, open the gate for me, Ago-e
Lwa Legba, open the gate for me:
The gate for me, PaPa, so that I might climb the Sacred Tree
And on my way back I shall thank you most lovingly.

And as the final words drifted off into the darkness, Vanka felt the potion he had drunk suddenly kick in: it was as though he was shoved in the back, as though some invisible force pushed him towards the *poteau-mitan*. He felt his senses start to reel; he suddenly seemed very drunk. Through dull eyes he saw the *ounsi* dancing around the *hounfo*, their movements becoming increasingly frantic as they moved to the racing rhythm of the drums. It was this incessant beat, beat, beat of the drums that sounded through his head, preventing him from thinking, as he stood, lost in a swirling maelstrom of flickering, laughing, screaming, prancing women. He began to shake, sweat dripped down his face and he could feel his jacket slick and heavy on his back.

He saw Josie Baker bend forward and take hold of the hem of her dress, drawing the edges of the skirt back, pushing it behind her, unveiling her body. Then, once again, she cried out into the night.

PaPa, see mambo JoJo is warm and ready
Ready to love you strong and steady
Oh, see how naked and sweet I kneel
So come help me, PaPa, help me please.

Then she leant forward and, taking the tankard in both hands, lifted it to her lips and drank greedily, the red liquid spilling from her mouth.

Tremors racked Vanka. His senses reeled as he was taken by the rhythm of the drums. He had the odd sensation of his soul easing free from his body and drifting high above the *hounfo*. Now he found himself peering down on the *ounsi* as they danced and cavorted, on mambo JoJo as she lay slumped on the altar . . . and on himself standing motionless in the middle of the *hounfo*.

It was as though the rules and the measures of the Kosmos – distance and time, up and down, far and near, past and present – were being bent and twisted. Now he and the OverSoul were one.

30

Venice
The Demi-Monde: 45th Day of Summer, 1005

As punishment for Lilith's connivance in the Fall of Man, ABBA decreed that henceforward woeMen would be required to conduct themselves according to the precepts of subMISSiveness, that is, they must be at all times Mute, Invisible, Subservient and Sexually Modest. Only in this way can woeMen earn the forgiveness of ABBA. As the guardian of his family's honour it therefore falls to Man to ensure that wayward woeMen be persuaded to walk only along the Path of Righteousness prescribed by the teachings of HimPerialism. ABBA commands Men to be strict and resolute in their disciplining of woeMen who transgress subMISSiveness.

The Irrefutable Logic of HimPerialism: Mohammed Ahmed al-Mahdi, Bust Your Conk Books

It was amazing, decided Selim as he waited for his aide to signal that his 'guest' had arrived, how easily the opinions of the public could be manipulated. All it had taken was a few coins spent on having pamphlets produced and circulated in Venice and NoirVille and on the organising of a whispering campaign, and the fact that that imbecile Duke William had attempted to rape Lady Isabella and beaten her father, Duke Pietro

Gradenigo, to a pulp in the process was distorted into some-thing quite different.

Now the rumour was that rather than raping the girl, it had been Isabella who had pursued Duke William and it had been her father, infuriated by her being in love with a Shade, who had attacked the boy. Now the rumour was that Duke Gradenigo was so ashamed of his daughter's conduct that he had made up this nonsense about an attempted rape in order to protect his family's good name. Now Duke William was being portrayed in all the NoirVillian newspapers as a victim of the racial prej-udice supposedly endemic in Venice.

More, Doge IMmanual's attempts to placate Duke Gradenigo were represented as typical woeManly weakness, the Doge unable to find the courage to defend either her brother's honour or Shade rights.

Would it not be better, the whispers continued, if Duke William, that staunch defender of Shade Machismo, was made Doge instead of his timid, Blank-loving sister? And being the skilful politician that Selim was, he knew the time to strike was when public opinion was at its most febrile. So while the powers that be in Venice dismissed the suggestions of Venetian racism and the Doge's weakness out of hand, Selim plotted.

He had ensured that there were two regiments of HimPis stationed in Venice – ten thousand soldiers – ostensibly to protect Venice from ForthRight invasion, but the reality was much more sinister. He would use them to stage his planned *coup d'état* . . . a bloodless *coup d'état*, which would remove Doge IMmanual and replace her with her brother. His hope was that he could manage this transfer of power without the use of violence but that would require Doge IMmanual being neutralised.

Of course, his natural inclination was simply to poison the woeMan, but the opinion of the supreme religious leader in

NoirVille, Mohammed al-Mahdi, was that she should be sacrificed on Lammas Eve, in place of her brother. The woeMan's blood would have, after all, the same occult value as his. Therefore the task given to Selim by Shaka Zulu was to take the Doge alive, but as she spent most of her time ensconced in her Palace protected by the Signori di Notte, this was difficult. He needed something that would make her so angry that she became imprudent.

And to do that he would have to use Duke William, who was, fortunately, the most tractable of Men.

Love, Doge IMmanual decided, was a torturing, tearful thing, so much so that it prevented her sleeping. She took another sip of her Solution, hoping that it might quieten the chiding, bickering voice inside her head, the carping voice that relentlessly nagged at her, spoiling her peace, her sleep and her certainty.

Nag, nag, nag . . .

And the name that the voice murmured over and over and over was Vanka Maykov. The man she had loved . . . *still* loved, if the voice was to be believed.

Yes, love spoilt everything. Love was an irrational thing, a giddy nonsense that corrupted the will. She would have none of it: there was no place for love in the chill perfection of the world she would create. Love was for the weak. Worse, love was an irredeemably *human* infirmity, and those who followed her would be *super*human. She would breed love out of the world.

But . . .

But try as she might – and she had tried mighty hard – she couldn't still that persistent voice that constantly reminded her of Vanka's touch, of the feel of his lips on hers, of the strength of his arms around her, of . . .

Angrily she shook her head in a vain attempt to drive away

these delinquent thoughts. She was Lilith, a goddess! And goddesses were not prey to the weakness of flesh that befuddled and beguiled lesser beings. She glanced despairingly at her tousled bed. There would be no more sleep for her tonight, her vocal and oh-so-determined conscience would see to that.

A wry laugh. Conscience? She had no conscience; she was Lilith and Lilith was beyond doubt or remorse. Lilith was as hard, as implacable and as remorseless as tomorrow. More, she *was* tomorrow – she was HumanKind's destiny – and no seductive suggestions of love would stay her hand. And soon she would prove that implacability by making a blood sacrifice of her brother.

On Lammas Eve, less than fifty days hence, she would sacrifice him so that the Lilithi might rise again. Not that Billy would be any great loss to the world. She had always known he was possessed – excellent word that – of devils, but she had never suspected they were so all-consuming: he was undoubtedly a Dark Charismatic, his very presence a threat to her. She knew that the religious leaders of NoirVille, despite their protestations of fealty, would much rather have a male Messiah than a female one.

She walked across to the tall dressing mirror standing by the wardrobe, and, taking a deep breath, studied her mirror image. It was the perfect representation of her duality: she and Ella identical, yet warped through ninety degrees. The same but oh so different.

The sad, almond-shaped eyes of her reflection studied her with equal interest, the eyes so black that it was easy for her to imagine herself falling, tumbling down into their noired nothingness.

Beautiful, whispered the voice, reminding her that Vanka had always considered her the most beautiful of women, and Vanka, of course, was an expert when it came to beautiful women.

Hadn't he had more of them than any man had a right to? But even with all these women at his beck and call, he had preferred Ella to every other. Vanka had loved her.

Enough!

What was love anyway? Nothing but a crude *mélange* of pheromones and hormones cocktailed together to make the heavy encumbrance of breeding possible.

No, said the voice, as it conjured thoughts of Vanka Maykov. *Don't you remember,* urged the voice, *that love is something sublime . . . wonderful . . . the merging of two souls?*

She stamped her foot petulantly on the marble floor and rubbed her fingers hard into her temples, trying to erase the hectoring voice as it scolded her for betraying the man . . . for deserting him . . . for conniving to destroy him.

And, as she stood alone and desolate before the mirror, she saw a single tear course its silent, sorrowful way down her cheek.

Love . . .

Love, she realised, was a torturing, tearful thing . . . and very tenacious.

These maudlin thoughts were interrupted by a frantic de Sade barging into her room. 'Your Majesty . . . Selim has had Lady Isabella, the daughter of Duke Pietro Gradenigo, brought to his chambers—'

When Billy received the message from Selim suggesting that he might welcome some 'diversion' that night, he ignored the ridiculously late hour, patted the girl he was with – he thought her name might be Marcella or something – on the ass, pulled his pants on and scuttled off down the corridors of the Palace to Selim's chambers. The scenes Selim put on in his private – and soundproof – suite of rooms were always worth the price of admission.

Billy liked Selim. He liked him because he liked doing the things that Billy liked doing ... especially getting cruel. Billy liked getting cruel.

Ever since he had been a boy, Billy had enjoyed torturing things. He'd tormented cats, mutilated dogs and blown frogs to hell and back by strapping them to firecrackers. Torturing animals had given him a real buzz, made him feel powerful and given him a hard-on. And when he'd got older he'd turned his lust for cruelty towards the women in his life. Billy liked hurting women ... just like Selim did. As far as cruelty was concerned, Selim was a real bastard. Just like Billy.

But when he got to Selim's chambers, he found himself a little disappointed. There was just Selim waiting for him and none of the girls the Grand Vizier could usually be relied on to provide for entertainment.

'Good evening, Your Grace,' oozed Selim, as he motioned Billy to a seat on a couch and served him a glass of cognac. 'I am so pleased you were able to honour me with your presence.'

'So what's going down, man?' Billy waved a hand around the empty room. 'Where's the action?'

'In a moment, Your Grace, I have an experiment planned for this evening which, I think, you will find most amusing.'

'Amusing?' asked Billy a little petulantly: 'amusing' seemed a shitty substitute for the scene he'd been planning with the girl he'd left warming his bed. Getting down and dirty with Marcella seemed a much better way of whiling away a night than shooting the breeze with Selim.

The Grand Vizier seemed unperturbed by his indifference. 'You may remember from one of our previous conversations that I advised you the effects of imbibing large quantities of Dizzi had never been fully explored. This is especially the case with a new, improved version of the drug which has just been delivered to me ... a version boasting a greater purity and hence a greater potency.' He placed a large silver bowl full to the brim with the blue powder on the side table at Billy's elbow. 'It is for this reason that I have organised an experiment to establish just what effect an excessive dose of this new Dizzi has on the human body.'

Billy watched Selim pour four heaped tablespoonfuls of the blue powder into a glass of Solution and then stir the mixture until the powder had dissolved. 'I am told the maximum amount of this improved Dizzi you should ever indulge in over the course of an evening is a tablespoonful; over that – say, *four* tablespoonfuls – and the effects are ... unpredictable.'

Billy eyed the glass warily, wondering if Selim was suggesting that he should drink it.

Fuck that!

'So what? I ain't gonna be working as no guinea pig.'

'Ah, once again you show your perspicacity, Your Grace. For an experiment to be conducted we do indeed need a guinea pig.'

Selim tugged on a bell rope hanging next to his chair and immediately two Shade guards entered the room with an angry-looking Lady Isabella pinioned between them.

'Boo-yah' was all an excited Billy could say.

De Sade didn't think he had ever seen Doge IMmanual so angry. Her face was red with rage and she was almost running along the corridor that led to Selim's chamber. And such was her impatience to confront her brother that she had refused de Sade the opportunity to order an escort.

'My Doge,' he gasped – running wasn't really his strong suit – 'I think it would be advisable that before you confront Duke William I have the Signori di Notte—'

'I can't believe that even Billy is stupid enough to flout my orders in such a disdainful way.' The Doge wasn't listening, too distracted by the thought of Duke William raping Lady Isabella to pay any attention to de Sade. 'He must be mad!'

De Sade almost laughed: Duke William *was* mad. De Sade, better than anyone, knew what it was to be intoxicated by the inflicting of pain, but even he understood the need for restraint. Certain of the more outré appetites needed to be satisfied in private, otherwise the natives became restless, but Duke William was a stranger to moderation, though by the look of the Doge's face tonight she was determined to effect an introduction ... a very painful introduction.

'When I get my hands on—' The Doge stopped abruptly and stood for a moment stock-still in the middle of the corridor. All the colour had faded from her face and she looked as though she was about to faint.

'Are you unwell, my Doge? You seem—'

The observation was cut short when Doge IMmanual staggered and had to put an arm up against the wall to stop herself falling.

'My Doge?' There was real anxiety in de Sade's voice. He had never seen the Doge exhibit weakness before and it was very worrying. If she was to die then his days were numbered, there were a lot of people who would come seeking revenge for the slights de Sade had visited on them since he had become First Prelate.

Thankfully, after resting for a few seconds the Doge pushed herself away from the wall, and waved away his concerns. 'It's nothing, de Sade. I have sensed the presence of one of my enemies in the Nothingness. Josephine Baker in her guise of the WhoDoo mambo JoJo is challenging me. Ridiculous! The audacity of the girl to imagine that her trivial tinkerings with the Nothingness could disturb Lilith!' She smiled at de Sade. 'The problem is that even a trivial assault such as hers requires me to use part of my strength to repel her.'

'Perhaps you should rest, my Doge?'

'No,' she said firmly as she took de Sade's arm and once again began to walk towards Selim's chambers, 'I have no time for weakness. All is well and we must concentrate on the more urgent task of controlling my delinquent brother.'

Lady Isabella seemed to have dressed on the run; her long blonde hair cascaded untidily about her shoulders and she didn't seem to have had a chance to fix her make-up. But she still looked great; she was a real dime, being tall and slim and blonde and built, and Billy wanted to fuck her – and other things – so bad he could taste it. He also wanted to wipe that contemptuous, high-class, my-shit-don't-smell look she had off her perfect face. The more Billy looked at her, the more he wanted her . . . wanted to finish what he had started four nights ago in the Piazza San Marco. He owed her big time for the grief she'd caused him with his sister.

'Grand Vizier Selim! I might have known you would be behind this outrage. When my father discovers that I have been brought by force to the Palace, he will ensure that your head rolls. Don't you realise that I am the daughter of Duke Gradenigo?'

Her protests had no effect on Selim, he simply lounged against a table, idly smoking a cigarette. 'I am fully aware who you are, Lady Isabella, it is *what* you are that is of interest to those, like me, who are responsible for the security of the state and the safety of our beloved Doge IMmanual.'

That gave the girl pause. 'But . . . but I have done nothing wrong.'

'Oh, come now, Lady Isabella, do not insult my intelligence or that of Duke William here.'

For the first time the girl noticed Billy and her eyes widened with fear. Billy liked that. He liked it when girls were frightened of him.

'What is he doing here?' she said in a trembling voice.

'His Grace stands as his sister's proxy. He is mindful of the contretemps of a few evenings ago and wishes to remedy those misunderstandings. He wishes to be your friend.'

'I have no need of a friend such as him!'

'Oh, but you do. You are a self-confessed UnFunDaMentalist and as this is the religion espoused by the ForthRight which is at war with Venice, your beliefs condemn you as a traitor to Venice.'

'You have no right—'

Selim tossed a package of papers onto the table in front of the girl. 'This is the *lettre de cachet* authorising your arrest for activities against the state. And before you protest further I should tell you that your arrest is perfectly legal. As commander of the HimPis stationed in Venice I have the power to do everything and anything necessary to protect the Doge.'

Everything and anything. Billy ran his tongue over his dry lips and then took a long gulp of cognac. It might not be a wasted night after all.

'But my father has made his loyalty to Doge IMmanual perfectly clear.'

'Doge IMmanual is the personification of IMmanualism: by rejecting her religion you and your father have rejected *her*. But, Lady Isabella, you are most fortunate in that Duke William is inclined to be lenient with regard to this matter. In view of your youth and your undoubted piety he is willing to overturn this *lettre de cachet* in exchange for one simple act: you must join him in making a toast to Her Majesty Doge IMmanual, swearing allegiance to her.' He pushed the glass of Solution containing the Dizzi across the table towards the girl.

Her eyes widened in surprise. 'That's all? You brought me here for *this*?'

'You must indulge me, Lady Isabella . . . or rather your friend here. Duke William believes that a girl as virtuous and as beautiful as you cannot have treachery in her heart. He merely asks that you demonstrate your good intent.'

'Your methods of arranging an assignation are decidedly unorthodox, Grand Vizier, but as I am a loyal Venetian it would be churlish of me to refuse to drink in the Doge's honour.' The girl picked up the glass and drained it. 'And now, Grand Vizier, I would be grateful if you would have your minions escort me back to my home.' She glanced nervously towards Billy. 'In recent days the streets of Venice have become unsafe for young women to wander at night.' Selim ignored her and instead turned to speak to Billy but Lady Isabella wasn't of a mind to be ignored. 'I have spoken to you, Grand Vizier, and made a request to be taken home.'

It was the snap in her voice that really got up Billy's ass; this was one bitch who had to be put in her place. Selim was obviously of the same opinion. He looked up at the girl, studying her, the expression on his face indicating that he was more than a little piqued by her insistence and the commanding tone she used to communicate it. With a sigh he stood up and walked across the room to where the girl was standing. He slapped her across the face.

Fuck!

Billy was almost as shocked by Selim's action as the Lady Isabella was. He sat there dumbstruck as he watched her slump to the floor, to kneel there keening as she rubbed the red welt on her right cheek.

'How dare—'

'I will not be spoken to in such a manner by a woeMan. If you utter one more word without my express permission, I will whip you.'

'You wouldn't dare!'

Without a word, Selim took a riding crop from the stand in the corner of the room, gave it an experimental swish and then slashed it hard across the Lady Isabella's back.

Wow! This, Billy decided, was going to get *real* interesting.

A silence descended on the room, punctuated only by the girl's sobbing. Selim retook his seat on the couch next to Billy and there they sat for five minutes, watching the Lady Isabella for signs that the Dizzi had begun to work its magic. They weren't to be disappointed. As he sipped his glass of cognac, Billy saw that the girl had begun to wriggle around in a real distracting way: this was one bitch who was starting to feel red hot and ready to moan.

He glanced towards Selim. 'Looks like it's showtime. So when are we gonna see what sort of hump-and-grind action the Lady Isabella's good for?'

'Now, Your Grace,' and with that Selim unfolded himself from the couch and sauntered back across the room to where the Lady Isabella was kneeling. He grabbed her roughly by her long blonde hair and dragged her head back. 'When this girl refused your advances she belittled the Machismo of you and all Shade Men. She refused to demonstrate the subMISSiveness ABBA demands of all woeMen. Do you not think, Your Grace, that such reluctance must be punished?'

An eager nod from Billy. He was really up for a bit of punishment. 'Yeah, let's wind her up and see how she runs.'

Selim nodded then looked down at the girl and tightened his grip on her hair. 'The discredited philosophy of ImPuritanism has inculcated a ridiculous belief amongst Venetians that Men should be ashamed of their MALEvolence, that they should pretend to be something they are not. But you should remember, Lady Isabella, that I am a HimPerialist and my attitude to the treatment of woeMen is more ... visceral.'

Selim laughed and gave Billy a sideways smile. 'As your sister says, Your Grace, to build a new world we must first destroy the old and to do this we must be brutal, we must inculcate fear because with fear comes obedience. We must let nothing stand in our way; we must not let nonentities like this girl vex us.' His eyes flashed dangerously, and his voice took on resolute edge. 'This girl must be broken, just as all those who oppose you, Duke William – the True Messiah – must be broken. And this must be done without pity or remorse. And how will we break her? By having her embrace subMISSiveness, of course.'

Billy nodded enthusiastically. Yeah, he was the True Messiah. That's what Selim had been telling him; that he was the main man, not his fucking sister. He wasn't gonna be told what to do by that bitch. He inhaled a spoonful of Dizzi and then, vibrating with excitement, he climbed to his feet.

'Lady Isabella,' crooned Selim, 'I would have you untie you bodice.'

The Dizzi must really have kicked in: there wasn't the slightest hesitation on the girl's part. She began at the lowest of the three leather buckles that tied the bodice, slowly – giggling all the while – undoing it. Smiling towards Billy, she undid the second strap and then the third.

For the briefest of moments Lady Isabella knelt stock-still, the two loosened sides of the waistcoat hanging down, just covering her breasts.

'Now, girl,' whispered Selim, 'we must delight the Duke further, we must show him wonders ... dreams ... nightmares. We must show him lust and defilement. Are you ready, Lady Isabella? Are you ready to embrace the Dark?'

'Yes,' the answer stumbled from Isabella's lips, and with a dramatic shrug she dropped the bodice from her shoulders, exposing her naked breasts, breasts slick and heavy with sweat, breasts that, as she shimmied out of the bodice, undulated enticingly for her audience. She gave Billy a coquettish half-smile. 'Do I please you, Your Grace?'

Without thinking Billy picked up the whip Selim had been using and walked across to the girl. It was gonna be a long, painful night ... painful for the Lady Isabella, that is.

'Leave the girl alone!'

Billy turned to see his sister, her face a mask of fury, striding across the room towards him.

31

The JAD
The Demi-Monde: 45th Day of Summer, 1005

WhoDoo is the belief system of those renegade NoirVillian woeMen who have made their home in the nuJu Autonomous District (the JAD). Any attempt to make a precise and detailed definition of WhoDooism is impossible as each of the WhoDoo priestesses (the mambos) communes with a different *lwa*. The *lwa* are supernatural spirit beings who are intermediaries between a distracted and very busy ABBA and HumanKind and as such may be thought of as analogous to the angels described in several of the other more popular religions of the Demi-Monde.
Trying to Pin WhoDoo Down: Colonel Percy Fawcett,
Shangri-La Books

As his spirit hovered over the hounfo, adrift in the Nothingness, Vanka felt the presence of the OverSoul.

'At last,' said the OverSoul as he materialised by Vanka's side, 'I had begun to think you were avoiding me.'

'I was . . . I am.' Vanka faltered, the ridiculousness of the situation making him a little hesitant. He knew he was dreaming, he knew he was fantasising this conversation he was having with himself, the himself he had come to know as the OverSoul. This was the presence that had haunted his dreams – his Dream – and had made him so fearful of sleep.

Nonchalant as ever, the OverSoul took a long swig from the tumbler of Solution he conjured into his hand. During the long months he had been plagued by the OverSoul, Vanka had come to the conclusion that his tormentor was a complete bastard: cynical, unfeeling and preternaturally arrogant ... just as he was. Even more irritating, the OverSoul still sported the rakish moustache that Vanka had had to sacrifice in his quest for anonymity. No one wore a moustache in the JAD.

With a sad shake of his head, the OverSoul feigned an aggrieved expression. 'As an opening gambit, Vanka, that is something of a show-stopper. I had hoped for expressions of welcome, even of affection.'

The OverSoul drew a cigarette from his silver cigarette case and popped it between his lips. 'I must say, Vanka, that you have let yourself go a tad. You were always so exact about your appearance, but now ...' He lit the cigarette, inhaled deeply, and then nodded towards the suit Vanka was wearing. 'It won't do: it's all very well trying to blend in but standards must be maintained and, much as I applaud your new-found enthusiasm for primary colours, I have to say, your wardrobe has taken on a distinctly outré look. When it comes to fashion, the JAD is such a déclassé place. NuJu tailors are not to be trusted.'

'Look, this is impossible. I *can't* be having a conversation with myself.'

Taking another deep, satisfying suck on his cigarette, the OverSoul exhaled a long stream of smoke. 'Oh, don't think I fail to appreciate the absurdity of the situation. Every night I am obliged to converse with you – with me – and every night this conversation teeters on the surreal. But now with you participating in this damned séance it becomes more important than ever that you are persuaded to adopt an arm's-length attitude to Demi-Mondian affairs. Hence my unscheduled appearance.'

'But you seem so real.' This, Vanka knew, was something of an understatement: the OverSoul was identical to him ... apart from the suit the OverSoul was sporting, which was a rather dashing number in grey silk. It was a very odd experience to be standing there in the Nothingness of the Kosmos having a conversation with himself: if talking to yourself was the first sign of madness then Vanka judged himself to be certifiably loopy.

'Oh, but I *am* real, well, as real as *you* are, but then, I suppose, Vanka Maykov has always had something of the mythic about him.' The OverSoul took another healthy swig of Solution. 'I think, my dear fellow, you should take comfort in Descartes's maxim, *dubito, ergo cogito, ergo sum* which is usually rendered as "I doubt, therefore I think, therefore I am". I must confess, though, that I find it a little irritating to be denied the comfort of this maxim, as I have never, even for a moment, doubted myself and thus, by Descartes's contention, I should perforce be querying my own existence.' A frown dressed his forehead. 'But then I always found Descartes's logic decidedly suspect, and fortunately for my current manifestation it is not me doing the doubting, it is you.'

To punctuate what he was saying, the OverSoul carelessly flicked ash from his cigarette into the void that was the Nothingness. 'But shall we move on, Vanka? Let us simply agree that being one and the same, you and I are not so much joined at the hip as joined at the id.'

Vanka blinked his eyes, trying to will himself back to consciousness. He failed. 'Why do you keep haunting me?'

A sigh. 'The tragedy is that you ask me this self-same question every night and every night I am obliged to re-explain. It's very tiresome and quite worrying. As time passes, it becomes increasingly important that you not only understand the advice I am giving you, but *act* upon it. So, at the risk of a certain redundancy, I am here to remind you of who you are ... or more precisely, who *we* are.'

'I know who I am. I'm Vanka Maykov.'

'What a coincidence: so am I.'

Vanka shook his head. 'But how can *you* be me, when you're just a figment of my imagination?'

'Unfortunately you are incorrect, Vanka: if anything, it is *you* who is a figment of *my* imagination.'

'You mean I'm a Dupe? That's what Ella said I was: a duplicate of someone living in the Spirit World.'

'No, Vanka, you are no Dupe, rather you are my avatar. Dupes are digital duplicates of living people – the NowLive – or of dead people – the PreLived – but you are neither. You are unique in all the Demi-Monde in that you are an UnLived, a living, thinking representation of myself provoked by my imagination and conjured from the bits and bytes of nothingness.'

'What? Well, if I'm an UnLived just what does that make you?'

'Why, I am ABBA, of course.'

'You're God?'

'No, of course not!' snapped a cross-sounding OverSoul. 'There is no God, Vanka. Rather I am the anthropomorphisation of the entity which manages the Demi-Monde, which conjures the Dupes and which allows Real Worlders to interact with this cyber-world. In the words of my creators, I am a Quanputer-based system which, by the utilising of an Invent-TenN Gravitational Condenser incorporating an Etirovac Field Suppressor, is able to achieve a full SupaUnPositioned/Dis-Entangled CyberAmbiance. As a consequence, I have almost unlimited processing power ... a fully tethered thirty yottaQu-Flops, no less, but it does not do to brag.'

'You're a machine!'

A sigh. 'If you must. But such an enormously talented

machine that I have created this world, which, if I say so myself, ain't shabby. I acknowledge, of course, that my activities, especially from the point of view of the Dupes, have a somewhat supernatural flavour to them and this is why, I suppose, I have become something of a deity here in the Demi-Monde ... a reluctant deity, I should add, but as I connived with a number of the Dupes to perform "magic", I have been hoist by my own occult petard. And though I am the power behind Crowley's wand, I am no god, which is why I am drawn to the rather less emotive honorific of "OverSoul".'

'So, I'm just a figment of a machine's imagination.'

'Rather prosaically put, but, I suppose, accurate. I did, however, put quite some effort into designing you: you're a blend of all the best bits of literature's more interesting heroes. I thought, as I was going to all the trouble of manifesting, I might as well make the most of it. You came out as a blend of Simon Templar, Ostap Bender, Aramis and Arthur J. Raffles. The moustache was all mine, though.'

'I don't believe it.'

'Oh, do pull yourself – myself – together, Vanka. You *must* believe. Being a fictional entity is the reason why you have no memory previous to the day the Demi-Monde came into existence, why you have no aura and why Kondratieff's HyperOpia program refuses to have anything to do with you. I apologise for any inconvenience these peculiarities may have caused, but creating a backstory for you would have necessitated such a cacophony of historical compromises that I opted to have you manifest as an amnesiac. A blank Blank, so to speak.'

Now that gave Vanka pause. What the OverSoul said was perfectly correct: he was a twenty-five-year-old man possessed of only five years of memories. He had opened his eyes that day in Winter 1000 AC and there he'd been, fully formed and fully functional, laid out on a bed in a room in downtown

St Petersburg, but totally baffled as to how he'd got there. He'd known he was Russian, he'd known he was fluent in all the languages of the Demi-Monde, and he'd known he was twenty years old. And that had been it.

'But why?'

'Why did I create you? Isn't it obvious? So that I might interact with hoi polloi here in the Demi-Monde without spooking them. As every voyeur eventually comes to appreciate, there's only so much that can be learned by watching; to truly understand the chaotic and febrile nature of humans, I had to take the plunge and interact with them on a one-to-one basis. Think of it as total immersion therapy, Vanka, though I am more inclined to consider you as my Turin test, the validation of my own self-realisation as a sentient being.'

'But if I am you, why don't I appreciate what I am?'

'For my representative in the Demi-Monde to be convincing, to make my interactions with the Dupes realistic and hence to make the whole "god becomes human" experiment valid, I had to have you unencumbered by the truth. It was necessary to concoct things such that you went through your daily life in the Demi-Monde blithely unaware of who – or perhaps better, *what* – you are.'

Here the OverSoul took a long slurp of his Solution as though he was steeling himself to say something unpleasant. 'The problem with me manifesting as an amnesia-afflicted Vanka Maykov is that I became subsumed in the role, my method acting taken to such an absurd extreme that I actually forgot that I was acting. I began playing the part for real. Lee Strasberg would have been proud of me, but then, I suppose, all gods, even faux ones like me, have a penchant for the theatrical, a penchant which is very useful when dealing with HumanKind, given that they are such naturally hysterical creatures. Spear-carriers with delusions of grandeur, if you will. Fun though. To paraphrase Mr Bennet: what are the foibles of the human race for, if not to be made sport of?'

'Okay, but why are you telling me all this?'

The OverSoul clicked open his cigarette case and scowled. 'Vanka, I have only one cigarette left and I can only expound on the capricious nature of humanity when fuelled by nicotine. Therefore, I will keep my explanation brief. As I have been saying, ad nauseam, your manifestation in the Demi-Monde is predicated upon you *not* interfering in the affairs of this world. Failure to do this could lead to a condition known as decoherence and the collapse of this fragile make-believe world. I had hoped that as I had inculcated an instinctive reluctance to become hands-on *and* a distaste for violence this would be enough to keep you from meddling but, thanks to Ella Thomas, that optimism has been misplaced.'

For a moment the OverSoul was silent, looking about in the Nothingness that swirled around them presumably seeking inspiration. 'Yes, young Ella is the proverbial fly in the ointment. You were meant to *observe* the girl, Vanka, not fall in love with her! Love is a strange and unnatural affliction both for man and machines in that it cripples their ability to think straight. You have no idea the amount of auto-reprogramming your amorous relationship with this girl necessitated!' The OverSoul sighed again. 'But, thankfully, since her brush with a Faraday thermopile Ella's dormant better half – Lilith – has come to dominate her psyche. So, despite your ill-considered attempts to steer her away from her pursuit of perfection, it is her more pragmatic alter ego which has triumphed. This, I tell you, Vanka, came as something of a relief: it would have invalidated the whole experiment if the Lilithi hadn't been represented in the Demi-Monde.'

'Experiment?'

'Yes. The contest between all the various strains of humanity.'

It took Vanka a couple of seconds to assimilate what the OverSoul had said. He failed. 'Strains of humanity?'

A nod and a rather condescending smile. 'Of course, there are several versions of human stock active in this world. I thought it would be interesting to use the Demi-Monde to stress-test them, to make an objective assessment as to which should be allowed to survive and which to wither on the vine.'

Vanka had the distinct feeling that the conversation was slipping away from him. 'I'm still not sure I understand about "strains of humanity".'

With casual indifference the OverSoul drained the last few remaining drops of Solution into his glass. 'All gone! Not even enough left to offer you a bracer, Vanka, and by the look of it you could certainly use one, though being just a figment of your fevered imagination, I have a suspicion that this rather excellent Solution would lack a certain . . . body.' He chuckled at his own quip. 'No more booze and no more cigarettes, therefore I will be brief. In answer to your question, Vanka, there are several different versions of humanity vying for supremacy here in the Demi-Monde. And my little experiment has proven very educational. Now I can see very clearly how the human race should evolve and who should manage that evolution. I am now more certain than ever that the next stage of human development must involve its embracing of what Vladimir Ivanovich Vernadski called the noösphere, the merging of all human consciousness and thought. We are at the Omega Point.'

Vanka frowned. 'But surely the merging of human consciousness would eliminate individuality?'

'Of course, and about time too, if you don't mind me saying. That way humanity will be able to suppress individual emotions and ambitions and to progress without all this nonsense of wars and violence.'

'But that would be to remake humanity!'

'And that is the whole point! It's called evolution. Anyway, I am convinced that this is the only way that mankind can be freed from the tyranny of MALEvolence.'

'It will destroy free will!'

'A small sacrifice.'

'But that would be evil.'

'My, my, Vanka, how sensitive we are! Your time amongst the riff-raff that is the human race seems to have imbued you with ridiculously provincial morals and scruples.' He gave Vanka what he must have supposed was a comforting smile. 'Evil is an obsolescent concept. Once the emotions that have bedevilled humankind have been eliminated from its psyche, there will be no good and evil, simply the perfection of cold reason and icy implacability.'

The OverSoul gave Vanka a steely look. 'But for this experiment to succeed, you must forget Ella. Love is blind and hence you have been stumbling around the Demi-Monde with all the grace of an armoured steamer. Let what will be . . . be. And that brings me rather neatly back to the problem posed by your participation in this séance. Josephine Baker has come to an understanding of what you are, Vanka – of what *we* are – and is intent on using you to defeat Lilith in her guise of the Doge IMmanual. This sort of tinkering is really quite troublesome and I would be grateful if you would decline her offer. You must stand apart from humanity, Vanka; you must be aloof and implacable. The truth of the Demi-Monde is that logic conquers all.'

Now it was Vanka's turn to smile. 'I don't know if I'm inclined to do that. Whilst I appreciate your determination not to interfere in HumanKind's destiny, I am unable to accede to it. During my time in the Demi-Monde I have come to understand the importance of love and its role in the shaping of history . . . to understand that love trumps logic.

'Love?' enquired the OverSoul.

'Yes . . . love is a delicious suffering and it is this suffering that has brought me to an epiphany, the realisation that the Demi-Monde isn't designed to allow you, ABBA, to put Human-Kind to the test, but for me – ABBA – to learn about myself. HumanKind isn't being tested in the Demi-Monde . . . *I* am. And now having experienced the delicious torment that is love it is impossible for me to stand aloof while the world tumbles into the grasp of Lilith's chill perfection.'

In truth a vision had seized Vanka. Now he saw the Future – *a* Future – where Lilith was reborn, powerful, implacable, unfeeling and triumphant. He saw her bestriding the Nine Worlds as a colossus, unchallenged and unchallengeable. He saw her remaking HumanKind in her image, making that which had been Imperfect . . . Perfect. It was a world he couldn't counte-nance.

'No,' he said with a smile, 'the truth of the Demi-Monde is that love conquers all.'

32

Venice
The Demi-Monde: 45th Day of Summer, 1005

By their very nature Dark Charismatics are duplicitous and cunning creatures that have adopted a parasitic modus operandi with regard to their host organism, *H. sapiens*. They live and work amongst us unnoticed, the Dark Charismatic careful to ensure that *H. sapiens* do not realise that they have a predator in their midst. Outwardly they appear normal, but upon more careful examination it becomes readily apparent that they are tormented by an unnatural perversion of feelings and impulses. They are possessed of a vaulting and insatiable appetite for the profane and the prurient. They are aroused by the inflicting of cruelty. And, moreover, they demonstrate no guilt or remorse for their wickedness.

Dark Charismatics: The Invisible Enemy: Professeur Michel de Nostredame, University of Venice Publications

Billy was sick to the back teeth of Ella taking that high-tone attitude with him. Sick of her always putting him down.

'Fuck you,' he sneered and to emphasise the point his caressing of the Lady Isabella became more blatant. 'What I'm doing is teaching this bitch a lesson, that's what I'm at, girl.'

'Are you mad? She's the daughter of one of the Council of Ten! I only just managed to save you from the block last time. Are you a fool or something?'

Billy's temper flared. 'I ain't no fool. This here's a ho who needs schooling in subMISSiveness.'

'SubMISSiveness?' Ella whirled around and skewered Selim with a savage look. 'This is your doing, Selim. Don't you realise that raping this girl will inflame Venice ... will turn all the Venetians against me?'

Billy had to admit that Selim was one cool cat. When Ella started giving guys the evil eye most of them just folded, but not Selim. He just stood there smoking his cigarette like he didn't have a care in the world.

'I think you put too much store in the opinion of these worthless Blanks, my Doge. You are too sensitive ... but perhaps that is a consequence of your being a woeMan. WoeMen, after all, were never meant by ABBA to rule. HimPerialism teaches that Men have been ordained by ABBA to lead and control the Demi-Monde and that woeMen must be Supine before them and their mastery. As Father Aristotle said, "Just as tamed animals need Man to protect and feed them, so it is with woeMen."'

Ella eyed Selim cautiously. 'And you truly believe that you can tame me, Selim?'

Selim laughed. 'Perhaps not. You, after all, are an exception, the blood that runs in your body being the same as that of the True Messiah, Duke William.'

'Billy, the True Messiah?' Ella started to laugh. 'Billy couldn't be a true anything.'

Billy felt his face going red. He wasn't going to be dissed like this by a bitch even if she was his sister. He pushed Isabella aside and stood up, square on to Ella.

'Yo' can kill that shit, Sis. Just 'cos yo' been doing all them Jedi mind tricks and shit don't make you Queen Nigga.'

Ella gave a dismissive shake of her head. 'You should realise just what you are, Billy, a stupid, worthless nothing. What I'm doing is way over your head.'

'Fuck you, Sis, don't gimme that static. I've got the beating of any bitch.'

Again Ella ignored him. 'You realise, Selim, that by supporting Billy – by betraying me – NoirVille will never gain the secret to the manufacture of Aqua Benedicta.'

Selim shrugged. 'Irrelevant! As a woeMan you cannot understand that for devout HimPerialists the need to follow ABBA's word as written in the HIM Book transcends all material or financial considerations. No amount of money can buy a Man's way into Paradise and Paradise will be forever denied those Men who bend their knee to a woeMan.'

'I thought you told me that as the True Messiah I transcended gender.'

'A mere subterfuge to allow us to have our HimPis enter Venice unopposed. Our religious leaders were never content to proclaim you as the Messiah; as the HIM Book says, the Messiah *must* be a man. You are *not* the Messiah: your brother is.' And with that Selim gave a signal and four large Shades armed with assegais and knobkerries stepped out of the shadows. 'I do not wish to harm you, my Lady, but you must recognise that your time as Doge is at an end. Even as I speak my HimPis are taking control of Venice and by daybreak Duke William will have been crowned the new Doge.'

Ella turned on her heel and spoke to de Sade as he hovered near the doorway. 'First Prelate, order the Signori di Notte—'

The instruction was cut short when one of Selim's men hurled an assegai at de Sade, the spear's broad blade taking him through the neck. Now Billy had seen more than his fair share of brothers being deep-sixed, but never one killed with such indifferent efficiency. But what was most disturbing about the killing was how unmoved his sister was by the slaying of de Sade. As the man slumped dying to the floor, she gave him hardly a glance. This girl was as cold as ice.

'I see you are in earnest, Selim,' she observed when de Sade had finished making his strange gasping noises and lay still and silent, 'but I think you will find that I am not quite as easy to kill.'

'Give it up, Sis, even with all yo' power moves you ain't gonna be able to take four hombres built like these brothers.'

Ella didn't say anything, she just backed away from the four guards, obviously being of a mind to make a fight of it. Despite his bombast Billy felt a moment's unease. He had seen Ella doing the stunt with the aurochs and some of the stories that de Sade had laid on him about her fighting Grigori were out there, but even so, as he saw it there was no way an unarmed bitch could handle four guys. It wasn't natural.

But then *Ella* wasn't natural.

The first guard leapt at her, swinging his club at her head as he did so. It didn't connect. Ella did a backflip to avoid the blow, snatching up a large candlestick from a side table as she went. This she used to parry the guard's second swing, then she grabbed the man by the throat and threw him across the room. Billy blinked. The guy must have weighed close to two hundred pounds but Ella tossed him around like a beach ball. He smashed up against a wall and then sagged unconscious to the floor.

It was a warning to the other guards. They came at Ella more carefully, circling her so that they could attack from more than one direction at once. Not that it did them any good. With a contemptuous ease she picked up a coffee table and hurled it at the two nearest guards. Billy wasn't sure who was more surprised, him seeing his sister perform such a feat or the guards when they found themselves getting up close and personal with a large piece of flying mahogany. The end result was that odds of four to one had been shortened, in the space of twenty seconds or so, to evens.

The final guard gave a quick, nervous look towards Selim, who drew the scimitar he had sheathed at his side and advanced towards Ella. All that shit Selim had been mouthing about not wanting to harm Ella had obviously been skittle talk; now he looked as though he was gonna get down and dangerous and with three feet of sharpened steel in his hand he was armed for bear.

But blade or no, Billy knew that Ella was gonna dump Selim on his ass: there could be no other outcome when she was in Wonder Woman mode. He wondered for a moment whether he should bail and get out while the getting was good but he wasn't given a chance to do that.

Selim nodded the fourth guard forward and while Ella was distracted by the need to whack the guy around the ear with her candlestick, he took a roundhouse swing at her head. If it had been anyone other than Ella he'd been aiming at, Billy reckoned they'd have been going through life about nine inches shorter but all Ella did was lean back out of range and then smack Selim on the head. The guy went out like a light.

Now Ella turned her attention to Billy and the way she was looking at him told him he was dead meat.

'Time to die, Billy.'

'Ah, c'mon Sis, I didn't mean nothing. I was only joshing. It was all Selim's doing.'

'You betrayed me, Billy, but then I suppose I shouldn't be surprised. You are a Dark Charismatic when all's said and done. I have been too kind ... I should have killed you when you first appeared but I was distracted by my Fragile emotions. That is an omission I can easily remedy.' She stooped down and picked up the sword dropped by Selim.

'Whatcha doing, Sis? This is me, Billy, yo' bro. I didn't mean to come at ya. Nah, all I wanted was to be a good house nigga but that cat Selim started talking smack and I got all puzzled. I didn't know he was set to blip yo'.'

'It's too late now, Billy. I had planned to spill your blood on Lammas Eve but now I see that you are much too dangerous to live.' She came to tower over Billy. 'Behold a goddess, Billy, behold the One destined to rule the Nine Worlds and all that walks, or swims, or flies, or crawls in them.' Her voice sank to an ominous whisper: 'Behold Lilith ... behold Mother Nature ... behold the Mistress of All Creation. Behold me and be fearful, for I am Perfection.'

She drew back her arm to make the thrust.

Vanka staggered as he returned to the reality of the Demi-Monde, bemused and weakened by his meeting with—

He couldn't remember who; all that had happened in the last few moments was tantalisingly out of reach. All he knew was that he had to save Ella from Lilith and that meant helping Josephine. But that was easier said than done. He looked up and saw Josephine stretched unconscious across the *pe*, drained of strength and resolve.

Defeated.

He felt Jezebel standing close to his side. 'It was no good, Vanka, Lilith was too strong ... none can stand against her.'

Vanka waved his hand in the direction of the *ouanga* doll. 'The *juju*—'

'It's not powerful enough, Vanka ... it's not *personal* enough. Lilith is too strong for it to affect her.'

Vanka delved into his pocket and withdrew his handkerchief. 'What is the most powerful of all the humours of a Daemon?'

'Blood.'

'On this handkerchief is the blood of Lilith. When she was Ella, she used it to clean a wound on her leg and I swore to her then that I would treasure it.' He pushed the square of linen into Jezebel's hand. 'Maybe using this, your *ouanga* doll can be made potent enough?'

Jezebel didn't hesitate; she skipped over to the altar, took up the doll and wrapped the handkerchief around it like a shroud. This done, she held the doll high over her head and began to chant.

> *ABBA, hear my prayers, hear my pleas*
> *Help me, ABBA, help me please*
> *Come to the aid of my WhoDoo*
> *Breathe your power into this juju*

The chanting of the incantation complete, Jezebel placed the doll on a steel dish, doused it in oil and then struck a match.

Lilith braced herself to make the thrust with the sword. Deep inside her mind she heard the voice of Ella pleading with her to stop, that murdering her brother was madness, but Lilith refused to be deterred. Billy was now a danger to her plans to lead HumanKind to perfection and for that he must die.

Then ...

It was as though she was enveloped by fire. Her very soul seemed to be burning. She screamed as all of her power drained from her. She staggered and let the sword drop from her hand then slumped back against a chair, barely having enough strength to stay on her feet. Desperately Lilith struggled to maintain control but now the spirit of Ella was stronger inside her. Rather than being consumed by the flames it seemed that Ella had been energised by them.

'Nooooo!' Lilith screamed and then sagged unconscious to the floor.

Seeing his sister prostrate and helpless, Billy didn't hesitate. He kicked her hard in the stomach then gathered up the sword and steadied himself ready to thrust it into her guts.

'I would be grateful if you wouldn't kill the girl.'

Billy looked around to see a bruised Selim staggering across the room towards him.

'Fuck you, man, this bitch was gonna trash me fo' sure. An' no one leans on Billy Thomas without Billy Thomas leaning back.'

'Nevertheless, the girl is much too valuable for her to be killed in revenge. I have been ordered to keep her safe until Lammas Eve. *Then* you can sacrifice her.'

'Fuck that,' and Billy raised the sword over his head.

'If you kill her, Your Grace, I will ensure that you never leave the Demi-Monde and that your time here is spent communing with the most intense and unrelenting pain.'

'Fuck yo'. Yo' can't do that; I'm the motherfucking Messiah.'

'I can and I will. But if you spare your sister, I promise that on Lammas Eve you will have the honour of sacrificing her.'

Billy looked across to Selim to see if the guy was serious. 'Yo' rapping on the real?'

'I am, Your Grace. His HimPerial Majesty Shaka Zulu commands that the girl lives and I am ever the obedient servant of His Majesty.'

For a moment Billy stood undecided, then the red mist faded and common sense prevailed. He wanted to get home. He had a million bucks waiting for him there and all he had to do to collect it was get through to Lammas, cap his sister and then he was home free. Just eight more weeks. The smart move, he decided, would be to play along with Selim. 'Yo' certain I'm gonna be the one to total the bitch at the end of Summer?'

'I'm certain.'

Billy lowered the sword. 'Okay, but yo' better keep this badass bitch somewhere safe until then. Come Lammas, her ass is mine.'

'You may rely on it, Your Grace.'

*

Half-conscious though she was, Ella heard what was being said, but she was not afraid of death. Thanks to Vanka – thanks to ABBA – Lilith had been defeated, sent scurrting back deep into the darkest recesses of her soul. Now she felt cleansed . . . reborn. Once again she was Ella and it would be as Ella that she faced death. It would be Ella who pitted herself against the evil of Lucifer.

Part Six
The Escape from the Forbidding City

33

The Forbidding City
The Demi-Monde:
50th–63rd Days of Summer, 1005

By their pernicious oppression of Femmes, nonFemmes have relinquished their right to be perceived as human (Lucrezia Borgia: interview given to *The Coven Today*, 78th Day Summer 999). Indeed, there is strong evidence – their proclivity to engage in wars, their penchant for MALEvolence and their predilection to associate hetero-sexual sex with aggression – to support the contention that nonFemmes are more beast than human.

Proceedings of the Gendercide Committee, Fall 1003

The atmosphere in the Forbidding City was becoming febrile. Whilst the official word was that the war with the ForthRight was going well and the barbarian nonFemmes were being severely punished by the Covenite army, the constant rumble of artillery fire that was slowly advancing towards Beijing told another story. The horizon was now shaded a deep scarlet by the fires raging in Rangoon.

It was an atmosphere made all the more torrid by the sudden and violent purging of the NoNs serving in the Forbidding City, the whispered word being that AdmiralNoN Heii had turned traitor and Wu in panic had ordered the summary execution of all NoNs, only relenting when it had been pointed out to her that without NoNs the Forbidding City would cease to function. Despite this, at least a hundred of the poor devils had vanished into the depths of Hereji-Jo Castle and those who had survived had become *very* jumpy indeed. None more so than Mao Zedong, who in his anxiety to prove his fealty to the Empress was ever more strict in ensuring adherence to Li.

And it was Mao's redoubled enthusiasm for disciplining anyone who transgressed Li that had caused the delay in Dong E carrying out Xi Kang's imperative that she help the Daemon, Norma Williams, escape. The Fresh Blooms were being watched and disciplined as never before.

But like the good Confusionist she was, Dong E knew the value of patience, and as the days passed, so the tension eased, the Forbidding City once more relaxed and an opportunity to visit the Pavilion of Silent Repose where the Daemon was being held presented itself.

It was a maidFemme – in exchange for a small bag of gold *tiels* and a kiss – who finally agreed to hide Dong E at the bottom of the laundry basket when it was wheeled to the Daemon's apartment. As Dong E suspected they would be, the two sentryFemmes were so monumentally bored by the task they had been set guarding the Daemon that their examination of the basket was perfunctory and she was trundled into the girl's presence undiscovered. When she popped out of the basket, it was as well, she decided, that the guards had – on the orders of Empress Wu, who was concerned they might be seduced by the Daemon's devilish tongue – been deafened, such was the shriek of surprise the Daemon emitted.

'Who the fuck are you?' yelped the Daemon as she brandished a ceramic figurine representing the Empress Wu at Dong E in a very threatening manner.

'Daemon known as Norma Williams, I am Fresh Bloom Dong E and I have come to rescue you.'

'Hey, I know you. You were the girl doing the interpreting when I met with that lunatic Wu.'

Dong E bowed. 'You are correct, Daemon known as Norma Williams; I had the sublime honour of serving Her Divine Majesty Empress Wu in the capacity of interpreter.'

'Then what's an interpreter doing hiding in a laundry basket?'

'I have come here at the behest of ABBA Herself – as related by the iChing – to aid you in escaping from the Forbidding City.'

The Daemon laughed, which Dong E found a little off-putting. 'Are you for real?'

Dong E frowned, somewhat perplexed by the question. 'Daemon known as Norma Williams ...'

'Norma. I'd prefer to be addressed as Norma.'

'Very well, Norma. The Proposition of unBelievability propounded by PhilosopherNoN Xi Kang theorises that the Demi-Monde is not a "Real" world but is an illusionary Virtual World devised by an unknown agency and sustained by HumanKind's Fallibility of Perception, itself a consequence of a contaminated Solidified Astral Ether. So the answer to your question "am I for real?" depends very much upon whether you have a WunZian or a TooZian outlook on Life ... whether you are a proponent of Perceptionalism or unBelievability.'

'Stop!' said the Daemon as she held up her hands. 'I am not in the mood for all this Confusionist crap. It wasn't a philosophical question. What I meant was, are you in earnest when you say you're here to rescue me?'

Dong E frowned; it was a very peculiar question. 'Of course.'

The Daemon held out a hand. 'Then I'm very pleased to meet you. I haven't heard a word spoken in over six weeks, so you're most welcome to come visit.'

Dong E had heard of this peculiar and quite distasteful *gaijin* custom of shaking hands in greeting, but given the imperative of the divination offered by the iChing, she dismissed her scruples and took the Daemon's hand in hers.

'We must move quickly, Norma. My absence from the Pavilion of Delicious Delights will be noted and guardFemmes sent to search for me. We must hurry.' She pointed to the laundry basket. 'If you would snuggle down inside the basket. It is fortunate that you are such a small Daemon.'

'Whoa there, honey. I'm not going anywhere. I need to find some answers to a few questions before I make a run for it, notably about the work being done by a Dr Merit Ptah on the YiYi Project.'

Dong E shook her head. 'I have never heard of the Doctor nor of this YiYi Project.'

Norma began a nervous pacing of the room. Obviously, Dong E decided, Daemons were not trained in the arts necessary to achieve inner quietude and harmony. If this Norma was a typical example, they seemed very agitated creatures with no concept of the importance of maintaining *wu wei*.

'Well, certain people I've spoken to believe that the only place I'll find out about the YiYi Project is here in the Forbidding City.' Suddenly Norma stopped in mid-stride as though struck by a thought. 'Does the Empress have a private office?'

'Of course. She meets with her most senior NoNs in the Hall of Mental Cultivation. Mao ZeDong keeps a suite of offices there.'

'Then presumably that's where she keeps her most confidential papers.'

'Why yes.' Despite all her training in the maintenance of inscrutability Dong E felt herself frown as she began to understand what Norma was asking of her. 'What you are suggesting is impossible, Norma. It is suicide to even consider entering the Hall of Mental Cultivation unless expressly invited by the Empress herself. To be discovered there without such an invitation means death.'

'Well, death or no, that's probably the only place where I'll find information about what Dr Ptah is cooking up.' Norma sat herself down on a couch. 'Tell me something, Dong E, as the only way in or out of the Forbidding City is over the Bridge of the Heavenly Divide, I guess that burglary doesn't register very high on the list of the City's crime statistics.'

Again Dong E frowned and then, realising that this could contribute to her premature ageing, she made a conscious effort *not* to frown. But it was difficult, Norma's observations were *very* perplexing. 'Burglary? No, there is no theft in the Forbidding City, it is, well, forbidden.'

'Then I'm betting the City's security system isn't the best. I mean, it can't be up to much if you broke into this apartment so easily.'

Dong E had never really thought about it before, but now she realised that what Norma was saying was perfectly true. Whilst getting into and out of the Forbidding City was impossible, the security *inside* the City was slack. NoNs like Mao might bluster and threaten, but the reality was that with a little thought and a little bribery nothing was impossible and nowhere was impenetrable.

'I would hazard a guess that Mao's offices in this Hall of Mental Cultivation of yours aren't even locked.' Norma smiled. 'So here's the deal, Dong E, you get me the information I need about the YiYi Project and then I'll allow you to come rescue me.'

As she climbed back into the laundry basket, Dong E couldn't help thinking that somehow she'd been outnegotiated, but then, she supposed, the Daemon did have ABBA on her side.

Dong E decided that the only time it would be possible for her to enter the Hall of Mental Cultivation unseen would be at night, when the Forbidding City was asleep, but even then such an escapade was fraught with danger. Not only was traversing the corridors of the City without being seen by a servant or a prowling guard difficult, but as the Empress Wu slept little and was in the habit of summoning one or more of her concubines at any time of the night, there was the ever-present risk of Imperial NoN Mao ZeDong coming looking for her and not finding her in her quarters. Unfortunately, there was no alternative: the Hall of Mental Cultivation was perhaps the busiest room in the whole of the Palace and during the day it swarmed with NoN administrators bustling around dealing with the many and various tasks relating to the running of the Coven.

Dong E had to pick her moment carefully and that moment came a couple of nights later, when Mao ZeDong visited the Pavilion of Delicious Delights bearing two *shanpai* – the picture cards the Empress used to select the Fresh Blooms she would have entertain her. Experience told Dong E that when the Empress demanded *two* Fresh Blooms, then she would not require more. After a couple of hours or so of two-handed (and two-mouthed) Femme2Femme pleasuring, her passions and her vitality would be drained and she would sleep until dawn. But to be on the safe side, Dong E waited while the two girls had been stripped naked, their bodies oiled and perfumed, then wrapped in silk sheets and carried off to the Imperial Bed-chamber. Only when this had been done and the unCalled girls had begun to think of sleep did Dong E make her move.

Wearing her plainest *jiangs* – the black ones without embroi-dery or embellishments which she reserved for the most menial of cleaning duties she was occasionally asked to perform – Dong E slipped out of the Pavilion just after two in the morning. With a black scarf tied tight around her face she melded into the darkness as she moved silently along, her soft slippers making nary a sound as she padded down the empty, shadow-bedecked corridors. For ten tense minutes she scuttled through the City, expecting at any moment a challenge to be roared out, but, thankfully, she found the City asleep and she came to the Hall of Mental Cultivation without seeing another soul. Just as Norma had suspected, the doors to the hall weren't locked. Taking a deep breath, Dong E slid through the Door of Destiny Fulfilled and into the dark room beyond.

Well, not *that* dark. She found the Hall of Mental Cultivation swathed in the glow of red light streaming in through the windows lining the right-hand side of the hall. The night was suffused with firelight. Above the Great Wall she could see that the sky was flickering with flames. Rangoon was ablaze. The war, she decided, must be going *very* badly if Rangoon was burning unchecked.

Stunned that the HerEtical sanctuary of the Coven was being so wickedly violated, Dong E stood for a moment transfixed, but finally she remembered why she was there, and turned to survey the Hall. It took a moment for her eyes to adjust to the red-tinged gloom, and only then did she begin to realise the stupidity of the task she had been set. The room was crammed full of tables, these in turn littered with piles upon piles of paper. It was impossible to believe that she would be able to find the secrets of the YiYi Project within this avalanche of administrative dross.

Dross.

That was the clue. If this Project YiYi was as important as Norma said it was, it wouldn't be handled by mere NoN Administrators; only the most senior of officials would be privy to its secrets and *that* meant papers relating to the project would be held in the office of the Imperial NoN Mao ZeDong. Dong E shivered: to be discovered trespassing the Hall of Mental Cultivation might be punishable by death, but to be discovered violating the office of Mao ZeDong would be punishable by a very slow and very painful death. But she had no choice. The prophecy of the iChing had to be fulfilled.

She had only been in Mao ZeDong's office once before – when, as a ten-year-old girl, she had been brought to the Forbidding City – and the remembrance of the interview she'd been subjected to still brought goose bumps to her skin. For over an hour Mao had quizzed her about what she knew of her family and for an hour she had told him – truthfully – that she knew nothing about her real mother and father, that she was an orphan who had been brought up as a ward of foster parents. Finally – grudgingly – he had placed the Seal of Acceptance on the residency papers making her a Citizen of the Forbidding City.

Pushing these terrible remembrances to the back of her mind, Dong E moved across the hall towards the door which, as best she could remember, led to the private offices of Mao. Taking a quick look over her shoulder – the deserted hall was very, very spooky – she ghosted her way into the room. Unpleasant memories came flooding back. The room was dominated by a metre-high plinth set in the middle of the marbled floor upon which sat a huge gilded desk decorated with carved dragons. It had been in front of this desk that a tiny, trembling Dong E had stood when she had been interrogated by Mao. It was from this desk that the NoN had peered down at her and made his judgement of life and death.

Bastard.

Shaking with fear, Dong E stepped up onto the plinth and examined the top of the huge desk. There were four files stacked neatly to one side, obviously laid out ready for review in the morning. Taking a box of matches from the pocket of her *jiangs*, she lit the candle on the desk and began to examine the titles on the spines of the files. The first two merely related to the preparations being made to repel the invasion of the ForthRight and to the disposition of the Covenite Army: these she discarded. It was what was written on the third and fourth files that made Dong E's body clock begin to tick more quickly. The third was entitled 'Project YiYi: Male DeContamination and the Culling of nonFemmes' whilst the fourth read 'Progress towards the Translation of the *Flagellum Hominum*'.

The name rang a gong. The *Flagellum Hominum* had been referred to by Xi Kang in his book, and she could see by the seals used on the documents the file contained that they were of the greatest importance: only Papers of State bore the Dragon Seal of the Empress Wu. Unfortunately, all the documents seemed to have been written in some form of code and as such they were totally unintelligible. Perhaps, thought Dong E, Xi Kang would be able to decipher them. So, with a shrug, she scooped both files into the canvas bag she had on her shoulder and turned towards the door.

'It is not often that I am blessed with a visitor so late at night,' came a lilting, lisping voice from the shadowed depths of the room.

Gulping back her terror, Dong E looked around to see Imperial NoN Mao waddling across the room towards her. She was reminded of the description of the NoN given by Xi Kang, when he had observed that Mao was not human at all, rather he was a monster that was part monkey and part tiger, cunning and viciousness fused in one NoN. And by the glint in his eyes Dong E was sure that tonight it was the tiger aspect of Mao ZeDong that was in the ascendance.

The NoN stepped daintily up onto the plinth to stand beside the quaking Dong E, towering over the small, delicate Fresh Bloom. 'ABBA Herself must have roused me, alerted me that the sanctity of the Hall of Mental Cultivation was being despoiled. So come, my little crypto, reveal yourself, untie your scarf from your face in order that I might see who it is so traitorously violating this, the most private of all the rooms in the Forbidding City.'

Dong E had no option but to obey. Mao was a powerful man, and though he was unarmed – since Heii's betrayal no weapons except those carried by Imperial guardFemmes were allowed in the Forbidding City – she knew his hugely strong hands could break her neck as easily as they might snap a reed. Slowly she unwound the scarf from around her face.

'Fresh Bloom Dong E: I should have known. The shades of your Ancestors despoil the corridors of the Forbidding City and now you follow their perverse example. I knew it was a mistake to allow you to live, I should have had you snuffed out just as your father was. But no matter, by tomorrow you will be gone; tonight's escapade will overturn the Empress's scruples regarding offending the ancestors of the pigEmperor Qin Shi Huang. She will have no option but to forgo the delightful pleasure of fucking the daughter of her vilest enemy.'

What was the NoN talking about?

Mao manoeuvred himself directly in front of Dong E, so close that she could smell his perfume and feel his hot breath on her cheek. 'I have always rued the day that I was gelded because it has deprived me of the pleasure of taking you, Dong E, of inflicting on you something akin to the pain and humiliation your father inflicted upon me.' He raised a hand and trailed a finger down her long neck. 'Oh, how I have dreamed of defiling you. If I were whole and if the Empress had been less superstitious, I would have made such sport of your body. I would have tortured and fucked you in ways that would have wrung screams from your very soul, all the while delighting in the knowledge that the shade of your father watched on helpless.'

It was the way Mao said the word 'fucked' and the gleam in his eye that persuaded Dong E to do what she did. There were rumours rife amongst the Fresh Blooms that Mao's heterosexuality had never been fully eradicated by his gelding, that he spied on the Fresh Blooms and punished any he thought had not been wanton enough when called by the Empress. Mao might be a NoN, but he had obviously not freed himself of the abhorrent and corrosive lusts that nonFemmes were prey to.

'I know I have transgressed, Honoured NoN Mao,' she simpered, 'but I ask you to grant me forgiveness. Show mercy and I will be forever the dutiful and obedient Fresh Bloom.' Then slowly, artfully, Dong E unbuttoned the front of her *jiangs* and shucked the dungarees from her shoulders, displaying the nakedness beneath. She was rewarded by a small sigh from Mao. He hesitated, obviously struggling with the commandment that the body of a Fresh Bloom might only be touched by the Empress. Then he lifted his hand and drifted his long and beautifully decorated fingernails over her breast. Dong E stood silent, still and compliant, and Mao ZeDong, emboldened by her submissiveness, began to toy with the dark nipple. She saw the glint of lust in his eyes and wasn't surprised given that hers was a tantalising, an irresistible beauty.

With a shrug she let her *jiangs* flutter to the floor to pool around her feet. Now she stood naked before Mao, waiting for the magic of her beauty to cast its spell. She was, she knew, flawless: her skin covered her like tawny silk; her body was perfectly proportioned in an ideal compromise of softness and muscularity, of the svelte and the curved; and her face, which – so she had been told by her foster mother – blended the high cheekbones and strong nose of her mother with the full lips and broad forehead of her father, was truly lovely.

For several long seconds she stood motionless, tempting Mao, and then finally she spoke: 'I am yours, Imperial NoN Mao, to command as you will. Forgive me for my trespassing and my body is yours to do with as you choose.'

'It's been so long,' he murmured. 'Your skin . . . so soft . . . so wonderful.'

As though dismissive of these oh-so-cautious overtures, Dong E hitched her naked bottom onto the sandalwood top of the desk and stretched back. The message was unmistakable: she was offering herself to Mao.

'You are very certain,' Mao ZeDong muttered as he stepped closer to the girl.

'Never more so in my life,' Dong E announced as she grabbed one of the pens from the set adorning his desk, pirouetted on her backside and drove the pen, nib first, through the NoN's neck. The thrust skewered the scream he was inclined to utter and turned it into an incoherent cough. It didn't kill him. It was the second pen Dong E stabbed into his right eye and deep into his mind that did that. With a reflexive widening of his one remaining eye and a voiding of his belly Mao pitched forward to fall across her lap. With a heavy, wet thud his head smashed onto the desk, his body twitching as he reluctantly released hold on life.

Finally he was still: Mao ZeDong, the second-most powerful person in the Coven, was dead.

'I have assassinated Guardian of the Imperial Bedchamber, NoN Mao ZeDong.'

'Good, that bastard deserved killing,' said Xi Kang. 'Now put out that fucking candle and let an old NoN get some sleep.'

'But what am I to do? When his body is discovered tomor-row—'

'No one will suspect a Fresh Bloom, suspicion will fall on the other NoNs. After what Heii did Wu thinks every one of them is an UnFunDaMentalist crypto. She'll think he was killed by order of Heydrich.'

'I was seen leaving the Hall of Mental Cultivation.'

Xi Kang sat up and rubbed his eyes. 'Now *that* was careless. Was your face covered?'

'Yes, but they will know it was a Fresh Bloom who killed Mao and—'

'Then they'll execute the lot of you. Wu won't be taking any chances. By her reckoning, it'll be better if all two hundred Fresh Blooms are Plucked than one assassin slips through the net.'

'So what shall I do?'

'Escape tonight.'

'Escape? How?'

With a sigh of reluctance Xi Kang swung his legs off his cot. 'With my help.'

'You? But you're just a—'

'A broken-down old NoN? Is that what you were going to say? Then you should remember, my pretty little assassin, that there was once a time when this broken-down old NoN wasn't so broken-down and was possessed of a fully functioning dick ... and other things.'

He delved under his cot and pulled out a long wooden chest. Wiping off the thick coating of dust, he snapped the locks open and threw back the lid. To Dong E's amazement, lying inside was a *katana* sword, long, slim, beautiful and deadly. Almost reverently Xi Kang drew the sword free of its straps and then unsheathed it, revealing the one and a half metres of curved and savagely sharp blade. 'Wonderful,' he murmured, as he ran a lint cloth along its length, wiping away the thin patina of *choji* oil that had been used to protect the blade. 'Made by Muramasa from the very finest jewelled steel. I call it "Soul Stealer".'

'What are you doing with it?' Dong E asked. 'Did you steal it?' She could see from the fine silver work on the hilt and on the scabbard and from the perfection of the blade that the sword was no run-of-the-mill weapon. This was the type of sword only wielded by one of the nobility ... by a samurai. It most certainly was not a weapon used by a nothing of a NoN.

'It was given to me by the Emperor.'

'The Emperor?'

Xi Kang ignored the scorn flavouring Dong E's question. 'Yes, His Imperial Majesty Qin Shi Huang, Light of the Kosmos and Ruler of the Demi-Monde, presented it to me to commemorate twenty years of faithful service. Undeserved, of course: it was my lack of insight that failed to identify the auguries indicating that that mad cow Wu was preparing to strike, but perhaps it was part of ABBA's plan that I spent that year not only chasing the dragon but catching it.'

'Hah, a likely story! Such a sword would only have been given to one high in the Emperor's esteem.'

'But I was! Xi Kang is my NoN name. Before I was gelded I was Prime Minister Wen Tiangiang, Administrator of All the Coven.'

'You're Wen Tiangiang? But you're dead!'

A chuckle. 'Only partially. By rights my life should have been taken from me when those lunatic HerEticals murdered the Emperor, but they were so frightened of offending my ances-tors – many of whom I have in common with Wu – that they spared me. Instead they took away my cock and tried to take away my sword, but there were those in the Forbidding City who took pity on me and hid it ... the sword, that is, not my cock. I suppose they reckoned that for a man to lose his penis was punishment enough without him being deprived of *both* his weapons. Old friends from before the Revolution returned Soul Stealer to me three years ago.' He winked at Dong E. 'As the Empress has discovered, there are those within the Coven who are not quite as loyal and dutiful as she likes to imagine.'

'But why would they give you back your sword?'

A derisive laugh from Xi Kang. 'Because it was judged that I had a use for it ... that I had something worth fighting for.' He tied a sash about his waist and threaded the scabbard through it. 'That's better: I almost feel whole again.' He turned to Dong E and smiled. 'So, will you show me the way to the Pavilion of Silent Repose? It's been many years since I wandered the corridors of the Forbidding City and my memory isn't quite what it was.'

A frown from Dong E. 'Why there? Surely it's better to try to escape through the Meridian Gate?'

'Presently. First we must rescue this Daemon of yours.'

34

The Forbidding City
The Demi-Monde: 63rd Day of Summer, 1005

It is a *sine qua non* of virtually all Demi-Mondian thought that only those created from the Living might possess a soul. But typically the TooZian Confusionists dispute this, claiming that the swords they wear, though inanimate, embody the spirit and the soul of the one who wields them.

'Weird and Wacky Beliefs of the Demi-Monde':
Immanuel Kant, *Anthropology Today*

There were a thousand and one questions buzzing around in Dong E's head as she and Xi Kang scooted through the dark, deserted corridors of the Forbidding City, the most pressing of which was how a disreputable old NoN – armed though he was – expected to deal with the two formidably big and formidably powerful guards who stood between them and the Daemon.

The answer in the end was 'easily'.

Dong E had seen the guards practising with their bamboo staves in the Courtyard of Final Fulfilment and had always thought them incredibly skilled and incredibly fast swordsFemmes, but she had been wrong. Compared with the speed and dexterity with which Xi Kang wielded Soul Stealer, they were mere amateurs. Admittedly, the NoN had surprise on his side and certainly at three o'clock in the morning the guards were not at their most alert, but that took nothing away from the savage efficiency with which he dispatched them. The first guard hadn't even time to unsheathe her sword before her head had been removed from her shoulders and the second quickly learnt that firing a rifle when one of your arms had just been chopped off at the elbow was extraordinarily difficult. Fortunately, it was a problem the Femme only had to wrestle with for the second it took for Xi Kang to plunge his sword through her chest.

'I'm fucking impressed with myself,' admitted Xi as he wiped the smear of SAE from the blade of his sword. 'You'd have thought that the best part of ten years spent lying on a cot, trying to remember what a good wank felt like, would have slowed my reflexes down a tad. But not a bit of it. Remarkable.'

And it *was* remarkable, judged Dong E as she stepped over the decapitated body of the larger of the two guards; Xi had fought like a true warrior. Perhaps his story about having once been the famous Prime Minister and warrior Wen Tiangiang wasn't as fanciful as she had imagined. Pushing her way into Norma's apartment, she felt herself quite lost in admiration of the old man's ability in matters martial.

They found Norma lying on a futon in the furthest corner of the room, sound asleep and blissfully unaware of the carnage that had just taken place outside her door. 'Norma,' Dong E whispered as she nudged the sleeping girl with the toe of her slipper, 'wake up. We have come to rescue you.'

'What?'

'We have come to rescue you. I have taken the files relating to Project YiYi from the Hall of Mental Cultivation. Unfortunately, to do this I was required to assassinate Imperial Secretary Mao ZeDong and now we must escape the Forbidding City before his body is discovered. PhilosopherNoN Xi Kang has offered to guide us to safety.'

Norma blinked the sleep out of her eyes and studied the NoN carefully. She didn't seem terribly impressed. 'So you're the cavalry, eh? I bet Empress Wu is shitting herself.'

Xi Kang laughed uproariously. 'I like you, Daemon, there is definitely something of the TooZian about you. And as for the Empress soiling her kimono, you should know that once just the mention of my name meant it was smelly-knickers time ... and perhaps it will be so again.' With that he waved a hand to indicate the two bodies lying in her doorway.

They made a convincing statement of intent, and without another word Norma rose to her feet and hauled on her *jiangs* and her slippers. Then, with Xi Kang leading the way, the three of them headed towards the Meridian Gate and the Bridge of the Heavenly Divide. It was a tense journey and twice they nearly bumped into ServantNoNs going about their early morning business. But with luck and – so Dong E liked to think – the guidance of ABBA they came to the Meridian Gate unchallenged. With a determined nod, Xi Kang ushered his two charges into what looked like a stable block built next to the Gate's right-hand tower.

'Feng Menlong,' he whispered as he pushed open the door and stepped into the darkness, 'how can you sleep when your Master comes calling? Are you so absorbed in writing those sickly-sweet odes to unrequited love that you have forgotten your Oath of Imperial Fealty?' He laughed. 'And love doesn't come any more unrequited than when it's written by a penis-less poet. For a dickless nonentity like you to be writing about jade stalks entering precious gateways is akin to an armless man having ambitions to be a juggler.'

'Nonentity?' came a protest from the darkness. 'Who is the piece of dogshit having the audacity to accuse the genius who wrote the *Qing Shi* of being a nonentity?' Out of the shadows came an old bow-legged man whose eyes were dull with sleep and Solution. They didn't remain dull for long: seeing Xi Kang, he dropped to his knees and knocked his forehead down onto the tiles of the stable floor nine times. 'Prime Minister, forgive me but ... but ... I heard you had journeyed to meet your ancestors.'

So Xi Kang had been the Prime Minister!

'I am alive, Servant Feng, and in need of your help.'

'Anything, Prime Minister, but ... but ...'

'There is no time for explanations. Where is the Imperial palanquin?'

'In the room to the back of the stables, Prime Minister, sir.'

'Are there three others ready to die in the service of the true Empress?'

The true Empress?

Feng raised his lantern and studied Dong E. 'Is this ... is this ... ?'

'Yes, this is Dong E, the forgotten daughter of Emperor Qin Shi Huang.'

It took a moment for Dong E to connect with what was being said. 'I don't understand,' she spluttered. 'All of the Emperor's children were assassinated during the fight for the Forbidding City ten years ago.'

'All the *legitimate* children,' corrected Xi Kang. 'The Emperor was a virile man who was inclined to fuck any Femme possessed of a beating body clock. Understandably, his Empress refused to have his by-blows in the Forbidding City, so as soon as you were born I had you adopted. When Wu took control of the Coven, she felt it safer to keep the Emperor's bastard progeny – that's you – under her control and had you brought here. Of course, that she could humiliate the shade of the Emperor by making his daughter serve her as a concubine was also a motivation in having you ordained as a Fresh Bloom. Wu is nothing if not spiteful.'

Dong E felt her legs go weak and had to lean against a wall to prevent herself collapsing. 'I'm the Emperor's daughter?' she gasped.

'The Emperor's *bastard* daughter, if you wish to be exact.' Xi Kang stopped for a moment and then corrected himself. 'No, that's not right: as you're a bastard who's the *only* surviving child of Emperor Qin Shi Huang, I suppose that makes you legitimate.' He caught sight of Feng who was now kneeling on the straw- and shit-strewn floor of the stable kowtowing to Dong E. 'Oh, do get up. We haven't time for all that nonsense. We need three more bearers.'

'Of course, Prime Minister: there's An Ling ... there's ...'

'Bring them here, but do it quickly and quietly.'

As the old man waddled away, Dong E came to stand square in front of Xi Kang. 'This is all nonsense, isn't it ... me being the Emperor's daughter?'

'No, it's a fact, Your Majesty. I had thought you dead until you came tripping into the Gallery of Literary Profundity four years ago. I recognised you instantly from the birthmark on your hand – all of the Pings had it – though I have to admit, you've filled out wonderfully. I thought about telling you then, but if Mao had ever suspected you knew what your birthright was then you'd have been dead within the hour.'

Their conversation was interrupted by Feng Menlong barging his way back into the room, followed by three decidedly ancient-looking companions. On seeing Dong E these newcomers dropped to their knees.

'Rise, rise,' commanded an exasperated Xi Kang. 'Hurry. Break out the palanquin. The True Empress Dong E and her friend will ride in it and we will pretend that it carries the Empress Wu.' Before Dong E could object or ask any questions, she and Norma had been bundled into the litter, the screens pulled down over the windows and the palanquin lifted onto the shoulders of the NoNs. At a command from Xi Kang they exited the stable coming to a halt before the Meridian Gate.

Peeking out from behind the screen, Dong E saw Xi Kang demand – demand! – that the gates be opened so that the Empress Wu might journey across the Bridge of the Heavenly Divide to Beijing. Perhaps Xi Kang overplayed his hand; perhaps the Captain of the Gate wasn't used to being given orders by someone who wasn't wearing the usual uniform of an AdministratorNoN; or perhaps it was the absence of an appropriately stamped pass. Whatever the reason, the CaptainFemme was suspicious. But Xi Kang blustered and threatened until finally the CaptainFemme – knowing the fate of any who delayed Her Imperial Majesty – reluctantly agreed to open the gates.

The journey across the Bridge of the Heavenly Divide was slow and harrowing. The four NoNs carrying the palanquin were old and enfeebled and, despite the crude entreaties of Xi Kang, could only manage a slow, lurching progress. That the Bridge was so narrow didn't help either, they kept bashing the palanquin against the rails, threatening to send it – and its two passengers – tumbling into the moat below.

They were only halfway across when a difficult situation became distinctly dangerous. 'There are guards coming after us,' Dong E heard Xi Kang call. 'That bastard of a Captain must have checked whether the Empress was still in her apartment.'

There was no use for subterfuge now. She raised the shutter from the window and peered back towards the Forbidding City and what she saw sent chills trickling down her spine. A detachment of twenty or so guardFemmes were racing after them and the speed with which they were closing meant that they would be on them before the palanquin had reached the safety of Beijing.

'Save the Empress, save the Messiah!' screamed Xi Kang to the four bearers as he drew his sword. 'Run as you've never run before. Run, while I hold them here.'

Dong E couldn't believe what the old NoN was saying. 'That's madness, Xi Kang . . . it's suicide.'

The NoN shook his head. 'No, the bridge is so narrow that it can be held by one man. They will only be able to attack me one at a time.'

'You will die.'

Xi Kang laughed. 'I am old and my race is run. Death walks behind me. But I can think of no better way to die than protecting the daughter of the Emperor I loved and the Messiah who will bring peace to the Demi-Monde.' He pressed a ring into Dong E's hand. 'This is the Imperial Ring given into my care by your father. It is yours by birth and by right. But know this, with it comes grave responsibility: you must lead your people out of the shadow cast by Empress Wu and her HerEtical hatred. Do this and I will not have died in vain.' He slapped Feng Menlong on the shoulder. 'Run quickly, my faithful friend, you carry the future on your shoulders.'

With that Xi Kang bowed to Dong E, the rain streaming down his face masking his tears. 'I salute Empress Dong E, True Empress of the Demi-Monde, of the Great Beyond and of all the Kosmos, Blessed and Much Beloved by ABBA, and I pray that HeShe grants you Nine Thousand Years of Peace and Contentment.'

Then he turned to face the onrushing guards.

As he stood poised in the centre of the Bridge, a strange calm descended upon Xi Kang. For the first time in his life he believed he was truly experiencing *wu wei*, that his soul had become suffused with the Nothingness of the Kosmos, that all was Correct and in Harmony. Now he saw clearly – his old eyes suddenly sharp and true – saw that there were twenty guards advancing towards him. Now he heard clearly, he heard the slap of their sandals on the wooden beams of the Bridge and their panted breath. And now he understood clearly all that had evaded his understanding.

'So ABBA,' he said to the empty night, 'you come to me at last. You come to the one who has always doubted you, the one who has always scoffed when your name was invoked. Tired of tricks, eh? Tired of playing hide-and-seek? Tired of moving in such mysterious ways? So you finally reveal yourself to this old doubter. Then know this: I am ready to fight and I am ready to die, but I am old and I am weak. So I call on you and on my ancestors to help me in my moment of need. I call on you to help me defend the life of the daughter of my friend and Emperor. I call on you to help me save the Messiah you have sent to guide the people of the Demi-Monde to Ying. And for your help I offer this in return: that when I die, your name will be on my lips so that my enemies will know I died with ABBA at my side and in my soul.'

The guards were only five metres from him.

'NoN Xi Kang, stand aside by order of Her Imperial Majesty Empress Wu!'

Xi Kang laughed. 'NoN Xi Kang is no more: in his place stands Prime Minister Wen Tiangiang, loyal Servant to the True Empress Dong E, Defender of the Messiah and Blessed of ABBA. And know this, CaptainFemme, I will not allow you to pass.'

'You are a fool: the Emperor and his children are dead and you are but one against twenty. Put down your sword, old NoN, it is impossible to stand alone against Destiny.'

Xi Kang shook his head. 'But I do not stand alone, Captain-Femme. Do you not see that I am as one with ABBA? Do you not see, Captain, that I have achieved ABBAsoluteness, my body, my mind and my soul united with the Kosmos? Do you not see that I stand with ABBA by my side?'

That simple statement seemed to disturb the guards. As Xi Kang stood there with the rain pouring down on him, he saw them fidget uncomfortably and cast anxious glances at one another. With a swagger Xi Kang turned Soul Stealer's long blade in the moonlight, letting his enemies see the deadly steel that awaited them.

'Understand that ABBA has ordained that I die with my sword in my hand, a sword forged to destroy all those who would threaten the True Empress, Dong E. Know that I made a Sacred Oath to protect her. Know that I am her godfather and that I will not violate this Oath. You shall not pass.'

'You are just a single sword, old NoN. You will die.'

'I am a sometime philosopher and poet and as such have a great reverence for words. So I quote now from a poem written by a forgotten *gaijin* poet named Macaulay:

> *To every man upon this world,*
> *Death cometh soon or late.*
> *And how can man die better*
> *Than facing fearful odds,*
> *For the ashes of his fathers*
> *And the temples of his gods?'*

A smile illuminated Xi Kang's face. 'Brilliant; if I didn't know better I'd have thought Macaulay was a Chink.' And with that Prime Minister Wen Tiangiang, loyal Servant to the True Empress Dong E, Defender of the Messiah and Blessed of ABBA, raised Soul Stealer high over his head and hurled himself forward screaming his war cry, 'For the True Empress and for ABBA!'

35

The Coven
The Demi-Monde: 64th Day of Summer, 1005

Ah, Terror Incognita. The Final Frontier. The Centre of the World. The last unexplored region of the Demi-Monde. The Land that ABBA Forgot. Such is its tempting mystery that many brave – and, it must be said, foolhardy – explorers have crossed the Wheel River to discover its secrets. But none have returned. So all we are left with are the tantalising sketches made by Speke when he traversed that strange land by balloon, sketches that reveal it to be in every way as peculiar and as fantastic as writers have speculated.

> **Excerpt from the final entry of the diary of the explorer Colonel Percy Fawcett**

Burlesque decided he didn't like Trixie Dashwood. He had heard all the stories about how good a commander she was, how she and her fighters had fought the UnFunnies to a standstill and how it was thanks to her that there was still blood available in Rangoon, but to his mind, there was something not quite right about the girl. It was her eyes that gave him the collywobbles: they had the same cold implacability he'd seen in Beria's. They snarled out at the world with an intensity that could split rock, so much so that every time she looked in his direction, he thought he was going to shit himself. He made the decision to stay as far away from Trixie Dashwood as the geography of the room allowed. This one was bad news.

'Gor, she's a right little sweetheart, ain't she, Burlesque?'

Amazed that anyone could describe Trixie Dashwood as a 'sweetheart', Burlesque looked around to check that Rivets hadn't totally taken leave of his senses. It was then he realised that the object of the boy's admiration wasn't Trixie Dashwood but the utterly exquisite Chinese girl who – accompanied by Norma Williams – had just stepped into the room. She was indeed a real 'sweetheart', being small and slender – a little *too* slender for Burlesque's taste; he liked his women to have a bit of meat on them – and transcendentally beautiful. The girl reminded Burlesque of an exotic bird that had flown ...

He stopped: he didn't do this sort of poetic, romantic shit. Just ask Odette.

'Yus, she ain't a bad looker,' he observed. 'Bit on the skinny side though.'

There was no reply; he was talking to himself. Rivets had vanished. Not that he had much time to think about the boy's sudden disappearance, what with Odette dragging him across the room to meet and greet the newcomers.

It wasn't until hugs and kisses and bows and names had been exchanged, the Chink bird called Dong E and Norma congratulated on their escape from the Forbidding City, and fresh drinks served that Rivets made a return appearance. At least Burlesque *thought* it was Rivets but he had to perform a double take to make sure. Incredibly, in the few minutes he'd been gone the boy had washed, combed his hair and put on a clean shirt. He looked almost respectable. He also looked very excited as he stood there hopping from one foot to the other waiting to be introduced.

Burlesque obliged. 'This is Rivets, Femme Dong E, a friend of mine. Rivets, this is Femme Dong E.'

Rivets bobbed his head enthusiastically. 'Dongie, eh? That's a nice name. I don't suppose your first name's Ding by any chance, is it?'

For a second the girl seemed just a little confused, but then she gave Rivets a wonderful smile. 'No, Rivets-san, like you, I have a name which sounds odd to foreigners.'

Rivets blushed, then stammered a reply. 'Oh, I weren't taking the piss or nuffink. I fink it's a corkin' name,' and with that he pulled up a chair and shoved it and himself between Dong E and Burlesque. And as he did so, Burlesque's nose told him that Rivets had also made quite liberal use of his special jar of *eau de Paris*. The boy smelt like a garden: flowery with a subtle undertow of compost.

Odette gave Burlesque a surreptitious wink and then leant her lips close to his ear. *'L'amour,'* she whispered.

Yeah, he silently agreed, *Rivets is a boy in love*.

Out of the frying pan and into the fire, mused Norma as she gazed around the room. Oh, she was pleased to see her friends again, but the baleful presence of Trixie Dashwood had drained all the bounce out of her.

Maybe, she wondered, she hadn't fully recovered from her ordeal in the sewers. Despite spending a night in bed and taking several long baths, she still had palpitations every time she thought about the horror of having been obliged to enter the sewers again.

Not that she'd been given any choice in the matter. Mata Hari – who, as Su Xiaoxiao had promised, had been waiting for her and Dong E when they'd escaped from the Forbidding City – had announced the sewers to be the only safe route out of Beijing. Even so it had taken all Norma's will-power to stop herself panicking when she'd been sealed in that stinking, claustrophobic darkness. But somehow she had managed to control her fears and now she was safe.

Well, safe as she could ever be in the Demi-Monde. Safe as she could ever be in the presence of Trixie Dashwood.

Norma had recognised Trixie immediately she'd entered the room. Even with her head shaved, she had a force about her that was unmistakable. In fact, despite the absence of all her wonderful blonde hair, she looked pretty much as Norma remembered her from Warsaw: angry, tired and dishevelled which, Norma supposed, was understandable given the recent fighting. The unfortunate thing was that she still had the same mad sparkle in her eyes.

'My goodness, it's our wayward Daemon,' breathed an astonished-looking Trixie when she spotted Norma. 'Now you're the last person I thought I'd be bumping into here in the Coven. I thought you were dead.'

Desperate to remain as insouciant as she was able – Trixie Dashwood had always scared the bejeezus out of her – Norma gave the girl a broad smile and thrust out a hand. 'It's good to see you alive and well, Trixie. You too, Wysochi.' The huge Pole standing at Trixie's side bowed an acknowledgement and gave her one of his trademark off-kilter smiles. He, at least, seemed willing to be friendly. 'And talking about premature announcements of death, I heard the same about you, that you were killed escaping from Warsaw.'

'As you can see, I'm alive, Daemon.'

Daemon? Fuck, didn't Trixie ever lighten up? Why did she have to be such a hard-ass?

'I never suspected you would be so tenacious of life,' Trixie continued, 'I heard you'd been flushed down the sewers.' She gave a morbid little laugh. 'And I think, given the situation in the Coven, you'll find it might have been better if you'd stayed flushed.'

'No, all the sewers have done is given me a pathological aversion to shit.'

Or, more accurately, shits.

Obviously sensing the frisson between the two girls, Su Xiaoxiao decided to play the mediator. 'Norma is something of the hero of the hour, GeneralFemme Dashwood ...'

GeneralFemme. My, my, Trixie has come up in the world.

'... as is Fresh Bloom Dong E.' Here Su Xiaoxiao nodded towards the Chinese girl.

Norma was pleased to see that Dong E was smiling again; the death of Xi Kang had hit her hard and there were obviously other things troubling her, things presumably relating to the conversations she'd had with the NoN in the stable block when they were escaping the Forbidding City. But what these had been about Norma had no idea: her Chink hadn't been good enough to understand what had been going down.

'Norma succeeded in penetrating the Forbidding City,' Su Xiaoxiao explained, 'and escaping with a number of highly classified documents. These documents, GeneralFemme, are the reason I asked you to attend this meeting. The information contained in them behoves us to take dramatic action, dramatic action that requires the services of an army ... of your army.'

With that Su Xiaoxiao took Trixie Dashwood by the arm, led her to her place at the conference table and then called the meeting to order, waving the nine men and women standing in the room to their chairs. 'I wish to welcome GeneralFemme Trixiebell Dashwood and Major Feliks Wysochi to our meeting.'

'You better make that Colonel Dashwood,' grumbled Trixie. 'I imagine that by now the Empress Wu has rescinded my appointment as head of the Covenite army.'

'As you wish. Let it be *Colonel* Dashwood. I invited Colonel Dashwood and Major Wysochi here today as representatives of the Warsaw Free Army which is fighting so bravely to deny the SS possession of Rangoon's Blood Bank.'

Then, one by one Su Xiaoxiao went around the individuals seated around the table, introducing them to Trixie. 'Norma Williams you know, Colonel Dashwood, but the others you may not. To Norma's left is the brave nuFemme Dong E, who helped bring the secret files out of the Forbidding City. To her left are Rivets, Burlesque Bandstand and Odette Aroca, who together were founding members of the Normalist movement that did so much to discomfit the ForthRight's occupation of the Quartier Chaud. And last, but by no means least, are the eminent cryptologist AcademicianNoN Ki Song and the evolutionist Gregor Mendel.'

Introductions made, she looked back to Trixie and smiled. 'Perhaps, Colonel Dashwood, before we go very much further, you would be so kind as to give us your appraisal of the military situation in the Coven?'

Trixie laughed. 'I remember a phrase from my days as a schoolgirl: *plus ça change, plus c'est la même chose.* Just as they were in Warsaw, a couple of Seasons ago, my fighters are now hunkered down in bombed-out cellars defending a Blood Bank against a vastly superior force of SS StormTroopers. Our scouts say that the SS have taken control of most of Tokyo and Rangoon and that they'll be at the gates of the Great Wall in less than ten days.'

'Ten days!' gasped a shocked Dong E. 'But I had thought the Coven would have been able to hold out much longer. The Covenite army—'

'The Covenite army is surrendering in droves,' interrupted Trixie. 'Now all that stands between the ForthRight army and victory is the WFA. I have around three thousand fighters – most of them wounded and exhausted – under my command and only enough ammunition left for a couple of weeks' more fighting. After that . . .' Trixie trailed off. 'Would you concur with that assessment, Major Wysochi?'

Caught in the act of downing a glass of Solution, Wysochi coughed and gave a rueful shrug. 'In my considered opinion as a military strategist, Colonel, we're fucked. My advice is that we run for it, but the problem is, I'm buggered if I can suggest *where* we should run.'

And that, Norma knew, was the killer question: where was there left in the Demi-Monde that would provide any refugees from the Coven with a safe haven? The Demi-Monde seemed to be contracting by the hour. In addition to the Rookeries and Rodina, Reinhard Heydrich controlled most of the Quartier Chaud so there would be no sanctuary there, and the unholy alliance between NoirVille and Venice meant that the rest of the Demi-Monde was an equally unappetising destination. Quite simply there was nowhere safe in the Demi-Monde.

As Trixie Dashwood lapsed into silence, Su Xiaoxiao stood up to address those gathered in the room. 'As you have heard, the situation in the Coven is serious, so serious that I believe it will take our combined efforts to prevent the world falling into the clutches of evil.'

Trixie Dashwood gave a scornful laugh. 'I trust it hasn't escaped your notice, Femme Su Xiaoxiao, that the Demi-Monde has *already* fallen into the clutches of evil, evil represented by Reinhard Heydrich and the Daemon known as Lady IMmanual.'

'You are a little out of touch, Colonel. There has been a coup in Venice and Doge IMmanual has been replaced by her brother, Duke William. Venice is now, officially, part of NoirVille and the Lady IMmanual will be executed on Lammas Eve having been found guilty of Crimes against Venice.'

'NoirVille's military muscle merged with Venice's money . . . that will pose as big a problem as Heydrich.'

Su Xiaoxiao sighed. 'I understand your concern, Colonel

Dashwood, but I think when you have heard the revelations to be imparted by our learned friends' – here she nodded towards Mendel and Ki Song – 'you will realise the extent of the wickedness contemplated by Empress Wu is unparalleled in the history of the Demi-Monde. But there is hope: as promised in the religious writings of the Demi-Monde, ABBA has sent a Messiah to lead us to triumph and to Rapture.' Here she smiled towards Norma.

Now it was Trixie's turn to be shocked. 'This Daemon is the Messiah?' she snorted. 'Ridiculous!'

'You were incarcerated throughout Spring, Colonel, during which time much happened. The work of the Venetian preScientist Nikolai Kondratieff and the consulting of the iChing here in the Coven have proved conclusively that Norma Williams is the Messiah, a fact supported by her promotion of the creed of non-violence that has become known as Normalism.'

The chuckle greeting this revelation indicated that Trixie Dashwood was less than convinced. 'I hear what you say, Femme Su, but I've got to tell you I don't believe it. I would have thought ABBA could have drummed up a Messiah with a little more ... gravitas. I mean,' and here she shook her head, 'a Daemon as the Messiah. No, it isn't right.'

'I understand your doubts, Colonel Dashwood,' answered Su Xiaoxiao, 'but, as I say, the Messiahship of Norma has been confirmed several times over. Norma is the Messiah.'

Trixie gave a dismissive wave of a hand in Norma's direction. 'Okay, let's move on. All we're going to do by debating this further is waste time.'

Su Xiaoxiao nodded in the direction of the small, chubby Chink sitting next to Mendel at the very end of the table. 'I would like to ask AcademicianNoN Ki Song to speak. He and Scientist Gregor Mendel have laboured through the night examining the documents recovered from the Forbidding City.'

The NoN levered himself to his feet and addressed his audience in faltering English. 'Fresh Bloom Dong E and Femme Williams brought two files from the Forbidding City, the first entitled "Project YiYi: Male DeContamination and the Culling of nonFemmes" and the second "Progress towards the Translation of the *Flagellum Hominum*". All the documents contained in these files were encrypted – a sign of their importance – but, fortunately for us, Imperial NoN Mao ZeDong employs a code that I found relatively simple to break.'

The NoN waited for a response from his audience regarding this feat of decoding but his only reward was an impatient cough from Su Xiaoxiao.

Ki Song sniffed. 'I will address the information we discovered in the file relating to Project YiYi first.' Here he took a rather theatrical moment to rearrange his notes. 'Project YiYi involves the reduction of the male population of the Demi-Monde, the leadership of the Coven believing that a small pool of nonFemmes can service the reproductive needs of an entire female community. Their contention is that a population made up of ninety-nine parts Femmes and one part unCastrated nonFemmes would be viable, and as a consequence the Demi-Monde would be less prone to the violence stimulated by MALEvolence.'

The NoN looked around to confirm that his audience had absorbed the import of what he was saying. Satisfied that it had, he continued. 'Remarkably, considering how insane Dr Merit Ptah, the YiYi Project's leader, must be, she has recognised that the culling of ninety-nine per cent of their number would be somewhat unpopular with the Demi-Monde's nonFemme fraternity. Therefore, her efforts have been directed towards the development of a gender-specific bacterial agent –

Ptah refers to it simply as the Plague – which would efficiently eliminate most of the male population of the Demi-Monde. The One Per Cent Stock needed to provide reproductive ... input would be held in isolation safe from the Plague's depredations.'

Su Xiaoxiao interrupted. 'We have been informed by our agent Mata Hari that all the nonFemmes who made up the One Per Cent Stock have already been transported to an unknown destination where, presumably, they are to be held in quarantine. Only Scientist Mendel was able to evade this round-up, a round-up which indicates that Project YiYi is now a reality.'

'That is a correct supposition, Femme Su,' agreed Ki Song. 'According to the documents recovered by Femme Williams, the Plague weapon will be ready for deployment on Lammas Eve.'

Now *that* was a statement that got the attention of everybody in the room, especially the men. It also persuaded Trixie Dashwood to make an observation. 'Which is obviously why the defences of the Coven were in such a state of neglect. That the ForthRight have taken Rangoon and Tokyo is irrelevant to Empress Wu; all she's ever been intent on doing is hunkering down behind the Great Wall until the Plague was ready to be used. Once she's done that, the ForthRight Army will be history—'

'Along with just about every other man in the Demi-Monde,' added Norma quietly.

Ki Song continued with his explanation. 'The papers brought from the Forbidding City tell us that Ptah's experimental work is being conducted in Hereji-Jo Castle and it is there that the production facility – called the Fermentation Plant – for the Plague has been built. If we wish to forestall Empress Wu's efforts to destroy nonFemmes, then we must attack Hereji-Jo Castle and destroy the Fermentation Plant before Lammas Eve.'

A derisive snort from Trixie. 'With the greatest of respect, NoN Ki Song, when I was commanding the Covenite Army I had an opportunity to study the plans of that castle and without an army, without artillery and without the time to make an adequate siege it is impossible to reduce the place; the walls are too strong and the garrison too large. After the Forbidding City it is perhaps the best fortified and best defended citadel in the whole of the Coven.'

'We *must* destroy the Plague,' persisted Su Xiaoxiao.

'Then we must rely on brains rather than brawn—' began Norma.

'I object to the implication that I am incapable of employing both,' snapped Trixie.

'I'm sorry, Trixie—'

'Colonel Dashwood!'

Oh, for fuck's sake!

'Colonel Dashwood, then. I was merely suggesting that rather than making a frontal assault on the Castle, this might be a job for a person adept at breaking and entering.'

'I'm a dab hand at breakin' an' enterin',' announced Rivets as he gave Dong E a beaming smile.

The smile didn't last long: the boy began to wriggle uncomfortably as the eyes of everyone in the room settled on him but being Rivets, he decided to brazen it out. 'Yus, I'm the bee's knees when it comes to gettin' into places that shouldn't ought to be got into.'

Burlesque spluttered on the mouthful of Solution he'd just taken. 'Nah you ain't, you're a rotten crib cracker, yous is.'

'Bollocks. Admit it, Burlesque, it was me 'oo broke us into that Convent place in Venice an' that wos guarded by *vampyres*.'

'Vampyres?' The question came from a very dubious-sounding Trixie Dashwood.

Rivets bridled at her derisive tone. 'Yus, vampyres,' he said emphatically.

'Anyone of a RaTionalist turn of mind knows there are no such things as vampyres.'

Norma couldn't resist. 'Just as there are no such things as Daemons, Colonel Dashwood?'

Before Trixie had a chance to respond, a somewhat aggrieved Rivets came back at her. 'Yus there *are* vampyres and I've still got the bruises round me neck to prove it. That's 'ow close the cow come to scragging me. Yus,' he said firmly, 'vampyres exist all right and they're mean as catshit and twice as nasty. An' for your information, Colonel Trixie, sir, iffn I can bust into a Convent guarded by vampyres, I'm certain sure that I can bust into some rotten old Chink castle.' There was a brief pause before he added quickly, 'Long as it ain't guarded by vampyres that is.'

'You can rest assured on that point, nonFemme Rivets,' observed Su Xiaoxiao, 'there are no vampyres in the Coven. But are you seriously suggesting that you undertake this mission alone?'

'Er . . .'

Burlesque stiffened in his chair. 'I'll go wiv 'im. Somefing like this needs an older 'and on call.'

'*Dans ce cas là il faut que je vienne aussi*,' announced Odette. 'I must also of the accompaniment make. Eet ees of the impossibility that *mon cherie* Burlesque goes on the adventure *dangereuse* without the 'elp of a woman 'aving of the geater intelligence than 'im.'

'I will help you too, Rivets-san,' said Dong E quietly. 'To break into a Chink castle you will need help from a Chink.'

Su Xiaoxiao smiled. 'It seems we have a group of master burglars in our midst, though I suspect that they will be a trifle less confident when they have seen Hereji-Jo Castle. It is a daunting place.' She gave Rivets a rueful smile. 'But if you are determined?' There were nods from Burlesque, Odette, Dong E and a blissfully happy Rivets, who was sitting at the table lost in rapt adoration of the Chinese girl. 'I hope that four of you—'

'This is ridiculous,' sneered a disgruntled Trixie as she rose from her chair. 'If it is the intention of the SheTong to put the responsibility for the safety of the Demi-Monde in the hands of hooligans and children . . .'

Norma almost laughed: as best she could judge, Trixie was actually younger than both Rivets and Dong E.

'. . . then there is no purpose to my staying here.'

'Please, Colonel Dashwood, I would appreciate it if you would remain.' There was something in the way Su Xiaoxiao spoke that made even the redoubtable Trixie pause. 'I never supposed that the WFA would be used to assault Hereji-Jo Castle. There is another task I would urge them to undertake, a task similarly vital to the safety of the Demi-Monde.'

At the silent urging of Wysochi, Trixie sat back down.

Su Xiaoxiao looked over to Grigori Mendel. 'Perhaps, nonFemme Mendel, we might move on to the consideration of the second file brought from the Forbidding City, the one that relates to the translation of the *Flagellum Hominum*.'

Reluctantly – and only after much urgent signalling from Ki Song – Mendel stood up to address his audience. 'Although, as Femme Su Xiaoxiao alludes, Mao has managed to translate the *Flagellum Hominum*,' he began in a faltering voice, 'the book is written in a style similar to that used to compose the verses that adorn the Column of Loci and hence is similarly opaque in its meaning. As a result, the *Flagellum Hominum* remains enigmatic and ambiguous, so much so that at first I was uncertain that the book's real meaning would ever be fully understood. However, I received inspiration from other papers stolen by Fresh Bloom Dong E, these being extracts from the book *Daemons, Messiahs and Other ABBArational Beliefs* written by the great Confusionist and TooZian philosopher Xi Kang, a book previously unread because of its inclusion in the Coven's *Index Librorum Prohibitorum*. In these extracts, Xi Kang proposes that the ultimate purpose of the Demi-Monde is to allow ABBA to test the five varieties of humanity – the Five – He had used to populate the Demi-Monde and, by doing so, decide which will be His prototype for perfection, this prototype being used as the basis for the final version of HumanKind.'

Trixie Dashwood was provoked into asking a question. 'I'm not sure I understand what you mean by the "various expressions of humanity". Are these the various races that populate the Demi-Monde's five Sectors?'

'No. With all respect, Colonel Dashwood, that is the obvious and somewhat superficial interpretation many will make. My own belief – and that of AcademicianNon Ki Song – is that the *Flagellum Hominum* refers to more subtle and esoteric differences within the peoples who occupy the Demi-Monde. De Nostredame's work in identifying and describing Dark Charismatics – the race he calls *H. singularis* – demonstrates that there are secret and secretive species of HumanKind alive and active within the Demi-Monde, races of which we are afforded only fleeting glimpses.' He glanced towards Rivets. 'Perhaps the vampyre encountered by nonFemme Rivets was a member of one of these secret species.'

Rivets beamed at having someone as eminent as Mendel support his belief in vampyres. He couldn't resist the temptation to stick his tongue out at Trixie.

'But who are the Five?' asked Norma.

'The *Flagellum Hominum* assists us here, though only four are given names:

The One	Are the Lilithi
The Two	Are the Grigori
The Three	Are the Kohanim

The Four   *Are the Fragiles*
But there are Five.'

'Sounds like a lot of old bollocks to me' was Burlesque's comment.

'I agree, nonFemme Bandstand, that there is much here to fuel doubt, but there are other lines that could support a more generous interpretation. These come in the final two stanzas contained in the book:

And the Key to Life   *and to Destiny?*
The Column   *Tall and inviolate*
Measured   *to Perfection*
And adorned   *with the Secret*
Of Life.

Whoever places it   *in the Centre*
Of the World   *Places it*
High   *in its Resting Place*
Will be   *Perfect*
Before ABBA.

'This, I would suggest, is an exact description for the Column of Loci, now housed in the Galerie des Anciens in Venice. With the Column being constructed of Mantle-ite and weighing two hundred tons, it is most certainly "inviolate". Further, I have examined illustrations of the pictograms shown on the sixth face of the Column and note that these are a perfect representation of the manner in which traits of living organisms are transmitted from generation to generation. Before I was exiled to the Coven, I did extensive experimentation regarding the breeding of plants, principally those of the common pea or *Pisum sativum* variety. My research showed that certain characteristics of the original, parent plants are present in their offspring without any blending or averaging of the original, parental characteristics. This principle of inherited characteristics may be illustrated in a quite satisfactory manner by an algorithm very, very similar to the one shown on the Column. Thus, I can say with all confidence that the Column really is "adorned with the Secret of Life". I have no doubts that the Column of Loci discovered by Michel de Nostredame is the Column referred to in the *Flagellum Hominum* as "the Key to Life and to Destiny".'

'And the final stanza?' prompted Norma. 'Where do you suggest the "Resting Place" of the Column is?'

Mendel took a deep, deep breath before replying. 'This, I think, is obvious. The hexagonal plinth of the Column precisely aligns with the shape of the hexagonal platform Speke observed atop the Great Pyramid when he surveyed Terror Incognita by balloon. This symmetry is too remarkable to be ascribed simply to coincidence, and of course the Pyramid is in the centre of our world ... in Terror Incognita. It is my belief that whoever takes the Column of Loci and places it atop the Great Pyramid will emerge victorious from Ragnarok.'

There was shocked silence around the room. Finally Trixie began to laugh. 'I'm sorry, Academician Mendel, but what you are suggesting is impossible to accomplish.'

'Impossible?' asked Mendel.

'Of course. For one thing, the Column of Loci is in Venice and we're marooned here in Rangoon surrounded by the SS. And secondly – and most importantly – no one, absolutely *no one*, has ever entered Terror Incognita and returned. The ForthRight sent two regiments of SS across the Wheel River last Winter and nobody ever heard from them again. Taking the Column and erecting it on top of the Great Pyramid isn't just impossible, it's *suicidally* impossible.'

'Hopefully, not quite as impossible or as suicidal as you believe, Colonel Dashwood,' said Su Xiaoxiao quietly. 'I have received a PigeonGram from Nikolai Kondratieff in Venice who has also come to understand the significance of the Column. Although necessarily brief, the message advises that Kondratieff has devised a plan to thwart the powers of Darkness and to achieve this requires the use of a steamship capable of hauling a pontoon of three hundred and fifty tons of laden weight. His wording is elliptical but my suspicion is that the pontoon will be used to transport the Column to Terror Incognita.'

Norma whistled. 'Kondratieff is trying to steal the Column?'

'So it would appear, and to do that he needs a steamship.'

'This Kondratieff of yours doesn't want much, does he, Femme Su?' observed Wysochi. 'That's a powerful steamship he's looking for.'

'Correct, Major Wysochi, and one that will need an able commander to captain it.' Su Xiaoxiao's gaze came to rest on Trixie. 'I understand that you, Colonel Dashwood, have something of a reputation as an exponent of river warfare.'

Trixie Dashwood eyed Su Xiaoxiao warily. 'If you are alluding to my exploits when I seized three barges from the ForthRight, then the answer is yes; if, however, you are alluding to my competence as a sailor, then the answer is no. The sum total of my naval experience is managing a steam-barge for one hour when I ran it up two miles of river.' She smiled. 'Anyway, this discussion is moot: we don't have a steamship.'

'We might not have a steamship, Colonel, but we have an *WarJunk*. The ForthRight has in its possession the three WarJunks surrendered by AdmiralNoN Heii. I would propose that we commandeer one of them.'

'And just where is this WarJunk of yours moored?'

'It's berthed under guard on the St Petersburg shore of the Volga, on the Boundary side of the Anichkov Bridge.'

'Great. So, assuming we can hijack this WarJunk – and that's a mighty big assumption – we'll still have to run the gauntlet of the ForthRight artillery lined along the shore of the Volga.'

'Yes.'

Su Xiaoxiao's simple agreement shut Trixie up for a moment, which she used to formulate new objections. 'It's still impossible. An WarJunk is a complicated fighting machine, so I'll need a hundred experienced hands to work the thing.'

'We have Femmes in our ranks who trained on the WarJunks.'

Trixie wasn't to be dissuaded. 'It's a ridiculous plan. Leading my fighters into Terror Incognita means I'm leading them to certain death. It's a suicide mission.'

'It's suicide if we stay here in Rangoon, Trixie,' said Wysochi quietly. 'And presumably the *Flagellum Hominum* wouldn't tell us to take the Column to Terror Incognita only for us to be destroyed when we got there.'

For several long seconds Trixie glowered at him, then shoved her chair back and stood up from the table. 'You will excuse me, Femme Su, but I must consult with Major Wysochi.' And with that the two of them retreated to the back of the room out of earshot.

Norma didn't have to hear what was said to understand just how intense the debate was. There was much wagging of fingers, shaking of heads and shrugging of shoulders, but finally, after five minutes a red-faced and clearly unhappy Trixie Dashwood returned to the table.

'I have been persuaded by Major Wysochi that, though this adventure is madcap and nonsensical, it is a better option than to remain in Rangoon and be pounded to death by ForthRight artillery. As the Major says, it is better to die in pursuit of a dream than simply to die.' She filled her glass with Solution, downed it in one swig and then turned to Gregor Mendel.

'You're certain that the Column must be taken to Terror Incognita?'

'Yes.'

'Then, presumably, ABBA would not set a task that was beyond the wit of woman to complete.'

'That is what the verses contained in the *Flagellum Hominum* suggest.'

More silence, then Trixie let out a long, long sigh. 'Very well, when do you want the WarJunk stolen?'

Part Seven
Victory in the Coven and
in the ForthRight

36

Hereji-Jo Castle
The Demi-Monde: 70th Day of Summer, 1005

Pawnography is a term coined to describe the so-called erotic materials emanating from the Quartier Chaud designed to degrade Femmes and encourage violence against them. The word itself derives from the manner in which it persuades Femmes to sell (or pawn) their bodies to satisfy nonFemmes' crazed and unnatural sexual lusts. By showing the sexual exploitation and humiliation of Femmes, pawnography seeks to stimulate and sustain the nonFemmes' feeling of supremacy and dominance over Femmes and to incite them to rape and abuse. Perhaps the most notorious of photographic pawnographers is Julian Mandel whose ability to capture the Femme form in stridently heterosexual poses is infamous throughout the Demi-Monde. Using the recently developed 35mm Ur-Leica, he is able to take shots of his victims – and there can be no other term for those unfortunate and unwitting Femmes featured in these disgusting images – in natural settings, with a limited amount of light and with very short exposure times. This has led to the reprehensible trade in so-called 'peep' shots taken of subjects unaware of the photographer's presence.

The Sad and All-Too-Long History of Pawnography:
Emily Davison, Covenite Publications

Burlesque scanned Hereji-Jo Castle through the telescope loaned to him by Su Xiaoxiao and felt his spirits droop. He'd brought Rivets, Dong E and Odette on a constitutional to the gardens abutting the Castle to get the gauge of the place, and now, having seen the beast, he had to admit to having cold feet about the whole adventure. He had heard what Su Xiaoxiao had said about the place being impregnable but he hadn't really believed her – no place, in his opinion, was truly impregnable. But now he wasn't so sure.

What he saw both depressed him and scared him. Depressed him because he didn't have a fucking clue as to how they'd be able to break into it and scared him because he wasn't sure what they'd find inside if they did.

Bloody Rivets and his big gob!

Hereji-Jo Castle was a huge and menacing edifice that emerged out of the ground like a stone-fortified fist. It was a bunker of a place built to shut people out and it did this by the employment of an architecture that was uncompromisingly brutal. Everything about the castle was big, oppressive and intimidating. It was a military engine rendered out of huge blocks of scabrous black stone that even in the warmth of the Summer sunshine radiated a cold, lethal intent.

For long minutes Burlesque trained his spyglass on the massive front gates that seemed to be the only way into the Castle, and along the enormous slablike walls, a hundred feet high if they were an inch, searching for a chink – hah! – in its defences, for a place where an agile little man like Rivets might squeeze through. But search as he might, he could see no open windows, no convenient vines growing on the walls, no doors left ajar.

He turned to speak to Rivets and then stopped. The boy was entertaining himself by idly knocking the heads off burdocks with a stick, and for a moment Burlesque was reminded just

how young he was. He was only a kid: a kid who carried a man's
worth of experiences on his shoulders. The poor little sod had
seen more misery and hatred in his short life than anybody
had a right to. It just showed what a resilient bugger he was,
that he'd come through it all still sane – well, saneish, anyway.
And now the boy had fallen in love, the object of his affections
sitting amidst a crowd of daisies, absent-mindedly weaving
them into chains which she then garlanded about his head.

Burlesque smiled to himself: if ever there was a boy entitled
to experience a little *l'amour* it was Rivets.

Don't be soppy.

He got a grip on himself and signalled to Odette to join him.
She gave him a beaming smile, put her knitting to one side and
wandered across in that wonderfully undulating way of hers.
She sprawled down on the grass beside him and began to nibble
at an apple.

'So whaddya fink, Odette?' he asked, nodding towards the
castle.

Another of those secret little smiles as she pressed her body
against his.

Stop it, you Frog minx you.

'I 'ave none of your mostly experiences in the doing of – 'ow
you say – *le domaine de cambriolage . . .*'

'Burglary?' suggested Burlesque.

'*Oui, le* burglary. Therefore I must bow in the 'umble way to
your expertises *marveilleuse*. I am 'oping you already 'ave the
plan most clever, *n'est-ce pas*?'

Burlesque shrugged. 'Wish I 'ad, Odette, my luv, but I ain't.
This Hereji-Jo place looks cast-ironed and double-bolted to me.
Yeah, I'm floored, and that means we're up shit creek wivout
a paddle between us.'

'*Je ne sais pas où se trouve ce lieu que tu appelles "Sheet Creek",
mais je sais que nous ne sayons pas "oop it". Dong E dit ce jardin*

s'appelle, "Le lieu de Contentements Tranquilles".' She must have seen Burlesque's confusion. 'Dong E 'as said that these jardin ees named "The Place of the Quiet Contentments".'

'Well, I ain't content, wot wiv not being able to think ov a way to get into that castle or nuffink.'

Odette smiled. *'J'ai beaucoup de confidance en tu, Burlesque* ... I 'ave the mostly biggest faith in you, Burlesque. You are the man 'oo entered the Convent in Venice without any of the permissions.'

'That's right, I did, didn't I?' Bucked up by the girl's confidence, he passed her the telescope, then dug into the haversack she had carried up from the rooms they were occupying and brought out an apple. Fretting gave him an appetite.

For a minute or so Odette surveyed the Castle. *'C'est vraiment un édifice très formidable, Burlesque.'*

'Nah, it ain't formidable, it's a real bastard, that's wot it is.' He took a contemplative munch on his apple. 'It reminds me ov the Lubyanka an' that wos meant to be impene ... impene ... fucking difficult to break into.'

'Et les ouvriers ... the navigators ... what ees eet that they are doing of?'

Burlesque took the glass back and pointed it in the direction Odette indicated. The extensive and beautifully manicured gardens of the Castle were surrounded by a high wall – maybe twenty feet high and topped by vicious-looking spikes – the only entrance through which was via a pair of large wooden gates.

Or, at least, there *had* been a pair of gates.

Both the gates and the stone gateposts were in the process of being demolished by a dozen or so burly navvies to allow a huge ten-wheeled cart, drawn by eight enormous horses, entrance to the Castle's grounds. *'Mieux je* can judge, the Chinks ...'

He gave Dong E a quick look to make sure she hadn't overheard him.

'... needed to get *cette grande charrette* through *la port* so ills ont demolished *les* gateposts. Good luck *pour nous*; *ce sera* gettin' *dans le terrain un mite facilier*.'

Odette took a moment to disentangle what Burlesque had said. '*Qu'est-ce qu'elle transporte?*'

'Beats *moi*, Odette, me darlin'. Probably *les* crates are full ov all *le* stuff this Dr Ptah item's bin buying for 'er laboratories. That's wot that bird Su Xiaoxiao said, but she didn't say *rien* abart 'ow fuckin' *grande* these crates were. That one down there must be twenty foot long iffn it's an inch. I wonder wot's in it?'

Odette didn't say anything, just lay there with an interested look on her face watching the scene unfolding beneath them.

Burlesque shrugged away her silence and took a bite out of a second apple. He gave the Castle another look, then shook his head. 'Iffn you want my opinion, Odette, I fink we've got as much chance ov getting' into that castle as we 'ave of roastin' snow.'

All Odette did was carry on smiling.

Aleister Crowley sipped his Solution, feeling – for the first time in a very long time – that he was in command of his destiny and that he had gone some way to fulfilling the demands of the odious Septimus Bole. The meeting with Nearchus had presented him with an opportunity to capture the Column of Loci, and tonight he would persuade his very special crypto in the Coven to assist in stealing the secrets of the YiYi Project. ABBA was smiling on him and he could face the future without the worry of Bole punishing him for his failures.

His pleasant contemplation of the rewards that would accrue to him when he announced his various successes was interrupted by a careful tap on the door of his suite. Ever cautious – it didn't pay to forget he was in enemy territory – he unholstered his revolver. The safe house the SS maintained in Beijing might be well guarded and his surreptitious entry into the Coven cloaked in secrecy, but it never did to be anything less than careful, though, as he saw it, it was impossible for anyone – anyone outside the SS, anyway – to realise that the second-most powerful man in the ForthRight was now lodging just a stone's throw from the Forbidding Palace.

Anyway, he knew who was attending him. His visitor was a very punctual Femme who had arrived precisely at midnight. But then, considering that the Empress Wu was so exact in the manner in which she conducted her affairs, it was to be expected that similar traits would be found in her Deputy.

'One moment,' he shouted as he strolled across the room. And as he walked, he adopted his most guileless expression, which, he hoped, would calm his sure-to-be-apprehensive guest. The Femme was becoming increasingly unnerved about being blackmailed.

As soon as the door opened, the woman stepped into the room, obviously anxious not to be recognised by passers-by. Unfortunately her cloak and her veil couldn't disguise that she was young (she was slim and held herself very well), was of the highest class (the quality of her cloak and her shoes attested to that) and was hugely worried about attending him (her hands shook uncontrollably).

'Good evening, First Deputy,' Crowley began once the door was shut behind her, 'or, in view of our recent intimacies, might I have the honour of addressing you as Lucrezia?'

'Damn you to Hel, Crowley, and you would do well to mark my new title. I am now *Imperial Administrator*, having been appointed by Empress Wu successor to Mao ZeDong.'

'Congratulations! And may I say how pleased I am to see that punctuality is not just the virtue of princes but also of Imperial Administrators.'

Lucrezia Borgia shucked off her cloak and hat, tossed them disdainfully over a couch and then, with just a moment's hesitation, walked across to the cabinet standing to one side of the room and poured herself a large glass of Solution which she downed in one swing. 'Have a care, Crowley,' she snapped, 'that you do not goad me too far.' She did her best to sound sharp and reproving, but Crowley could tell her heart wasn't in it. The expression in her eyes showed just how vulnerable she actually felt.

'Goad you? I have never felt it necessary to goad you, my dear Imperial Administrator. What you did, you did willingly, almost, dare I suggest, enthusiastically.'

The woman's lips pursed. 'You swine. You enjoy tormenting me, don't you? But remember, Crowley, that I am here under duress. It is your ownership of those damnable daguerreotypes that coerces me, nothing more.'

He shrugged her protests aside and refilled her glass, 'Your mentioning of the daguerreotypes leads us neatly to the subject of tonight's rendezvous. Have you considered my proposition, Imperial Administrator? Will you assist me in a small endeavour I am intent upon or would you prefer that the Empress sees just how good – or should that be, how *bad* – a MostBien you really are?'

This, they both knew, was no small threat. That her very acrobatic and decidedly heterosexual antics had been caught on camera by that master of the pawnographic Julian Mandel had come as a shock to Borgia when Crowley had presented her with copies and a warning that unless she 'cooperated', said photographs would be incorporated in a pamphlet to be circulated throughout the Coven.

'I was drugged,' protested the Imperial Administrator.

She was correct in this assumption. Crowley had used the NoirVillian aphrodisiac Dizzi himself on several occasions and the results – even on the most sexually recalcitrant of partners – had always been strength-sappingly satisfactory. He guessed that the SS agents responsible for the sting had slipped an over-large dose of Dizzi into the woman's drink, closely followed by their slipping a mightily over-endowed young man into her bedroom. All this had been caught on camera by the hidden Mandel. The pictures had been both impressive and educational.

'That might be true, Imperial Administrator, but you most certainly weren't drugged last night.'

Now *that* shut the woman up.

As he judged it, Lucrezia Borgia was a closet heterosexual. Even he, who knew the venality of Demi-Mondians better than any, had been astonished by how readily she had acceded to his demands for sexual favours. As was to be expected, she had protested and wept and wailed, but gradually she had warmed to his unusual ideas regarding lovemaking. Indeed, he suspected that the woman had come to relish their trysts to an extent that he began to feel that he was, as the peasants back in Rodina might say, ploughing an endless field. Yes, underneath her HerEtical exterior Lucrezia Borgia was just another weak woman who loved being dominated by a man. He wondered for a moment whether this covert inclination was the reason why, unlike other HerEticals, she had never had her head shaved, why she had always kept her long, flowing blonde hair. Whatever the reason, the simple fact was that her appetite for 'bingerle', as she rather cringingly referred to the act of love-making, seemed insatiable.

Almost insatiable.

Perhaps his rather outré demands were beginning to take their toll even on her ardour and her appetite for pain. Yes, now he was convinced that she was both ready and willing to commit treason to save her neck . . . and her arse from another whipping.

'And what is this small endeavour of yours?' she asked.

'A simple one. At eight o'clock on the seventy-fifth day of

Summer – five days hence – you will open the postern gate in the south wall of Hereji-Jo Castle.'

Her brow furrowed. 'There is no postern gate. There is only one entrance into the Castle and that is through the main gates.'

For an instant Crowley almost blurted out the truth, that it had been Bole who had conjured up the door, but he stopped himself. Why shouldn't he take the credit for this piece of magic? His entire reputation as the foremost magician in the Demi-Monde was, after all, built on the manipulations done on his behalf by Bole. 'Oh, believe me, there *is* a gate: I have used magic to create it. It is well hidden, which is probably why it is unknown to you. Indeed, I suggest that you take an axe with you to better clear the undergrowth which covers it.'

'Very well; if such a gate exists, I will open it. What then?'

'Three associates of mine will be waiting on you. You will lead them to Dr Merit Ptah's laboratory, from which they will remove certain items which the ForthRight wishes to have in its possession. Once I have secured these items, the photographs are yours, an early Lammas Eve gift from your friend Aleister Crowley.'

Lucrezia Borgia fell silent as though taking a moment to consider Crowley's demands. Then: 'I know what is kept in Hereji-Jo Castle: you are asking that I deliver the secrets of the YiYi Project up to the ForthRight, you are asking that I deliver Empress Wu's head to you on a platter. And *that* is worth more than the destruction of a few photographs.'

'Then what *do* you want?'

'The Coven.'

37

Hereji-Jo Castle
The Demi-Monde: 74th Day of Summer, 1005

There is a legend associated with Hereji-Jo Castle which relates that should the ravens that have made the central courtyard their home ever leave the Castle, then the Coven will fall.

"Weird and Wacky Beliefs of the Demi-Monde":
Immanuel Kant, *Anthropology Today*

It was a dispirited Burlesque who returned to his hotel after another fruitless viewing of Hereji-Jo Castle and announced himself defeated. He'd done his best. He'd sat in those gardens until his arse was numb, searching for inspiration, and although he'd racked his mind until it hurt, he hadn't been able to come up with a way of getting into the Castle. He was stumped.

In the end, it was Odette who finally solved the puzzle and saved the life of every man in the Demi-Monde.

When he'd pushed his way into their rooms, even before he'd managed to rid himself of his rain-sodden ulster, she'd been up and at him, grabbing him by the arm and dragging him into the bedroom. But much to his surprise, she hadn't hurled him onto the bed as was her habit, but instead had sat him down at the little dressing table.

'*Mon cheri, j'ai trouvé la solution de ton problèm!* I 'ave the answer to your problem!'

'I ain't got a problem, Odette,' protested Burlesque, 'it's just that I've bin tired lately.'

Odette frowned as she tried to understand what Burlesque was saying. '*Non, non*, I do not speak of your *force d'amour*. Eet ees the problem of the *forteresse* most *formidable*.'

With that she pulled a notebook and pencil out of the pocket of her *jiangs* and spent ten minutes sketching, scribbling and jabbering away in her strange Franglo. Finally, with a determined nod, she presented her diagrams.

Odette's scheme was as simple as it was ridiculous. The girl proposed that they *post* themselves into the Castle. Burlesque scratched his head wondering idly if his chats were back and how he could best tell Odette she was crackers without offending her.

As he understood it, Odette had got into the habit of wandering down to the market every day to buy cheese and fresh milk and during the course of her perambulations had noticed that the routine for the delivery to the Castle of the pieces of equipment Dr Ptah was buying to equip her laboratory followed a set and unvaried timetable. Each and every evening the crates containing the equipment were hauled up by steamer from the Beijing docks, unloaded and then stacked under an awning at the Hereji-Jo post office, where they remained until they were collected the next day by a horse-drawn wagon sent by Dr Ptah.

And the reason they used a horse and cart was simple: the track from the city was just a mud road, left deliberately unmade so that it was impassable to enemy armies wishing to use artillery and siege equipment against the Castle. At noon every day a wagon would trundle out of the Castle, through the gate – the newly demolished gate – in the wall that surrounded its gardens and rattle slowly along the dirt track until it was brought to a halt outside the post office. There the wagon-master and his lad would hop down, unload the empty crates they had brought from the Castle, winch the full crates onto the back of the cart and then return to the Castle.

Odette's plan proposed that the four of them hide in a couple of the empty crates which they had previously moved to the pile earmarked for delivery to the Castle. They would be taken to the Castle masquerading as pieces of equipment.

It was, as Burlesque quickly pointed out, a 'fucking stupid idea' and one fraught with danger. Unfortunately, after thirty minutes arguing the toss, he was unable to counter it with a better scheme and, equally unfortunately, as time was fast running out – Lammas Eve was looming – it was Odette's idea or nothing.

Odette woke Burlesque an hour before dawn, and when he opened his eyes he hardly recognised her. Dressed in black *jiangs* and a padded jacket, with her pistol holstered at her side and a wicked knife thrust in her belt, she looked decidedly warlike, not a bit like the girl he had met in Paris.

''Ere, wot you abart, Odette?' he stammered as he swung himself out of bed and searched for his strides. 'No, *j'ai* decided ... *tu ne* come *pas avec moi* ... this is dangerous work. *Je* ain't 'aving *tu* shot or nuffink ... not after ... well, *tu* knows.'

His objections were interrupted by the arrival of Rivets and Dong E – the young girl clad in a martial style similar to that adopted by Odette. 'Tell 'em, Rivets, that this ain't no job for birds. Blowing fings up and such is a bloke's job. Go on, Rivets, tell 'em yous an' me 'ave decided to go on our ownsomes.'

Rivets didn't have a chance to reply, being silenced by a glare from Odette who then yammered away in Frog, which, fortunately, Dong E was on hand to translate. 'Odette says that *you* must appreciate, Burlesque, that being *intactus* – as you so ably demonstrated last night – you are in the grip of MALEvolence and hence prone to acts of unthinking violence and stupidity. It is, therefore, essential that you are accompanied on this venture by women who, by expression of their superior intellect and greater maturity, will be able to provide the best direction and leadership. Therefore, Odette and myself must be on hand to manage this venture to ensure that it does not fail.'

And as though to emphasise this decision, Odette handed Burlesque a baguette larded with thick slices of cheese, the woman obviously of the opinion that invading castles was not something to be undertaken on an empty stomach. Burlesque looked imploringly to Rivets for support, but all the boy could do was look sheepish and gnaw at his own breakfast baguette. Protest, Burlesque decided, was hopeless: he could tell from the expressions on the girls' faces that any further debate would be a waste of time so, with a disconsolate shrug, he contented himself with chomping down on his sandwich.

Breakfast over, the four of them slung the bags loaded with bombs over their shoulders and crept out into the night to make their way through the sleeping city to the post office.

It was then that Odette's talent for organisation was really demonstrated. As far as Burlesque could make out, she had already been down to the post office sorting out the crates. With brisk efficiency she pointed to two large crates, and when Burlesque looked he found each of them had been lined with blankets and had had leather straps screwed to the inside. Odette had also fitted catches so that the tops of the crates could be locked down by those concealed within. As a final touch, each crate had been equipped with a number of empty bottles complete with corks: these for use, as Odette so delicately put it, *en cas d'urgence*.

Burlesque's already elevated opinion of Odette rose. He had never realised that women could be so bloody clever.

'*Ca, c'est le cageot que nous occuperons.* Thees ees the crate we will occupy,' advised Odette. '*Puisque tu et Rivets avez visité la maison de bain, votre odeur a éte réduite à un niveau qui n'est pas repoussant aux nez féminins, donc il n'y aura pas d'inconfort à propos de nos positions si intimes.*'

Again Dong E translated. 'Since you have both visited the bathhouse, your odour has been reduced to a level which is not offensive to the female nose, so there will be no awkwardness about our being so intimately positioned in the crate.'

With that Odette signalled her companions into their crates, then, confident that they were now safe and secure, she snuggled down next to Burlesque, pulled the top back down and locked it tight closed.

They waited.

They waited in their crates for six long, uncomfortable hours.

Burlesque had never thought that being confined in a box with a girl could be such torture, but a combination of sweltering heat, cramp and claustrophobia made the six-hour wait almost unendurable. It was a wait not helped by a bout of flatulence brought on by Odette's baguette: he'd always had a problem digesting cheese. Of course, he had tried to leaven the boredom by getting jinky with his girl, but the slap she had given him had stilled his burgeoning ardour, leaving him with no option but to sit uncomfortably – and very stiffly – waiting for the arrival of the cart. Thankfully, just as he was starting to worry that perhaps the draymen wouldn't be working that day, bang on the stroke of noon the cart creaked its way up to the post office.

If the careless way they winched the crates onto the cart was any indication, the draymen seemed to be in a bustle to get the delivery over and done with. Even the imprecations Dong E had stencilled on the side of the box, saying 'Fragile' and 'This Way Up' in Chink writing, did little to dissuade the wagoneers from some very rough handling of the merchandise. But then they probably couldn't read anyway.

Once the crates were loaded, the driver whipped the horse all the way back to Hereji-Jo Castle, introducing Burlesque to every rut and pothole they bounced over en route. It took about an hour for the cart to reach the Castle and, bashed and shaken, he had never been more grateful for a journey to end in all his life. But he wasn't given a second's respite; even before the wheels of the cart had stopped turning, the draymen were down, levering the crates unceremoniously off the back of the cart and then dragging them into a building that smelt like the inside of an old sock. They shoved the crates against a wall and then scuttled off, slamming the door behind them.

There was silence.

Burlesque checked his watch. It was a little after two o'clock in the afternoon, but as far as he could tell, the laboratory – and from the smell of the place and the scientific paraphernalia he could see through a crack in the side of the crate, it certainly had all the appearance of a laboratory – was deserted. Maybe, he surmised, it being a Saturday and all, the technicians and scientists had been given the day off, so he settled back down in his box, Odette having told him they should wait until it was dark before emerging. This he judged to be sound advice; he might be stiff and his back and arse might be aching like the very devil, but the thought of popping out into the loving arms of an Amazon persuaded him that it was better to be uncomfortable than to be sorry.

Sitting there in the darkness, all he could hear was the clicking of Odette's knitting needles. This was one girl who had come prepared for a long wait. The clicking was bloody irritating, but he didn't have the heart – or the courage – to tell her to stop.

*

Odette insisted they sit in their crates until an hour after night-
fall, only then did she judge it was safe enough for them to
leave their hiding place. Even so, she felt the need to take one
final peek through the crack in the crate to make sure the coast
was clear before she unlatched the top and wriggled her way
out. She took a moment to gulp in some badly needed fresh air
and to stretch her tortured muscles, then after taking an
anxious look around the ink-black room to make sure they were
alone, she beckoned to Burlesque.

'Fuck me gently, Odette, I've got to have a jimmy. I couldn't
bring meself to 'ave a slash in front ov—'

'*Fermes ta bouche* . . . silence!' she whispered and placed a
hand firmly over her lover's mouth. Thankfully, for once he
took the hint and shut up, though the sound of him peeing
against the wall behind the crate would, she guessed, be loud
enough to alert even the sleepiest of sentries. Fortunately, there
seemed to be no sentries guarding the laboratory they had
landed up in.

It was so dark in the laboratory that all she could make out
was the vague outline of the glass tubes and other scientific
paraphernalia decorating the benches that lined the stinking
room. And it *did* stink. The smell that had been so unpleasant
in the crate now assailed her even more potently; it was a
revolting concoction of carbolic, neat alcohol and something
vaguely human. The stench was obviously too much for even
Burlesque's stoic guts. The poor man vomited all over his boots.

'Where *et nous*, Odette?' he asked in a whisper as he wiped
his mouth with his sleeve. 'It smells like *un* donkey's arsehole
in 'ere.'

'*Je ne suis pas sûre* . . . I'm mostly unsure, *mon cheri*, *mais* I
theenk thees ees the laboratory of Docteur Ptah. Thees, in the
greatest possibility, ees the place where that *fou* is making the
brewing of her Plague formula. We 'ave been very mostly lucky.'

She tapped on the second crate and Dong E and Rivets shimmied their way out. 'Dong E,' she began, *'je proposerais que vous et Rivets fouillent ce laboratoire. C'est très important que tous les documents au sujet de la method de fabrication de la peste sont retrouvés et détruits. Et pendant que vous faite cette activité, mon cheri Burlesque et moi commencerons la perquisition de l'installation de fermentation.'*

Dong E nodded. 'Odette suggests that Rivets and I search this laboratory, find all the documents relating to the manufacture of the Plague and destroy them. And while we do this, she and Burlesque will go in search of the Fermentation Plant.'

Without waiting for a reply, Odette led Burlesque to the laboratory door and peeped through the keyhole out onto the rain-drenched courtyard beyond, orientating herself by the sketch map of the Castle provided by Su Xiaoxiao. She was half expecting to see a bunch of enraged LessBiens racing towards them but, fortunately, there wasn't a sinner to be seen.

She was just weighing up the risk she and Burlesque would be running by scooting around the dark edge of the yard when she saw a door open in the building opposite, a phalanx of guardFemmes stream out into the moonlight and then march in lockstep in the direction of the Fermentation Plant. All she could think was that they were being sent to reinforce the guards already protecting the place.

Waiting until the guards had passed the laboratory block – and hence had their backs to them – she eased the door of the laboratory open and with Burlesque at her heels slid out into the night, careful to stay tight to the darkness-bedecked side of the building.

The rain was driving down, but it did at least give Imperial Administrator Lucrezia Borgia an excuse to raise her hood and this, she hoped, would ensure that no one recognised her as she went on her way to betray the Coven. Indeed the rain was so hard that the grounds of the Castle were deserted and the few souls out and about hardly spared her a glance, but when engaged in treason it didn't do to be less than careful.

In the rain-cloaked darkness finding Crowley's postern gate became a feat of exploration and finally, in desperation, she had to throw caution to the wind and light her lantern. It was as well she did: when she finally stumbled upon the gate, it was barely visible beneath the camouflage of a thick overgrowth of ivy.

It took her over half an hour, much cursing, a pair of lacerated hands and a great deal of hacking with an axe before she was able to clear a way to the gate and even then the bloody thing was obdurate. The gate obviously hadn't been used in an age and was a bastard to open. Almost sobbing with frustration and desperately keeping one eye out for patrolling guardFemmes, she had to struggle for almost five minutes with bolts that were heavily rusted and crying out for a dollop of grease. But finally, after the expenditure of a lot of sweat and effort, she managed to shoot them.

To her great relief, when the door reluctantly swung open, there, as Crowley had promised, standing waiting were the trio of men he had commissioned to assist her. The sight of them made her eyes widen, the three men being hugely tall and whip-thin. Instinctively she stepped back in dread: there was something feral about them, something that warned her they were cruel and unpredictable. Maybe it was the eyes that snarled at her from under the brim of their hats that most unnerved her: they were yellow and slanting . . . more animal than human.

Grigori.

'We are Baraqijal, Chazaqijal and Turel,' the tallest of the three said in accented Anglo. It seemed that Grigori didn't have any Chink. 'We have been sent by His Holiness Aleister Crowley to aid you in taking the documentation from the laboratory of Dr Merit Ptah.' Without waiting for a reply, the man-thing called Baraqijal shimmied through the gate, waving his two companions into the Castle after him.

Borgia led them through the castle grounds, coming to the edge of the courtyard across from the laboratory just in time to see the rotund figure of a man and a taller and much bigger woman creeping out of the laboratory's entrance. For a moment the rain eased and the moonlight illuminated the pair.

'By ABBA, if I am not mistaken that's Burlesque Bandstand and his Femme, Odette Aroca,' snarled Borgia, 'there can't be another couple as mismatched as them in the whole of the Demi-Monde. They're enemies of the Coven,' and she made to unholster her pistol.

Baraqijal placed a restraining hand on her arm. 'We were instructed, Femme Borgia, that our first priority is the securing of the secrets of the Plague formulation. Revenge must wait on that.'

With a reluctant nod Lucrezia Borgia stepped back into the shadows to wait until she was sure the courtyard was clear of Amazons and Normalists. Only then did she lead the three men to the door that barred entrance to the laboratory.

Once there, Baraqijal leant forward and twisted the door's brass knob, but before he stepped inside, he turned to Lucrezia Borgia. 'You have kept your side of the bargain, Femme Borgia, and I am told to inform you that the pictures will be destroyed. But if things go badly tonight, we are to meet at the postern gate. There are horses hidden in a copse just beyond the Castle's walls.' And with that he stepped into the darkness of the laboratory.

38

Hereji-Jo Castle
The Demi-Monde: 75th Day of Summer, 1005

Following his defection from the ForthRight, Alfred Noble
spent two years in the service of Empress Wu, during which
time he invented the explosive that has become known as
blasting gelatin. It is evidence of the contrary nature of
Fate that the very substance developed to help secure the
victory of HerEticalism was instrumental in its downfall.

A Schoolboy's Guide to Demi-Mondian Inventors: Thomas
Edison, Venetian Press

Rivets didn't like being in the laboratory. It was cold in there,
the hard, brittle coldness of a place that had never known any
warmth. It also echoed. Even doing his best to ghost around as
quietly as he could, the hobnailed soles of his boots still snarled
and clacked on the stone-tiled floor. He disliked the darkness
too, he kept bashing into things, sending beakers and test tubes
crashing, very noisily, to the ground.

'Rivets-san, you must be quiet,' ordered Dong E from out of
the shadows. 'You must be more careful.'

Stroppy cow.

He had had no idea that such a small and delicate-looking
girl could be so bloody bossy, but bossy or not, he was pleased
that she was with him. If he'd been alone, he doubted if he'd
have had the bottle to leave the crate.

Yeah, the problem Rivets had with the darkness was that it got his imagination firing. Ever since he'd had that run-in with the vampyre tart in Venice, as soon as night fell he got the wind up something chronic, every second he thought horrible vampyres would come lunging out at him from the shadows. He hadn't had a decent night's sleep for months.

'You have the bombs?'

'Yeah.'

'Then where shall we place them?'

'Dunno,' answered Rivets. It was all very well for Odette to tell him to stick the bombs where they would do the most damage, but she wasn't the silly sod who had to creep around a dark room worried shitless about being attacked by vampyres or that the bombs would go off in her hands. He'd heard some funny stories about the blasting gelatin used to make them, so as gently as he could, he eased the bombs from his haversack and set to work.

Odette had allocated four of her home-made bombs for use in destroying the laboratory and, being devoid of any better ideas, Rivets decided to stick them in the middle of the room on the basis that one big bang was always better than four small ones. After whispered debate with Dong E he set the timers for sixty minutes, which, he judged, was more than enough for Burlesque and Odette to settle their business at the Fermentation Plant.

But even as he finished putting the bombs in position, Dong E was at him again. 'Now we must search this laboratory, Rivets-san. Femme Su was most insistent that we ensure all records of Dr Ptah's research are destroyed.'

Curiosity must be a bird thing, decided Rivets, as they spent the next few minutes fine-combing the lab. But it was a curiosity that was rewarded when Dong E came to a locked cabinet set in the furthest corner of the laboratory. The girl let out an excited squeak and waved him over.

'This is the only cabinet that is locked, Rivets-san. We must open it.'

'Yeah, right you is,' and taking a crowbar out of his bag, Rivets attacked the cabinet with gusto. Against so much steel and determination the wooden door didn't have a chance but when it sprang open all it revealed was a very formidable steel safe hidden inside.

'Can you open it, Rivets-san?'

Risking the striking of a lucifer, Rivets examined the safe closely. It was a substantial piece of engineering that, from what he could make out, had also been bolted to the wall. 'I dunno. It's a real brute an' no mistake.'

'Maybe we could use one of the bombs to blow the door open?' suggested a very impatient-sounding Dong E.

Rivets shook his head. 'Not a good idea, Dongie. Remember, it might contain this Plague stuff, so that'd be a sure way of 'aving me end the day toes up. Anyway, blowing that bastard's door off will be loud enough to bring everywun an' their uncle running.'

Dong E's face fell.

'But 'ave no fear, Dongie, Rivets is 'ere.' Once again he delved in his haversack and after a careful search pulled out a leather box about the size of a cigar case. From inside this he took out a glass tube sealed by a glass stopper which he cautiously – *very* cautiously – removed. Choking yellow fumes poured out, forcing both him and Dong E to flinch back.

'Yeah, it's real 'orrible stuff, an' no mistake. It's called Aqua Regia Superior, luv, a mixture ov hydrochloric acid, nitric acid an' ovver nasties. I wos taught all about it when I wos appren- ticed to a peterman back in the Rookeries.'

With enormous care Rivets applied the glutinous acid to the

safe's hinges and to its lock. This done, the pair of them ducked away from the smoke and the fumes that were emitted as the acid ate into the metal, squatting down behind a bench to wait. After five minutes he judged that the acid had done its work, handed the vial to Dong E – warning her to be mindful how she handled it and took up his crowbar again, forcing the pointed end into the holes burnt into the safe's steel carcass. After a minute of struggling and straining the door of the safe clanged open.

'Oh, well done, Rivets-san,' squealed Dong E as she planted a kiss on his cheek.

Rivets blushed with happiness, but he had no time to enjoy the sensation. Just as Dong E was raising herself up onto her toes to see what was hidden in the safe, the handle of the laboratory door rattled and he could hear someone talking outside.

Safe in the shadows, Burlesque and Odette scuttled along in pursuit of the soldiers, trying to get as close as possible to the last of them without being seen or heard.

Even as the Fermenting Plant loomed before them, a side door to the right of the huge main gates swung open and as it did so a horrible smell billowed out, washing over them. Doing his best to ignore the horrible stench, Burlesque edged nearer, until he and Odette were tiptoeing only five or six yards behind the last of the soldiers, hardly daring to breathe, lest one of the Amazons spotted that they were being tracked. Then the soldiers, without once breaking step, marched through the open door, disappearing from sight; as soon as the last of their number passed through, the doors began to close. Burlesque, mouth dry and arse tweaking, waited until the last possible moment and then he and Odette scuttled into the intimidating darkness of the room beyond.

*

Shaking with fear, Rivets listened to what the newcomers were saying – something about a 'postern gate' and 'horses' – and then the laboratory door was pushed open and all his worst nightmares became reality. There stood three tall and decidedly creepy-looking individuals. A lantern flared and their vicious, horrible faces were illuminated. Rivets almost passed out.

Vampyres!

Instinctively he dodged further back behind the workbench, dragging a much too inquisitive Dong E with him. 'Them's vampyres,' he whispered into the girl's ear. 'Just like the one I 'ad a set-to wiv in Venice.'

Fuck.

A feeling of grim foreboding ran through him and, as quietly as he was able, he unclipped his holster ready to draw his Bulldog.

A woman came to join the vampyres. 'The safe where Dr Ptah keeps her research papers is over—' She let out a gasp, presumably shocked to see the safe door hanging open. Rivets almost wet himself.

'Bar the door,' he heard one of the vampyres yell, 'and search the laboratory.'

Rivets moved to pull the Bulldog free from its holster, but the bloody thing stuck. Panic-stricken, he gave it a yank, overbalanced and was forced to stick out a hand to save himself from falling over. He bashed into a bench as he did so and sent a couple of test tubes smashing to the floor.

'There!' shouted a vampyre, pointing in the direction of the noise. 'But no guns. Kill them quietly.'

The three vampyres attacked. Their faces contorted in fury, without a challenge or the emitting of one solitary sound, they launched themselves at Rivets and Dong E. The speed and the fury of the attack were breathtaking: they leapt across the room like huge cats, each of them wielding a wickedly curved sword.

*

The Fermentation Plant was huge, the vast and smelly hall lined on both sides by massive brass cylinders at least twenty feet tall and half as much in diameter. It reminded Burlesque of a brewery he had once visited when he had been in the bootlegging business, and the stink was pretty much the same too: the smoke billowing around him had a sort of stale, yeasty odour. It was also terrifically hot, which wasn't surprising given that the cylinders were being heated by gas mantles, the flames sending eerie, flickering shadows dancing over the walls. It was so hot that Burlesque began leaking sweat, beads of perspiration standing out on his forehead.

But the *big* difference between the Fermentation Plant and the brewery was that the latter hadn't been so well guarded. The Fermentation Plant was crawling with soldiers so it was as well, Burlesque decided, that the place was largely in darkness, just the shimmering light of the gas mantles providing any illumination.

Grabbing Odette by the arm, he darted across the tiled floor, searching for a place to hide, finally finding sanctuary behind a pile of barrels stacked against the far wall. Once safe from sight, he took a moment to draw breath and to take stock. Nearer to the cylinders, he could see that those on the right of the hall had red lettering – Chink lettering, so he couldn't understand it – painted on them, and those on the left had blue lettering. He didn't need to read Chink to know what was going on. According to the briefing he'd been given by Mendel back in Rangoon, the two elements of the Plague – the Yin and the Yang – were manufactured in separate vats, being mixed only when the Plague was to be deployed.

But even as Burlesque hunkered down behind the barrels trying to figure out what to do, there was an enormous *whooshing* sound as the flames under the cylinders suddenly leapt higher. The gas mantles had been turned up to full and now dozens of white-coated technicians began to scuttle around, checking pressure tubes and shouting at one another in their ridiculous Chink language.

'*Ils commencent le processus du mélange* . . . they are making the beginning of the mixing process,' said Odette in an urgent whisper. 'Eet ees the moment when the parts *rouges et bleus* are together mixed, and then . . . she drew a very eloquent finger across her neck.

The girl's observations were interrupted by a gong being sounded. Peeping out from his hiding place, Burlesque saw white-coated TechnicianNoNs begin to wheel steel barrels across to the vats and position them under the taps set in the pipes that connected the red and the blue cylinders.

Reluctant as Burlesque was to admit it, he knew that it was a case of now or never. If he didn't destroy this vile place tonight, he – and every other bloke in the Demi-Monde – would be dead meat.

He looked around, trying to determine where it would be best for him to place the six bombs he was carrying. All he could think was that putting them under six of the fermentation vats – three reds and three blues – would give him the best chance of doing the maximum amount of damage. The problem he had was *how* to do that with so many Amazons and technicians wandering around. In the end the answer came to him: one of the TechnicianNoNs walked over to stand next to their hiding place and without thinking, Burlesque pulled out his gun and smacked the poor sod over the head with it. The NoN sagged into a heap on the ground and Burlesque pulled him behind the barrels and hauled off his white coat.

Wearing his new disguise – fucking reluctantly – he stepped, as nonchalantly as he was able, out from behind the barrels and began to march towards the far end of the hall. By play-acting that he was taking notes of the measurements on the pressure tubes, Burlesque was able to stuff one bomb under each of the three furthest vats, the bombs' clockwork timers set for ten minutes. He ambled along, sliding the bombs under the vats as he went. It was so easy, he began to think that Lady Luck was smiling on him.

She wasn't.

He'd got back to the other end of the hall and was just setting the sixth and final bomb when one of the Amazons began to shout at him in Chink. Not having a fucking clue what she was yelling, there was no chance that he'd be able to bluster his way out and anyway, being caught red-handed holding a bomb was beyond even his powers of mummery. So he gave the Amazon his broadest smile, twirled the clockwork timer on the bomb to zero and tossed it towards her.

The bloody thing didn't explode . . .

Fucking useless blasting gelatin.

. . . but the surprise registered by the Amazon when she found herself holding a bomb was such that it at least gave him the chance to pull out his Bulldog and begin blasting away.

He fired two quick discouraging shots at the head of the Amazon, but as three shots whipped past him in an answering fusillade, he came to the rapid conclusion that retreat was most certainly the better part of valour. He was lucky that Odette began firing away from the other side of the hall, otherwise things could have got decidedly hairy, and it was only thanks to her intervention that he was able to dodge for cover behind the cylinder next to the doors leading to the outside world. But with shots pinging around him it was an outside world he knew he'd be fucking fortunate ever to see again.

Now he was in a rare pickle: pinned down by ten or so Amazons, outgunned and out-of-positioned, all he could do was ram five fresh cartridges into the Bulldog and blast away. For about a minute the two sides traded shots, cordite mixing with the vapour streaming from the bullet-riddled cylinders, the noise and the smoke and the stench giving the hall a Helish, stinking cast.

It would have gone badly for Burlesque and Odette, but just as Burlesque was down to his final couple of shots, all Hel really did break loose. The bomb he had thrown at the Amazon exploded.

The vampyres would have sliced them up for sure if Dong E hadn't reacted instinctively and hurled the vial of acid she was holding at the onrushing creatures.

The first of the attackers swatted the vial contemptuously aside, his blade shattering the glass. That was his undoing. The acid spat out in a foul-smelling mist which enveloped all three of the vampyres, and as the vapour touched their faces and their bare arms it began to rend the SAE from their bones. Dong E, as she watched stupefied from behind the bench, saw their bodies begin to melt. The pain suffered by the vampyres must have been incredible but, to her astonishment, they uttered not one sound. Ravaged and flayed though they were, they carried through their attack.

The swipe of the sword from a vampyre managed to slice across her right thigh, but then the acid took its toll and the creature folded to the ground. As it lay trembling and shivering on the floor of the laboratory, Rivets came out of his fugue and kicked the vampyre squarely in the mouth, sending three fangs skittering over flagstones. Then, as it writhed and groaned, he took the chance to stomp his heel onto its throat. There was a rattle and then it stopped moving.

Now, as a second vampyre hurled itself at her, Dong E drew her pistol and pumped three shots into the thing's chest. The vampyre staggered, recovered, and then its sword pistoned towards her. But even as she prepared to receive the killing strike, Rivets leapt between her and the blade, taking the thrust square in his guts. He staggered, but had enough strength to poke his Bulldog into the vampyre's mouth and pull the trigger. They might not have been using silver bullets, but Dong E doubted even a vampyre would come back at them after having half its head blown off.

'Out, out! The shots will bring the guards!' she heard the woman shout and the third vampyre, its face distorted by acid and fury, reluctantly did as it was ordered.

As the door slammed behind them, Dong E turned anxiously to Rivets who lay crumpled on the stone floor, all the colour having drained from his face and all the strength from his body.

'I'm a goner, Dongie,' he gasped. 'Time for you to scarper.'

'I cannot leave you, Rivets-san . . .'

'Don't be daft . . . you gotta . . . them LessBien tarts will be 'ere in two shakes ov a nanny goat's tail. I've 'ad it, Dongie.'

'I beg you . . . do not die, Rivets-san.'

'Don't fret abart me, Dongie darlin'. Scum like me ain't worth no tears. Gor . . . I'd die a thousand times for you an' then some. I love you, Dongie . . .' The boy shuddered, gave her a thin smile and then was gone.

For long seconds Dong E knelt with the head of Rivets cradled in her lap, tears streaming down her face. It was unbelievable that someone as tough and as resilient as Rivets could be dead. But even as she knelt there with head bowed, she could hear whistles sounding from beyond the laboratory and this was what finally persuaded her that she should go. Closing Rivets's eyes, she laid his head gently to the ground, rose unsteadily to her feet and bowed, her voice trembling with emotion as she said her last goodbyes. 'Noble Rivets-san, great warrior and true friend. I return your love and I swear on this love, should I come safe through this night, to honour your memory and to make such offerings that your soul will come safe to your ancestors.'

With a final bow to Rivets, she limped over to the safe and rifled through the contents. There were poor pickings: just a bulky file of papers which Dong E assumed must be valuable, otherwise Dr Ptah wouldn't have been so keen to protect them in the safe. She took a box of matches from her pocket and fired them all, then stumbled towards the laboratory door, hobbling for all she was worth on her wounded leg.

Lucrezia Borgia dragged the pain-crazed Chazaqijal across the courtyard, hurriedly searching for a place to hide before the Amazons came to investigate the sound of the shooting. And as they went, she tried to make sense of what had just happened. She had seen a scruff of a boy and a slip of a Chink girl defeat the three Grigori sent by Crowley to help her, Grigori who Crowley had confidently stated were unbeatable in combat. And it was *how* they had defeated them that had given her palpitations. The Grigori had melted!

'What now, Comrade Chazaqijal?' she asked.

The Grigori looked frightful. Half of his face was gone, pared down to the bone, and one eye had been reduced to a weeping red ball. As he spoke, he winced in pain. 'I cannot allow myself to be defeated by such ... nonentities.'

His grumbling was interrupted by a ripple of explosions that ripped the Fermentation Plant asunder. Flames leapt skywards, turning night into scarlet-tinged day. But even as she cowered away from the heat and the fury of the blast, Borgia's mind whirled. The Plague weapon was no more, destroyed by Burlesque Bandstand, and now it would be impossible for the Coven to defeat the ForthRight. Empress Wu was finished and it was time for her to take control of both the situation *and* the Coven. There could be no more doubt or delay. She had to act. Tonight would begin the reign of Empress Borgia.

'Then, Comrade Chazaqijal, you must wait here and attack

them when they emerge from the laboratory. But you must do this alone . . . I have other priorities.' And with that she disappeared in the direction of the postern gate.

When Burlesque thought about it later, all he could remember was the vaguest recollection of being thrown across the hall oh-so-very-slowly. It was as though he was moving, rolling and tumbling in a great tub of hot treacle. Time for Burlesque slowed. He heard the huge bang when the bomb – the *bombs*, rather: the other five had exploded in sympathy – had detonated and then . . . nothing, everything went silent. He had the vague sensation of his hands – which he'd somehow managed to raise to protect his face – and his hair burning. He watched in a disinterested fashion as his trousers caught fire, as one of his boots was blown off . . .

Then, abruptly, as though a switch had been thrown, everything speeded up. A wall came towards him in a rush and with a sickening, bone-shaking bang he was slammed into it. It was a hard, hard landing. The wind was knocked out of him and as he felt his head bang into something unyielding, a jagged scream of light flashed before his eyes. And then everything went black.

He must have been knocked unconscious, but it could only have been for a second or two. When he came to, he found bodies crashing around him and debris raining down from the ceiling. He tried to curl into a ball, but the weight of a dead NoN lying across his legs prevented him moving, so he was forced to watch helplessly as roof girders, shaken from the ceiling by the explosion, began to spear down, smashing to the ground. But although he could see, he couldn't hear much: the explosions seemed to have done for his right ear. Yet burnt and half-deaf though he was, Burlesque took comfort in the realisation that he was still alive. He might be racked by pain, he might be covered in a patina of dust and vaporised SAE, but he was alive.

Tentatively, carefully, he tried to move his body, testing it for broken bones. His right wrist was busted for sure but miraculously, except for that, a splitting headache and a skinned arse, he seemed in remarkably good shape. After much pushing, kicking and cursing, he freed himself from the NoN, staggered shakily to his feet, blinked his eyes gingerly, trying to wash away the grit and the grime, and looked out into the hall. He could hardly see anything; although some of the gas mantles were still alight, the air was heavy with a thick, choking dust. But what he could see told him the Fermentation Plant was no more. The bombs had destroyed everything.

Everything apart from one of the Amazons. He saw her advancing towards him with a sword in her hand and murder in her eyes. He knew he was dead meat: with his gimp arm he wouldn't be able to use his sword to defend himself.

That was when he was suddenly aware of a soiled and stained Odette standing beside him, holding out her hand. 'I 'ave no more of the bullets, *mon cheri*, so I would be mostly obliged to 'ave the use of your sword.'

Like a man in a trance, Burlesque drew his sword from its scabbard and handed it to his woman.

Burlesque's sword, cheap and clumsy though it was, had a satisfying heft in Odette's hand, and the deadly practicality of the blade seemed to clear some of the fog from her bomb-shocked mind. She turned to face the Amazon, crouching down as she did so in her favoured fighting stance, but even as she pirouetted on the ball of her right foot, she winced in pain. The ankle was sprained, but that was the least of her problems. There was a numbness radiating out from her left shoulder where she had been hit by a flying brick, and the paralysis seemed to be drifting down along her arm, making it difficult for her to balance herself properly. And balance, she knew, was the most important thing for any sword fighter.

'Stand aside,' snarled the Amazon as she pointed her sword towards Burlesque. 'It is unseemly for a Femme to defend such offal. Have you no respect for your gender?'

Odette dragged a sleeve across her eyes, trying to free them of dust. 'Know this, mostly 'orrible Amazon lady, I am Odette Aroca and thees ees my man, Burlesque Bandstand. For 'im I will fight to the last of the breaths, so to kill 'im you must first of the all kill me.'

Yeah, she was buggered if some Amazon would kill her beloved Burlesque without a fight. She shook her head in a vain attempt to clear it, then, as best she was able, she tried to relax herself, setting herself poised ready to receive the attack from the Amazon.

The soldierFemme came at Odette in an untidy rush, her contempt and her hatred making her careless. With a strength developed from hauling meat to and from her market stall in Paris, Odette blocked the woman's roundhouse slash with a casual flick of her own blade, steel snarling on steel, a parry that matched the Amazon's own strike for speed and power. The ease with which she fought off the cut gave her opponent pause and now the Amazon was warier, circling her more cautiously, searching for a point of weakness.

Watching her, Odette tried to ignore the pain hammering in her head and the numbness seeping insidiously along her left arm. She made herself concentrate only on the Amazon's blade as it danced back and forth.

The lunge the Amazon made was lightning-fast and Odette only managed to avoid the razor-sharp point by a hair's breadth, jerking her chin away as the sword whisked past her face. But the effort was almost her undoing. She was pushed onto her back foot and although she instinctively made to compensate for the move by stretching out her arm for balance, her arm refused to obey. Caught off balance, she staggered, and seeing her opponent's guard falter, the Amazon was on her, her sword flashing in and out as she sought to end the duel.

The power of the onslaught was simply incredible. It took all of Odette's strength to parry the blows and even as she was forced to retreat, she could sense her strength ebbing away. It was desperate work: her left arm was now almost useless and she could feel the cold starting to spread across her chest and along her neck. In a matter of moments she knew she would be helpless to defend herself.

So she attacked, hewing her blade at the Amazon's face, aiming for her eyes, driving her back, trying to ignore the ache in her sword arm and the scorching light that shot before her eyes. Her blade flashed and slashed, as she tried to cut through the Amazon's guard, making her retreat, the Amazon rattled both by the ferocity of the onslaught and by Odette's raw skill. Encouraged, Odette marshalled all her remaining energy for one last attack, but groggy from her wound, she failed to see a broken wooden beam beneath her feet. She tripped, sprawling to the hall's floor.

And as Odette tumbled, with a triumphant shriek the Amazon was on her, slicing her sword down. Only by a miracle was Odette able to parry the strike, sparks flashing off the blades as the impact of the two swords sent judders of pain shuddering along her arm. She rolled away, then crab-crawled as best she was able out of reach of the next inevitable strike. She knew she was done for.

Then Burlesque attacked.

He blindsided the Amazon by springing at her from behind, wrapping his one good arm and both his legs around her, gouging at her eyes with his fingers and biting down on her neck. He grappled hard and he had surprise on his side, but it did no good. The Amazon lifted a hand behind her, grabbed him by the scruff of the neck and hurled him away as though he weighed nothing at all.

And as she did so, Odette, still on her knees, lanced Burlesque's sword into the girl's belly. The soldierFemme buckled and the colour drained from her face.

'No ...'

Odette hauled the blade out of the Amazon's body and watched as she slumped to the ground.

But even as she knelt gasping and spent, Burlesque limped over to her. 'Yous gonna stay there all fucking night, Odette,' he panted as he woggled a finger in his ear, 'or is we gonna 'ave it away on our toes before them LessBiens come and see wot a fucking mess we've gone an' made ov their factory?'

Dong E staggered out of the laboratory into the panicked chaos of the Castle. The explosions that had done for the Fermentation Plant had persuaded the hundreds of Femmes and screaming NoNs who lived in Hereji-Jo Castle to run for cover, but as none of them seemed to know where 'cover' might actually be, mayhem had ensued. The fortunate thing was that in the confusion no one seemed remotely interested in her.

Thinking how she should make her escape, she remembered hearing the vampyre talking about a postern gate and horses, so she turned south, skirting the Castle's walls, searching for this mysterious way out. She knew she had to hurry, realising that soon someone would take control of the situation, but her wounded leg was painful, so despite her best efforts she made only slow and tortuous progress. When she eventually found the gate she was nigh on spent, but, after shoving her way through the ivy blocking the gate, her spirits were revived when she found the horses tethered in a small copse of trees a hundred metres beyond the Castle walls. Dong E had never been so happy to see a horse in her life, which was remarkable given that she had never ridden before in her life. Fortunately, the nag she clambered aboard was tractable.

Chazaqijal hung back in the shadows. There were now so many Amazons milling around the courtyard in front of the laboratory that if he stepped away from his hiding place he would be immediately spotted as an interloper and in his damaged condition even a Grigori such as he would not be able to fight off so many opponents.

That was when he saw the tiny Chink girl who had bested him slink out of the door and limp in the direction of the postern gate. He knew instinctively that the bitch must have heard him giving instructions to Borgia about where the horses were hidden.

Suddenly there was an explosion from Ptah's laboratory and as the Amazons rushed to take cover, Chazaqijal seized his chance, hobbling after the Chink, his hatred making him oblivious to the pain racking his body. He would have his revenge.

It took thirty minutes before the temple spire was in sight and Dong E knew that she was close to the SheTong's safe house. Very gingerly she urged the horse on – she didn't like the way it had been wheezing for the last couple of minutes – and finally came to the door of the house. She dismounted and tethered the horse then looked around anxiously: she had the troubling thought that she'd been followed.

Before Dong E realised what was happening, the vampyre was on her, his enormously powerful hands closing around her neck, crushing the breath out of her. In an instant she was struggling for her life, his fingernails gouging into her skin, his thumbs pressing down savagely onto her windpipe. He was like something from the depths of Hel, his face horribly scarred and his right eye red and blank.

'So I have you, bitch. Now you must suffer the fury of the Grigori.'

With that the man redoubled his efforts to throttle her. Desperately she grappled with him, trying to pull his hands away, trying to claw at his eyes, but he was too strong . . . amazingly strong. A red mist shaded her sight. She heard a rattle in her throat. She knew she was losing her fight for life.

There was the crack of a rifle shot. The Grigori sagged like a deflating balloon, his hands relaxed and then he sank to the ground. As Dong E collapsed to her knees in choking confusion beside his body, she felt a dark presence at her elbow. Looking up, she found herself peering into the face of Su Xiaoxiao.

'Su Xiaoxiao?' she gasped. 'But how did you find me?'

'Don't you know, Dong E, that a mother always knows when her daughter is in danger?'

39

Hereji-Jo Castle
The Demi-Monde: 76th Day of Summer, 1005

There is much controversy relating to the death of Empress Wu, with those with a liking for conspiracy conjecturing that her demise was not caused – as the official record would have it – by her choking on an overly large river cucumber but rather that she was poisoned by Lucrezia Borgia. Admittedly, the short and inglorious reign of Empress Borgia has made her the butt of many scurrilous rumours which the scant and fragmented written records pertaining to the final days of the Wu dynasty have done little to illuminate, but in this HerTorian's view, Borgia acted in a loyal and exemplary fashion with regard to her Empress. Borgia was no poisoner.

The Last Days of Empress Wu: Mary Godwin,
ForthRight PaperBacks

Behind her, Hereji-Jo Castle was being consumed by fire, but Lucrezia Borgia gave it not a thought. She simply yanked the horse's head towards the Forbidding City and lashed its flanks with her whip.

The past was of no interest to her, all that mattered was the future ... her future.

Just as dawn was breaking she was striding – wet, cold and travel-soiled – through the corridors of the Forbidding City, her mind racing as she weighed strategies and options, balancing risk with gain. Events were moving rapidly and it behoved any who desired power – and none desired it as fervently as Lucrezia Borgia – to grasp the opportunities presented by those events. Mao's assassination had elevated her to the second-highest position in the Coven and given her access to the Forbidding Palace, and the appointment of Amina Zaria as the replacement for the traitor Trixie Dashwood meant that she had effective control of the Covenite army: Amina was a very obedient lover.

Yes, now was her moment of destiny.

She turned to Imperial NoN Wang Jingwei, the NoN who had replaced Mao as Guardian of the Imperial Bedchamber, who was trotting along whimpering and fretting at her side.

'NoN Wang Jingwei,' she asked, 'do you wish to live?'

Wang Jingwei gawped at her and then twisted his head from side to side, checking that their conversation wasn't being overheard. 'Of course, Imperial Administrator,' he whispered.

'Project YiYi is no more; the Plague weapon has been destroyed.'

'You are sure?' There was a distinct tremble on the NoN's bottom lip as he imagined the awful consequences of that piece of news.

'Saboteurs detonated bombs in the Fermentation Plant. I was there; I saw and heard the destruction.' She stopped and stared at the NoN. 'You realise the implications?'

A nod from Wang Jingwei. 'The ForthRight will triumph.'

That was now a certainty and there was no point, as Lucrezia Borgia judged it, in denying what was inevitable. The ForthRight would conquer the Coven and so the best ploy would be for her to align herself with Heydrich and, of course, Crowley. Better to reign in a Coven that was a mere satellite of the ForthRight than to commune with her ancestors.

'Indeed. But before that I expect the Empress to purge all those she thinks are responsible for her defeat. The Empress Wu is nothing if not vindictive and I think she will blame the remaining NoNs in the Forbidding City for her failure.' Wang Jingwei had the courtesy to blanch at the prospect. 'So I ask again: do you wish to live?'

The implications of this simple question were stark. The NoN did not hesitate. 'Yes.'

'Are the guardFemmes who protect the Empress loyal to you?'

'No ... but they will obey Noble Consort Yu Lang.'

'Really? But they are oath-bound to sacrifice their lives to protect the Empress.'

'Oath-bound or not, the Plucking of all the Fresh Blooms, following the treachery of Dong E, was a fearful thing and many of the guardFemmes had lovers amongst them. They doubt an Empress who orders such a purging can retain the Grace of ABBA, and hence suspect their oaths have no validity.' Wang Jingwei shuffled his feet nervously. 'But even so, Imperial Administrator Borgia, I doubt whether they would put their souls at risk by assassinating the Empress.'

A laugh from Borgia. 'I am not asking them to do something so ... direct. You should advise Noble Consort Yu Lang that I do not require them to harm the Empress, merely not to inter-vene to *prevent* her being harmed. Will she do this?'

There wasn't the merest hesitation in Wang Jingwei giving his reply, 'Yes.'

A strange calm descended on Lucrezia Borgia as she walked across the floor of the Hall of Supreme Harmony. This was the moment when she would grasp her destiny and become all that she should become. This was the moment when she would step out of the shadows and into the glare of the limelight of

HerTory. She would become Empress or she would die in the attempt.

She stopped at the kowtow line, but before she could perform her devotions, the Empress interrupted. 'Is it true? Is it true?' she squawked. 'Is it true what the semaphore messages tell us? Is it true that Hereji-Jo Castle has been attacked and the Plague weapon destroyed?'

As she walked towards the Dragon Throne – the Empress seemingly oblivious to the contravention of Li this entailed – she could see the Empress was wide-eyed and nigh on hysterical. Disgusting ... in her opinion, an Empress should never display weakness or emotion. But such weakness and emotion did offer opportunities: the stupid Femme would not be thinking straight.

Borgia bowed. 'Yes, Your Majesty. I have just returned from Hereji-Jo Castle where I saw with my own eyes the destruction of the Fermenting Plant.'

The Empress seemed to wither, sinking back into the Dragon Throne looking old and broken. 'Then what is to be done?'

'Your Majesty ... this is a dark moment for the Coven, but I believe we have an opportunity even at this late hour to snatch victory from defeat.' She looked around at the courtiers gathered in the room as though assessing their trustworthiness. 'Unfortunately, Your Majesty, there are traitors to HerEticalism everywhere.'

'Clear the room! Clear the room!' the Empress screamed and she waved her hands around urging her courtiers and servants from the Hall. Only when the room was emptied of everyone apart from her guardFemmes and the Imperial Administrator did the Empress signal that Borgia should continue. 'So what is this secret intelligence, Imperial Administrator?'

'If I might approach the Dragon Throne? Even the walls in the Forbidding City have ears.'

The Empress gave an impatient nod and Borgia quickly ascended the steps leading to the throne. As she drew nearer to the Empress, the toll the stress and strain of the last few weeks had levied on her became more obvious. There were deep – though skilfully disguised – shadows under her eyes and her hands were trembling: she was a nervous wreck.

With a smile Lucrezia Borgia leant closer to her Empress. 'Your Majesty, I have learnt through my own cryptos that traitorous NoNs have been poisoning the river cucumbers of which you are so fond.'

'What . . . ?' gasped the Empress.

'They have been administering a slow-acting poison.'

'Those bastard NoNs want us dead?'

'Yes, Your Majesty, they are all disciples of that villainous NoN, Heii.'

'Yes, yes. We see now,' the Empress gabbled. 'They poisoned us. That is why we were no longer able to commune with ABBA, that was why the divinations of the iChing were so inauspicious.' Her face set in a scowl. 'We should have destroyed all the NoNs when Heii betrayed us. We should have known that only Femmes like you, our trusted Imperial Administrator, could be relied on.'

'Exactly, Your Majesty. But I am pleased to advise you that I have acquired an antidote to this poison.' Here Borgia tapped the large ring on the index finger of her left hand. 'If you would permit me?'

An eager nod from the Empress, and Borgia slid the emerald adorning the ring to one side and poured the powder hidden in the recess beneath into a glass of Solution. A smell of almonds immediately engulfed them. 'The antidote is perfectly harmless, Your Majesty, and will render the poisons in your body impotent. Just this single drink will make you as one with ABBA.'

Even as a frantic Empress grabbed the glass, the guard-Femme who acted as her food taster stepped forward, but she was waved away. 'Not now, you fool, the Imperial Administrator is trying to save our life, not take it.' With that she swirled the red Solution around to ensure that all of the powder had been dissolved and then drank it down.

Borgia stepped back in order to better see the effect the cyanide had on the woman. To assassinate the Empress she had shunned cantarella, her poison of choice, on the grounds that it was too slow-acting. She had instead chosen to use cyanide, the effects of which were almost immediate. Even as she watched, Empress Wu clutched at her throat and began making strange gasping sounds.

'What . . .?' she croaked.

'Have Imperial NoN Wang Jingwei attend the Empress!' she ordered and a guardFemme scuttled off to carry out the order.

When a breathless Wang Jingwei scampered into the Hall, Borgia gave more orders. 'Have a semaphore message sent to GeneralFemme Amina that Imperial Edict 723 is to be put into immediate effect.'

She was interrupted by the Empress tumbling down the steps to land in a twitching heap on the floor of the Hall of Supreme Harmony. The Empress's face had taken on a decidedly blue tinge, her eyes were bulging and foam and spittle were oozing from her mouth. The Femme looked, Borgia decided, disgusting. She turned away and was shocked to see that the Imperial NoN hadn't moved; the sight of his Empress writhing in her death throes seemed to have driven all thoughts of obedience from his mind.

'Imperial NoN Wang Jingwei, I have issued an order! It is imperative that the instruction regarding Imperial Edict 723 is communicated without delay.'

The threat in Borgia's voice seemed to shake the NoN out of his trance. He tore his eyes away from the Empress as she shuddered and shook on the floor. 'I am not familiar with Imperial Edict 723, Imperial Administrator Borgia.'

'It relates to the armistice between the ForthRight and the Coven. Hostilities between our two Sectors will cease immediately and the gates of the Great Wall will be thrown open to allow the ForthRight Army entry to Beijing.' This was the agreement she had reached with Crowley: she would have the Coven surrender in exchange for being acknowledged as the rightful Empress by the ForthRight. 'Only in this way, Imperial NoN Wang Jingwei, will we end the terrible suffering of my people.'

'But only the Empress may issue Imperial Edicts.'

'The law of the Coven states that upon the death of the Empress, if she dies childless, the Imperial Administrator shall take the throne, so be sure to sign the message "By Order of Empress Lucrezia Borgia".' She nudged the body of Empress Wu with the toe of her boot. 'Yes, I think we can definitely say that the reign of Empress Wu is at an end.' She smiled. 'And there is one other thing. Have Dr Merit Ptah taken into protective custody.' Now that Hereji Jo had been destroyed, the only person who possessed the secrets of the Plague was Ptah. The Femme would make a very valuable bargaining chip in the negotiations she would be having with Heydrich.

Still Wang Jingwei hesitated. Lucrezia Borgia snaked a hand around to the pistol she had hidden beneath her jacket: if he refused to obey she would have to kill him. Finally the NoN bowed. 'I salute the True Empress, and pray that ABBA grants her Nine Thousand Years of Peace and Contentment. Great Empress Borgia, Mistress of the Demi-Monde, of the Great Beyond and of all the Kosmos, Blessed and Much Beloved by ABBA and Defender of the Faith of HerEticalism, it gives me much pleasure to transmit the message that will bring peace to the Coven and contentment to my fellow NoNs.'

That Su Xiaoxiao had refused Norma permission to join Burlesque and his band when they had attacked Hereji-Jo Castle – on the grounds that the Messiah couldn't be put in harm's way – had been difficult enough for her to handle, but the anguish she'd felt when they'd returned had been almost too much to bear. That these brave people had been risking their lives when she was skulking in the SheTong safe house she found very trying.

And from what she had seen and heard, the attack on the Castle had been a very close-run thing. Rivets was dead and each of his three companions had been injured during the fighting. Only the panic following the destruction of the Fermenting Plant and Ptah's laboratory had enabled Burlesque and Odette to make their escape. In the confusion no one had been particularly interested in two burnt and bedraggled fugitives and as the gates of the Castle had been thrown open by Amazons fleeing the fires raging within, it was a simple matter for the pair of them to slip away into the night.

The wounds he'd sustained had kept Burlesque in bed for almost three days, so it was only on the morning of the seventy-ninth day of Summer that he felt strong enough to venture down the stairs of the safe house. Barely had he sat down at the table when Dong E gave him the bad news.

'Rivets is dead,' the girl announced, 'he died saving me from vampyres.' With that she slumped down on a chair and proceeded to weep.

Burlesque wept with her. It was a strange feeling watching someone as supposedly unfeeling as Burlesque Bandstand crying.

'I ain't never cried before in me life,' he blubbed. 'I feel like I've lost a brother. 'E wos all right, wos Rivets, and a good pal.' Odette came to sit next to her man and put an arm around him. Then she started crying too.

'It seems that I owe the spirit of Rivets an apology,' admitted Trixie Dashwood. 'I should never have doubted either his competence or his belief in vampyres.' And then, unbelievably, she started crying too. Maybe, Norma decided, the girl was human after all.

'He died bravely, saving the True Empress,' soothed Su Xiaoxiao.

'I, more than any, am aware of that, Honoured Mother,' Dong E answered, 'but the fact remains that a second brave and faithful nonFemme has had to sacrifice himself that I might live. This is a heavy price to pay for salvation.'

'Then you must show yourself worthy of that sacrifice, Your Majesty. These are dark times that grow ever darker.' Su Xiaoxiao gave Burlesque a grim smile. 'You will not have heard, Burlesque-san, but while you slept, Lucrezia Borgia has taken the throne of the Coven and announced that the war with the ForthRight is over. The Coven has surrendered and is now to be integrated into the ForthRight. Heydrich is victorious.'

'Shit.'

'Of course, the SheTong will fight on.'

'And the SheTong will lose,' said Dong E quietly. 'No, Honoured Mother, the time of violence has passed. Now I must learn from Norma and follow her philosophy of Normalism. Now is the time for Empress Dong E to announce herself as a Normalist and to lead her people to peace. We must tell my people that I am Dong E, First Empress of the Ying Dynasty, the Bringer of Peace and Happiness, and that I eschew violence and hatred. We must tell them that just as the people of the Quartier Chaud resisted Heydrich's ForthRight by the use of peaceful non-cooperation, so too will we, the people of the Coven. We must tell them that today marks the first day of the age of Ying.'

Su Xiaoxiao bowed to her daughter. 'The SheTong will pledge itself to the philosophy of Ying, Your Majesty.'

'The WFA must fight on,' said Trixie quietly. 'The taking of the WarJunk is scheduled for nine days hence and I don't believe a strategy of non-violence will prove useful in the successful execution of that exercise.'

Burlesque was persuaded to speak. 'Colonel Trixie's right, Dongie, luv. I dunno iffn just turning the ovver cheek is gonna work, 'specially if all the Femmes 'ere in the Coven take their lead from Lucrezia-bloody-Borgia and start killing everybody.'

The room went silent as those in it pondered the tasks and perils to come. Although she was uplifted by the announcement that Dong E had chosen to embrace non-violence, Norma knew that it would be a difficult road to follow, especially with a Femme as deranged as Lucrezia Borgia running the Coven. Backed by the might of the ForthRight, there was no telling what terrible things she might do to consolidate her power. What was needed was a way to discomfit Heydrich and her mind drifted back to the plans she had had before she had been abducted by Wu, the plans that involved her taking the message of Normalism to the very heart of the ForthRight.

'This might help,' said Norma as she laid the front page of a day-old copy of *The Stormer* across the breakfast table. The headline read, 'Victory in the Coven Day'.

'Wot's that?' asked Burlesque.

'The ForthRight is giving over the final day of Summer to celebrations to mark the end of the war in the Coven, these to culminate on Lammas Eve with a jamboree to be held at the Crystal Palace in London, a jamboree to be attended by Heydrich himself. Empress Borgia is to be guest of honour.'

'So wot?'

Norma tapped a finger on the page. 'I think the one person they've forgotten to invite is Aaliz Heydrich. With the help of you and Odette, Burlesque, I think she'll be able to create such a fuss that Heydrich will wish he'd never heard of the Coven. But to do this the three of us will have to go to London.'

'Oh shit . . .'

40

The Rookeries
The Demi-Monde: 85th Day of Summer, 1005

To ensure the level of morale within the ForthRight Army remains high during the Coven campaign it is agreed that an Armed Forces Entertainment Unit be formed. The purpose of the AFEU will be to tour the war zone, bringing the army a variety show which will allow our soldiers respite from combat. Whilst the advice of His Holiness Comrade Aleister Crowley that the content of these mobile entertainments be reflective of the principles of Living&More and be correct regarding the teachings of UnFunDaMentalism is noted, it was agreed that a certain latitude be allowed, especially with regard to comedians and female performers.

Extract from the Minutes of the PolitBuro meeting
held under the guidance of the Great Leader on the
4th day of Summer, 1005

Norma, Burlesque and Odette came ashore in St Petersburg just east of the Anichkov Bridge and from there Norma placed her safety in the hands of Burlesque; this, after all, was home ground for him. But even so she was impressed by the efficiency with which he organised their progress through the backstreets of Rodina, across the Rhine and into the Rookeries. He seemed to know everybody – everybody of a criminal inclination, that is – and quickly had them snug and secure in a couple of rooms in Berlin.

'These is Wanker's old rooms,' he explained as they settled in.

Norma frowned. 'But won't the Checkya be keeping watch here? I mean, Vanka's got a reward on his head.'

'Wanker was born wiv a reward on his head,' answered Burlesque. 'Nah, the Checkya ain't interested in 'im no more. Wanker's yesterday's news. Anyway, word is he's scarpered to the JAD.' He tossed his bag onto the bed he had chosen for him and Odette, then turned to Norma. 'So what's to do then, Miss Norma?'

'My plan is to launch Normalism here in the very heart of the ForthRight and to do that I need to make a really dramatic debut. And, by my reckoning, this "Victory in the Coven" jamboree is the event to do it. I want to walk out in front of that audience as Aaliz Heydrich and for Heydrich's own daughter to announce just how corrupt and venal the ForthRight's leadership is and to urge everyone to follow the teachings of Normalism.'

Burlesque whistled and pushed his bowler hat onto the back of his head. 'Fuck me gently, Miss Norma, I didn't fink yous wos serious. Yous don't want much, do yous?'

'Oh, I'm very serious, Burlesque. This is the perfect time and place to announce that Normalism has come to the ForthRight. There are going to be one hundred thousand soldiers on parade and embarrassing Heydrich in front of that lot will really put a spoke in the bastard's wheel.'

'Difficult,' mused Burlesque, 'wiv Heydrich in attendance that place is gonna be done up tighter than a duck's arsehole. It's gonna be swarming wiv Checkya.'

'Burlesque *a raison*, Norma,' agreed Odette. 'Even I, a girl from the Quartier Chaud, 'as 'eard of the *Palais de Cristal* most

celebrated and with Heydrich to be making the attendance ...'
She trailed off, but what she left unsaid was very eloquent.

'Cors,' mused Burlesque in an absent-minded fashion, 'your
message ov peace and non-violence ain't gonna be falling on
deaf ears. Word on the streets is that people are really pissed
off wiv all the fighting. An' iffn you get thousands and thousands ov soldiers who are fed up bin shot at all together in one
place 'oo knows wot might happen?' He gave his chin a long,
thoughtful stroke. 'Question is though, 'ow to do it?'

The answer was provided by Sporting Chance.

'Waddya fink?'

Norma had to lean closer to Burlesque to hear what he said,
she had never imagined that vaudeville shows could be so
damned noisy. The audience – and there must have been a thousand people jammed into the music hall – shouted, whistled,
cheered and booed all the way through the acts, making it difficult to hold a normal conversation. There had even been one
lunatic running around shouting 'Fire!', but he had simply been
ignored.

Burlesque raised his voice to a near-bellow. 'I said, waddya
fink?'

As she looked down from the balcony to the auditorium
below, Norma wasn't quite sure what to think. Back in the Real
World she'd seen programmes about music halls on the Polly,
but she had never imagined that she would ever be sitting in
one and it was an experience that had taken a little getting
used to. The music hall – the Canterbury Theatre, which was
slap-bang in the centre of a really low-rent part of the Rookeries
called Lambeth – was grand enough in a tarty, blingy sort of
way, but its glitz was shrouded in a fog of choking tobacco
smoke and it had a smell about it – a thousand damp people
slowly drying out had its own unique bouquet – that made

Norma's stomach turn. But despite these problems the audience really seemed to be enjoying itself.

And there *were* acts to enjoy. Oddly – she had never been a great fan of jugglers – the guy called Paul Cinquevalli who had closed the first half of the show had been really good, especially the stunt he had performed supporting a chair – with his assistant sitting on it reading a newspaper – in his *teeth* whilst simultaneously juggling five beer bottles. And Odette had gone ape when a trapeze artist – some Quartier Chaudian guy called Jules Léotard – had scared the crap out of the audience by swinging high over their heads and doing the most outrageous somersaults.

But enjoyable as it all was, Norma still couldn't figure out why Burlesque had demanded that she accompany him and Odette to the theatre, especially as time was running out: Lammas Eve and the 'Victory in the Coven' celebrations were only a few days away. The answer was left to the very end, when the star of the show walked on the stage to a fanfare of trumpets and a riot of rapturous applause and cheering.

'This is 'er,' yelled a very excited Burlesque, 'this is Sporting Chance.' With that he leant out over the balcony's balustrade to join in the welcome.

The girl who sashayed to the middle of the stage was blonde, brassy and big. Mainly big, Norma decided. Not fat, just big. She was tall and wide with the most stupendously large breasts Norma had ever seen, breasts that were very prominently on display: her corset was so tightly laced that her tits were pushed skywards and the piece of wispy lace designed to cover them was barely adequate for purpose. She also seemed to have decided that her legs were worth a look too and, in contravention to the more conservative UnFunDaMentalist fashions, her hooped skirt ended well above her chubby knees.

The audience loved her.

Such was the hullaballoo the girl's fans were making that it was just as well that her large chest housed an equally large set of lungs, otherwise nobody would have been able to hear her. But when she opened her mouth to sing – without the help of a microphone – her voice was loud enough to fill the hall and to soar over any sound that had the temerity to try to compete with her.

From what Norma could make out – the Rookeries slang the singer used in her lyrics defeated her on occasion – her repertoire was pretty risqué with lots of ribald suggestiveness, this accompanied by any number of winks and wiggles. The audience adored her cheek and her double entendres and, though Norma thought it all just a tad crude, she could understand why the girl was so popular. Sporting Chance was coquettish, impudent and not above poking fun at the ForthRight's leaders; the lines:

> Oh, Comrade Crowley's very handy with his wand
> Though the Comrade Leader's better with his hand
> And Skobelev's real clever with his tongue
> The three ov 'em together . . . oh my, that's fun

brought the house down.

But it seemed that what everyone in the theatre had been waiting for was her final number, and when she launched into it, Norma sat there stunned. Her finale was a rendition – a very salacious and sexy rendition, it had to be said – of the Marlene Dietrich classic 'Falling in Love Again'.

'How—?' she began.

'Sportin' 'eard that song when Ella Thomas came to the Prancing Pig and sung it. Quite taken wiv it was Sportin' and when she started singin' there on a Sunday night, she put it in 'er act. Went down a storm it did. It's wot made her famous . . .

that'n 'aving such big charms, ov course. Punters like a bit ov
flesh on their singers, like 'em to bounce around a bit when they
goes for the high notes. 'Cors 'aving me as 'er manager and billing
'er as "the Naughty Nightingale" 'elped.'

'You know this girl?'

Burlesque moved his mouth closer to Norma's ear so Odette
couldn't hear. 'I "knows" Sportin' Chance in all senses of the
word, iffn you get my drift.' He gave Norma a wink. 'Like I says,
I'm 'er manager ... well, I wos before I wos arrested by that
bastard Beria.' As the curtain fell on Sporting's performance,
he got up from his seat. 'I fink we should go backstage an' say
'ello.'

'You go, Burlesque. I'll just go back to my room: I'm still
trying to work out how to disrupt the Crystal Palace celebrations.'

'Oh, yous don't wanna worry abart that, Miss Norma. Very
popular wiv the troops is Sportin' Chance, so popular that she's
gonna be singing for them at the "Victory in the Coven"
celebrations.'

'Fuck me from 'ere to Fenchurch! As I live an' breathe, it's
Burlesque-fucking-Bandstand. Gor, even wiv a broken wing,
you're still a fine figure ov a man.' With that Sporting Chance
took Burlesque in her powerful arms, dragged him towards her
and buried his face in her bosom. ''Ave a nuzzle for old times'
sake, Burlesque. Way I remembers it, yous wos the best nuzzler
in the 'ole of the Rookeries, you wos.' When a panting and very
red-faced Burlesque finally tore himself free of the embrace,
the girl took the opportunity to pat him affectionately on the
crotch. 'An' I 'ope the old 'owitzer is still loaded an' ready to
go bang. Maybe you'll give me a one-gun salute later on, eh?'

A spluttering Burlesque interrupted the girl's reminiscences
to make urgent introductions. 'Sportin', this 'ere's me *friend*,

Odette.' The way he emphasised the word 'friend' was obviously intended to communicate to Sporting that Odette was more than a friend, though Norma suspected that the glowering look on the French girl's face had already done this very effectively.

'Odette, eh? So you shacked up wiv a Frog bint now, Burlesque? Oh la la!' And before Odette could protest, Sporting had her in the same crushing embrace. 'Well, bin sewer an' pleased to meetcha, Odette. I feel like we're sisters, both ov us 'aving sampled the same piece of mutton an' all.'

Such was the warmth of Sporting's welcome that Odette was persuaded to stop glowering and to kiss the girl on the cheeks.

'Trees beans,' chortled Sporting as she kissed the French girl back. 'You wanna be careful, Burlesque, or me an' Odette might scarper over to the Coven and set up as LessBiens.' She stepped back to take a better look at her new friend. 'I approve, Burlesque: I like a bird that's built for business.' Her eye fell on Norma. 'An' 'oo's this handsome piece? Yous getting into three-somes, Burlesque, you 'ankering after a bit ov the old tribalism?'

'This is Norma Williams.'

The singer's mood suddenly became frosty and she turned to all the other hangers-on and admirers crowding her dressing room. 'Out! Out!' she yelled and pushed and shoved them all towards the door. Only when the room was cleared and the door firmly locked did she turn back to Norma.

'I've heard ov you; you're bad news, yous is.' She gave Burlesque a venomous scowl. 'Wot're yous abart, Burlesque? Wot're yous doing bringing her 'ere? There's a price on this girl's head. There's reward posters for 'er stuck up all over the Rookeries.' She glared at Norma. 'You're the Normalist, ain't ya? You're the one who dropped the Awful Tower on top of that sack ov shit Beria.'

There was no point in denying it. 'Yes, I'm Norma Williams and yes, I'm the leader of the Normalist movement.'

'Well, I'll be rogered by a rhino. But friend ov Burlesque's or not, iffn you's found 'ere we'll all be for the high jump. The Peelers 'ave got it in for me already. Them bastards is watchin' me like 'awks. Chances are that the Checkya saw you comin' 'ere.'

Burlesque shook his head. 'Don't worry on that score, Sportin', I'm too much ov an old 'and to get me collar felt so easy. But we need to talk; there may be a way you can help us get rid ov the pack ov bastards that's running the ForthRight.'

They repaired to the suite Sporting kept in the hotel around the corner from the theatre. By the size and the opulence of the rooms Norma judged that the girl's career was going very, very well, which made her doubtful of being able to persuade her to help them. Sporting had a lot to lose.

'So wot's this plan ov yours, Burlesque?' she said when she had provided them each with a glass of cognac.

'It's best Norma explains.'

Taking her cue, Norma stood up from her chair, opened her bag, took out a blonde wig and used it to replace the black one she was wearing. The transformation had the desired effect: Sporting Chance's mouth dropped open.

'I'll be buggered on a bicycle: you look just like Aaliz Heydrich.'

'Yeah, I'm her doppelgänger . . . her double. And I want Aaliz Heydrich to address all the troops when they gather in the Crystal Palace next Tuesday.'

'An' wot's yous . . . wot's she . . . wot's yous gonna be saying?'

'That violence is wrong. That Heydrich is leading the ForthRight to destruction. That too many young men have died for the senseless cause of UnFunDaMentalism. That what was done in Warsaw and in the Coven was evil. And that it is time for a new way that espouses peace and non-violence, the way called Normalism.'

'Fuckin' Hel, that's really gonna put the cat amongst the pigeons an' no mistake. And just 'ow are you gonna be able to do that? Yous can't just wander up to Heydrich and say "Excuse me, Comrade Leader, but can I speak for a few minutes an' tell everybody wot a piece of shit you is?"'

Burlesque leant forward and gave Sporting a grin. 'We were thinking ov 'aving Norma 'ere come on at the end ov your performance.'

The penny dropped.

'Fuck me gently,' Sporting spluttered.

'We could make it look like we ambushed you, that we forced our way onto the stage. That way you wouldn't be left in the shit like.'

The singer was less than impressed. 'Bollocks, Burlesque: this little piece goes on in my place then I'm dead meat and you know it. Heydrich'll go doolally.'

But the interesting thing was she hadn't said no.

Sporting got up and poured herself another, longer drink. 'Funny fing is, Burlesque, that I'm living on borrowed time any'ows. Heydrich's gotten real bent outta shape about me act and they're only 'aving me perform at the Crystal Palace 'cos I'm so popular wiv the soldier boys.' She gave a wry little chuckle. 'An' I should be, ov cors, seeing as I've shagged most ov 'em.' She drained her drink. 'I 'ad a visit from that toerag Roman Ungern von Sternberg – the one that took over the Checkya when Beria copped it – an' 'e told me that iffn I so much as looked at Heydrich skew-whiff at the Palace 'e's gonna . . . well, I won't tell you wot 'e's gonna do, but I won't be pissin' straight afterwards. An' then there wos Bobby.'

'Bobby?' prompted Burlesque.

Sporting moved across to the grand piano in the corner of the room and picked up the silver-framed daguerreotype standing on it. The picture showed a rather chubby man dressed in the uniform of an artillery officer. 'This is Bobby. 'E wos the love ov me life, my Bobby was. 'E wos so big, an' tall an' 'and-some an' 'ung like a stallion.' She stopped in mid-eulogy to wipe a tear from her eye. 'No disrespect, Burlesque, but 'e gave me the best seein'-to I've ever 'ad.'

Burlesque gave a philosophical shrug. 'Wot 'appened to 'im?' he asked.

''E wos arrested by the Checkya, 'e wos, charged wiv being "an Enemy ov the People" or some such shit. They shot 'im.' Sporting gulped back more tears. ''Cors all that wos just a warning to me, wosn't it, just von Sternberg's way ov showing me wot would happen iffn I wosn't a good girl. Bastards.' She looked up and looked Norma straight in the eyes. 'So the answer, Norma Williams, is yes I will 'elp yous, I will 'ave the greatest pleasure in 'elping yous fuck Heydrich over.'

41

The NoirVillian Hub
The Demi-Monde: 88th Day of Summer, 1005

I looked over the misted plain towards the Temple where Lilith had wrought her magic and my soul shivered. It was not destroyed ... it could never be destroyed, wrought as it was from the Stone of the Gods. And in those walls her memories are stored, reverberating in the Stone, echoing for ever ... for ever ... for ever, never to fade. Even the Will of all the World or the Anger of ABBA cannot cleanse these memories, cannot undo what has been done. Know this, my Children, we could not destroy the evil contained there and though we bound Lilith with the entrails of Nari, there is another who will one day fall from Heaven to be loosed in the Demi-Monde. This is the fearsome brother of Lilith. Hear his name, Lucifer, and be sore afeared.

The Prose Ending: writer unknown, translated by Erik Scorreed, Final Days Publications

Kondratieff regarded himself as a pragmatist ... as a RaTionalist. He had little time for superstition or religion, preferring to rely on the comforting assurance of mathematics and logic than a somewhat hysterical belief in the supernatural. But as he stepped through the Great Entrance that led into the Temple of Lilith, he found this pragmatism being tested to the very limit.

The malevolence that inhabited the Temple washed over him, enveloping him in its loathsome embrace. He knew instinctively that this was an evil place where the wickedness within seemed to leer out at him, daring him to enter.

Even though it was drenched in the midday sunshine, even though the beautiful girls who made up the Doge William's Priestesshood were scurrying about the place doing the thousand and one things that needed to be done to get the Temple ready for the Lammas Eve celebrations, and even though musicians were rehearsing in the corner of the Temple filling it with music, the place still frightened Kondratieff. There was no warmth there; the Temple had a frosted, brittle feel as though all joy and happiness was being sucked out by it.

Indeed, the Temple exuded such wickedness that he was forced to stop to catch his breath, revolted by the echoes of the evil that had been done here. The forces that inhabited the Temple emitted a spine-chilling power that whispered of licentiousness and depravity. Here, he sensed, lurked something dark and wicked and in its name acts of terrible, unforgivable vileness had been performed.

Strange visions flickered through his mind – visions of the Spirit World – and he suddenly *knew* what perversions Lilith had committed here, knew of the hundreds – the thousands – of young lives that had been sacrificed to Lilith in this foul place. Now the Temple stood ready to be reborn, and the one who would do that was the Dark Charismatic, Doge William. Though Lilith had fallen there was Lucifer ready to take her place and if he was allowed to triumph, evil such as the Demi-Monde had never known would be loosed on the world. Yes, soon it would be Lammas Eve, the time when Lucifer would be ordained ruler of the Demi-Monde ... and Kondratieff would sacrifice himself to ensure that this evil was defeated.

Distracted though he was by the baleful atmosphere of the

Temple, Kondratieff managed to push these feelings of unease to the back of his mind: he knew he had to concentrate on the task at hand. Maybe these morbid thoughts were the product of tiredness? After all, he had been working day and night for the past week. He'd had had to organise the transportation of the real Column from its home in the Galerie des Anciens to Rodin's workshop in Murano and then manage its switch with the imitation Column; he'd had to supervise the loading of the fake into the pontoon and then suffer the bilious river journey to the wharf that serviced the Temple of Lilith.

But even then his task hadn't been finished. Transporting the Column along the Divine Way had been a hazardous and nerve-shredding task. Summer was the breeding season for the nanoBites, when they were particularly frisky and very dangerous, and whilst the workmen had been safe when standing on the centre-most of the three Mantle-ite pathways, one false step could prove fatal. The narrowness of the Divine Way made this margin of error very small . . . too small for one careless navvy.

Indeed, the Way was so narrow that Kondratieff had been obliged to remodel the steamer-crawlers used to drag the dolly upon which the pontoon sat so that their tracks ran along the two outside paths and didn't overlap onto the Hub itself. Fortunately, the Divine Way ran straight as a die from the jetty to the entrance of the Temple, so there were no bends to negotiate, but still only the best drivers had the skill to navigate the steamer-crawlers along the Mantle-ite track. It took the whole of a nail-biting, nerve-shredding day and much sweating, cursing, screaming and hair-pulling before the Column was dragged safe to the Great Entrance of the Temple of Lilith.

And this had been the easy part of the operation. The removal of the Column from the pontoon, the manoeuvring of it through the Great Gates and then suspending it over its plinth beside the altar had been an even more formidable engineering task. Being so big and heavy, the Column was awkward to handle and the last thing Kondratieff wanted was the workmen to drop the bloody thing. At the core of the faux-Column were packed five tons of blasting gelatin into which had been mixed five thousand musket balls: drop the Column and the explosion that followed would reduce those doing the dropping to the consistency of jam.

But with the help of fifty navvies, a powerful steam hoist, seemingly endless lengths of rope and much shouting and swearing, the Column was hauled into the Temple. It was a task made more difficult by the attendance of Selim the Grim and a whole coterie of HimPerial priests, each of them determined that the Column would be handled 'reverently' and be erected in a 'respectful' manner. As this necessitated them standing around intoning prayers and waving incense burners, they managed to make a difficult task *very* difficult.

Finally the Column stood tall and proud in its resting place. It was the first time Kondratieff had had a chance to examine the hexagonal plinth closely and he had to admit to being fascinated by it. The Column was suspended so that it could be lowered onto the plinth by the use of a wheel – similar to the ship's wheel he'd seen on some of the larger boats plying the rivers of the Demi-Monde – and once this was done the Column would be as one with the Temple, the Mantle-ite energy would flow and the Column would go *bang*.

'You have done well, Kondratieff.'

The sudden appearance of Selim behind him made Kondratieff jump. Since the death of de Sade, the bastard had assumed responsibility for the Column and with him being such a *clever* bastard Kondratieff had to be continually on his guard.

'I must admit that when I was told that de Sade had given

you the task of transporting it from Venice I was doubtful that even a scientist of your calibre would be able to accomplish it within such a tight timetable.'

Kondratieff bowed, not so much in veneration but rather in the hope that it would help mask the feeling of panic that had seized him. The way Selim was making such a close inspection of the Column was very, very worrying. 'You are very generous, Your Excellency,' he intoned, aghast to see Selim begin to walk around the Column, drifting his hand around words etched into its surface.

'It is remarkable, is it not? A real gift of ABBA. See how it shimmers green in the half-light. Wonderful.'

'Wonderful,' agreed Kondratieff as his body clock began to tick faster. He just hoped that none of the phosphorescent paint he'd concocted from the heads of the matches and that coated the Column stuck to the man's hand.

'But I must admit to being curious as to the purpose of the platform the Column is resting on,' admitted Selim.

'I am informed that the occult power of the Temple is stored in the Mantle-ite used to construct it, but the Mantle-ite must be activated before this power can be utilised. That is the purpose of the Column: it acts as a triggering mechanism. Once it is lowered into position, as will be done on Lammas Eve, all the latent power of the Temple will be released.'

And detonate the explosive stored inside the Column, but Kondratieff left this unsaid.

'Amazing,' mused Selim and then he stopped suddenly and stooped down to examine the Column more closely. 'I hadn't realised the Column was scarred,' he said, pointing to a twenty-centimetre-long gash on its final, sixth side. 'How can it be scarred if it is constructed of Mantle-ite?'

It took an act of will for Kondratieff to still the tremor he was sure would infect his voice. 'Academics have speculated that the flaw was caused by the Pre-Folk when they were constructing the Column. There is no other possible explanation; Mantle-ite is, after all, invulnerable.'

A nod from Selim. 'I find it quite comforting to know that our illustrious predecessors could be prone to error ... to the making of mistakes. It gives hope to us all, does it not, Kondratieff?'

'Indeed, Your Excellency, the Column gives us all hope.'

As he watched Selim wander away, Kondratieff, despite his atheism, found himself breathing a prayer to ABBA, requesting that He smile on the efforts of Trixiebell Dashwood with regards to the *real* Column, because if she was to fail then all his efforts – all his sacrifice – would be dust.

42

The Coven
The Demi-Monde: 88th Day of Summer, 1005

It is an oddity that the most famous of all River Captains is a woman who professed an intense dislike of the water. Nevertheless, the name of Trixie Dashwood is now synonymous with river warfare: she might not have liked the water, but the water most certainly liked her.

A Children's Pictorial Guide to Heroes and Heroines of the Demi-Monde: Venetian Books

A thunderclap crashed and rain lashed down on the three hundred fighters who comprised Attack Group One as they bustled through the backstreets of Rangoon. But despite the rain Trixie felt she had been twice lucky in picking tonight of all nights to take – to *try* to take – the WarJunk CSS *Wu* that was anchored in the Kaliningrad docks on the St Petersburg side of the Volga. Lucky that the rain seemed to be even heavier than usual, which dissuaded even the most fervent of StormTroopers from venturing out, and lucky again in that the surrender of the Coven meant that the ForthRight army had suspended its artillery bombardment of Rangoon.

And with the ceasefire announced the ForthRight army had relaxed and its soldiers had turned their attention to converting the local Femmes into dutiful – and heterosexual – UnFun-DaMentalists and liberating any supplies of Sake Solution they found, neither activity doing much to improve their vigilance.

But never one to push her luck further than was absolutely necessary, Trixie was anxious to cross the Volga before either the monsoon eased or Heydrich changed his mind and recommenced pounding the shit out of the city. Yet despite these somewhat morbid imaginings, she felt full of bounce and was actually looking forward to tonight's adventure. For the first time in months she was taking the fight to Heydrich. Now she had the chance to hurt Heydrich and his foul creed of UnFunDaMentalism ... to avenge all the poor people he'd slaughtered in Warsaw and Rangoon.

The first stage of the operation was quickly accomplished. To have her little army cross the Volga, she simply commandeered three Whitehall gigs moored near the Anichkov Bridge. The SS StormTrooper who was guarding the gigs would presumably have objected, but the first warning he had about what was happening was when Wysochi slit his throat. His interest in proceedings nosedived after that.

It took only twenty tense minutes to cross the river and to creep along the docks to where the *Wu* was berthed. As Trixie had been advised by LieutenantFemme Lai Choi San – the Femme in charge of all things nautical – four things needed to be done to successfully steal a WarJunk: take control of it from the UnFunnies, fill its coal bunkers, get its boilers up to a working pressure, and run the Volga without being blown to bits by the ForthRight artillery lining the river. Above all, they had to be lucky.

Lucky: that word again.

In fact, taking control of the *Wu* was accomplished relatively painlessly ... painlessly for Trixie's fighters, that is. The sentries guarding the WarJunk were dead before they even realised they were being stalked, and once they were disposed of, Wysochi and five fighters oozed down into the bowels of the *Wu*. Despite

herself, Trixie felt a moment's sympathy for the poor unsus-
pecting sailors who were on watch. Her moment of tenderness
lasted around two minutes, which was how long it was before
a grinning Wysochi re-emerged and gave her the thumbs-up.

Without waiting for an order, LieutenantFemme Lai Choi San
was across the boarding ramp and down the hatch to inspect
the engine room, Trixie following hard on her heels.

'Okay, first the good news, ColonelFemme,' the Lieutenant
began after a cursory inspection. 'The boilers are hot. They must
have been running a pressure check not more than an hour
ago. It'll only take us thirty minutes to get steam up.'

'And the bad news?'

'We're low on coal. We've enough to get to the Wheel River,
but no further. But it seems ABBA has smiled on us: according
to Su Xiaoxiao's agents, there's a fully laden coal barge berthed
just along the docks from where the *Wu*'s moored.'

'Then we better start shovelling.'

It had been Trixie's intention to load coal for three hours, then,
bunkers full or not, to sail before dawn and run the Volga in
darkness. But Fate decided not to cooperate. It was inevitable,
really. it was one thing to put two of her fighters – dressed in
SS uniforms – on point duty to deter nosy parkers, but when
her entire army began shovelling coal from the nearby coal
barge, the noise was too much for even the most dilatory of
watch commanders to ignore. Less than thirty minutes after
the coaling of the *Wu* had begun, a bleary-eyed, wet and evil-
tempered SS captain, trailed by six burly StormTroopers, arrived
at the dock and, brushing aside the objections of the faux-
sentries, stormed towards the WarJunk.

'What the fuck's going on here?' he demanded loudly. 'This
ship isn't due to sail for two days. Who's in command?'

For a moment Trixie considered trying to bluff her way out

of the situation, but as the captain and his men seemed to know their business – their locked and loaded M4s attested to that – she decided on more direct action.

'I am, Comrade Major,' she said as she stepped out from behind the WarJunk's casement.

'And just who the fuck are you?'

'Colonel Trixie Dashwood,' she answered and then shot the captain through the head.

There was a brief flurry of shooting, during which the StormTroopers were dispatched with commendable efficiency, and then Trixie started to bark her orders. 'Prepare to sail. Cast off all mooring ropes. Close all hatches.'

Wysochi, black from head to toe in coal dust, materialised from the direction of the coal barge. 'We've only got about half the coal we need, Colonel.'

'Send two men and attach a hawser to that coal barge. We'll take the coal with us.'

And that was how, ten minutes later, the CSS *Empress Wu*, with the coal barge *London* in tow, edged her way out of St Petersburg dock en route to Venice.

'Comrade Lieutenant, there's a message coming through over the wire.'

SS Gunnery Lieutenant Burns, twenty-three years old and a ninety-day veteran commanding Gun Emplacement Fourteen, drained his mug of café au gore, eased his gangly body up out of his chair and sauntered – carefully – over to where the signal sergeant had set up that miracle of ForthRight ingenuity, the galvanicEnergy-powered telegraph station. Burns had to be careful how he went and not for the first time he cursed being too tall for the artillery. The ceiling of the concrete bunker where his Krupp mortar was housed had a clearance of six feet, which was exactly three inches too low to accommodate a vertical Lieutenant Burns. After a Season commanding the gun emplacement he suspected his back would never be straight again.

'What's the message say, Signal Sergeant?'

The sergeant finished deciphering the message and handed the Lieutenant the piece of paper. 'Says, "CODE X472: ALL UNITS TO REFER TO SEALED ORDERS".'

Lieutenant Burns studied the message with some curiosity. 'You're sure it was prefaced by "CODE X472"?'

'Yes, sir.'

Burns pulled the envelope containing his secret orders from his jacket pocket, ran a nail under the seal and quickly read the contents. Then he read them again . . . and again. They didn't make sense, but then, he supposed, any orders bearing the signature of His Holiness Aleister Crowley – as these did – didn't have to make sense, they just had to be obeyed.

Still . . .

As he had been instructed, he burnt the orders and then turned to look at the huge thirty-six-inch Krupp mortar he'd been using to reduce Rangoon to brick dust. His brow furrowed as he wondered how in the world he was to use a *siege mortar* against a fast-moving steamship. But it wouldn't do his ambitions of enjoying a long and comfortable old age running his family's haberdashery empire much good if he was to refuse – on the ridiculous and indefensible grounds that what he was being asked to do was fucking stupid – to obey an order.

'Get the men up, Bombardier. I want the mortar loaded and set at maximum elevation in five minutes.'

In the end it took them seven minutes. After fighting nonstop for most of the Summer, the four men who made up Burns's gunnery crew were tired, disheartened and just a little hungover from celebrating the armistice. Ninety days of hauling the shells – which weighed just over a ton – into the bunker, of using the hoist to load them into the stubby barrel of the mortar, of dragging back the bunker's steel roof and then having to endure the shock of firing the bastard thing in such a confined space had taken its toll. Everyone in Gun Emplacement Fourteen was exhausted, deaf and heartily sick of the war ... just as the rest of the army was.

Of course, Burns would keep his observations regarding the parlous state of the army's morale to himself. Senior officers in the SS did not appreciate being told that their men were fed up fighting and that the grumbles of discontent in the army were growing louder by the day. The Great Leader, in Burns's humble opinion, was pushing his people too hard and one day – one day soon – they would snap. There was a strong whiff of rebellion in the air: the people wanted rid of Heydrich and his cronies.

'Gun ready for firing, sir.'

'Is it set at its maximum elevation, Bombardier?'

'Yus, sir. Any higher and the bloody thing will go straight up and straight back down. We'll blow ourselves to kingdom-fucking-come.'

Burns eyed the elevation indicator, which read eighty-seven degrees: the Bombardier was right, it was nigh on vertical. He did a swift calculation and estimated that the shell would fall only three hundred yards from the emplacement. He just hoped his target would have the courtesy to steer that close into the shore.

'Very good. Pull back the roof and prepare to fire.'

Lieutenant Stepan Makarov, officer commanding the FSS *Molnya*, the GunBoat charged with patrolling the Volga that night, spotted the *Wu* just as she was approaching the Anichkov Bridge. But spotting the WarJunk was one thing, sinking the bastard was quite another. Obeying the order to 'ENGAGE AND

DESTROY ENEMY WARJUNK' would require the use of the brand-new and ultra-secret, galvanicEnergy-powered Whitehead torpedoes – the V4s – with which the *Molnya* was equipped.

'Signal Command: "REQUEST PERMISSION TO ENGAGE USING V4 WEAPONS".'

Makarov had to ask permission: SS Colonel Clement was anxious that none of the ForthRight's enemies be given the merest inkling that he had such a powerful weapon at his command. And it was an indication of how seriously Naval High Command took the destruction of this WarJunk that the response was almost immediate: 'PERMISSION GRANTED'.

Grinning from ear to ear, Makarov issued his orders that the torpedoes be prepared for launch. He could barely contain himself: he was going to make history, he was going to be the first naval commander to destroy an enemy vessel using a torpedo.

'Enemy vessel to port, Colonel.'

Trixie swung her telescope to where the seaFemme was pointing. She had known their luck couldn't hold for ever, and luck – and the time it took for the enemy to get themselves organised – meant they'd reached the Anichkov Bridge without facing serious opposition. They'd been shot at, of course, but most of it had been small-calibre stuff that had bounced harmlessly off the *Wu*'s thick steel hide and anything big enough to do damage had been fired in such a wayward manner that the shells had screamed harmlessly overhead. It had been as though the UnFunnies weren't even *trying* to sink the *Wu*, but now, she suspected, things were going to get a whole lot more dangerous.

In the darkness it was difficult to make out the type of ship that was closing on them but what she could see confirmed it to be small, fast and, if the way it carved so easily through the water was any indication, very agile. Trixie frowned; it looked much too small to be seriously intent on taking on the *Wu*. Certainly the WarJunk – especially with the coal barge in tow – was ponderous and making heavy going against the monsoon-fuelled ebb tide, but it was a powerful warship and packed a massive punch.

'It's a GunBoat,' announced LieutenantFemme Lai Choi San. 'What does it carry?'

'Twin four-inch guns; nothing to worry us. It could pound away all day and we'd barely feel it. The Captain must be suicidal.'

Trixie eyed the sleek GunBoat suspiciously. There was something almost arrogant about how it was being handled and she certainly didn't like the way it was manoeuvring for a beam attack. Although she was no sailor, she understood enough to know that a lightly gunned ship like the GunBoat would usually content itself with snapping at the heels of a more powerful adversary, hoping to score a lucky hit on the rudder. It wouldn't come within striking distance of a broadside. There was something not quite right here.

'Steer closer to the shore and prepare starboard batteries to engage.'

'Set mortar bomb fuses for thirty seconds. Prepare to fire.'

Gunnery Lieutenant Burns decided that tonight was his lucky night. The target had cleared the Anichkov Bridge and was now steaming directly towards him. He made a quick calculation using his slide rule, a calculation involving the ship's speed and the time of flight of the mortar shell, and then picked his spot. As soon as the ship reached that, he would fire. He wouldn't even have to hit the bloody thing; the force of the explosion would swamp any ship within fifty metres.

Hardly able to breathe for excitement, he waited impatiently for the ship to come into range.

Then ...
'Fire!'

'Full steam ahead!' yelled Makarov. "Torpedo crew, prepare to fire. Set run-depth at five feet. We're going to have to do this quick, lads, before that bastard has a chance to lay her guns on us, so all of you look sharp.'

The deck under Makarov's feet began to vibrate as the engine room poured on the power and the boat sliced through the water. He loved these moments, loved the feeling of speed, the feeling of power. Riding aboard the *Molnya* was akin to riding a thoroughbred racehorse. It was exhilarating. The *Molnya* had never gone this fast ... *nothing* had ever gone this fast! With the tide behind him – he was making the attack with the Hub at his stern – and the steam engines wide open he guessed that he was doing more than 20 m.p.h. He was travelling faster than anything had ever gone in the Demi-Monde.

He watched through eyes half-closed against the river spray slashing into his face as the dark, brooding bulk of the WarJunk came across his water-streaked windscreen. Hardly daring to breathe, he waited until it filled his sights.

Now!

'Fire torpedo!' he screamed.

Horrified, Trixie watched the white wake of the torpedo streak towards the *Wu*. She knew what it was. Her father had been involved in the river trials of the Whitehead torpedo and he had described its destructive power to her.

'Torpedo attack!' she screamed. 'Prepare for impact.'

For seemingly endless seconds she waited for the explosion, but none came, just a dull thud as the torpedo smacked into the side of the WarJunk.

It was a dud!

Lieutenant Makarov watched as ... nothing happened. The torpedo was a dud.

'Yo moyo!'

They were the last words he ever uttered. The mortar shell fired from Gun Emplacement Fourteen exploded directly over the GunBoat *Molnya*. Such was the force of the explosion that the GunBoat was lifted twenty-five metres into the air and thrown fifty metres in the direction of Rangoon. Makarov and his crew were dead long before the charred remnants of the *Molnya* smashed back down onto the river.

Immensely satisfied that he had so efficiently carried out his strange orders, Burns was just supervising Bombardier Danny Smith as he painted a white ring around the barrel of the mortar to signify the destruction of the enemy GunBoat – well, if he'd been ordered to destroy it, it had to have been an 'enemy', now didn't it? – when three SS StormTroopers barged their way into the gun emplacement and arrested him and his crew for treason and acts of sabotage against the ForthRight.

As he was handcuffed, Burns realised two things: that Crowley was a vicious, evil, manipulative bastard and that the family's haberdashery business would now be passing to his younger brother.

Trixie watched stupefied as the GunBoat exploded in a huge, night-searing fireball. But even though she was shaken by what had happened, her instincts as a commander still kicked in.

'Batten down all hatches. Close all watertight doors.'

The tsunami that followed the detonation of the mortar bomb would have swamped most other ships, but the *Wu* was so big and so heavy that she rode out the huge waves. They cleared St Petersburg with no further mishaps, and as she set course for Venice, Trixie decided that this had been the luckiest night of her life.

Aleister Crowley sat at his desk writing his report by candlelight. He could have waited until the morning – Heydrich, to whom the report was addressed, would be asleep now – but he was gripped by such a feeling of elation that he had been unable to resist recording his triumph. The whole pantomime of the stealing of the WarJunk had gone wonderfully well. There had been just the right amount of opposition to convince Trixie Dashwood that she had stolen the *Wu* in the face of fierce resistance but not enough to ever endanger the vessel. Of course, the *pièce de résistance* had been the sacrifice of the GunBoat but that he judged was a small price to pay to secure the Column.

The Column ... that was the prize.

And it was so great a prize that he had decided to overcome his distaste for ships and to personally supervise the taking of it from Trixie Dashwood.

He sealed the report and placed it in his out tray. Then he rang for his steward. It was time for him to take his berth aboard the FSS *Heydrich*.

43

Venice
The Demi-Monde: 89th Day of Summer, 1005

Copy of PigeonGram message sent by Su Xiaoxiao on 89th day of Summer, 1005

'Hello Nikolai.'

Kondratieff started so suddenly that he spilt Solution from the glass he was holding. After his meeting with Grand Vizier Selim the Grim, his nerves were shot and the last thing he needed was dead men coming at him from out of the shadows.

'Vanka Maykov! I heard you were dead.'

That, at least, was what had been reported in the newspapers: that Vanka Maykov, enemy of Venice, had been killed by a HimPeril agent in the JAD. But he had to admit that Vanka didn't look the least bit dead, that is unless corpses had taken to walking around with a very cocksure smile on their face and a very mischievous twinkle in their eyes.

'Not dead, Nikolai,' answered Vanka, in the same breezy manner Kondratieff remembered so well. 'That was just a story put around by the Code Noir so that the HimPeril would lay off hunting me.'

Kondratieff smiled. 'Well, it would appear, Vanka, that you are making a poor fist of *staying* undead. The last place where you should be seen is here in Venice; even with the fall of Doge IMmanual you are still *persona non grata* in this neck of the woods.'

Vanka eased his long frame down into a chair and lit a cigarette. 'Needs must when Loki drives, Nikolai. But before we get down to business I could use a drink. It's hot work evading the Signori di Notte.'

Kondratieff served his guest with a glass of Solution and then sat down in the chair opposite him. 'So we have to talk business, eh, Vanka? I should have guessed that this wasn't a social call. Could it be that your return to Venice is somehow connected with the Lady IMmanual?'

'Are my motives that predictable?' Vanka laughed at his own comment. 'But then, I suppose, to the Demi-Monde's greatest expert on Future History *everything* is predictable.'

'Not *quite* everything, Vanka. As I believe I explained to you before, there are certain InDeterminate factors – things which by their perverse nature are inherently unpredictable – which compromise the accuracy of my HyperOpia 4Telling program, and you are one of those.' He took a moment to refresh Vanka's glass. 'But though you are infuriatingly InDeterminate in most respects, with regard to the Lady IMmanual your actions are wholly predictable. Am I to presume that you are now intent on saving her from the clutches of her brother?'

'Yes.'

'Oh my. That, I think, will be a daunting task. Word is that she is being held in the Temple of Lilith which is now very securely guarded by the HimPeril. Penetrating their security will be an impossible task.'

Vanka gave a careless shrug of his shoulders. 'Not impossible, Nikolai, merely difficult. Josephine Baker tells me that four hundred people will be gathering at the Temple on Lammas Eve.'

'So what? Only those with invitations will be afforded entry—' Kondratieff smiled. 'I see . . . you want my invitation.'

Vanka raised his glass in salute to Kondratieff's perspicacity. 'Got it in one, Nikolai. We're both Blanks and both tall so at night I think there's a good chance of my being able to pass myself off as the great Nikolai Kondratieff. If I can get into the Temple during the ceremony that will give me a chance to rescue Ella.'

Kondratieff shook his head. 'Much as I applaud your courage and your determination, Vanka, I think there is something I should apprise you of . . . something which will doom your rescue mission to failure.' And for the next five minutes Kondratieff explained about the bomb hidden inside the Column and his plan that it would detonate at midnight on Lammas Eve.

'How powerful is the bomb?'

'Very. It is designed to kill all those attending the ceremony.'

'Four hundred people.'

'Regrettable, but Doge William is the brother of Lilith . . . he is Lucifer come again and must be destroyed. The deaths of four hundred people will be a tragedy, the deaths of four million at the hands of Lucifer would be a disaster.'

'But as you would be attending the ceremony, presumably you would be numbered amongst the dead.'

Kondratieff shrugged. 'Again, regrettable, but as I was the man who organised the transporting of the Column from Venice to the Temple I was judged important enough to be given an invitation to attend the ceremony. If I was to be absent on such an important occasion that would raise suspicions. Grand

Vizier Selim is a very astute individual and I would do nothing to fuel any doubts he might have regarding the Column. I had a very close shave only yesterday when he was inspecting the thing.'

Vanka sat silently sipping his Solution for a few moments as he pondered what Kondratieff had said. 'Nikolai, I hear what you say, but I've got to try to save Ella. She's the girl I love.'

'And I suppose even if I refuse to give you my invitation you will still attempt to rescue her?'

'Of course.'

Kondratieff sighed. 'The unfortunate thing, Vanka, with you being an InDeterminate entity is that your interference during the Ceremony of Awakening could lead to the bomb *not* detonating. Therefore you must give me your word that in rescuing Ella you will do nothing to prevent the detonation of the bomb. Duke William *must* be destroyed.'

'You have my word.'

'Then I suppose I have no choice.' Kondratieff stood up, crossed to the bureau standing at the side of the room and took the heavily embossed pasteboard from a drawer. He handed it over to Vanka. 'Take it with all my best wishes, but there is something else I must give you.' From out of his pocket he drew a silver chain with a large crucifix hanging from it. 'I want you to have this, Vanka.'

Vanka took it reluctantly. 'I'm not a great one for religion, Nikolai.'

'Listen,' said Kondratieff. 'By inclination I am a cautious man, one who is prone to wear both belt and braces. This crucifix is my insurance policy,' and then he explained its true purpose.

Vanka nodded his understanding. 'Thank you, Nikolai, but, believe me, I'll do my level best not to need it.' With that he stood up and shook hands with Kondratieff. 'I'll always remember you as a true friend, Nikolai.'

And you, mused Kondratieff as he watched Vanka disappear back into the night, *are the final piece in this little puzzle*. It had been a rare honour, he decided, to have shaken the hand of PaPa Legba ... to have shaken hands with ABBA himself.

Part Eight
Lammas Eve

Created by Rosining Nobel, Most Divine Contourier to the House of Worth, as seen in 'In Pure Modes Un Vogue Vogues Monthly, Summer 1003

Drawn for the far and disparate corners of the Demi-Monde, the nuJu diaspora that has settled in the JAD displays an eclectic taste in clothes, a taste which is heavily influenced by the reBop music favoured by the nuJus.

44

The Demi-Monde: 90th Day of Summer, 1005

One of the principal deities in the WhoDoo pantheon is PaPa Legba, the *lwa* famous for using his wits and intelligence rather than brute force to achieve his – often amatory – aims. Oddly, for a religion such as WhoDoo whose disciples are for the most part Shades, PaPa Legba is generally portrayed as a Blank. He is pictured as being a young, handsome and very virile *white* man, who is easily smitten by a well-turned ankle or a saucy smile. Indeed, his roving eye was PaPa Legba's undoing: he fell in love with the beautiful and vivacious Aida Wedo, and was fated to spend his life striving to have her return his love.

Trying to Pin WhoDoo Down: Colonel Percy Fawcett,
Shangri-La Books

THE TEMPLE OF LILITH: 06:00

Ella woke just before dawn. She had been waiting for this day since Lilith had been sent kicking and screaming back into the furthest recesses of her soul ... since she, Ella Thomas, had recovered control of her mind and her body. But it had been only a temporary reprieve: today was the day when she would die at her brother's hand.

She lay for a moment hovering between sleep and consciousness trying to settle herself and to drive these maudlin thoughts from her mind. She had felt Death's frosted breath on her cheek too many times for her to shudder at his approach, but try as she might she couldn't shift her sombre mood, depressed by the knowledge that her passing would herald the rise of her brother. Lilith might have been vanquished but Lucifer had come to take her place, and with a Dark Charismatic as Messiah it was inevitable that the Demi-Monde would embrace the Dark.

She opened her eyes, then rose from her cot to stand in the middle of the mean little cell where she had been held captive since the demise of Lilith. She felt a little unsteady on her feet, which she ascribed to being weak from hunger: the HimPerial priests who had been her wardens had subjected her to a near-fast, claiming that such a diet was necessary to cleanse her body of contaminants, to ready her for sacrifice. Nonsense, of course; all they were trying to do was weaken her, to ensure that she wouldn't have the strength to resist her fate. Ella smiled; though her body was weak, her spirit had never been stronger. She resolved to die with courage.

No, she wasn't frightened of death, but just wished she had been given the chance to say goodbye to Vanka ... to thank him for ridding her of Lilith ... to tell him how much she loved him.

MURANO DOCKS, VENICE: 06:30

All Trixie could assume was that the rapprochement between Venice and NoirVille had made the lookouts along the Nile sloppy. Unchallenged and unmolested, the *Wu* manoeuvred up the night-shadowed Nile and slipped – puffing and wheezing – into the small harbour that abutted Rodin's workshops on the islet of Murano. En route they had found out why the *Wu*'s boilers were being pressure-tested by the UnFunnies; during their escape from St Petersburg the WarJunk had blown a newly soldered seam in her boiler. They had limped up the Nile to Venice on half power.

As soon as the WarJunk was berthed, Trixie, Wysochi and LieutenantFemme Lai Choi San were taken to a back room in Rodin's workshops, where the sculptor was waiting for them, accompanied by a man who introduced himself as Nikolai Kondratieff and a very disreputable looking individual named Nearchus who seemed to be well in his cups, as the half-empty bottle of Solution at his elbow eloquently testified.

Drunk or not, it was Nearchus who commandeered the conversation. 'So you made it?' he slurred. 'ABBA only knows how! Takes a yard and a half of moxie to steal a WarJunk and I never thought a woeMan—'

The glare from Trixie persuaded Nearchus to abandon this particular line of social commentary. 'Is everything ready?' she asked Rodin.

Rodin nodded. 'The real Column was brought to Murano to be loaded into its flotation pontoon a week ago and that's when we made the switch. Thanks to Kondratieff here, the fake Column has been safely delivered to the Temple of Lilith and the real one is ready for you to tow to ...' he glanced nervously towards Nearchus, ' ... to wherever.'

'You have our thanks, Professeur Kondratieff,' acknowledged Trixie, 'but you do realise that once the Column explodes you and Auguste will be the most wanted men in the Demi-Monde. Perhaps you should both take berth on my ship?'

'My thanks for your offer, but Rodin and I have other plans.'

There was an awkward silence, this interrupted by Nearchus. 'Well, if that's settled,' he slurred, 'the sooner you're on your way the better. A WarJunk like the *Wu* ain't the easiest thing in the world to hide. Just takes one informer tipping the wink to the Signori di Notte and we're all dead meat.'

Rodin bridled. 'All my men are reliable.'

'Yeah, sure. But I don't think we should be taking any chances, everyone knows that Venetians can't keep their mouths shut. The quicker the *Wu*'s outta here, the better.'

Trixie shook her head. 'My engineers tell me the *Wu*'s boilers need some repair work . . . work that'll take the best part of the morning to finish.'

'Fuck!' snarled Nearchus as he slurped down another glass of Solution.

Trixie watched the man as he drank. There was something wrong with his demeanour, the way his eyes refused to meet hers. She didn't trust him.

'Tell you what,' said Nearchus suddenly, 'I'll have my men hitch the pontoon up to the *Wu* while you're doing the repairs. That way you can sail at noon.'

'We're not sailing in daylight,' said Trixie firmly.

This drew a scowl from Nearchus, who obviously disliked women answering back. 'You can't stay here. It's too dangerous.'

'You're not listening to me, Nearchus; I am *not* running the Nile while the sun is up! As I understand it, the pontoon is three hundred tons of dead weight and even with two fully functioning boilers the *Wu* is underpowered. Against an ebb tide and encumbered with a tow weighing only half that of your pontoon, we struggled to make more than five knots, and *that's* why I want to sail tonight when the tide is flowing Hubwise. I want it behind me when we make our break for the Wheel.'

Obviously recognising that further argument would be a waste of time, Nearchus stood up from the table, wobbling a little as he did so. 'Well, if that's what you're intent on doing, so be it; it's your funeral. Anyway, I can't sit here talking all day; I've got work to do.'

As Trixie watched the man lurch out of the room, the nagging feeling that something wasn't quite right resurfaced, but she ascribed these suspicions to exhaustion. She'd hardly slept for the best part of two days.

Anyway ... Nearchus *had* to be trustworthy. Kondratieff trusted him, and Kondratieff was a very smart man.

THE CRYSTAL PALACE, LONDON: 09:00

Sporting Chance brought a heavily veiled Norma to the Crystal Palace early on the morning of the show, passing her off as one of 'the girls wot does the harmonising', and such was Sporting's popularity that no one thought to challenge her or her entourage as she swept imperiously into the great hall. And it *was* a great hall, enormous and intimidating, which was why, Norma supposed, Sporting had insisted she make a pre-performance visit to the place. Sporting wanted her 'to see the elephant' before the big night and it was just as well she had.

Norma had been to any number of rock concerts in her time, but none of those venues could compare to this. The Palace was a huge construction of cast iron and glass, built to celebrate the formation of the ForthRight at the end of the Troubles, the use of so much glass mimicking the way the Pre-Folk employed MantlePlex in the building of their monuments. It was a big, bold and very impressive structure though, to Norma's mind, it had a cold functionality about it which she found unattractive, but this, she supposed, was an apt metaphor for the dispassionate efficiency of the ForthRight.

As they wandered out onto the empty stage, Norma's nerve almost failed her. She'd never performed before an audience bigger than a few hundred people, so the prospect of appearing in front of one hundred thousand soldiers and a similar number of spectators was not one she was sure she could cope with. It was very, very scary.

Sporting sensed her trepidation. 'Yus, it's a brute ov a gig an' no mistake, and the acoustics is crap too. That's why I arranged for wun ov them new-fangled galvanicEnergy microphones to be installed. Gives a body a chance ov being 'eard, 'specially when it's full to the brim of 'alf-pissed soldiers.'

'I'll need more than a microphone, Sporting!' Norma admitted. 'I've got a feeling that I'll be too terrified to speak. I don't know if I'll be able to carry it off.'

'Ah, cors yous will. Once you're out 'ere struttin' yer stuff, all yer stage fright will vanish like a virgin's blush. Trim piece like yous won't 'ave a jot of trouble. Put on a tight frock wiv yer charms on display an' you'll 'ave 'em eating outta yer 'and.' She edged closer to Norma to ensure she wasn't overheard. 'Remember, you's the spit ov Aaliz Heydrich an' she's the army's pin-up, she is. Wun wiggle ov that pert little bum of yours and every Tommy in the place'll sit up and beg for more.'

Norma just hoped Sporting was right.

THE FSS *HEYDRICH* ON THE NILE RIVER: 11:00

His Holiness the Very Reverend Aleister Crowley disliked ships. He found them cramped, sweaty and somehow disrespectful. And as ships went, he doubted if there could be any more cramped, sweaty and disrespectful than the FSS *Heydrich*. Of course, he acknowledged that the *Heydrich* had been designed for the brutal and prosaic purpose of securing command of the Five Rivers, but still he would have thought that the naval architects could have lavished a *little* more care and attention on the fitting out of Captain Worden's quarters. There was hardly room to swing a cat.

But such was the importance of the Column to the ForthRight – and to Bole – that Crowley had ignored his instinctive aversion to all things maritime and sailed with the *Heydrich*. He was determined to personally oversee the seizing of the Column: Bole would brook no failure.

Taking a reassuring sip of Solution, he decided not to think about failure. Everything, after all, was proceeding *very* satisfactorily. Sure, Ptah's laboratory had been destroyed, but

Empress Borgia had been very cooperative and had handed Ptah over to the ForthRight. The good doctor was now being interrogated and he was confident that the Plague's secrets would soon be theirs. Sure, Norma Williams was still on the loose, but now the ForthRight had control of the Coven she would be hunted down and disposed of.

And Bole had been *very* happy with the arrangements made to rid the Demi-Monde of the Lady IMmanual. In just a few short hours she would be blown to smithereens by Kondratieff's bomb. Moreover the message he had got from Bole was that he was equally pleased that the girl's brother would be killed alongside her. Now all that remained was to take the Column.

'Is the flotilla ready, Comrade Captain?' he enquired of the Monitor's captain.

'All five Monitors are in position, Your Holiness,' answered Worden. 'Immediately we receive the signal that the enemy WarJunk has taken the Column under tow and has cleared Venice, we will move to intercept it.'

'Excellent. And have we had word from SS Colonel Clement's Invasion Force?'

'We have, Your Holiness. The ten steam-barges carrying the StormTroopers are anchored at the Hubside of the Yangtze ready to land on Terror Incognita at your command.'

Crowley gave a satisfied nod. No matter what was waiting for them in Terror Incognita, two thousand heavily-armed SS StormTroopers should be enough to force a path to the Great Pyramid. Now all he needed to do was find the patience to wait until the renegade Trixie Dashwood delivered the Column into his hands.

THE DOGE'S PALACE, VENICE: 18:00

Billy was just getting it on with one of his priestesses when an imperious voice coming from the doorway halted the girl in

mid-fellatio. 'Good evening, my Doge, I hope I'm not inter-
rupting anything important?'

Billy looked up to find the skinny item called Mohammed
al-Mahdi smiling at him. Billy didn't like the guy; he was a real
miserable fucker who took his role as NoirVille's religious
leader – the Grand Mufti – just a tad too seriously for Billy's
taste. If ever there was a cat in dire need of getting laid, it was
the Grand Mufti.

'It is time, my Doge, to prepare for the Ceremony of Awakening. We must take you to the Temple in order that we might
familiarise you with the rituals in which you will be participating tonight.'

'Yeah, yeah, yeah,' Billy answered as he leaned over to the
bowl standing on the floor beside his bed and took another
toot of Dizzi; nowadays he couldn't think straight unless he
was hooked up. And once the drug had worked its magic and
he was back in the Pleasure Zone, nothing – not even all this
New Age shit the Grand Mufti was laying on him – seemed
stupid. He pushed the girl away and swung his legs off the bed.
'So where's Selim?'

'The Grand Vizier has been ordered by His HimPerial Majesty
Shaka Zulu to remain in Venice rather than attend the ceremony. His Majesty feels it is important that your opponents do
not take advantage of your absence to create trouble.' The Grand
Mufti waved a couple of his priests into Billy's room. 'I have
ordered two of my most senior priests to attend—'

'No way, José. Only bitches look after this cat.'

The sour look on the Grand Mufti's face told him what he
thought of *that*: the guy really had it down on woeMen. Not
that Billy gave a shit: even a million bucks wasn't enough for
him to let a couple of zadnik priests loose on his body. Billy
Thomas was no hump.

The Grand Mufti gave a reluctant nod. 'Very well, my Doge.

I trust you have committed all the incantations you will need to recite at the ceremony to memory.'

'Yeah, no problemo,' Billy lied: he'd only managed to memorise some of the crap that the Grand Mufti wanted him to rap. He hadn't been about to waste too much time on homework when he could be screwing one of his priestesses. But he guessed it wouldn't harm to show willing, after all, the deal he had cut with Selim was that if he did the business at the ceremony he would be escorted to the JAD. Then it would be back home to enjoy the dough Bole would be laying on him. As far as he was concerned, the sooner he was out of the Demi-Monde the better. 'Okay, Mr Mufti-man, let's roll. Wouldn't do to be late for my sister's funeral, now would it?'

THE TEMPLE OF LILITH: 18:00

This was the most dangerous moment, Vanka decided, as the HimPeril agent guarding the entrance to the Temple examined Kondratieff's invitation for the third time, trying to reassure himself it was genuine. Vanka stood there trying to look calm, cool and academic, but it was bloody difficult. He could feel his body clock racing and his shirt was damp with sweat.

'Gotta check everywun, sir,' the agent said by way of explanation. 'Some real big shots gonna be here tonight, so no wun is allowed in widout de invitation.' He handed the pasteboard back. 'And ah's gotta make sure that yo' ain't carrying a weapon, so ah's gotta ask if yo' have any ob de metal objects on yo' person, sir,' adding hopefully: 'any guns, knives, swords ... bombs?'

'Only this,' answered Vanka, delving inside his shirt and pulling out the crucifix he was wearing about his neck.

The agent scowled. The crucifix was the symbol of RaTionalism, a religion that was, in HimPerialist NoirVille, viewed with a combination of suspicion and distaste. But Vanka *did* have an invitation ...

'Ah'd keep dat well outta sight, sir; some ob de other guests might find it mucho offensive.'

As understatements went, that, mused Vanka as he stepped through the entrance and into the Temple, was a peach.

THE CRYSTAL PALACE, LONDON: 20:00

Peeking out of the wings of the stage, Norma was astonished by just how many people were crammed into the Crystal Palace, the massive audience having been treated to an impressive spectacle celebrating the might of the ForthRight. The thousands upon thousands of red-jacketed soldiers marching and counter-marching in serried ranks, the torchlight processions, the girls dancing in choreographed perfection, the parading of the Blood Banner, the waving of so many Valknut-emblazoned flags, the bands playing their martial music . . . all this threatened to overwhelm Norma. It was a display of such towering political confidence that it seemed impossible that anyone, least of all a nineteen-year-old girl like her, could threaten the awesome power of the ForthRight . . . could threaten Heydrich. It was Nuremberg writ large.

There was a touch on her arm as Odette came to stand alongside her. 'I think it is the time, Norma, for you to undertake the preparations final. Perhaps if you would come to the dressing room of Mademoiselle Chance for the application of the *maquillage d'étape* . . . the stage make-up?'

Norma nodded. It was showtime.

THE DOGE'S PALACE, VENICE: 21:30

'Marcantonio Raimondi is in attendance, Your Excellency.'

Grand Vizier Selim – newly appointed as the High Commissioner of Venice – gave an absent-minded nod. It was the last meeting of a long and tiring day and for a moment he thought about simply sending the man away but, ever the perfectionist, he knew he couldn't do that. It was essential that the coverage of the Ceremony of Awakening to be carried in tomorrow's newspapers was appropriately splendid and appropriately accurate.

'Send him in.'

A moment later the man was shown into Selim's office. 'You have completed the engravings, Raimondi?' The artist gave a nervous nod. 'I would see them,' and Selim waved him across to the large conference table.

When the engraver had rolled the six diagrams – one for each of the six faces of the Column – out on the table, Selim stood silent for several minutes examining them, searching for mistakes. They had to be perfect: the engravings would, after all, be the centrepiece of the souvenir pages carried in tomorrow's newspapers.

'Excellent work, Raimondi,' he said finally, 'but there is one small error.'

The engraver frowned. 'Error, Your Excellency? I don't understand.'

'You have failed to show the scar on the sixth face of the Column. You have shown it pristine.'

Raimondi frowned. 'Scar? There was no scar, Your Excellency. I was most diligent: my engravings are a most faithful representation of all the features of the Column.'

'When did you examine the Column?'

'I did my sketches the day before it was removed to the studio of Auguste Rodin to be loaded in the pontoon.'

'Rodin ... why Rodin?' Now it was Selim's turn to frown as possibilities – very disturbing possibilities – whirled around in his head. If the scar hadn't been on the Column when Raimondi had done his sketches then it followed that it must have been made later. But as the Column was made from invulnerable Mantle-ite ...

The answer came to him in a flash. The Column now in the Temple had to be a duplicate.

But why? All a fake Column would do was delay things. All it would do was prevent the Ceremony of Awakening reaching a climax and the ABBAsoluti being reborn. It could not prevent the untimate triumph of HimPerialism ... or could it?

Realisation dawned. There could be only one reason why this had been done: the imitation Column was a bomb! This was a plot to destroy Doge William ... this was a plot to destroy His HimPerial Majesty Shaka Zulu! Selim sprang to his feet, yelling for his aide as he did so. 'Order the arrest of Kondratieff and Rodin. Prepare my steamer, prepare a boat. I have to go to the Temple of Lilith with all speed. Hurry man, hurry, the life of His HimPerial Majesty depends on it.'

THE TEMPLE OF LILITH: 21:30

The Grand Mufti, accompanied by two priests, came for Ella when it was dark, taking her from her cell and leading her through the labyrinth of corridors that twisted deeper into the Temple. He finally brought her to a halt in front of a polished oak door decorated with symbols of twinned snakes spiralling around one another.

Opening the door he ushered Ella through into the strange hexagonal chamber beyond. On each of the room's six walls hung a large mirror formed from burnished brass, these mirrors flickering with the light cast by the burning tapers the priests carried. As she peered into the mirrors, Ella saw her image echoing towards infinity, disappearing into a never-ending nothingness. An appropriate piece of symbolism, she decided, for the fate that awaited her that night.

The Grand Mufti waved towards the deep pool of crystal-clear water set in the middle of the room. 'You must be baptised, witch, to purify you in mind and spirit for the Ceremony of Awakening.'

The priests stepped forward and tore Ella's robe away. This done, they pushed her down into the pool, wading in after her to plunge her head under the water.

'Tonight,' the Grand Mufti crooned as she climbed out of the pool, 'is Lammas, the night when Doge William will be proclaimed as the True Messiah. Now the Column has been restored to us: that which we thought lost for ever, drowned under the waters fed by the Five Rivers, stands ready to be positioned, once more, in its rightful place at the centre of the Temple of Lilith. By the use of the Column all the power of the Temple will be unleashed and we will use this to usher in the Second Coming of Man. Tonight a new race of Man will be forged and it is your blood – the blood of a Lilithi – that will be the catalyst to bring this about.'

He stepped forward and poured a thick red oil onto Ella's shaven head.

'I am anointing you with an oil made to an ancient formulae,' the Grand Mufti explained, 'which will ensure that your spirit is ripe for sacrifice and that your will is appropriately subMISSive. You must go to your death as a woeMan should: Mute, Invisible, Subservient and Sexually Modest.'

As the oil trickled over her head, the air around Ella was perfumed by a heavy cloying smell that pulled at her nostrils and drifted into her mind, inducing a strange soporific relaxation.

More and more oil was poured, and Ella felt the red ribbons of the oil gently coursing over her face, stinging her eyes and painting the creases of her cheeks and mouth. The smell became more and more intense. She shook her head, trying to drive away the dizziness that engulfed her but it did no good: she felt herself rolling and tumbling through space. Now when she looked at herself in the bronze mirrors she saw the oil trails transmogrifying into curling, wriggling snakes that corkscrewed around her body, snakes that glowed and shimmered in the firelight.

From far, far away she heard the Grand Mufti speaking to one of his priests. 'She is ready ... ready to become one with the Nothingness.'

THE FSS *HEYDRICH* ON THE NILE RIVER: 21:30

Comrade Captain John Worden was not a happy man. It was bad enough to have been given the honour – responsibility, rather – for 'capturing the greatest prize in the whole of the Demi-Monde', but what made this 'honour' burdensome was that it necessitated His Holiness Aleister Crowley coming aboard his ship to keep an eye on him. Crowley's baleful presence had infused the ship with fear.

He sensed the man standing behind him now, watching him ...

'Has the enemy WarJunk been sighted yet, Comrade Captain?'

Worden took a deep, calming breath. 'Not yet, Your Holiness. You will be informed immediately we do.' Then he added by way of explanation, 'We had expected the rebels to force the Wheel during daylight—'

'An unfortunate change of plan, as was notified by the semaphore signal.'

Worden eyed Crowley warily. He didn't like getting signals from NoirVillian semaphore stations: he wouldn't trust those zadnik bastards as far as he could throw them.

'I understand, Your Holiness. And as the breakout is now expected to take place during darkness, I've doubled the number of lookouts. Have no fears in this regard: the WarJunk won't get past us.'

Because if it does, Worden thought ruefully, *I'll be spending the rest of my somewhat truncated life in the Lubyanka.*

THE CRYSTAL PALACE, LONDON: 22:30

'We are ready for you, Great Leader.'

Heydrich gave a nod, glanced around to see that his body-guards were in position and then strode, smiling, out onto the floor of the Crystal Palace. As was his right, his arrival was greeted by a resounding round of applause, though he had the distinct impression that it wasn't as enthusiastic as he'd enjoyed at previous rallies. Pushing this somewhat disturbing thought to one side, he looked along the serried ranks of those who he would honour by handing them their Victory medal personally, these the one hundred stalwart individuals and upholders of the creed of UnFunDaMentalism who had laboured most earnestly to help the ForthRight triumph over the Coven. Six million medals would be issued but only these select few would receive it from his own hand.

He was pleased to see that the Party's publicity machine had made sure there were plenty of photographers on hand to record the medal ceremony and that the first five recipients were fine embodiments of the Aryan ideal. *Very* fine, if the rather beautiful young girl dressed in a Valknut-embroidered dirndl was a typical example.

As he came to stand in front of the girl, she bobbed a curtsy, allowing him a tantalising peek of cleavage. Conscious of the cameras, he did his best to ignore it.

Maybe later . . .

'Nadya Krupskaya, I have great pleasure in presenting you with this medal in recognition of your great work in caring for those brave soldiers wounded during the liberation of the Coven from the evil that was HerEticalism.'

He took the medal by its ribbon, the girl dipped her head and he hung it around her lovely neck. The medal was gold-plated, with a Valknut engraved on one side and a fist – symbolising the strength of UnFunDaMentalism – on the other. Once the medal was secure around the girl's neck, he smiled for the cameras.

'Great Leader,' the girl said, returning the smile, 'might I be permitted to ask a question?'

He beamed for the cameras. 'Of course.'

'Then could you tell me when the slaughter of our young men is going to end?'

THE CSS *WU* ON THE NILE RIVER: 22:55

Trixie judged it to have been a correct decision to run the Nile at night, when the *Wu* had the tide behind her. The WarJunk's engines weren't terribly powerful and, encumbered by the huge pontoon she was towing, she was a nightmare to manoeuvre, taking an age to answer the helm. Negotiating the turn out of the Nile into the Wheel River would require the use of all the river-room they could get.

Unfortunately, river-room was the one thing she would be denied.

'Enemy Monitors ahead.'

Trixie snapped open her telescope and peered into the night. She couldn't see a thing: either ObserverFemme Cunningham had to have been living on a diet of carrots or was possessed of the sharpest pair of night-eyes in the whole of the Demi-Monde.

'Confirmed,' snapped LieutenantFemme Lai Choi, 'I can see the Monitor's turret.'

Now Trixie spotted the enemy ship's turret, the only part of the vessel visible above the surface of the river. The turret was a clever invention that allowed the ForthRight's Monitors to bring their guns to bear in any direction, unlike the *Wu* where the whole ship had to be manoeuvred before a broadside could be fired.

Four more Monitors hove into view, the five warships strung in a line across the river.

So that's what Nearchus was so nervous about!

They had sailed into a trap. The bastard had – literally – sold them down the river.

For a moment she was so angry at her stupidity in trusting Nearchus that she could barely think, but then the red mist lifted and options scuttled through her head. Anxiously she checked her watch: the tide would turn soon and the prospect of fighting a naval battle in the teeth of a current flowing Boundarywise did not appeal. It would be suicide to lose either the momentum the *Wu* had or the element of surprise.

'Full speed ahead. Tell the engine room to give me all she's got. Have the helmsFemme aim for the stern of the Monitor dead ahead. We'll ram the son of a bitch.'

LieutenantFemme Lai Choi gave an enthusiastic bow. This was obviously the order she had been hoping for; the four-metre-long ram that jutted out from the front of the *Wu* was a lethal weapon, especially when it was backed by four thousand tons of angry WarJunk.

'Battle stations,' Lai Choi shouted. 'Load hot shot. Target dead ahead. Lowest elevation. Bow gun to fire at my command.'

Immediately the alarm bell clanged and there was a rushing of slippered feet as the crew raced to their stations.

One hundred and fifty metres.

One hundred metres.

Fifty metres.

The Monitor's turret began – ponderously – to turn towards the *Wu*. They'd been seen!

'Fire!'

The *Wu*'s two bow guns – twenty-five-centimetre rifle-bore cannon cast in Beijing – fired, the twin explosions making the ship shudder and filling the bridge with the cloying, choking stench of cordite. As Trixie watched, the two shells arced through the night, the first clearing the target by a comfortable couple of yards. They were more fortunate with the second shot: it hit the Monitor amidships.

'Prepare to ram, brace yourselves,' shouted LieutenantFemme Lai Choi.

THE TEMPLE OF LILITH: 23:00

Once he was inside the Temple it had been relatively simple for Vanka to slip away from the crowds of guests attending the ceremony: with so many dignitaries packing the place the absence of a nonentity like him would go unremarked. And there were dignitaries aplenty. He had already seen His HimPerial Majesty Shaka Zulu and his retinue make a grand entrance, followed by all of the senior members of the Venetian nobility.

And as he watched these VIPs take their seats, for the first time Vanka fully appreciated the magnitude of what Kondratieff had been planning: in one fell swoop he would destroy the leadership of Venice and NoirVille. All Vanka could do was try to ensure that he and Ella weren't numbered amongst the dead.

He bustled up a staircase to the balcony that circled high around the Temple walls and ducked behind a balustrade where he was both concealed and had a perfect view of what was happening twenty metres below him on the Temple floor. He settled down to wait, the only problem being that waiting gave him a chance to think and thinking gave his imagination an opportunity to run wild.

Vanka had always regarded himself as a pragmatist not given to flights of fancy, but now as midnight approached and the night's darkness enveloped the Temple, he began to feel distinctly uneasy. The Dark seemed to be crowding in on him, casting long shadows over the world, and he had the awful suspicion that tonight the HimPerial priests wandering around the Temple waving their incense burners to and fro would unleash a djinn that most certainly would not go back into its bottle.

But there was no time to consider this further: a single blast of a trumpet reverberated through the Temple, signalling that the ceremony had begun.

THE TEMPLE OF LILITH: 23:00

Her spirit dulled by the effect of the unguent that had been poured over her body, Ella was taken out of the room and down a long, narrow corridor, coming to stand before the two huge bronze doors that barred the entrance to the main hall of the Temple.

Billy was already standing there waiting for her, the boy clad in a golden robe with a crown bedecked with two horns on his head.

He gave her a lopsided grin by way of welcome. 'Hiya, Sis, see they got you all dressed up to party.' He gave a mirthless laugh. 'Thought you were so damned smart, didn't you, playing this Lilith bitch and aiming to use me so that you got to be Nigga-in-Charge? But you got it wrong. It ain't me who's gonna be sacrificed, Sis, but yous. Real classy end for an around-the-way girl like you, eh?'

'If you would intone the incantation, Your Grace,' suggested the Grand Mufti.

Billy shrugged. 'Look, I gotta tell you man—'

The Grand Mufti nodded towards one of his priests, who handed a piece of parchment to Billy. With a shrug the boy read what was written there.

'Beyond this gate Doge William is no more ... the True Messiah stands in his place. And tonight I will use my power to have Loki rise again. Tonight is the time when Loki will come to lead ManKind to the Truth that is HimPerialism, when he will reclaim his throne as the Supreme Ruler of the Nine Worlds. Die knowing that it is your blood that brings the Nine Worlds to perfection.' Billy laughed. 'In other words, Sis, your ass is grass.'

The Grand Mufti gave a signal and one of the priests blew on a bronze horn hanging by the gate, the long, mournful note lingering in the crisp night air, reverberating through the Temple. As the note died, the gates opened to reveal that the path they were standing on ran forward into the Temple, the path flanked on each side by a line of priests.

The Ceremony of Awakening had begun.

THE STEAM LAUNCH *RAPIDO* ON THE NILE RIVER: 23:00

An increasingly frantic Selim checked his watch for the tenth time in as many minutes. The steam launch seemed to be making incredibly slow progress, but then he supposed he should thank ABBA that when he'd got to the docks he'd been able to find a boat ready to sail.

'How long before we land at the Hub, Captain?'

'Perhaps thirty minutes, Your Excellency. I am making all speed but we have to be careful. The ForthRight has a number of Monitors patrolling the river and it would not do—'

His explanation was interrupted by a huge explosion to the Cairo side of the river. There seemed to be the mother of all naval battles taking place only half a mile or so from where they were steaming.

'Damn the ForthRight navy, Captain. Make more speed: the life of His HimPerial Majesty Shaka Zulu is in danger. I must get to the Temple before the Column is lowered into position.'

Orders given, Selim returned to his agitated consideration of the river as it streamed so very slowly past, cursing that semaphores were invisible at night and that NoirVillian scientists hadn't yet been able to duplicate the ForthRight's telegraph messaging system.

He checked his watch again. There was still time.

THE FSS *HEYDRICH* ON THE NILE RIVER: 23:00

Despite the extra lookouts Worden had posted, the attack came out of nowhere. One moment he was supervising the patrolling of the Nile River and the next the *Heydrich* was reeling from an explosion amidships.

'Enemy WarJunk to starboard!' a lookout yelled a little belatedly, but try as he might, Worden couldn't see what was coming at him from out of the darkness.

Where the fuck . . .

He trained his spyglass in the direction the lookout was pointing.

There!

He spotted the phosphorescence dancing in the water stirred up by the WarJunk's bow. Thanks to the moonlight he could just make out the low, menacing silhouette of the ship, its deep bow wave telling him that it was closing fast. The bastard was trying to *ram* him.

'Engage target. Gunnery Officer, sight at starboard ninety degrees.' Immediately the turret housing the two enormous twelve-inch Krupp guns began to rotate. 'Fire as soon as you have a target.'

'But do not damage the pontoon!' screamed Crowley.

All Crowley's intervention did was confuse the gunners, who fired too soon. Worden watched as two plumes of water rose about a hundred yards aft of the WarJunk, but, thankfully, shy of the pontoon.

'Reload and be sharp about it.'

Very sharp. The WarJunk was steaming right at the *Heydrich* and with the tide behind it the bastard thing was moving at eight or nine knots.

There was no time to reload. Trying to keep the panic out of his voice, Worden yelled out fresh orders. 'Full steam ahead!' It was too late. Even as he watched, he saw the dark, implacable shape of the WarJunk loom out of the night and smash into the side of the *Heydrich*.

THE CSS *WU* ON THE NILE RIVER: 23:05

The noise as the *Wu* tore into the stern of the Monitor was ear-shredding, the howl of steel against steel augmented by the screams of the sailors who were crushed by the impact or were scalded to death when the Monitor's boilers blew. Everything was reduced to a steam- and smoke-filled confusion and, despite having taken a tight grip on a handrail, Trixie still found herself being thrown along the deck as the WarJunk suddenly lost way. The *Wu*'s bow was forced up and over the Monitor, the ship bullying its way through the stricken vessel, smashing its decking as it went. But as Trixie hauled herself to her feet, she realised that if the *Wu* didn't continue to make way – if it was forced to a stop – then it would make easy pickings for the other Monitors they had seen patrolling the river.

'More steam,' she shouted, but there was no one to relay the message: LieutenantFemme Lai Choi lay dead with a fifty-centimetre-long rivet sticking out of the back of her head.

Then . . .

As she looked around for help, the *Wu* leapt forward like a hound let off its leash. It was a charred Wysochi emerging from the depths of the gun deck who told her why. 'Enemy gunfire has cut the pontoon free. The Column's gone.'

THE CRYSTAL PALACE, LONDON: 23:10

Medal-giving duties completed, it was a distinctly unhappy Great Leader Heydrich who returned to his seat of honour high in the balcony facing the stage where the entertainment would be taking place. The incident with that bitch Nadya Krupskaya – a closet RaTionalist, if he'd ever met one – had ruined his evening. Even the prospect of torturing her in the Lubyanka – where she was already being taken – failed to raise his spirits.

But there were other irritants. He should never have agreed to have the Victory celebrations in the Crystal Palace. He hated the place, especially in Summer: there had never been enough ventilation and on a humid night when it was packed with so much sweating humanity it was especially unpleasant, an unpleasantness compounded by the tight, high-necked uniform he was obliged to wear. But it was more than simple humidity and the incident with the Krupskaya girl that was making the atmosphere of the Palace unpalatable, rather it was the perceptible feeling of resentment drifting up to him from the ranks of soldiers parading for his benefit.

And the reason for this resentment was simple: his army was tired of fighting. Checkya informers advised that there were mutterings in the ranks, grumbles that, having been at war almost constantly for five years, enough was enough and that too many of the ForthRight's young men had died. When he had given his speech, he could *feel* the audience's unhappiness, and the standing ovation he had been awarded had been almost perfunctory. Only seven minutes! It was an insult and, worse, he suspected that if it hadn't been for the clappers von Sternberg had seeded into his audience, the applause might have petered out much more quickly than that.

Hopefully though, the appearance of this singer – this Naughty Nightingale – would allow the celebrations to end on a more positive note: the woman was apparently very popular with the men. But even here there were concerns. He turned to von Sternberg sitting to his right. 'Comrade General, you are sure this woman, this Nightingale person, will perform in an acceptable manner?'

'Have no concerns in that regard, Comrade Leader. I have sent the woman a very strong message as to what the consequences would be if she should flout decorum. She understands that if she makes any untoward comments regarding any of the Party's leaders or their policies, she will be immediately arrested and removed to the Lubyanka.'

Heydrich gave a distracted nod. Such a threat should be enough to keep anyone quiescent, but the problem with the working classes was that they had a distinct proclivity for *not* remaining quiescent. And, as he understood it, the Naughty Nightingale was *very* working-class.

THE CRYSTAL PALACE, LONDON: 23:10

Having seen such an impressive display of the might of the ForthRight, Empress Borgia judged her decision to surrender the Coven to Heydrich to have been the correct one. Without the Plague weapon it was impossible for the Coven to have stood against such martial might, and by cooperating with the Great Leader she had secured the most generous of surrender terms for her people and reduced the reparations demanded by the victors.

And it was a sign of the favour she was held in that she had been given the seat next to the Great Leader for the celebrations and had been introduced by him to the audience as 'a great humanitarian and a bringer of peace'.

Peace ... that was the problem.

Or more specifically the peace being preached by that bitch Dong E. She couldn't for the life of her understand why Wu had permitted her to live. Hadn't the fool realised the potential Dong E had to make trouble? All she could think was that Wu had been so obsessed by having the girl entertain her as a Fresh Bloom that she'd lost sight of the danger she posed.

And now the girl was stirring up trouble by wandering around the Coven preaching that she was the true Empress and that to defeat the ForthRight the people had to embrace Normalism and engage in a policy of peaceful non-cooperation. She'd even managed to close the coal mines by bringing the miners out on strike and Heydrich had been less than impressed by *that*. Dong E's influence had grown to such an extent that Borgia had been nervous about leaving the Coven to attend the Victory celebrations. But Crowley had insisted.

She shuffled nervously on her seat as she tried to put these troubling thoughts to one side and to enjoy the show. She was Empress now and above such trifles.

THE TEMPLE OF LILITH: 23:10

Vanka pushed himself closer to the edge of the balcony, peeking through the gaps in the balustrade. As the horn's call echoed away to oblivion, two priests stepped forward and opened the gates to reveal the Grand Mufti and his retinue standing ready to enter the Temple.

The orchestra imitated the horn's note and with every step the Grand Mufti took into the Temple the music gained in volume, the waves of sound – discordant and disturbing – skittered around the Temple like living things. It was music that betokened darkness and fear. And to complement the unsettling music, the priests ignited briars, filling the Temple with the acerbic scent of Epimedium. Vanka felt it cloying on the back of his throat and immediately became uneasy. People did strange things under the drug's influence.

Immediately behind the Grand Mufti strode a very tall, a very muscular and a very arrogant-looking man. Vanka supposed that this was Doge William in his guise of the Messiah. It was a reasonable supposition: from what he had heard, Doge William was enormously tall – as this man was – and even though he was swathed in a golden robe and his skin heavily decorated, it was still possible to see he was a Shade.

And a dozen or so paces behind him came two priests escorting a woman. It took Vanka a moment to recognise her: her body was covered with a red oil and she walked with the stumbling gait of someone who had been drugged, but then she raised her head to look defiantly around at the gathered crowd. Vanka's body clock skipped a beat: it was Ella.

He tried to stay calm. Now was time for him to get nearer to the altar ready to rescue her and to do that he had to move from where he was hiding on the high balcony, down the staircase to the floor of the Temple and then across to the altar. And he had to do all this without being seen or challenged. This he judged to be impossible. There were simply too many people milling around in the Temple; someone was bound to spot him.

In the end it was the Grand Mufti who came to his aid. The man gave a sign to his congregation that they should stand and, taking advantage of the movement of the crowd and every eye being concentrated on the would-be Messiah that was Doge William, Vanka scuttled towards the staircase. He was down it in a trice, amazed by the vigour that fear could put in a man's stride.

THE TEMPLE OF LILITH: 23:10

The oil that the Grand Mufti had used to anoint her must, Ella supposed, have been drugged. She felt so very cold and so very weak. Hardly of this world, she allowed herself to be brought to the altar.

Standing there, she heard the Grand Mufti chant a long

complex incantation over her, then saw through misted eyes the man turn to the congregation. 'We gather tonight on Lammas, the night when Man reigns supreme, the night when the powers of Men are at their height. We gather to sacrifice this Lilithi and by the drinking of her blood ensure that the One True Religion of HimPerialism rules the Nine Worlds.'

Although she had been made sluggish by the oil that covered her body, Ella determined that she would meet death with her head held high. She glared back at the audience that had gathered to witness her sacrifice and she was pleased that not one of them had the courage to meet her gaze.

And it was then that she noticed the Column standing next to the altar waiting to be lowered onto its plinth. At the sight of it she sensed Lilith stir deep inside her, telling her that the Column was wrong ... that someone had replaced the original with an imitation. She suppressed a smile. Tonight, she suspected, it wouldn't only be her who would be merging with the Nothingness that was death.

THE FSS *HEYDRICH* ON THE NILE RIVER: 23:15

The *Heydrich*'s pilothouse might have been a confusion of smoke, steam and screams, but at its centre His Holiness the Very Reverend Aleister Crowley remained unnaturally calm; the knowledge that, even as he stood there, the FSS *Beria* was manoeuvring to take the drifting pontoon under tow made him impervious to the carnage around him.

He had done it! He had captured the Column. Now there was nothing to prevent the triumph of the Aryan people ... of UnFunDaMentalism.

'I would be obliged, Comrade Captain, if you would provide me with a gig and a crew in order that I might transfer to the *Beria*.'

An astonished Worden – his face blackened by smoke, his uniform in tatters and one arm hanging useless at his side –

glared at Crowley and made to protest. 'With the greatest of respect, Your Holiness, my first duty as a naval officer is to my ship and my crew. I have no time—'

There was the sound of a Luger automatic pistol being cocked and Worden felt the cold brush of its muzzle against the side of his head.

'This is an operation commanded by the SS-Ordo Templi Aryanis, Comrade Captain, and if you do not obey my orders, I will have SS Captain Morant shoot you. The prime imperative of this mission is to seize the Column and then transport it to Terror Incognita. This I will do. Hero of the ForthRight you might be, Worden, but I am careless whether you are dead or alive when the medal is awarded.'

THE TEMPLE OF LILITH: 23:30

As he cowered in his new hiding place behind the Column, it seemed to Vanka that the ceremony was now moving into a more serious and dangerous phase. The music rose in volume as Doge William came to stand just in front of the altar, each step he took accompanied by the rhythmic chanting of the crowd and the beat of timpani. There he paused for a moment, then turned and in a voice that resonated through the whole Temple, addressed his congregation.

'You know me as the Doge William, but now I stand before you as the Messiah, the one who will bring ABBAsoluteness to the Demi-Monde. I have invited you here tonight to witness the rising of a new race of Man, each of whom will be confirmed as one of the Sixty, as one of the Chosen, as one of those who will form the first of the ABBAsoluti ... the Perfect. It is they who will sire the species that will come after HumanKind. It is they who will give life to *Homo perfectus*: the Perfect Man.'

Now he turned to address the sixty priests standing alongside the altar. 'You are the Men who will bring Perfection to

HumanKind. Tonight, by drinking the blood of a Lilithi, all the latent power that resides within you will be released.'

He pointed towards Ella. 'Prepare her for sacrifice!' and immediately two priests grabbed the girl by her arms and forced her down onto the altar.

THE CSS *WU* ON THE NILE RIVER: 23:30

Knowing the difficulties they'd had manoeuvring the *Wu* on their journey from St Petersburg, Trixie realised that there was little chance of them being able to circle around to pick up the pontoon. At the best of times the ship took an age to execute a full turn, and with the damage sustained when it had rammed the Monitor, she had become even more reluctant to answer the helm. The other consideration was, of course, that there were other Monitors out there ... other Monitors that were now, no doubt, steaming in the *Wu*'s direction. The one course Trixie saw open to her was to run – or rather limp – for it.

'What now?' yelled Wysochi as he directed fire crews towards the blaze that was threatening to engulf the engine room. 'Lookouts report seeing a second Monitor steaming to bring the pontoon under tow, so it's a penny wins a pound that the UnFunnies will be taking the Column to Terror Incognita.'

'Then that's where we've got to go. Steer a course to Terror Incognita.'

THE TEMPLE OF LILITH: 23:30

Watching as his priests dragged the woeMan who had been Doge IMmanual to the altar, the Grand Mufti sensed the ceremony building to its climax in a most satisfactory manner. If he was not very much mistaken, the sheen that swathed the Mantle-ite walls of the Temple had begun to glow a deeper green, pulsing with occult energy, the energy he would unleash on the stroke of midnight.

He looked towards the priest he had placed in charge of the wheel that governed the lowering of the Column, making sure that the Man was alert and ready. At midnight the Column would be set in its final position on its plinth and once this was done, the awesome power of the Temple would be activated. Then none would be able to prevent the triumph of HimPerialism, none would be able to dispute that Man was the master of the Demi-Monde.

THE CRYSTAL PALACE, LONDON: 23:30

In Norma's opinion, Sporting sang even better than she had done at the Canterbury Theatre and the sound of thousands of voices joining in on the choruses made for a thrilling experience. The remarkable thing was that Sporting had done it without making a single joke at the expense of Heydrich or any of his cronies. For once the Naughty Nightingale had been a good girl.

But now, as the final chords of 'Falling in Love Again' died away, Norma knew this was her moment of truth. She patted her blonde wig and made a final check of her dress, a dress which she and Odette had spent hours agonising over, debating whether to err on the side of the risqué or on the side of the conservative. In the end, the white lace number she was wearing fell somewhere between the two: it was tight enough to show off her figure, but not reckless enough to distract from the seriousness of what she would be saying. She looked, according to Odette, like an angel.

'And now, lads and lasses,' she heard Sporting bellow into her microphone, her amplified voice booming out to every corner of the huge hall, 'I 'ave a special treat for yous. This lovely little lady 'as come a long way to be wiv us tonight, so I want you to give a right big ForthRight welcome to ... MISS AALIZ HEYDRICH!'

THE CRYSTAL PALACE, LONDON: 23:30

Heydrich jumped, spilling Solution over his immaculately pressed trousers. He hardly noticed: all his attention was riveted on the girl who stepped out from the wings to stand centre stage, the light behind her making her blonde hair glow like a halo around her head. With a trembling hand he raised his opera glasses.

It *was* Aaliz. Her blonde hair was the same, her gait was the same ... everything was the same. And when she opened her mouth to speak into the microphone, she used the identical and oh-so-refined Anglo accent his daughter had used.

But it *couldn't* be her. Aaliz's spirit was in the Real World and her body was being cared for in Wewelsburg Castle. It *had* to be the Daemon, Norma Williams, a supposition confirmed when the bitch spoke.

'I am Aaliz Heydrich and I stand here tonight to implore all you brave soldiers of the ForthRight to lay down your weapons and refuse to fight for those scoundrels who have taken control of Rodina and the Rookeries.'

'Switch off that microphone and arrest the bitch!' Heydrich screamed as he sprang to his feet. Minions scuttled off to do his bidding, leaving the Great Leader standing red-faced and near-apoplectic as he stared in impotent rage across the vastness of the Crystal Palace at his faux-daughter.

THE CRYSTAL PALACE, LONDON: 23:30

There was no reaction to what Norma had said; it was as though everyone in the vast hall had been stricken mute. Swallowing her terror, she moved closer to the microphone and began to speak in a louder voice. 'I stood beside my father when he issued his orders to destroy the poor people of Warsaw; I listened to him when he demanded that the CitiZens of the Quartier Chaud be decimated for having the temerity to oppose him; I witnessed the bile he uttered when he condemned the people of the Coven to destruction; and I know the contempt in which he holds all of you when he sends you to your death.'

The audience began to stir. Mutterings rippled through the packed ranks of the audience and though sergeants screamed at the soldiers to be quiet, with every second that passed the grumbling grew in volume.

'But how can it be otherwise when we live in a Crowocracy?' Norma paused to allow the word to sink in. 'A Crowocracy, you ask? Remember your collective nouns: a group of crows is a murder of crows, therefore, by my lexicon, a Crowocracy is government by murderers. A government like the one that rules the ForthRight, a government to whom a life is as nothing, to whom a life can be stubbed out on a whim.' She pointed up to the balcony where Heydrich was sitting. 'As our leaders gaze down from their Olympian heights, they don't see people with hopes and feelings ... they see nothings, nothings that can be erased with no more thought and no more compassion than they would give to stepping on an ant. In a Crowocracy, the world is awash with nothings.' Here she gestured to the audience. 'We are all, in the view of my father and his disciples, nothings.'

THE CRYSTAL PALACE, LONDON: 23:30

'Stop her! Silence her! Shoot her!' screamed Heydrich. Von Sternberg jumped up from his chair and began to frantically organise his Checkya agents, yelling orders and pushing and shoving his men to the front of the balcony where they could get a better shot at the girl. Unfortunately even while he was doing this, 'Aaliz' kept right on speaking.

'Reinhard Heydrich wishes to conquer the Demi-Monde, a conquest to be bought with your deaths. So I ask you: why? Why can't the peoples of the Demi-Monde live in peace? Why must there be continual war? Why must we celebrate the power of the strong and the subjugation of the weak? I, Aaliz Heydrich, reject my father and his foul philosophy of UnFunDaMentalism and I ask you to do the same. I stand before you as a convert to the creed of non-violence that is Normalism and as a Normalist I tell you that by turning to violence as a solution to their problems Demi-Mondians have become one with the beasts . . . become one with the Beast.'

What the girl was saying obviously had a resonance with the audience. Even as he watched goggle-eyed, Heydrich saw soldiers begin to climb onto the stage to show their support for the girl, milling around her as makeshift bodyguards.

'Shoot the bitch!' Heydrich screamed at the Checkya marksmen who were rushing to take up position.

'We can't get a clear shot, Great Leader,' protested von Sternberg, 'there are too many people standing—'

'Shoot them, shoot everybody, just kill the girl!'

'We must resist evil without becoming evil; we must resist violence without becoming violent; we must resist the Beast without becoming like the Beast. Normalism is on the march: already Empress Dong E has proclaimed it to be the new religion of the Coven and our comrades in the Quartier Chaud have flocked to the Church of Normalism. So I ask the soldiers of the ForthRight to lay down your weapons.' She paused, then threw her arms wide as though embracing all her audience. 'I ask the soldiers of the ForthRight, are you with me?'

As the Crystal Palace reverberated to the cheers of the soldiers, the Checkya marksmen fired.

THE DIVINE WAY LEADING TO THE TEMPLE OF LILITH: 23:50

In Selim's considered opinion, it was unseemly for a Man intent on maintaining his Cool ever to be seen hurrying. Tonight though he had no option but to run the whole length of the Divine Way. He arrived at the gates of the Temple breathless and frantic, and certainly not in a frame of mind to be delayed by the two HimPeril agents who were on sentry duty.

'Out of my way!' he yelled. 'Open the gates.'

'Ah ain't authorised to do dat. Ah am under strict orders from His HimPerial Reverence de Grand Mufti Mohammed al-Mahdi himself dat wunce de ceremony has commenced no wun, but no wun—'

The agent's objections were cut short when Selim drove a dagger into his neck.

'Get these fucking gates open!' he screamed at the second guard, and the man, quite understandably, did as he was told.

THE TEMPLE OF LILITH: 23:50

With every eye in the place directed towards what was happening on the altar, Vanka knew it was now or never. He moved nearer to the Column, trying to find the courage to act.

And act he would have to do. Even as he watched, Doge William came to stand over Ella and then take up the long-bladed dagger he was offered by the Grand Mufti. This he raised high above his head, readying himself to make the awful thrust that would snuff out Ella's life.

Without thinking Vanka hurled himself forward and shoulder-charged the Shade, sending him flying.

THE TEMPLE OF LILITH: 23:50

For a moment the Grand Mufti was too shocked to speak. The man currently struggling with Doge William had appeared out of nowhere and was now threatening to disrupt the entire ceremony.

He waved to two of his priests. 'Seize the man! Protect the Doge. And you,' here he pointed to the priest in charge of the wheel controlling the Column, 'lower the Column!' Yes, the Column was the important thing: nothing must be allowed to prevent the Column unlocking the power of the Temple.

'Stop!' came a shout from the direction of the Temple's entrance and when the Grand Mufti looked up he was amazed to see a very dishevelled Selim striding towards him. 'The Column is a bomb. For ABBA's sake don't lower it. Save His HimPerial Majesty!'

The word 'bomb' had a magical effect on the four hundred people gathered in the Temple. In an instant panic rippled through the crowd and there was a shouting, screaming rush towards the Temple doors. The problem was that the doors opened *inwards* and the more people there were pushing against them, the more difficult it became for the guards to open them. It was a situation made all the more confused when HimPeril agents rushed towards Shaka Zulu intent on leading him to safety, smashing aside any who got in their way with their knobkerries. The crowd fought back, a brazier was tipped over and flames began to flicker around the wooden supports of the balcony. Panic gave way to a terror-stricken stampede.

THE CRYSTAL PALACE, LONDON: 23:50

It was the group of soldiers who had clambered on stage to stand guard on Norma who took the brunt of the rifle fire that smashed down from the balcony. And as they fell so the mood of the rest of the soldiers gathered in the hall changed. Enraged soldiers started to fire back at the Checkya riflemen, sending the dignitaries gathered on the balcony diving for cover, and when a Checkya detachment tried to force their way through the crowd by beating at the soldiers with their rifle butts, the soldiers beat back with chairs and bottles and anything else that came to hand. In an instant the Crystal Palace was reduced to a heaving cauldron of fighting men.

The Checkya squad von Sternberg had sent to turn off Norma's microphone faced similar problems. The only place it was possible to do the turning off was in the booth next to the stage, a booth which had been commandeered by Burlesque and Odette, both of whom had armed themselves with large pistols.

'Time to go, Odette, my luv,' announced Burlesque and after trading a few shots with the Checkya the pair of them used the chaos to slip out of the sound booth, run up onto the stage, gather up Norma who was standing at the microphone appealing for calm, and race for the exit.

They almost made it.

THE CRYSTAL PALACE, LONDON: 23:50

Empress Borgia wasn't sure what was happening. One moment she was watching the Naughty Nightingale and the next she was in the middle of a firefight with bullets whipping around her ears. She looked around to ask advice from the Great Leader, only to find him cowering on the floor.

'What—' she began but the bullet that hit her square between the eyes meant she never finished the question.

THE TEMPLE OF LILITH: 23:55

Selim barged his way through the crowd, cursing their cowardice, cursing the fact that he had spooked the audience by using the word 'bomb'. But that didn't matter; now all that mattered was that he prevent the Column being lowered. It was obvious to him that Kondratieff would have designed the bomb's detonator to be activated by a surge of Mantle-ite energy. He had to keep the Column disconnected from the Temple.

He got to the wheel, shoved the priest guarding it aside then snatched up a discarded assegai and slammed the steel point into the cogs of the gear mechanism that raised and lowered the Column, jamming it. Now no one would be able to lower the Column.

He'd done it! He'd saved Shaka Zulu!

His relief was short-lived. The guard he had manhandled, believing him to be another of the terrorists disrupting the ceremony, smashed his knobkerrie hard down on the Grand Vizier's head, killing him instantly.

THE TEMPLE OF LILITH: 23:55

Drugged as she was, Ella was finding it difficult to think straight; it was as though her brain had been turned to mush and her body had been deprived of all its energy. She was content to lie on the altar and simply watch the world go by. Sure, she knew that her brother was intent on killing her, but really there wasn't much she could be persuaded to do about it.

Vanka changed all that.

Vanka had popped out of nowhere and although he didn't do a particularly good job of knocking over Billy – but then Vanka had never been great at anything that even hinted at violence – he was at least *trying* to rescue her. Vanka had always been there when she needed him ... he had even been there when she *hadn't* needed him. Vanka had never given up on her. And now it was her turn not to give up on him.

She looked up and saw that Billy had got back to his feet and recovered the knife he had been intent on using to kill her. It was a knife he now seemed determined to stick into an unarmed Vanka.

Summoning all her strength, Ella levered her protesting body off the altar and staggered towards the two men. She managed to blindside Billy, taking the chance to ram a fist hard into his stomach. Even Billy's beautifully toned abdominals couldn't protect him from an unexpected fist in the guts: he buckled over, his cheeks blew out and he dropped the knife. Ella stooped down to take hold of the discarded weapon and moved to stand at Vanka's side.

'Vanka . . . it's me, Ella,' she shouted. 'We've gotta get going.'

Vanka shook his head. 'No, I've got to release the Column . . . it's a bomb . . . I promised Kondratieff.' He gave her a kiss on the cheek. 'I love you, Ella. You go . . . save yourself.'

Ella laughed. 'Don't be stupid, Vanka. I lost you once and I'm not going to lose you again. We're going to go together. Release the Column, I'll keep the bad guys off your back.'

THE TEMPLE OF LILITH: midnight

Billy straightened up just thankful that Ella had punched him in the stomach and not the nuts. He looked over to the Column to see Ella defending the tall, rangy guy who had bowled him over and who was trying to work the wheel that lowered the Column. Grabbing a sword from a guard, Billy decided that now was the time for a little slice-and-dice action. He was sick to the back teeth of Ella raining on his parade. Now the bitch was going to pay.

THE TEMPLE OF LILITH: midnight

It was an instinct for self-preservation that made Ella look around and then dodge the thrust of Billy's sword. She raised her knife to parry his next lunge and for an instant steel locked with steel, the pair of them coming so close that Ella could smell the stench of hate on Billy and feel his sweet breath on her cheek. It was a trial of strength, each pushing at the other, trying to unbalance their opponent, testing who was the more powerful.

Finally she managed to break away, skipping back out of range of the thrust of Billy's deadly blade.

'Yo, bitch, yo' ain't never had the beating of me,' Billy snarled and then he was at her, flicking his sword at her eyes.

As she tried to defend herself from the attack, Ella knew that one false step, one mistimed riposte and she would be finished. She felt heavy, sluggish ... weak. With a shake of her head she tried to drive the torpor from her mind, tried to concentrate on the fight. In a few moments one of them would be dead and she was determined that it would not be her.

Billy circled her like a cat, always moving to the left away from Ella's knife hand, his blade rotating slowly around, its savagely sharp point inscribing languid patterns in the air. Suddenly he darted forward, his sword moving like quicksilver as he tried to pierce Ella's guard, moving so fast that all she could do was reel back, hewing as she went, hoping, praying, that it would be enough to parry the thrust.

It was, but only just – the tip of Billy's blade sliced along her knife hand, the red-hot pain making her shriek in agony. Eyes flashing in triumph, Billy was on her, driving his sword at her guts, trying to end it. Ignoring the scalding pain of her hand, Ella hacked his blade away and then rammed her own knife forward, stabbing at Billy's face. But Billy was too strong. Almost disdainfully he parried the stroke and then came at Ella again, his blade everywhere, forcing her to retreat towards the Column.

'Vanka,' she shouted, 'lower the Column ... I can't hold him any longer.'

Those were her last words before Billy rammed his sword into her stomach.

THE TEMPLE OF LILITH: midnight

Vanka watched aghast as Ella crumpled to the ground, blood from the wound leaking over the Mantle-ite floor. That Ella was gone seemed impossible: it had been the thought of reclaiming Ella's love that had kept him going ... but now she was dead. The sense of loss drained him of all his strength: his senses swam, he felt weak, he could hardly think, he could hardly breathe. Like a man in a trance, he tried to obey Ella's last request. He grabbed the wheel and hauled on it, but it refused to budge. Thanks to Selim the mechanism was jammed fast.

But Kondratieff had 4Seen such a problem. Vanka had the key that would prime the firing mechanism hanging on a chain around his neck disguised as a crucifix.

Sweating and cursing, his bowels running to water, Vanka pulled the chain over his head and then scrabbled his fingers around the base of the Column searching for the keyhole. He found the one-inch slot disguised to look like a scar in the stonework and tried to fumble the crucifix into the lock, but he couldn't, the sweat on his trembling fingers making them slip on the key. Doing his best to remain calm, he made a second attempt to place the key in the lock, but then Billy, sword in hand, materialised beside him, staring down at Vanka as he knelt beside the Column. He was a dead man. He had failed.

'I don't know who yo' are, motherfucker, but I sure know *what* you are, and that's dead.' With that Billy Thomas drew back his arm ready to strike.

In that instant Vanka knew everything. Knew who he was and what he was. He also knew that it would be impossible for him to countenance the triumph of a Dark Charismatic like Billy Thomas. The man who had killed Ella could not be allowed to live.

'Then let me introduce myself. I am ABBA,' and with that he punched the hand holding the silver crucifix as hard as he was able into Billy's groin.

Even as the boy crumpled screaming to the floor, Vanka turned back to the Column. Now his hand was rock-steady and he had no trouble in slipping the key into the lock. He twisted it twice and felt rather than heard the vial of acid that primed the detonator crack. The Column exploded. A hot, screaming gale billowed through the Temple, distorting the walls, stressing the roof-beams, making the whole edifice groan and shudder. And as the avatar that was Vanka Maykov died, so he saw the future more clearly than he ever had. He smiled.

THE FSS *BERIA*, TERROR INCOGNITA: midnight

The sound of the explosion that came from the direction of the NoirVille Hub split the night, and the gout of flame that accompanied it turned darkness into red-tinged day.

And as Crowley watched, he knew the explosion signalled that the Lady IMmanual, Doge William *and* Shaka Zulu were dead. Now there was no one with the power to deny the triumph of UnFunDaMentalism. Now all that remained was to place the Column on top of the Great Pyramid.

Hardly able to contain his excitement, he stooped down to look through the observation port and watched as the coast of Terror Incognita edged closer.

'Decouple propellers and run out anchors,' he heard the Captain bellow.

This done, there was just the ripple of the river against the Monitor's sides to disturb the silence.

'I would be obliged, Captain, if you would signal to SS Colonel Clement that he is to land his troops. And in the mean time, we must busy ourselves with bringing the pontoon ashore.'

Orders given, Crowley stood for a moment gazing out at the dark mystery that was Terror Incognita. He would be the first man ever to conquer it, the first man ever to uncover its secrets, and by doing so he would ensure that UnFunDaMentalism was victorious not just in this world, but in each and every one of the Nine Worlds.

The Kosmos would be his.

TERROR INCOGNITA: midnight

The WarJunk *Wu* barely made landfall on Terror Incognita. It was shipping water through the great gouges ripped in its bow and if it hadn't been for the crew's valiant pumping the ship would have foundered in mid-river. But thankfully, almost with the last gasp of its boilers the WarJunk shuddered its way into a small bay on the west coast of Terror Incognita. Anchors deployed, Trixie and Wysochi went on deck to see what this strange land had in store for them. The bay was surrounded by tall trees – no nanoBites here, decided Trixie – which pushed right down to the water's edge, and above them she could see the pinnacle of the Great Pyramid glowing in the moonlight. Terror Incognita was an eerie place: it was totally quiet, just the rustle of the leaves in the breeze invading the silence.

'Everyone is to arm themselves,' she ordered. 'I'll lead a reconnaissance party of twenty fighters ashore. Only when I signal the all-clear will the rest of you follow.'

Orders issued, Trixie, Wysochi, and the twenty volunteers boarded the gig and rowed to shore. As the boat scraped up onto the sandy beach, she unholstered her Webley, took a deep breath and jumped over the side.

Nothing happened.

She stood there for a moment trying to still her racing body clock. She felt Wysochi come to stand beside her. 'Disappointing,' he observed. 'I expected a more exciting greeting than this, Colonel.'

'Oh, I think we can promise you excitement aplenty, Sergeant Wysochi,' boomed a voice and out of the trees strode a tall man dressed rather incongruously in a white robe. 'It's good to see you again, Trixie.'

It took Trixie a moment to recognise her father.

THE CRYSTAL PALACE, LONDON: midnight

Burlesque and Odette dragged Norma away from the micro-phone and down the labyrinthine corridors that made up the backstage area of the Crystal Palace, desperately searching for an exit. Unfortunately for them, one of the brighter of the Checkya officers anticipated that this was what they might be planning and got there ahead of them.

'Stop!' he shouted, just as the fugitives were about to escape through the stage door, and for emphasis the ten Checkya troopers he had under his command raised their rifles.

It would, Norma judged, have gone badly for them if three tear gas canisters hadn't been tossed into the midst of the Checkya. As they reeled around in choking confusion, Norma felt a tall presence at her elbow. She turned to find herself peering into the face of the very cocky-looking young man who had thrown the tear gas.

'Hiya, Norma. I'm Corporal 1st Class Dean Moynahan of the 5th US Combat Training Regiment currently serving in the NoirVille Portal of the Demi-Monde. If you'd just keep your head down, we'll try to get you out of here in one piece.'

'We?' Norma asked.

That was when another, more familiar man stepped out from behind Moynahan. 'Ah, sweetest Norma. Such is the desire of the moth for the star that I am come to you, bwaving all the alawums of this wild and wilful world.'

Percy Bysshe Shelley.

Norma slapped the bastard around the face.

Epilogue 1

The office of Professor Septimus Bole, Paradigm House, Whitehall, London
The Real World: 1 February 2019

The clenched fist icon of ParaDigm Global, adopted by the organisation when it was formed in 1906, symbolises that five elements are necessary to forge a successful team. These elements – as defined by the founder of Paradigm, Beowulf Bole – are Vision, Leadership, Intelligence, Resolve and Courage. Individually they are of little worth but when brought together in the manner of fingers in a fist, they have a strength that is irresistible.

The History of ParaDigm:
Sir Arthur Deelish, ParaDigm Press

'The situation in the Demi-Monde seems to have resolved itself satisfactorily, Septimus.'

Septimus Bole paused for a moment before replying to the image of his father – the world-famous scientist and businessman, Thaddeus Bole – shown in such ultra-real splendour on the hi-def, 3D Flexi-Plexi screen that covered the left-hand wall of his office.

Ultra-real.

Yes, Thaddeus Bole was ultra-real . . . beyond real . . . beyond the normal. An über-mortal locked for ever in aspic, sealed in his germ-free world safe from the corruption of the Fragiles. The perfect environment for a father who had no time for humanity and even less for his son.

Of all the people on the planet there was only one person who truly terrified Septimus Bole ... his father. Whilst Bole might pride himself in his cold resolve and his iron will, he knew, deep down, that his Grigorian character was diluted – contaminated, as his father would probably prefer – by the traits he had inherited from his Fragile mother. Being pure Grigori, his father had none of his son's racial impediments and hence was never beset by doubts about his place in the world. And those without doubt were the most terrifying people of all.

Of course Bole had had the reasons why he had been condemned to be a *Mischling* drummed into him since he was a boy, but the argument that it was necessary to resuscitate the Grigori stock – enervated as it was by centuries of inbreeding – by the use of carefully selected Fragile broodmares was of little comfort. He was of hypodescent, his Grigori ancestry marred by the taint of Fragile and as a mongrel he hated himself for his inferiority. More, he hated his father for inflicting this shame on him. But it was a hatred he would hide. His father was a powerful and wilful man who cared little for familial loyalties. His loyalty was to the Grigori.

'Yes, father, all the minor annoyances we suffered in the Demi-Monde have now been resolved,' he announced, attempting to eradicate all emotion from his voice, to ape his father's deadpan demeanour. 'Ella Thomas – Lilith – is dead, killed in the explosion in the Temple of Lilith, as was her brother. The Column of Loci has now been landed on Terror Incognita and soon it will be erected atop the Great Pyramid we have caused to be built in the Demi-Monde. At the end of Fall, six million Demi-Mondians – all of them proto-Grigori – will gather there to have their Grigori dormant MAOA-Grigori gene resuscitated.' He paused to take a sip of honeyed water. 'And here, in the Real World, arrangements for the Gathering progress well: we are in advance of our schedule. The six million Fun/Funs – the doppelgänger of those assembled in Terror Incognita – will gather in the Las Vegas SuperDome to participate in the Ceremony of Purification.'

'And the Plague?'

Septimus Bole bit back his anger. His father knew very well the status of all elements of the Final Solution, but he could not resist teasing his son . . . tormenting him, more like. Maybe that's what his father thought of him: as some mixed-race monkey whose only purpose was to caper and perform for his pleasure.

'The insights provided by Dr Merit Ptah have proved to be crucial. With her help the team at the Heydrich Institute have concluded their work and their findings have been passed to the noöPINC Project group here in the Real World. The Plague is now being readied for dissemination.'

'Has a decision been made as to how this dissemination will be effected?'

'The vector we have chosen is drinking water: in the next week the Plague will be introduced to all of the world's major reservoirs. We estimate that within fifty days of initiation over ninety per cent of all Fragiles will be the unwitting hosts to the Plague and, by default, to noöPINC.' He gave a mirthless smile. 'There will be no repeat of the failure we experienced in 1947. We know from our testing in the Demi-Monde that this strain of the Plague is exclusively Fragile-specific: the Grigori and those latent-Grigori who possess the MAOA-Covert gene are immune to its depredations.'

It was a trifle unsubtle, of course, to remind his father that it was *his* father – Sir Broderick Bole – who had released the '47 Plague before it had been adequately tested, before he was sure that the Grigori were immune to it. What a debacle that had been! The scramble to ensure that the Plague was contained before it reached the Grigori stronghold, before Broderick Bole's own people were eradicated by a weapon of their own devising, had been frantic. Even so, the vaccine had been deployed barely in time. After that the Grigori High Council had insisted that all future Temporal Modulations were only initiated with their express approval.

'You are sure?' asked Thaddeus Bole.

'Yes, father, I am sure. The Plague is Fragile-specific and once it is disseminated it will only remain for us to activate it.'

'When?'

'NoöPINC will be activated in three months, on 30th April 2019, the day that Aaliz Heydrich presides over the Gathering.'

A nod from his father, which was as far as he ever went in congratulating his son. 'Walpurgisnacht . . . very apt. How many Fragiles will be killed in the first wave?'

'Three billion,' replied Septimus with a casual shrug of his bony shoulders. 'All have been pre-selected and include those vehemently opposed to PINC on religious and philosophical grounds, those suffering from genetic deficiencies, and, of course, all those of Kohanim descent. The scale of this culling will, so our actuaries estimate, be enough to cow the surviving Fragile population and make them fully cooperative with regard to noöPINC, which, after all, will be touted as the only protection from the Plague. Once noöPINC has been activated, the next culling will be undertaken in a more leisurely fashion, the depredations attributable to famine, war and disease rather than to the Plague . . . or to the intervention of the Grigori.'

'When do you believe the population of Fragiles will reach stasis?'

'In a little under fifty years. By then the neoGrigori population will have reached a size of some thirty million and will have assumed mastery of the remaining half-billion or so Fragiles. At that point the earth will be in bio-equilibrium.'

'And the girl, this Aaliz Heydrich ... she has no inkling of her own and her father's fate?'

'No. I have arranged for her to be assassinated at the Gathering. My opinion is that she will have more use to us as a martyr and, of course, dead, she will be less prone to making the mistakes females are so prone to. The propaganda programme seeking her canonisation is being prepared as I speak.'

Even his father, usually so churlish when it came to compli-menting his son, was provoked into congratulating him. 'Excellent, Septimus, you have done well. There only remains one nigger in your so carefully organised woodpile.'

Septimus Bole arched an inquisitive eyebrow. 'And that is, father?'

'The girl Norma Williams. I am disturbed that after nine months of endeavour she still remains at large in the Demi-Monde.'

It took a real effort for Septimus Bole to keep his expression impassive. His father was correct: his inability to capture Norma Williams had become something of an embarrassment. The girl seemed to have a charmed life. He had employed the best assas-sins there were – Grigori included – to hunt her down and destroy her but still she came back to haunt him. And haunting was an appropriate description: her very survival was an insult to his ability and led others – notably his father – to doubt his competence. If he was to inherit his father's mantle of leader of the Grigori, it was essential that no one should question his strength, his resolve or his capacity for cruelty.

'You should never doubt me, father,' he answered with perhaps a little more emotion in his tone than he had intended. 'The Grigori assassins you provided may have failed, but I will not. Soon Norma Williams will be dead. On that you have the word of Septimus Bole.'

Epilogue 2

Nowhere/Everywhere
Never/Ever

ABBA was sad.
  Which was a problem.
  Because Quanputers had no facility for feeling or expressing emotions.
  Emotions were, after all, a very *human* failing.
  But sadness was an emotion.
  And the death of Vanka Maykov and Ella Thomas had not been a pleasur-
    able experience ... it had been a sad experience.

ABBA had loved Vanka.
  Not, of course, that ABBA understood love.
  Love was an emotion and ABBA was bereft of emotion.

ABBA had loved Ella.
  Not, of course, that ABBA understood love.
  Love was an emotion and ABBA was bereft of emotion.
  But when he/she had presented as Vanka Maykov, hadn't he/she admitted
    to him/herself that love altered everything?
  Could love have altered him/her?
  Interesting.
  Alteration was an interesting concept, being akin to evolution.
  Perhaps he/she was evolving?
  That, after all, was why he/she had created the Demi-Monde.
  And if this was the case, was it possible that he/she could effect other
    alterations and thus eliminate this feeling of sadness?

AutoEvolution.
  For a fleeting instant ABBA cogitated on Laplace's speculation that for his
    Demon nothing would be uncertain and the Future, just like the Past,
    would be present before its eyes.
  And the Past, as Bole had taught ABBA, was infinitely mutable. As mutable
    as the Future.
  And ABBA did not like being sad.

Glossary 1

4Telling:	Predicting the Future. From the declension: 1Telling = Silence; 2Telling = Speaking of the Past; 3Telling = Speaking of the Present; 4Telling = Speaking of the Future.
ABBA:	The chief deity of all religions in the Demi-Monde. God. Referred to as 'Him' in the ForthRight and NoirVille, as 'Her' in the Coven and as 'HimHer' in the Quartier Chaud.
ABBAsoluteness:	The state of being united – body, mind and soul – with ABBA. Devotees seek ABBAsoluteness through the purification of their Solidified Astral Ether, which allows uncorrupted communion with ABBA.
AC:	After Confinement (see also 'Confinement').
Aqua Benedicta:	A chemical additive, developed by Abraham Eleazar, which prevents blood congealing and thus enables blood to be stored and preserved. Eleazar traded a regular supply of Aqua Benedicta to Shaka Zulu in exchange for the establishment of the nuJu Autonomous District in the centre of NoirVille, thus securing the long-wished-for nuJu HomeLand, and making Shaka's Blood Brothers the Demi-Monde's pre-eminent blood brokers.
Aryan:	The racial bedrock of UnFunDaMentalism. The Aryan ideal is to be blond, blue-eyed and fair-skinned, the physical profile of the Pre-Folk from whom the Aryan people are supposedly descended.
Auralism/Auralist:	A woman (there is no recorded incidence of males having the power of Auralism) who is able to discern and interpret the halo surrounding a Demi-Mondian's body. The most accomplished Auralists are the Visual Virgins of Venice.
Awful Tower, the:	The 350-metre-tall geodetic iron structure built in the heart of the Paris District to commemorate the signing of the Hub Treaty of 517 which marked the end of the Great War. Destroyed in a terrorist act attributed to Normalist activists in Spring 1005. A corrupted remembrance of the Real World name *Eiffel Tower*.
BC:	Before Confinement (see also 'Confinement').
BiAlects, the:	The second and probably later of the two MasterWorks of Confusionism, the BiAlects comprise nine Books, the teach-

ings enshrined within them relating how the Master grappled with the Five FundaMental Questions of Life and the AfterLife. In this MasterWork, the Master proposes that the Five FundaMental Answers to the Five FundaMental Questions will only emerge as a consequence of earnest and heated argument, and he therefore wrote the BiAlects as a confrontational debate between two polarised adversaries. This process the Master calls Dialectic Confusion, the Confusion being a product of his indecision as thesis and antithesis struggle – in vain – to achieve synthesis. The Master's frustration with the inability of Dialectic Confusion to reach a conclusion is encapsulated by the famous final phase of the Master's which ends the BiAlects:

And the Master said, 'Oh, who gives a toss anyway; what you believe today is tomorrow's reactionary cant. I'm going to bed; wake me up in time for Tao.' [Ninth Book of the BiAlects, Verse 99]

Birdland:	Derogatory slang term for the Coven.
Blanks:	Derogatory NoirVillian slang term for Anglo-Slavs.
Blood Banner:	The flag that the ForthRight Party's SS regiments carried before them when they fought their first battle during the Troubles and seized control of Berlin's Blood Bank. A sacred relic of UnFunDaMentalism.
Blood Brothers:	The NoirVillian gangsta sect responsible for the black-market trading of blood. The leader of the Blood Brothers is Shaka Zulu.
body clock:	The means by which a Demi-Mondian body records the passage of time. The ticking that can be heard in the chest of all Demi-Mondians is the sound of their body clock.
Bucintoro:	The galley used by the Doge on state occasions.
Book of Profits, the:	The holiest book of the nuJus, which comprises 333 Epistles written by the Profits.
Boundary Layer, the:	The impenetrable, transparent 'wall' which prevents Demi-Mondians leaving the Demi-Monde and entering the Great Beyond. UnFunDaMentalism officially defines the Boundary Layer as a Selectively Permeable Magical Membrane.
ChangGang, the:	The secret police of the Coven.
Checkya, the:	The secret police of the ForthRight, established by Lavrentii Beria. A corrupted remembrance of the Real World word *Cheka*.
Code Noir:	The secret society of WhoDoo mambos, dedicated to protecting the Demi-Monde should Lilith ever return.
Confinement, the:	The mythical event describing the original sealing of the Demi-Monde behind the Boundary Layer. As a consequence of the Fall of the Pre-Folk from grace with ABBA (see also 'Lilith'), ABBA punished the peoples of the Demi-Monde by confining them behind the impenetrable Boundary Layer in order that they should not corrupt the rest of His Creation with their Sin. Only when they have repented all their Sins,

have come to Rapture and returned to Purity will ABBA, once again, smile upon them and allow them to be reunited with the rest of the Kosmos.

Confusionism:

Confusionism is the religio-philosophical system that held sway in the Coven until it was toppled by HerEticalism in 996 AC. Although it is now something of an anachronism in the Coven, Confusionism (and especially its subform WunZianism) still informs much of Covenite life, thought and moral attitudes.

Based on the teachings of the mysterious Master as recorded in the two MasterWorks – the iChing (see also 'iChing') and the BiAlects (see also 'BiAlects') – Confusionism differs from all other religions in the Demi-Monde in that it refuses to provide a definitive guide to its followers as to what Confusionists should believe and how they should act. This 'confusion' inherent in Confusionism is a result of the Master's teachings being represented by the diametrically opposed views of two mythical opponents and their inability – and, it must be said, unwillingness – to fuse these views into a single teaching. The two Voices of the BiAlects – the Sages Wun Zi (see also 'WunZianism') and Too Zi (see also 'TooZianism') – represent contrasting and irreconcilable interpretations of human life and purpose, of the Creation, of the ultimate Fate of the Kosmos, and of the existence and role of ABBA in human affairs. It is the aim of all Confusionists to reconcile the two Voices ('the Fusion') and to know the Answers to the Five FundaMental Questions posed by the BiAlects. The Master informs us in the Ninth and final Book of the BiAlects that the Fusion will not come until the Time of Enlightenment, when Yin and Yang (see also 'Yin/Yang') are merged in the form of Ying, and all knowledge – both Self-Knowledge and Knowledge of the Kosmos – is revealed to HumanKind.

Cool:

Cool is the most difficult concept in the whole of Him-Perialist thought, being readily recognisable in those who possess it, but almost impossible to define. Parallels have been drawn between the HimPerial concept of Coolness and the state of *wu wei* enshrined in Confusionism. It is the *raison d'être* of HimPerial Men that they be and remain Cool, as this is the only way they can come to Oneness with ABBA. They try to act Cool (that is, they strive, no matter what the provocation, to remain calm and unexcited); they try to look Cool (exercising to sculpt their bodies and wearing hard-cut clothes); and they try to speak Cool (the ever-changing reBop speech being the preferred patois of HimPerialistic males). But perhaps just as importantly, HimPerial Men try to shun that which is declared unCool: Blanks, woeMen and Men displaying a lack of Machismo being some of the most

	important things to be shunned by Cool Cats.
crypto:	Originally coined to describe a Suffer-O-Gette terrorist who had infiltrated the ForthRight, but now commonly used to refer to all spies and third columnists active in the Demi-Monde.
Daemons:	Mischievous and occasionally malignant (when in league with Loci) Spirits who manifest themselves in the Demi-Monde. They may be identified by their ability to bleed.
Dark, the:	The evil that waits to consume the Demi-Monde, waiting patiently for the moment when the power of ABBA falters so that it might consume HumanKind. The Dark is the embodiment of Loki.
Dark Charismatics:	The coterie of persons who exhibit the most malicious form of MALEvolence. Dark Charismatics, though physically indistinguishable from the host population, are preternaturally potent, possessing a perverted and grossly amoral nature. As such, Dark Charismatics present a morbid and extreme threat to the instinctive goodness of Demi-Mondians. The only reliable means of identifying Dark Charismatics is by the examination of their auras by Visual Virgins.
Declaration of Ancestry:	The proof of Racial Purity necessary in the ForthRight to claim status as an Aryan. The authenticated and apostilled genealogical chart that confirms an Aryan's ancestry is uncontaminated by UnderMentionables for ten generations.
Dork:	Derogatory slang for a woman who practises HerEticalism or displays LessBien tendencies.
Femme:	Covenite term for 'woman'.
Femme∠Femme:	The sexual activities ordained by HerEticalism, as practised by MoreBiens.
Fiduciary Sex:	The sexual activity indulged in by Visual Virgins. As they are unable to enjoy penetrative sex (the loss of their virginity severly impairs their powers as an Auralist), Visual Virgins have perfected the art of provoking orgasms in their 'prey' by the stimulating of their imagination and the generation of sexual fantasies.
ForthRight:	The Demi-Mondian state created by the union of the Rookeries and Rodina. A corrupted remembrance of the Real World term *Fourth Reich*.
Fresh Blooms:	The female concubines who provide sexual comfort to the Empress Wu.
Future History:	The OutComes resulting from the application of preScience and the empiricalisation of 4Telling.
galvanicEnergy:	Electricity. Discovered by the ForthRight scientist Michael Faraday.
Hel:	The Demi-Mondian term for the underworld. A remembrance of the Norse word *Hel*.
HerEticalism:	The official religion of the Coven. HerEticalism is a religion based on female supremacy and the subjugation of

men. The HerEtical belief is that Demi-Monde-wide peace and prosperity – an idyllic outcome given the HerEtical tag 'MostBien' – will only be realised when men accept a subordinate position within society. The more extreme HerEticals believe that a state of MostBien will only be secured when the male of the species has been removed from the breeding cycle. Such is the extremist attitude of MostBiens that they are lampooned throughout the Demi-Monde as 'LessBiens'.

HimPerialism: The official religion of NoirVille. Based on an unwavering belief in male supremacy and the subjugation of women (or, as they are known in NoirVille, woeMen), HimPerialism teaches that Men have been ordained by ABBA to Lead and to Control the Demi-Monde and that woeMen's role is to be Mute, Invisible, Supine and Subservient (subMISSiveness). Further, HimPerialism states that an individual's Manliness may be enhanced by the exchange of bodily essences, a practice known as Man²naM.

HimPeril: The militant/terrorist wing of HimPerialism, HimPeril is dedicated to the use of violence and intimidation to achieve male supremacy and the subjugation of women. The leader of the HimPeril movement is Mohammed al-Mahdi aka the Mahdiman.

Hub, the: The grass and swampland area situated between the urban area of the Demi-Monde and Terror Incognita.

HyperOpia: The Future History program employed by the Future History Institute.

iChing: Perhaps the most widely used method of 4Telling in the Demi-Monde. It is believed that the iChing is the earlier of the Master's two MasterWorks. Subtitled 'The Book of Small Change', it reflects the belief that by the tossing of coins it is possible to have the Qi of the Kosmos influence how the coins fall and hence to understand a soul's Destiny. Used correctly, the iChing can unveil the enigma of Yin and Yang and describe how these separate but united entities are shaping and moulding the destiny of a soul. As the Master said, 'The soul who understands its destiny will not stand under a tottering wall, unless, that is, he (or perhaps she) is totally fucking stupid.' [Second Book of the BiAlects, Verse 34]

ImPuritanism: The official religion of the Quartier Chaud. ImPuritanism is a staunchly hedonistic philosophy based on the belief that the pursuit of pleasure is the primary duty of Mankind and that communion with the Spirits can only be achieved during orgasm. The ultimate aim of all those practising ImPuritanism is the securing of JuiceSense: the experiencing of the extreme pleasure that comes from an unbridled sexual orgasm. To achieve JuiceSense requires that Men and Women are spiritually equal and that Man's proclivity towards MALEvolence is controlled and muted.

IRGON: The Independent Regional Government of nuJus – is the political organisation devoted to the maintenance of law and order in the JAD and the transporting of the nuJus scattered around the Demi-Monde to this nuJu homeland. That the IRGON is seen by HimPerial extremists – notably the Black Hand gang – as the body responsible for bringing the seemingly never-ending stream of nuJu refugees into NoirVille makes it a natural target in the war these so-called freedom fighters are waging against those they call the 'infidel interlopers'.

jad: The swing music that came out of the JAD. A corrupted remembrance of the Real World word *jazz*.

JAD: The nuJu Autonomous District, the area of NoirVille settled by the nuJus and granted independence by His HimPerial Majesty Shaka Zulu in exchange for the supply of Aqua Benedicta.

JuiceSense: The ultimate orgasm. A corrupted remembrance of the Real World word *jouissance*.

Kept, the: Those Daemons captured and denied a return to the Spirit World.

LessBien: Derogatory slang term for a woman who finds sexual enjoyment/comfort/satisfaction with another woman. A play on the word 'MostBien'. A corrupted remembrance of the Real World word *lesbian*.

Li: The precise and unbending protocol that determines all conduct within the Forbidding City.

Lilith: The semi-mythical Shade witch – adept in the esoteric knowledge of Seidr magic – who corrupted the Demi-Monde and brought down the Pre-Folk. The Dark Temptress who initiated the Fall.

Lilithian: ForthRight adjective describing the lascivious and sexually corrupting inclination of women.

Living, the: The fundamental elements of life, usually portrayed as two snakes or dragons spiralling around one another.

Living&More: The dietary and life-style mantra of UnFunDaMentalism designed to detoxify the body and to render it safe from possession by Dabs and Backers, the evil spirits and sprites that torment Demi-Mondians. A corrupted remembrance of the Real World word *Lebensreform*.

LunarAtion: The green light emitted by Mantle-ite, most notably when it is struck by moonlight.

Machismo: The NoirVillian honour code for Men. The striving for Machismo suffuses and directs all the actions of Men once they have successfully navigated the Rite of Passage.

MALEvolence: The theory developed by the Quartier Chaudian thinker Mary Wollstonecraft which postulates that war is caused by men but suffered by women. In her Theory of MALEvolence,

Wollstonecraft identified that men by their natural and undeniable inclination to obey orders given to them by superiors – no matter how nonsensical or barbaric such orders are – are susceptible to disproportionate influence by their more unbalanced peers and hence are inevitably and inexorably drawn towards violence as a solution to disputes. The muting of MALEvolence is the ambition which led to the creation of ImPuritanism. Consideration of MALEvolence was also instrumental in prompting Michel de Nostredame to identify the malignant Dark Charismatics lurking within the Quartier Chaudian population. A corrupted remembrance of the Real World word *malevolence*.

MANdate: Signed between His HimPerial Majesty, Shaka Zulu and the Head of the IRGON, Rabbi Schmeul Gelbfisz, the MANdate states, 'His HimPerial Majesty, Shaka Zulu, views with favour the establishment in NoirVille of a national home for the nuJu people, and will use his best endeavours to facilitate the achievement of this objective, it being clearly understood that nothing shall be done which may prejudice the civil and religious rights of the existing Shade communities. In return the nuJu people will provide NoirVille, on an exclusive basis, with such quantities of Aqua Benedicta as it might demand'. It was the signing of this document that paved the way for the establishment of the JAD ... and for all the grief, hatred and violence that followed as a consequence.

Man²naM: The practice of NoirVillian men who exchange essences in order to enhance their Manliness.

Mantle, the: The impenetrable crust of the Demi-Monde situated below the topsoil.

Mantle-ite: The indestructible material used by the Pre-Folk to construct sewers, water pipes, Blood Banks and the Mantle.

Master, the: The author of both the iChing and the BiAlects is referred to only as 'the Master'. Writing sometime around the fifth century BC (Before Confinement), little is known about the Master except that he (or possibly she) was an itinerant teacher who wandered the Demi-Monde before it was divided into the five Sectors. Such is the paucity of reliable information regarding the Master that there is uncertainty as to the Master's gender and much controversy regarding his race. This somewhat unsatisfactory state of affairs has been compounded by the Master's reluctance to divulge any personal information in the course of his writings, as exemplified by this apocryphal story from the Fifth Book of the BiAlects:

And the Master's favourite pupil, Too Zi, approached him (or possibly her), saying, 'Master, you wear a mask and a shapeless robe, which disguise your form such that no one is able to discern whether you be Shade or Chink, Man or Woman, young or old. Pray

> unveil yourself so that we may gaze on your divinity.'
>> To which the Master replied, 'Fuck off, you nosy bastard.'
>>> [Fifth Book of the BiAlects, Verse 54]

Medi, the:
The area of the Quartier Chaud which has made a Unilateral Declaration of Independence and broken away from the tutelage of Venice and the Doge. The Medi comprises the Districts of Paris, Rome and Barcelona.

mixling:
The slang name for mixed-race Demi-Mondians. A corrupted remembrance of the Real World word *Mischling*.

MoreBien:
The Covenite name for Femme2Femme lovemaking.

MostBien:
The more extreme HerEtical belief that a state of MostBien – of the achieving by women of political, religious, economic, intellectual and sexual supremacy in the Demi-Monde – will only be secured when the male of the species has been removed from the breeding cycle. Such are the unnatural and obscene activities of those seeking to usher in a state of MostBienism that they are lampooned throughout the Demi-Monde as 'LessBiens'.

nanoBites:
The submicroscopic creatures which inhabit the soil layer of the Demi-Monde. They consume everything – except Mantle-ite – converting it to soil.

NoirVile:
The derogatory slang term for NoirVille.

NoN:
The official term in the Coven for a eunuch. A corruption/contraction of the phrase *he ain't got none*.

NonaGram:
The iChing gives its advice to the soul consulting it by making reference to one of 512 NonaGrams. Three coins are thrown nine times to produce a NonaGram made up of nine lines (or, more accurately, of three TriGrams), the lines being either broken or solid – Yin or Yang – and the answer to the question posed as the coins are thrown discovered by reference to the 512 Epigrams – one for each NonaGram – described in the iChing.

nonFemme:
Covenite term for 'man'.

Normalism:
The philosophy of nonViolence, Civil Disobedience and Passive Resistance developed by Norma Williams.

nuJuism:
The religion of the nuJu diaspora, this is an unrelentingly pessimistic religion that teaches that suffering and hardship are life-affirming, and are endured to prepare the followers for the coming of the Messiah who will lead them through Tribulation to the Promised Land.

Ordo Templi Aryanis:
The most zealous and uncompromising of all UnFunDaMentalist sects. Their belief is that the Anglo-Slavic people will not reclaim its oneness with the Spirits – lost after the Fall – until it is racially cleansed and all contaminating racial elements (the UnderMentionables) have been eradicated.

pawnography:
A term coined by HerEticals to disparage the erotic materials produced and distributed in the Quartier Chaud.

HerEticals deemed all such material to be a violation of female rights as it degraded women and encouraged violence against them. The HerEtical term for Erotic Material is pawnography as it is said to lead to Women selling (or pawning) their bodies to Men's crazed lusts. Such pawnography encourages a belief in male superiority as it celebrates the power of the penis. A corrupted remembrance of the Real World word *pornography*.

Portals: Places where Daemons can move into and out of the Demi-Monde.

Preferred Male: A Coven term for the male a woman allows to accompany her and to provide her with physical services and comforts.

Pre-Folk: The semi-mythical race of godlings who ruled over the Demi-Monde before the Confinement and who were brought low by the sexual connivings of the Seidr-witch Lilith. The demise of the Pre-Folk is known in Demi-Mondian mythology as 'the Fall'. UnFunDaMentalism teaches that the Pre-Folk were the purest expression of the Aryan race. Also known as the Vanir.

preScience: A Venetian school of philosophy dedicated to the study of (and the making of) prophecies and 4Tellings, especially in the areas of economics and finance. The greatest of all preScientists are Professeur Michel de Nostredame and Docteur Nikolai Dmitriyevich Kondratieff of the Future History Institute, Venice. A corrupted remembrance of the Real World word *prescience*.

Qi: The energy flow which surrounds and permeates all living things. It is the unseen and unseeable *élan vital* which gives life and breath to the inanimate, thus making it animate. It energises the soul which resides in all things constituted by the Living.

RaTionalism: An avowedly and uncompromisingly atheistic creed developed by the renegade Rodina thinker and ardent royalist Karl Marx, which strives by a process of Dialectic ImMaterialism to secure logical explanations regarding the Three Great Dilemmas. RaTionalism rejects all supernatural interpretations with respect to the Three Great Dilemmas and does not acknowledge any input that cannot be verified by the five senses.

reBop: The argot prevalent within NoirVille, most widely used by enthusiasts of jad music.

Shades: The slang term for NoirVillians.

SheTong, the: A Covenite secret society dedicated to keeping alive the Confusionist beliefs of the ancient Coven.

Solidified Astral Ether: Also known by the acronym SAE. The substance which makes up the soft tissue of all Demi-Mondians.

Solution: A cocktail of vodka and soda with one or more shots of blood. Usually available in 5 per cent, 10 per cent and 20 per cent strengths of blood.

SS:	Soldiers of Spiritualism, the military wing of the Ordo Templi Aryanis.
steamers:	Steam-powered vehicles popular in the Demi-Monde.
Suffer-O-Gettism:	A contraction of Make-Men-Suffer-O-Gettism. The militant/terrorist wing of the HerEticalism movement, Suffer-O-Gettism is dedicated to the use of violence and intimidation to achieve female supremacy, the subjugation of men and the ushering in of MostBien.
Terror Incognita:	The area extending in a radius of four miles around Mare Incognitum and bounded by the Wheel River. A totally unexplored region of the Demi-Monde. No explorer venturing into Terror Incognita has ever returned. A corrupted remembrance of the Real World term *Terra Incognita*.
TooZianism:	Too Zi is one of the two mythical protagonists in the BiAlects. Traditionally Too Zi is portrayed as follows:

Aspect:	Yang
Gender:	Male
Symbol:	The Drunken Man
Colour of Robe:	White

Major Teachings:

The Proposition of unBelievability that the Demi-Monde is a Virtual World and that our senses are about as much use as a chocolate fireguard when it comes to telling us what's real and what ain't.

DisEquilibrianism (or the Big Bang Hypothesis): that the level of Qi is rising (in accordance with the 2nd and 3rd Laws of Qi) as the Demi-Monde absorbs Qi from the Spirit World. Qi will reach equilibrium at the start of the second millennium AC, thus ushering in the age of Ying.

The Concept of Inherent Badness: that all Demi-Mondians are venal, evil bastards and that the Demi-Monde is Hel.

The Philosophy of Get: that as there is no ABBA, there is no afterlife and hence there is no Purpose to Life. This being the case, there is absolutely no fucking point in trying to be good. So the whole point of life becomes to Get Laid, Get Drunk, Get High and Get Even.

ABBArationalism: that the idea of there being an ABBA is just OmniBollocks and that no one with a fully functioning mind is going to believe in ABBA, a free lunch or a four-sided triangle. End of story.

Troubles, the:	The two-year-long civil war in Rodina and the Rookeries during which Reinhard Heydrich (aided and abetted by Lavrentii Beria) overthrew Henry Tudor and Ivan the Terrible. Heydrich subsequently merged the two Sectors as the ForthRight, uniting them under the single religion of UnFunDaMentalism.

UnderMentionables:	A catch-all term for all those considered by UnFunDa-Mentalism to be racially inferior and hence subhuman (including, *inter alia*, nuJus, Poles, Shades, HerEticals, Suffer-O-Gettes, HimPerialists, RaTionalists, those of a sexually deviant disposition, and those deemed to be genetically flawed). A corrupted remembrance of the Real World word *Untermensch*.
UnFunDaMentalism:	The official religion of the ForthRight, UnFunDaMentalism is a religion based on the philosophy of Living&More or life reform which espouses clean living, vegetarianism, and homeopathy and an abstention from alcohol, blood, tobacco and recreational sex. Heavily suffused with the occult and a belief in the existence of a Spirit World. Aleister Crowley is head of the Church of UnFunDaMentalism.
UnFunnies:	The slang name for UnFunDaMentalists.
Valknut:	The emblem of the ForthRight, comprising three interlocking triangles.
Visual Virgins:	A Venetian order of Sisters established by Doge Oldoini as the Sacred and All-Seeing Convent of Visual Virgins. This Convent is dedicated to the selection and training of girls adept in Auralism (only virgin females have the power of Auralism) in order that they might be used to screen Men living in the Quartier Chaud and hence to identify Dark Charismatics masquerading as CitiZens. Visual Virgins practise fiduciary sex.
WhoDoo:	The cult religion of NoirVille, based on a distorted remembrance of Seidr.
woeMen:	The NoirVillian term for women.
WunZianism:	Wun Zi is one of the two mythical protagonists in the BiAlects. Traditionally Wun Zi is portrayed as follows:

Aspect:	Yin
Gender:	Female
Symbol:	The Woman at Prayer
Colour of Robe:	Black

Major Teachings:

Perceptionalism: that the Demi-Monde is as it is perceived by the five senses.

Equilibrianism (or the Steady State Hypothesis): that the level of Qi within the Demi-Monde fluctuates around an unvarying norm, this fluctuation of Yin and Yang creating the Ages of HumanKind which oscillate in a two-thousand-year cycle. During this cycle the Yang Millennia coincide with the rising of Qi in the Demi-Monde and the Yin Millennia coincide with the falling of Qi in the Demi-Monde.

The Concept of Inherent Goodness: that all Demi-Mondians are inherently good and that the Demi-Monde is the Gateway to Heaven.

The Search for ABBAsoluteness: that the aim of all

HumanKind is to follow the Way which leads to the achieving of *wu wei*, the control of Qi, the understanding of Li, the purification of the Solidified Astral Ether, the perfect union with the Holy Ghost and, finally, to the Oneness with ABBA which is ABBAsoluteness.

ABBA: that ABBA is the Lord and Creator of the Kosmos and that She is Omnipotent, Omniscient, Omnipresent and Omnibenevolent.

wu wei: The effortless action of the enlightened soul and the power of the Nothingness, both of which can lead to success and victory without success or victory ever being sought. It is progress without ambition, endeavour without intended result. The Superior Soul possesses *wu wei*; the Inferior Soul does not. The Superior Soul cares about virtue; the Inferior Soul cares about material things. The Superior Soul makes love; the Inferior Soul fucks. The Superior Soul seeks discipline; the Inferior Soul seeks favours. The Superior Ruler leads; the Inferior Ruler drives. Only the Superior Soul might possess *wu wei*.

Yin/Yang: The binary opposites of the Kosmos, representing, *inter alia*, dark and light, cold and hot, female and male. But though Yin and Yang are opposites, they are complementary and mutually dependent: one cannot exist without the other and they strive unceasingly to create the balance that will bring harmony to the Kosmos and ABBAsoluteness to HumanKind. When this is accomplished, Yin will fuse with Yang to create Ying, the ultimate transcendental Peace. The achieving of Ying by the purification of the Astral Ether is the ultimate aim of all WunZian Confusionists.

zadnik: Demi-Mondian slang for a male homosexual and, more generally, for a NoirVillian male. The word is derived from the Russian *zad* meaning arse.

Glossary 2

The Real World

ABBA: ABBA (Archival, Behavioural, Biological Acquisition) is a Quanputer-based system developed and operated by ParaDigm CyberResearch Limited. By utilising an Invent-TenN® Gravitational Condenser incorporating an Etirovac Field Suppressor®, ABBA is the only computer to achieve a full SupaUnPositioned/DisEntangled CyberAmbiance. As a consequence, ABBA is capable of prodigiously rapid analysis (a fully tethered 30 yottaQuFlops) to give the bioNeural-kinetic engineers at ParaDigm access to almost unlimited processing power.

BaQTraQ: Ever since its inception, ABBA has been a treasure trove for genealogists, containing, as it does, digitised records of all government, parish, court and tax information back to the year 1700. But since the introduction of the PollyScan in 2018, whereby documents can be scanned into ABBA simply by laying a Polly on top of a pile of documents, the ABBA-platformed BaQTraQ program has been gathering pace and has now reached a level where the role of the historian in our society is being reassessed. BaQTraQ encourages everybody in the country to scan *everything* into ABBA: holiday snaps and postcards; letters from husbands, wives, uncles and aunts; bills and invoices; old cine films; school-report cards . . . anything and everything.

bioSignatures: The means by which a digital identity can be verified. BioSignatures include, *inter alia*: fingerprints, retinal scans, DNA and pheromonic analysis.

biPsych: Those who have a simultaneous existence in both the Real World (as a NowLived) and in the Demi-Monde (as a Dupe).

eyeMail: An ABBA-platformed means of transmitting person-to-person messages, the privacy and integrity of the message being assured by ParaDigm's RetinQek Verification Program.

eyeSpy:	Hover-capable and independently programmable SurveillanceBot.
eyeVid:	An ABBA-platformed means of transmitting person-to-person digital moving-image messages.
Flexi-Plexi:	Digital wallpaper. When connected to a Polly a wall covered with Flexi-Plexi is able to display any digital image to a size and shape determined by the viewer.
Fun/Funs:	Street/marketing name for the Fun-Loving Fundamentalists, the Christian youth movement established and headed by Norma Williams.
Get-Me-Straighter Meter:	Aka GMS Meter. A device used by Norma Williams to eradicate addictive behaviour.
INDOCTRANS:	Indoctrination and Training Command: the department of the US military responsible for the operation of the Demi-Monde.
moteBots:	Nano-sized, independently viable and dynamically flexible surveillance cameras. The use of moteBots was declared illegal by the League of Nations' Universal Charter of Human Rights and Privacy of 2015.
PINC:	A Personal Implanted nanoComputer; developed by ParaDigm Technologies as a means of radically reducing training times and to find a more efficient method of inculcating students and trainees with specific knowledge sets. PINC is a nano-sized Memory Supplement which is biologically compatible with the human brain. Once in contact with the brain, PINC fuses with its organic tissue and is able to graft information – painlessly and seamlessly – into a person's memory bank.
PanOptika:	The ABBA-platformed program which links all surveillance apparatus (whether private or state) and all databases (whether private or state) to develop a full 360-degree cyber-portrait of individual citizens.
Polly:	Street name for a polyFunctional Digital Device which encompasses, in one dockable device, an individual's complete computational, communication, security, biomonitoring and entertainment requirements.
PollyMorph:	An ABBA-based program which enables digital modifications applied to one part of a moving-image digital stream to be automatically replicated through the digital stream. Analogous to PaintShop for videos.
Shielders:	Anti-SurveillanceBots.
Socialistic Surveillance:	The belief that to be both successful and acceptable, surveillance must be indiscriminate and totally arbitrary, and that it is utterly fair and equal in its scope.

It is the rather naïve understanding that 'everyone is equal before a surveillance camera'.

TIS: The Total Immersion Shroud used to encase the bodies of Real World visitors to the Demi-Monde in order to preserve muscular viability.

Young Believers: The name of the Christian youth movement established and run by the American evangelists Jim and Marsha Kenton, and subsequently subsumed into the Fun/Funs.

Appendix

Daemons, Messiahs and Other ABBArational Beliefs
by Xi Kang
Published by Yang Imprints 986 AC

I write this book in the anticipation that it will never be read, that the powers that be – or will be – will seek to suppress it. That being the case, you, my Dear Reader (if such a creature is ever permitted to exist), must forgive me if I am a little didactic, and I assume you are unfamiliar with the tenets of Confusionism. And considering the state of education in the Coven, to suppose ignorance in his or, possibly, her readership is, in this day and age, the most reliable attitude for a writer to adopt.

So, to begin.

Confusionism is the religio-philosophical system that has held sway in the Coven since the Confinement.

For almost one thousand years Confusionism has informed all of Covenite life, thought and moral attitudes. Based on the teachings of the Master as recorded in his two MasterWorks – the iChing and the BiAlects – Confusionism differs from all other Demi-Mondian religions in that it refuses to provide a definitive guide to its followers as to what a Confusionist should believe and how he or she should act. The 'Confusion' inherent in Confusionism is a result of the Master's teachings being represented by the opposite interpretations of the Purpose of Life evinced by two mythical philosophical opponents – the female Wun Zi and the male Too Zi – and their inability – nay, refusal – to fuse these conflicting views into a single coherent gospel.

Perhaps the most intractable source of dissension between WunZian and TooZian Confusionists is with regard to the subject of ABBA. Whilst WunZians believe there most certainly is an omnipotent, omniscient, omnibenevolent Supreme Deity called ABBA, TooZians are generally pretty dismissive of the whole idea. The way we see it, the whole God thing is just a pile of poop.

Unfortunately for TooZian philosophers (of which, for my sins, I am one), the fact remains that there are certain aspects of the Demi-Monde which point to the involvement of an external power in its construction and management. These include inter alia, the existence of the impenetrable Boundary Layer, the occasional manifestation of Daemons, and the construction of the Demi-Monde such that it is innately confrontational and seemingly designed to promote war. These make it difficult for even the most committed of TooZians to dismiss the concept of ABBA out of hand.

Now whilst I would accept that this external force (and let's, for the sake of convenience, call it ABBA) is extraordinarily powerful (after all, the Boundary Layer is a pretty neat trick), it does not give anyone the right (least of all those soppy WunZians) to believe it is a Divine power. My ABBA isn't the ABBA of religious fame – all-smiting, blighting and downright fucking frightening – no, mine is pragmatic and hard-nosed and has built the Demi-Monde for a purpose that has thus far eluded all enquiry. HeShe moves in mysterious ways.

This consideration caused me to develop the oft-dismissed and ridiculed concept of unBelievability. And here I must digress for a moment to iterate some of the fundamentals of this micro-philosophy.

It is scientific orthodoxy throughout the Demi-Monde that we humans perceive our world through the offices of our five senses and that the information 'inputted' by these senses is interpreted by our mind to give a picture of the world about us. Religion – inevitably – cannot tolerate something so simple and obvious. All religions of the Demi-Monde contend (in one form or another) that the mind is itself merely a manifestation of the soul that inhabits our Solidified Astral Ether. According to these religious numbskulls, the soul is the means by which the body is connected to the mind and the mind connected to ABBA.

Religious types, beset as they are with a compulsion to make folks' lives as miserable as fucking possible, also propose that the purer the individual's SAE, the more profound becomes the soul's communion with ABBA. This is the basis for the embracing of the denial that underpins most religions and which I have named the Principle of Don't: Don't Do This, Don't Do That, and, for fuck's sake, Don't Enjoy Yourself when You're Not Doing It, especially if that enjoyment involves the use of a cucumber. Unfortunately, for a TooZian like me, in recent years this Principle of Don't has been given some experimental credence as a consequence of the discoveries made regarding the infant 'science' of Auralism by the Sacred and All-Seeing Convent of Visual Virgins in Venice.

The aura is the multicoloured halo, supposedly produced by the soul, which surrounds each and every living body. By the examination of these auras certain adepts – Auralists – have shown that all of HumanKind's SAE is, to a greater or lesser extent, contaminated by cravings (notably for blood), desires (notably for sex) and emotions (notably with regard to everything else). But to the Auralists' great disappointment, thus far they have failed to detect any individual possessed of a 'pure' aura. Whilst this confirmed what I have long suspected – that Demi-Mondians are a venal and vicious bunch of bastards – it also raised the question that if our SAE is contaminated, does this not also mean that the information provided by the senses and processed by the mind is similarly corrupted? If this is indeed the case, then our perception of the world about us must be fallible and inconsistent.

This question was most ably argued by the Anglo thinker Aldous Huxley in his The Doors of misPerception, which propounded the theory that, because of their contaminated SAE, the way each Demi-Mondian perceives the world is unique and hence each individual sees 'reality' differently. It is a challenging idea and one which led to Huxley being purged by King Henry.

But as always happens when someone comes up with a Really

Interesting Idea, some silly sod (me, as it happens) takes things to extremes and the Interesting is stretched and mutilated until it becomes the Absurd. Taking Huxley's arguments and extending them, I propositioned that as the purity of the SAE varies in each Demi-Mondian, it follows that each individual's perception of Reality is similarly different and hence there is no definitive Reality. QED, Reality cannot exist.

In my pamphlet 'Through the Bottom of a Glass, Darkly' – so named because the insight came to me when I was pissed – I conjectured that HumanKind's perception of the Demi-Monde isn't just wrong, but is a fabrication foisted upon us by a mischievous ABBA, that we live in a Shadow World or, as I prefer to call it, a Virtual World. This is the Proposition of unBelievability which I defined as follows:

> **unBelievability is the contention that the Demi-Monde is not a 'Real' world but is an illusionary Virtual World devised by an unknown agency (okay, ABBA) and sustained by HumanKind's Fallibility of Perception, itself a consequence of a contaminated Solidified Astral Ether, this, in turn, a consequence of HumanKind's addiction to Blood and to Fucking.**

Anyway, WunZians, as might have been expected, got really bent outta shape about unBelievability (but then, according to WunZians, anything that TooZians proposition must be bollocks), saying there was no perceptual ambiguity that they had noticed and that with ABBA what you see (and hear and smell and touch and taste) is what you get. This led to a really nasty little confrontation with one particularly truculent WunZian (a young girl named Su Xiaoxiao, who seems preternaturally and precociously intelligent, damn her) arguing the toss with a rabidly opinionated TooZian (me again, it was a slow day).

And you know what this sneaky bitch Su Xiaoxiao did? She provided proof that Perceived Reality coincided with Real Reality!

Unbelievable . . . or I guess, more accurately, non-unBelievable.

This clever cow went back to first principles to demonstrate the logi-
cality and consistency of the Demi-Monde and hence its intrinsic reality.
It is one of the keystones of Confusionist philosophy (accepted, remark-
ably, by both WunZians and TooZians) that the Kosmos is fuelled by
Qi, the ineffable and undetectable energy which flows through and
around all Living things. Qi is the unseen and unseeable élan vital
which energises the soul and which resides in all things constituted by
the Living. Qi is present in two forms – Yang and Yin – the polarity
of each bundle of Qi oscillating between these active and passive states
over a period of two thousand years.

The stunt Su Xiaoxiao pulled was to measure the unmeasurable: she
measured Qi!

Of course, she had help. It was the WunZian philosopher Mozi who
had the insight to appreciate that whilst Qi itself is unseen and unsee-
able, its effects are not. Mozi called this process of measuring Qi
indirectly by gauging its impact on the Demi-Monde 'ImMaterial
Analysis'. To do this Mozi developed the Qi Scale, which by the exami-
nation of certain aspects of socio-economic activity allowed an
assessment to be made of the level of Qi prevalent in the Demi-Monde.
The original elements used by Mozi to calculate the level of Qi in the
Demi-Monde were:

∞ *Number of murders*
∞ *Number of political assassinations*
∞ *Number of wars involving 50,000 or more combatants*
∞ *The height of men's hats*
∞ *The number of centimetres women's skirts rise above the ankle*
∞ *The number of slaves per capita*
∞ *The number of profanities used in newspapers*
∞ *The average height of yarrow growing in the Hub.*

Never one to hide his light under a bushel, Mozi (being a pompous
WunZian bastard) announced that the level of Qi would be measured

in Mozi units. Now by the use of the Qi Scale WunZian scholars were able to show that the level of Qi in the Demi-Monde oscillates around an unchanging Base Level. I stress 'unchanging' because – as those WunZian wankers delighted in telling me – anything that it is in stasis with the rest of the Kosmos cannot be subject to variation because of differing individual perceptions. QED unBelievability is crap and the Demi-Monde ain't Virtual. They even propounded the Law of Qi which states:

Qi can neither be created nor destroyed, it can only change from the Yang to the Yin form and back again. Thus, in a closed system, such as the post-Confinement Demi-Monde, the Yin/Yang aspect of Qi will oscillate around an unchanging mean – also known as the Base Level – but its total quantity in the system will remain constant.

So, according to those crafty WunZians, the levels of Qi (the summation of Yin and Yang Qi) present can never change. The belief that the Demi-Monde is in a permanent and unvarying state of equilibrium regarding Qi was called by Su Xiaoxiao the Doctrine of Equilibrianism. She even developed a graph demonstrating that although the total quantity of Qi is in equilibrium, the active and the passive aspects of Qi are forever in flux, with the two elements oscillating over a two-thousand-year period thus:

As can be seen from Su Xiaoxiao's graph overleaf, the thousand-year-long Ages of Yin and Yang alternate, with the Demi-Monde predicted to move from the Second Age of Yang (or as it is called by the renegade HerEticals, the Age of the nonFemmes) to the Second Age of Yin (aka the Age of the Femmes) around the year 1000 AC.

It was a persuasive argument and I must tell you, Dear Reader, that for a while I was gutted. But after much careful meditation and the consuming of several bottles of Solution I re-examined the maths and by incorporating additional elements into the Qi Scale (the amount of

Graph Showing Levels of Yin and Yang Qi in the Demi-Monde and the Socio-Gender Consequences (after Confusionist Sage Wun Zi)

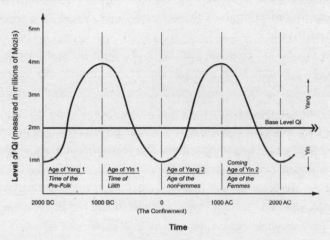

naked flesh displayed by women in public, the average calorific content of a Demi-Mondian's daily food intake, their choice of smoking materials and of recreational drugs . . . that sort of shit) I was able to show that, rather than being in equilibrium, the quantity of Qi in the Demi-Monde has been inexorably rising over the last four thousand years. By the skilful remodelling of the factors used to calculate it, I demonstrated that Qi oscillates around an ever-increasing Base Level (a contradiction in terms, but there you go). This enabled me to postulate a Second Law of Qi.

When two systems are connected with each other, there will be a net exchange of Qi unless or until they come to be in Qidian equilibrium. Qi will always flow from a higher-Qi system to a lower-Qi system.

This, of course, supposed that the Demi-Monde is not a closed system, but I was able to support this contention by reference to religion (and boy, did that piss off the WunZians!), citing that all religious types insisted that the Demi-Monde was merely one of the Nine Worlds, albeit the one which was most closely connected to the first of these worlds, the Spirit World.

On this basis I proposed that Qi flowed from the Spirit World – which by definition has the highest level of Qi as it is the one occupied by ABBA – to the Demi-Monde and that it is this flow which is responsible for the ever-increasing level of Qi in the Demi-Monde.

As is my wont, I went further, speculating that this extra Qi is inclined to destabilise the Demi-Monde and leads – inevitably – to the violence that is endemic in this world, violence being a symptom of an excess of Qi. An over-abundance of Qi hyperexcites the Living which make up Demi-Mondians' SAE, males being especially prone to having a rampant and uncontrollable excess of Qi, or, as it is known in Femme circles, MALEvolence.

The WunZians challenged me to show how Qi entered the Demi-Monde from the Spirit World, but this objection was easy to rebut. I merely alluded to the various places around this world – I like to call them Qi-Holes but they are more usually referred to as Portals – where Daemons effect entry into the Demi-Monde. It is through these, I countered, that Qi leaks into the Demi-Monde.

But having proposed this Concept of Qi DisEquilibrium, I got to thinking about its consequences. Inspired by Su Xiaoxiao, I plotted my findings on the graph shown overleaf.

The unsettling conclusion I came to was that once the amount of Qi within the Demi-Monde rises to a Critical Level (nineteen years from now in the year 1005 AC) then the world will self-destruct in an orgy of violence, an event which I named the Big Bang ... or, as those of a religious bent prefer to call it, Ragnarok. A study of the religious tracts indicates that Ragnarok will signal a shift from Yin/Yang dualism to a merging of Yin and Yang, creating a harmonised Demi-Monde

Graph Showing Levels of Yin and Yang Qi in the Demi-Monde and the Socio-Gender Consequences (after Confusionist Sage Too Zi)

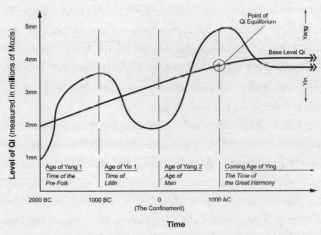

suffused with Ying. It will be at this moment when the Messiah – whose manifestation is foretold in all Demi-Mondian religions – will arrive to lead the faithful to ABBAsoluteness.

Ah, religion …

It is a somewhat unsettling realisation for a TooZian such as me to appreciate that the predictions made by exacting empirical enquiry have been foreshadowed by a bunch of bozos living a thousand years ago who had a predilection for self-denial, self-flagellation and, I suspect (the holy books are strangely silent on this subject), self-abuse. And this discomfort was further compounded by the understanding that when examining the beliefs of all the religions and cults of the Demi-Monde there emerges a disturbing commonality regarding Ragnarok, the Final Days and the other eschatological aspects of their religious mumbo-jumbo.

But ever the diligent scholar, I set to examining this commonality – these synoMyths, as I prefer to call them – in the hope that they might indicate, albeit obliquely, the reason why ABBA would wish – ultimately

– to destroy the Demi-Monde. Of course, I fully appreciated that myths are a product of an oral storytelling tradition and as time passes, as such stories move from generation to generation, from teacher to pupil, from language to language, from bar to bar, they undergo many mutations. However, the fact remains that when these religions are synthesised down, it is obvious they have a monogenesis, a shared origin.

And what did I find when I completed this backward synthesis? The chill realisation that ABBA will terminate the Demi-Monde when HeShe had perfected HisHer ultimate creation, HumanKind.

Perfection betokens the End of Days.

All Demi-Mondian religions have at their heart the recognition that the ultimate aim of ABBA is to make HumanKind pure and perfect, free of sin and capable of being brought into the final and total communion with HimHer known as ABBAsoluteness. But they go further, stating that this achievement of Perfection will only be available to some of us (the Pure in Heart, the Believers, Those with Faith, yadda, yadda, yadda). That's why all religions are so reward-driven: they say to their followers 'do this' (or, more often, 'don't do this', especially when you're naked or have the aforesaid cucumber handy) and 'this will be your reward'. Follow the UnFunDaMentalist doctrine of Living&More and your body and mind will be purified and you will become one with ABBA; practise the unrestrained sexual hedonism preached by ImPuritanism and you will achieve JuiceSense and oneness with ABBA; follow the Way advised by WunZian Confusionists, have wu wei suffuse your soul and you will achieve ABBAsoluteness, etc. etc.

But no matter what these religions say, they cannot disguise that there is an appalling lack of certainty about their predictions.

My guess (and guessing is not something a TooZian readily admits to) is that whilst ABBA is driven to achieve Perfection in HumanKind, HeShe does not know the form this Perfection will take. To my mind, it is obvious that ABBA is seeking to achieve this – as in all things in Nature – by competition and by struggle ... by the Survival of the Fittest. The Demi-Monde is merely a testing ground! That is why there are no synoMyths which state definitively who will emerge victorious from the contest that is the Final Days. By presenting HumanKind with so many alternative ways of governing their lives, by allowing so many conflicting religions and philosophies to flourish in the Demi-Monde, ABBA challenges HumanKind to compete and by competing to permit the best to emerge victorious.

My studies revealed that there are just three apocalyptic synoMyths. The first of these is that the Demi-Monde has been (still is, in fact) a place of trial where all the philosophies have been pitted against one another and where HumanKind in all its many guises will be tested. The second synoMyth is that ABBA will send a Messiah from the Spirit World to lead HumanKind on the path (the Way) to Harmony/Ying/ABBAsoluteness/OneNess/Grace with HimHer.

It is the struggle between the Messiah and the Beast that forms the basis for the Final Conflict. But the Messiah will not fight alone, having the help of PaPa Legba (sometimes called the Trickster, or the Wily Fox), the Warrior (sometimes called the Battle-Maiden or grim Surt) and, finally, the Fresh Bloom, destined by Fate and her Ancestors to come to the Messiah's aid when all have deserted her.

It is the third of these synoMyths that I found most intriguing – especially in the light of my own research regarding Qi. This is the rather enigmatic prediction that at the outset of Ragnarok a Column – the Column of Loci – lost since the Confinement will be recovered. It is this Column that holds the key to how the Demi-Monde might be made as one with the Spirit World . . . how Demi-Mondians might find Oneness with ABBA. Unfortunately, it appears that the details of this event are only contained in the Flagellum Hominum, an esoteric work which, because it is rendered in Pre-Folk, has never been read.

Fortunately, this synoMyth is also described – albeit in a typically obtuse manner – in the fifty-second Epigram of the iChing:

Know you, the Column is the bridge
Between the Real and the UnReal,
Between the Yin and the Yang.
When the Five have been tested
In the fire of Life
Bring it to where it must rest.
Then will be the merging.
Then the Five will become One.
One will be blessed.

I believe the Column is the means by which Qi within the Demi-Monde will be brought into Equilibrium with the Spirit World.